BURN THE PLANS
TYLER JONES

Burn The Plans
Originally published by Cemetery Gates Media
Binghamton, New York

Copyright © 2022, this Lethe Press edition © 2024 by Tyler Jones

ISBN 978-1-59021-779-5

For more information about Lethe Press publications, visit us at: lethepressbooks.com

Cover art by Ben Baldwin

Interior illustrations by Ryan Mills

Cover and interior design by Scott Cole | 13visions.com

For more information about the author, visit tylerjones.net

To Liam Patrick Jones,
you bend and shape the world around you into something better.
I am grateful for every second, minute, hour, day…every moment with you.
Whatever the future holds, I will be right by your side.
You are so loved.

BY TYLER JONES

Longsight M40

Night of the Long Knives

Turn Up the Sun

Heavy Oceans

Midas

Burn the Plans

Enter Softly

Almost Ruth

The Dark Side of the Room

Criterium

"In all chaos there is a cosmos, in all disorder a secret order."

—Carl Jung

INTRODUCTION
by Michael Marshall Smith 9

CORPORATION 15
TRIGGER 29
THE GOLDEN RULE 55
THE DEVIL ON THE STAND 65
BOO! 83
A SHARP BLACK LINE 97
CHARWOOD 113
CRATE 42 129
HOW WE LEARN 135
WARLOCK 151
LION'S DEN 165
DEEP DOWN 179
RED HANDS 199
WHITE GLOVE 221
STRIDOR 239
FULL FATHOM FIVE 287

AFTERWORD 319

STORY NOTES 323

ACKNOWLEDGEMENTS 333

INTRODUCTION

Picture a young man in his early twenties, just out of college, at the start of his adult life. He'll be hunched over a paper-back book, sitting outside a café or in a pub, or perched on stairs in lodgings or backstage at a provincial theatre. If you want to imagine what he's wearing, see a half-assed version of late 1980s fashion. His hair confirms the period. He'll almost certainly be smoking.

Why am I asking you to do this? I'll tell you in a minute.

I won't bury the lede. I'll tell you right here at the top: this is one of the best collections I've ever read.

That's not me being nice. Yes, I was asked if I'd write an introduction, but I wasn't asked to write *that*. Tyler and I have never met in person. I don't owe him money. There are a hundred ways of being kind about a book, of encouraging the reader to make up their own mind, of ushering a volume into the world without committing your own blood. You can introduce it without nailing your colours to the mast. But I'm not going to be cautious, and neither will it be generalized praise based on familiarity with the author's previous work, a breezy assumption this will be of that quality or thereabouts, and so anyway, what are we eating tonight.

I've read every word of what you're about to read. Just finished it, in fact. Personal circumstances meant I read it on planes, trains, and automobiles, on subway journeys, and when sitting on the stairs of an Airbnb. Re-opening this book and turning to the next page was like gratefully falling back into story-world, a strange dark place that was nonetheless home.

It strongly took me back to my early twenties (that's me, up there in the first paragraph), first discovering this kind of fiction, grabbing a break in random places during a long theatrical tour, and devouring the voice writers who first made *me* want to write—Stephen King, Peter Straub, Ramsey Campbell, Joe Lansdale, Nicholas Royle, Shirley Jackson, H. P. Lovecraft. Discovering their heady worlds, famous to others but new to me. Being transported from my present location into the places where their fiction happened, as if I'd become a shadow standing to one side, watching events unfold, a minor character in all the tales, one the authors simply happened to never mention.

You want to live in these stories. They feel like places. Even though the outcome may be horrendous or unnerving or disconcerting, they seem like home—and for that, you need both quality and consistency. You can't inhabit a collection if, once in a while, there's a story that knocks you out of absorption, which reminds you this is all made up by some person frowning over a laptop. There is no such tale here. No bum notes, no stories that don't make the grade, nothing that makes you think, okay, in general, this is working, but that one lost me, or I've seen this idea done better before, and actually, what *are* we eating tonight?

I'd have to reach way back to those first encounters with Stephen King to think of a group of stories that, one after another, left me this satisfied.

It's remarkably, undeniably, and unusually good.

How do you achieve this?

There's a *confidence* in good writing. There has to be. Prose is performance, like all art, and just as you know within moments whether a stand-up comedian will be funny (often before they've even told a joke) a secret and subtle part of the job of making stories is communicating to the reader, quickly and very firmly, that they're going to be engrossed. Their time, attention, and imagination are about to be well served, and this writer knows what they're doing. That you're in safe hands. And once you've sold the reader that idea, you're naturally free to do very *unsafe* things with those hands. You need the skill and confidence to beckon the reader forward and say: "Okay, I'm going to tell you something, and you're going to listen." And they do.

Tyler's narrative confidence is not pushy, however. It's never "look at me," and nor does it strive for effect. It's simply assured. So incredibly assured. He already shows mastery of evoking a world within a few paragraphs or even lines, so you feel bedded and comfortable living there for a while without questioning its reality. However uncomfortable that experience may eventually turn out to be.

It's like the grizzled dad you call round when your furnace is being weird and you know it's out of your league, and he knocks it with a knuckle and reaches for the levers with the quiet confidence of someone who's spent decades convincing these things to behave. It's the mom who'll immediately text you a recipe when you ask, and you know it'll work. It's the teenage daughter who'll lean over your dumb laptop and press a couple keys, and suddenly, it's not being an inexplicable ass anymore.

These comparisons feel appropriate because family is a common undercurrent in Tyler's stories. How they work, how they don't work, what happens when they break—the effects on children of that breakage, the slow-bleeding trauma of adults when they feel life slipping out of their grasp as everything stops making sense—and how these aftermaths play out in worlds where the symbolic and metaphoric can become disturbingly real.

Family is often where the horror starts. And though these stories deal with the unreal, they're embedded in places you believe in. That's why they hurt, but also why they sometimes warm.

Then, too, there's the writing itself.

In "Corporation," the very first story, Jones leads you in with an engaging, casually compelling voice. You think you know where you are, and then suddenly, you're somewhere else entirely, and only when you're thrown out the end of the piece—blinking and unsettled—do you realize there was a sly clue to your destination in front of you all along. That someone skilled built this rollercoaster and knew what they were doing from the start.

There's a mature sparseness in many pieces, too. The concision of "A Sharp Black Line"—superb, fast, and lean, sketching character and horror of genuine depth with a few deft strokes—and "Crate 42," where a few pages evoke a story big enough to bring down the entire world. Knowing when enough is enough is supposed to be a life's work. Apparently, Tyler's already done that work. Another story, "Lion's Den," though longer, proves the same point: achieving more in a short than many writers will attempt in a novella or even novel—then tossing in a couple of small but eye-opener ideas at the end, just in passing, as if they're free. As if ideas like that drop from trees.

But as any writer will tell you, they really don't.

Finally, there's variety. There needs to be variation in subject and voice in a collection, or it feels like one long note. On the other hand, you can't skip all over the place, or it begins to seem like you've stumbled into an anthology of multiple writers instead.

Tyler balances it perfectly. Some stories start in normality and swerve into horror—the standard journey in this genre. Some sneakily do the opposite. Others walk that line like tightrope artists, determinedly never committing themselves and encouraging you to do the same. "How We Learn," for example, tells a story that feels incredibly real and yet has an unexamined unreality at its core. Tyler poises it there in a way that makes it feel uncannily credible and true.

Variation in tone is also important. Some stories here feel very modern, imbued with a twenty-first-century uncanniness. Others, like "Warlock," resonate as if they've always been true and merely been waiting to be told, something the brothers Grimm decided not to include only because they knew it would freak people out. "Deep Down" comes on like the kind of black-and-white movie that would have starred Peter Lorre, but then unexpectedly, an idea takes it to a whole other and very contemporary place. And there's "White Glove"—another seemingly folkloric tale, where as soon as it starts, you sense where it's going, and there's a comfort and dark pleasure in that dread-laden walk into old woods—yet it still manages to punch you in the face at the end. That's why we have folklore. It doesn't age. And when it's updated like this, it's delicious. It also reminds you what a broad church this thing called "horror" is, and why it's not a diminishing term. People call fiction "horror" when it's too big yet subtle and profound—and cuts too deep—to be contained anywhere else. That's something to be proud of.

I'm not going to name-check every story—I don't want to risk giving anything away, and this is your town to explore, dark side streets for you to wander down without someone sketching you a map—but I will mention where we end: on "Full Fathom Five."

A treat and promise are hidden away in this story, but again, I won't tell you what. Just be reassured that this collection ends on a story that seems to gather up and re-present all the best qualities of the fiction you've just read, suggesting that this collection, however good, is but a precursor to what Tyler Jones is capable of. It's a high note. But honestly, they're all high notes. I would have been proud to have written *any* story here... but I'd give half a dozen of mine to have written this one alone.

One of the nice things about being a writer is it's not a zero-sum game. You can take simple pleasure in another's work without feeling diminished or in competition. Any really good writer does what *they* do, not what *you* do, and so where's the fight? The best ever is when someone's stories are so good, they make *you* want to write.

That's what I found in those writers thirty years ago, and this collection did exactly the same thing. It viscerally reminded me of how wonderful and true dark fiction can be and made me want to go out and once more hunter-gatherer the scary words into some disquieting pens. After all these years, it took me back to be that younger guy sitting somewhere with a great collection, and when I'd finished it, I decided: *I want to tell stories like that.*

I can't give it higher praise.

I'm done. An introduction is not a sales job. You've already bought the book. I'm just saying... *good choice*. I've either made my point by now, or (hopefully) you got the gist a while back and bailed from this part—and went straight to the stories.

Burn the Plans would be stellar as a selection of tales from any writer at any point in their career. As a debut collection, it's genuinely extraordinary. If there is any justice in the world—I accept there's plenty of evidence to the contrary, but I dare to hope—then Tyler Jones will soon become a household name.

That starts with you turning the page.

Do that. Do it now.

MICHAEL MARSHALL SMITH
London & Santa Cruz

CORPORATION

Sunlight blooms in the sky, rising from behind all those glass and steel buildings. It burns away the dark blue. The windows are still tinted from yesterday when I dimmed them. I touch the tablet to wake it up, then press the office icon. A new menu opens. I push the square with curtains. A control panel appears, and I drag the fader down.

The glass grows clearer, letting in more light.

A shudder moves through the building. Framed awards, signed photographs of CEOs and politicians rattle against the walls. A golden apple paperweight shivers across the surface of the desk. The window vibrates, warping my reflection.

Work here long enough you get used to this, this shivering building.

I'm always the first to arrive because I still have something to prove.

My dad taught me that. He said, "The moment you think you've made it, is the moment someone is waiting behind you with a knife."

The building I'm in, you know it if you live in the city. The tower at the center of everything is made of rust-colored stone. Some people say it gets redder every year.

I grew up walking past the tower every day on my way to school. There would always be a limousine, a Jaguar, or a Bentley parked in front, letting out some CEO or investor dressed to the nines in a suit that cost more than my dad made in a year.

I didn't know what they did in the building but I wanted to be there. Someday. Away from the single-bedroom apartment with stained carpets and mold-covered walls. The kitchen window looked out over an alley that always reeked of rotting food and dead animals.

My dad also used to say, "Anything worth having requires sacrifice."

But we didn't have anything, in fact, we had less than nothing. Mom died when I was still too young to remember her, and Dad worked as a machinist not because he wanted to but because he couldn't do anything else. And after forty years of never calling in sick, all he had to show for it was a hand missing a finger and a mind that couldn't remember which day of the week it was. The dementia stole him in pieces before it took him away for good.

He told me sacrifice was the only way to succeed. He told me this while I practiced basketball in the street. I didn't want to, Dad made me. He made me drill every evening while he sat on the stoop and smoked cigarette butts other people had dropped on the ground.

Everything was a lesson with my dad, but the ones that stayed with me were the ones he didn't even know he was teaching.

The foundation of the building was laid back when this massive city was only a small collection of farmhouses and fields when horse-drawn carriages rumbled down the dirt roads, and when the world seemed a lot smaller.

The foundation is still here, buried way down deep beneath the basement.

There used to be a name above the rotating glass doors leading to the lobby. But those letters rusted and fell off. You can still see the ghost letters on the stone, but they are so faded now that no one can read them. All that's left is the word "Corporation."

Dad hated being poor, but he never said it. He didn't have to. He just always told me how being rich would be better.

For me, it was the constant embarrassment of being dressed in clothes that other kids in my school had donated to the thrift store. It was not being able to buy a car at sixteen, which meant no dates. Or never having the money to go to the movies with my friends.

I would have done anything to have more. And the red tower represented everything I wanted. Sometimes, I'd walk by after school and look up at all that stone, imagine what it would be like to work in a place where you had to wear a suit and tie.

But no one knew what the Corporation did. I asked around and all I got were vague answers about finance and political campaigns. Some said it was stocks, others said it was international trade. Everything and nothing, is what I got.

Dad told me that everything hurts in two ways. "Your momma gets sick and goes to the hospital, now you're not only worried about her, but you also can't sleep because you don't know how you're gonna pay for her meds. Two ways—the pain of the thing and the money you lose taking care of that pain."

Every night, I'd lie on my sleeping bag in the living room with walls so thin you could feel the winter wind squeeze through the particle board, and promised myself I'd never be poor.

Dad told me my height was the only way it'd happen. Said God gave me a gift with my long arms and legs. I told him I didn't like basketball, and that was the only time he ever smacked me. His cracked and callused hand struck the side of my face. His fingers burned on my cheek even after the hand was gone.

Breathing heavily, he pointed one greasy finger at me and said, "You don't get to choose, boy." The finger moved and pointed at our apartment building. "This where you want to be? This the future you see? No, I didn't think so. You practice and you practice hard, because it's the only way you're gettin' into college."

As always, Dad was right.

Basketball got me a scholarship. I majored in business, and a few weeks after graduation, I'm standing just outside the red tower, waiting for Mr. Winters, the Corporation's vice president, to interview me for a job.

A few minutes before eight, a sleek black car pulled up. The driver got out and opened the back door for a tall, skeletal man with slicked white hair. So thin he looked like a skeleton draped in skin. He wore a navy blue, pinstriped three-piece suit. The gold chain of a pocket watch hung from his vest. He smiled with teeth that looked yellow because of the stark whiteness of his hair.

Mr. Winters shook my hand, his skin soft and cold. I wore a suit that didn't fit and still smelled like a thrift store because I couldn't afford to have it cleaned. My scalp itched under a fresh, slightly crooked haircut I had given myself the day before.

He held my hand for a long time and looked into my eyes. Instead of letting go, Winters moved my hand and lifted it to the building's stone. My fingers flattened against the cold, rough granite, Mr. Winters's skeletal hand on top of mine.

"Do you feel it?" His spearmint breath and aftershave filled my nose.

I tried to move my hand, but Winters pushed his down on top of mine harder. I was about to jerk my hand away when the stone under my skin shivered. I had to crane my neck to see the whole skyscraper, but I swear it swayed a little. The edges of the building blurred. From the roof, birds took flight and scattered into the sky.

Mr. Winters smiled, and I saw those yellow teeth again.

Our shoes clacked and echoed over the polished lobby tile. A security guard watched us cross and nodded at Mr. Winters as we waited for the elevator, the doors of which looked like they were right out of an old black-and-white movie.

Mr. Winters remained silent until the bell rang, and we stepped inside. His finger hovered over the twenty-four buttons. "Hmm," he said, "let's start at Asset Management, shall we?"

His thin finger pushed the button, and we rose with a shudder. The numbered buttons went all the way to 58, but the last floor's button only said "CEO."

"Will I meet him?" I asked, pointing to the button.

"Mr. Burke doesn't much like visitors," Winters said. "His concern is running the Corporation, not meeting new employees."

The elevator creaked and groaned as it moved. When the doors opened, we stepped out into a large open space. Doors lined each side of the room. A few young men in suits much better than mine walked back and forth, their faces serious and focused. One man came closer. His blonde hairline was slick, and sweat dripped from his nose.

"Good morning, Mr. Winters," he said.

Winters nodded.

The sweating man moved on, limping as he did. His face tightened in pain with each step.

Doors opened and closed. More young men crossed the large room, passed folders to other men in other rooms.

"Notice anything?" Winters asked.

One man opened his door to accept a file from someone who lurched across the room. The hand that accepted the folder was missing a finger. A white bandage covered the stump where his pinky finger should have been.

Winters patted my shoulder. "Let's move on, shall we?"

In the elevator, Winters pressed button 32, and once again the cage jerked a little.

The doors opened onto another floor that looked almost exactly like the other, only the men and women who moved through this space did so with an increased level of efficiency. None of them had sweat soaking the backs of their shirts. An overweight guy with a mostly bald head laughed as he talked with someone holding a tablet. One of the sleeves of his starched white shirt was pinned up at the elbow, just an emptiness where the rest of his arm should be.

An attractive woman in a black skirt and jacket walked by. Her dark hair swayed as she passed, and when the hair moved, I saw a twisted patch of scar tissue where her ear should have been.

I thought it was a joke, a prank-the-new-guy trick, but I couldn't stop the blood from rushing through my head.

A young man, not much older than me, hobbled over on a pair of crutches.

"Good morning, sir," he said to Mr. Winters.

One leg of this guy's pants was just dangling cloth.

Winters, hands folded in front, nodded slightly and asked, "Are you ready?"

The smile disappeared from the young man's face. He adjusted the crutches and nodded, then hobbled into the open elevator.

Questions tumbled through my head, but I couldn't find the right words to ask.

Mr. Winters lifted a chain from around his neck, a key dangled at the end of it. He inserted this into a slot near the bottom of the panel. When he turned it, three buttons glowed red. One marked LL, another TL, and the one below that, FOUNDATION. Winters pushed this last one and the elevator rumbled to life.

"Is that the sub-basement?" I asked.

Winters showed his yellow teeth. "Lower than that."

Crutch guy stood military straight, eyes closed, breathing in through his nose and out through his mouth. I tried not to look at the empty space under his knee.

The air got warmer as we descended. Deep, low sounds shook outside the elevator walls. The cables that lowered us thrummed as though plucked by a giant hand.

"Mr. Eisele here has made an important decision today," Winters said. "He has worked hard and proven himself to be diligent and dedicated. But today," the elevator caught for a moment and lifted my stomach, "today he takes the next step. Today he secures his place on floor 45."

Eisele's breathing came out even faster as the bell rang off each floor. 7, 6, 5.

"It's important for you to understand how one advances within the Corporation," Winters said, looking at me without any hint of a smile.

"Of course, sir."

4, 3, 2.

The air got so warm it hurt to breathe. It felt like being suffocated. Now Eisele started to sweat. Little beads of moisture formed on his nose, his forehead. His fingers squeezed the rubber handles of the crutches with damp squeaks. The smell of his sweat filled the elevator.

1, TL, LL.

At the FOUNDATION level, the doors slid open, and a blast of warm air hit us. Eisele crutched out into a long stone hallway. Winters and I followed.

There were no lights in the low ceiling, but a red glow came from the far end of the hall. It pulsed on the walls. Walls made of stacked stone that looked like what you'd imagine a castle was made of.

Metallic sounds echoed where the red light came from. Loud clanking noises, mechanical and rhythmic, filled my head. I walked behind Eisele, following his sweat-drenched jacket and the nervous reek of him.

At the end of the tunnel was a large circular space. I stopped walking when I saw what was at the center of the room, but Eisele and Winters kept going.

A massive hole in the ground, and from this hole rose a machine that looked like something out of a clockmaker's dream. A metal framework of pipes and joints twisted together to create a senseless shape. Gears, large and small, spun smaller cogs that pulled giant chains in and out of the hole. And that hole was the source of the red glow, the heat. So much stronger now. Pistons pumped deep into the brightness. Thick pipes ran from the machine and into the walls. Dark liquid leaked from around where the metal connected to the stone.

The whole thing looked like some metallic creature that just clawed its way up from the center of the world. Steam burst out of pipes above us with a loud hiss. The room filled with fresh heat.

Eisele made his way to a piece of stone that stood at the edge of the fissure. Eisele made his way to a piece of stone at the edge of the fissure—some kind of pedestal with a long trough that led down into the red light. The machine grew louder as he approached. A shudder moved through the floor. Black exhaust spewed from other pipes, a choking odor that smelled like burnt meat.

I could hardly breathe, and not just because of the steam and heat. This massive machine, whatever it is, I know it saw me. It sensed me in the room. I felt it as clearly as when the curtains of Dad's dementia pulled back a little whenever he saw and knew me. All those gears, pipes, and chains around us—something was aware at the center of it.

Red light glinted from something hanging above the bowl-shaped top of the pedestal—something I couldn't quite see.

Winters put a hand on the young man's shoulder and whispered something to him, before stepping back.

"If you want to advance within the Corporation," Winters said in a firm voice, "you have to make sacrifices."

Eisele let his crutches fall to the ground. He unbuttoned the left sleeve of his shirt.

"The more you sacrifice, the higher you go."

Eisele pushed the sleeve up past his elbow and rested his bare arm on the pedestal. Even from where I stood, I could see his chest moving faster and faster.

I followed Winters all morning, and the man hadn't limped once. He wasn't missing any fingers.

"What have you sacrificed?" I asked the man.

Winters smiled with rust-colored teeth. He reached out and grabbed my wrist then pulled my hand closer. I tried to pull back, but Winter's grip was stronger as he forced my hand toward his pants. His eyes never left mine. At the last moment, he twisted my hand until it opened and pushed my palm against his crotch.

My fingers touched a smooth slope between Winters's legs. His eyebrows went up. I couldn't help but press my hand against him, feeling for something that wasn't there.

"I gave up what no one else was willing to," he said.

Eyes closed, Eisele's head hung down, his mouth moved. Praying, no doubt. He unbuckled his belt, wrapped it around his upper arm, and tightened it.

"Burke," I said, "the CEO. What did he give?"

Winters turned his attention to the machine. "Burke gave more than any of us."

Eisele moved his other hand to a wooden lever sticking out of the pedestal. The machine continued to whir and clank, and the light from the hole glowed brighter.

"Burke opened himself here," Winters made a line across his stomach. "He cut through his intestines, fed one end to the gears, and let the machine pull from him as much as it wanted."

Eisele's hand opened and closed on the lever. The metal rattled and shook, pipes clanged together. Gears screeched and turned faster.

Winters nodded to the machine, "It left him just enough."

Red light glints above Eisele's head.

"Burke has led this Corporation for over twenty years," Winters says. "But he has wasted away. It is almost time for me to take his place."

Eisele looked over at us. His face was covered in beads of red sweat.

Winters took a small walkie-talkie from his pocket and pressed the button. "Make the call."

A sad voice came through the speaker. "Yes, sir."

Winters nodded at Eisele, who clenched his teeth together and pushed the lever down.

The glinting thing above his head fell, sliced through the air, and a large, rusty blade slammed into the pedestal with a loud crack. A moment of silence. Steam hissed, swirled around Eisele's feet, then he screamed. It echoed through the room. He fell to his knees, one hand held over the stump. Blood spurted from between his fingers. He writhed on the ground, still screaming, his one leg twitching.

I could not stop myself from moving closer. Eisele's arm slid down the trough and slipped off the edge. Blood flowed into the machine and ran into the gears. I saw the slickness as they turned, glistening on the teeth, pressing the blood deep into the shafts

Mr. Winters went over to the pedestal and pulled the lever. The blade slowly rose, pulled on a thick, oiled chain, until it hung in the shadows once more.

Eisele's screams became weaker until they were just whimpers. His face had gone stone grey, and his lips were pale blue.

"Help me get him upstairs," Winters said.

I lifted Eisele by the shoulders while Winters grabbed hold of the man's pants, and we hoisted him up.

In the enclosed space of the elevator, I heard sirens echo. Eisele moaned, moving his head from side to side, his mouth all twisted like he was determined not to cry. I tried not to look, but once I saw the bright white bone surrounded by all that raw, angry flesh, I couldn't look away. Blood oozed from the wound and dripped onto the floor. Mr. Winters's key still hung from the panel, its chain swinging back and forth.

When the doors opened, we carried him into the lobby. Three paramedics rushed inside, pushing a gurney. They got to work immediately, and none asked what had happened. Winters stepped aside as one paramedic plunged a needle into Eisele's arm to start an IV.

The choice wasn't made, not really, not until I heard the elevator doors begin to close, and I knew the only way to get to the FOUNDATION level was with Winters's key, so I sprinted across the lobby and shoved my arm into the cage. The elevator doors hit my arm and opened back up. I got inside and pushed the FOUNDATION button. The doors started to close again, and I saw Winters in the shrinking space, watching me.

I ran down the stone hall until I came to the room. The machine was quieter now, settled, but still in motion. The gears moved slowly. The structure towered above me, so high I couldn't even see the top.

I went to the edge of the hole and looked down. Nothing but smoke and red light. Two of the gears were close enough to reach.

I tried not to think of the pain, but I knew I had to hurry while the paramedics were still there.

Instead, I thought of what my dad told me: success requires sacrifice. I thought of him, poor and broken, and reminded myself of my promise in that single bedroom apartment.

I will not be poor.

I did what Eisele did: I took off my belt and tightened it around my arm. I was about to shove my arm into those gears when I saw Mr. Winters enter the room. He came over to me and put a hand on my shoulder. "You have to wait," he said. You don't understand yet how this all works. You will in time."

My hand reached up to my shoulder and covered his. Then I squeezed and grabbed his arm with my other hand. Winters's eyes went wide, and his shoes scraped the floor as I pulled him. But he was caught off guard, and he knew it. I planted my feet and swung him around with all my strength.

He started to say something, but the words caught in his throat when he lost his balance. The momentum took him right to the edge of the hole, half his body leaning out over all that red light. My hands still held him. His eyes were pleading with me, those yellow teeth clenched together.

I let both hands release at the same time, then shoved Winters in the chest. His feet left the ground, his body went horizontal, floated over the light and smoke, and crashed into the gears. His piercing scream, so loud and so full of pain, bounced around the room as the metal teeth tore through him. The screaming collapsed into a wet gurgle, then stopped. I heard the sound of bones snapping. Dark liquid flooded the gears.

The mess of ground-up flesh and pinstripe suit was crushed and carried from one gear to another. I saw a tangle of once white hair, now pink, fall into the red void below.

I knelt at the edge of the hole as the machine ingested Mr. Winters, and I felt that awareness again, watching me, assessing me. I closed my eyes and waited for whatever would happen next.

Sunlight blooms in the sky, rising from behind all those glass and steel buildings, burning away the dark blue.

There's a knock at the door. I tap the camera icon on the tablet and see Burke waiting outside. I push the button to release the three deadbolts so the doors can swing open.

Burke comes shuffling into the room with the help of a walker—a sickly looking man with grey sallow skin and dark flesh under his eyes. What little hair he has left looks brittle, and his crooked teeth are stained brown.

"Good morning, sir," he says. "The numbers are up again today. Senator Peyton will be arriving at eleven o'clock, and the sheik will be here shortly thereafter."

He looks around the office that used to be his. His gaze admires all the cameras I had installed, and he smiles slightly. He must know I wear a Kevlar vest beneath the exquisitely tailored suit. Or that I have a loaded gun secured to the underside of my desk.

"Will there be anything else, sir?" he asks.

"No. Thank you, Burke."

Burke turns and leaves the room. The doors close behind him automatically and lock again.

I go back to the window and look out at the thriving city. The stone of the tower is redder than it's ever been. We are in a new era. But I don't leave this building without an armed guard, never spend more than one night in the various properties I own around the city, and never eat food from our cafeteria or from any restaurant. Because, like my dad said, "The moment you think you've made it is the moment someone is waiting behind you with a knife."

TRIGGER

1

I falled asleep to Pa and Booker shouting, and I woke up to the high whine of Pa's electric saw. Somewhere in there, I heard the scream of a cougar echo 'cross the field. Probably took one a Jacoby's sheep again. I get outta bed and go downstairs. The table where we never eat is still covered in cards and poker chips and empty beer cans.

That saw sound is coming from the garage. High whine as it cuts through something. Low whine as it comes out the end.

Pa, Booker, and two other guys from the mill come over on Mondays after work to shoot the shit and play cards. Loser has to buy beer for the next week. But the way the chips is scattered, I can't tell who won. One chair is knocked down, and some of the chips is on the ground.

I go outside in bare feet, rubbing my eyes with one hand and my crotch with the other. Cold fall night with crickets singing in the fields. Big ole' moon hangin' there like a diseased eye. Nothing but field, as far as I can see. Our nearest neighbor is Jacoby's farm, and his house is just one light way out there in the dark.

The saw stops and starts and stops again.

I make it to the side door, wait until the saw stop, and knock. I know better than to walk in on Pa doing anything. Especially with a 'lectric saw. He's liable to cut a finger off, and he'd take off his belt and whip me good, even while blood still all spurting out the end of his stump.

It ain't unlikely. After all, that's what happened to Booker. He lost half his ring finger at the mill. Got a buncha time off work and some money 'cause of it, and he was always goin' on about his good fortune.

The saw drops to the dirt floor of the garage, and boots crunch over to the door. It opens a bit, and Pa's eye stares out the crack.

"What're you doing up, Travis?" His breath fresh Camels and Pabst.

"Did you hear the cougar?" I ask him.

Pa lowers his head, then opens the door wider and steps outside. He takes the pack of cigarettes out the pocket of his flannel shirt. Slips one out and lights it. His face glows all red in the cherry, and it makes him look like something outta one of them scary movies we ain't allowed to watch but sometimes do when he's at work.

"Listen," he says, "I need you to do something for me."

The gravel is sharp ice under my bare feet. I shove my hands into my pajama pockets and clench my teeth. I don't want him to see me shiver. Pa's car is still parked in front of the house. Old brown Chevy with black primer covering the spots where the paint's peeled. He calls it "the Turd."

"How'd Booker get home?" I ask him.

Pa takes a drag. His eyes squint in the smoke that goes up into his face.

"He walked," Pa says, his voice like he's sick.

There's a smell comin' off him, reminds me like when we butchered the hog. The smell of insides and blood. The cherry glows again, and I see dark little stains all over his shirt. One of his only good shirts. All the others have small burn holes, just like the couch.

Pa blows out smoke, squints at me. "Trigger got killed tonight. The cougar got 'im."

"Shit," I say.

Pa's two fingers with the cigarette slash down and point at my face. The cherry glows hot at my nose.

"Language, boy," he says.

"Sorry, Pa."

The fingers lift, and he takes another drag. "Jonah's gonna be hurt something awful. He loved that dog. I don't want him to know yet. He's still worked up about your ma."

I nod and a piece of gravel digs into the bottom of my foot, but it feels kinda good the way pain sometimes does.

"I need you to bury 'im out in the field. Didn't want your brother to see 'im so I cut 'im up, put 'im in trash bags and put those in some old duffels."

"Like the deer," I say.

Pa nods and breathes smoke out his nose like a dragon.

"You gotta bury it out there, too," he says.

I can't hold it anymore, and I shiver. Pa doesn't even notice.

"Bags'll be in here. Make your brother help. Tell 'im the cougar got Trigger."

"Yes, Pa," I say.

He drops the cigarette, and it hits the ground like a tiny Fourth of July. A spark lands on my foot, and it burns like the cold gravel.

Pa turns and starts to open the garage door. I let out a breath I didn't know I was holdin', and he stops and looks back at me. I swallow but it's one of those bad ones that makes your chest hurt.

"Why was you up?" he asks.

Pa don't like it when I shrug, says it's a dumb thing to do when God gave us words, but I shrug, and I'm glad he ignores it.

"Thinkin', I guess," I tell him.

Pa's hand is still on the garage door. "Your ma?"

It's been since school started up that she's been gone, and Pa didn't make Jonah and me go back, but since we ain't in school, we have to do lots of chores. He ain't said nothin' 'bout ma since he told us she run off, and I sort of believed he didn't feel nothin' over it 'cept maybe anger.

But his face now, it's what I see in Jonah sometimes when he's all worked up about ma leaving us. Usually when I look at Jonah, I see Ma all in his eyes and the way his smile is crooked, and that hurts.

Pa looks down at my bare feet. "Try not to think 'bout her," he says. "'Cause she sure as hell ain't thinkin' 'bout us."

He sighs, and the breath comes out like smoke, hangs there a little while. He comes closer and puts a hand on my shoulder. I feel the hard calluses even through my shirt.

"I gotta finish cleanin' up and get to work. Make sure your brother eats breakfast. He's lookin' weak, you know?" He jerks his head at the garage. "Job better be done when I get back. Don't wanna hear no excuses."

When he opens the garage door, that butchered hog smell comes out again. Pa turns around, tries to smile, but his face just looks like it does when he's lost at poker.

"We'll have chili for dinner tonight, okay?" he says, then he goes into the garage and shuts the door. I stand there in the cold to watch the smoke of my breath go up like a ghost leavin' my body.

2

I know Jonah's up 'cause I hear his piss hittin' water, and then he's walkin' like an elephant down the stairs. Each step bangs like a hand inside my head, and it makes me want to make him wear pillows on his feet.

When he comes into the kitchen, he's rubbin' his eyes and belly at the same time. Pa is right—Jonah looks all skinny and stringy.

"Mornin'," he says.

I slide him a bowl and spoon and fill the bowl with plain Cheerios.

"Pa says you need to eat," I tell him.

Jonah yawns and reaches for the sugar bowl, starts scoopin' one spoon after the other until there's a hill of the stuff.

He's got Ma's hair. It's thick and the color of the dust at the bottom of the Cheerio bag. He's got her green eyes too, and maybe that's why Pa is so hard on him. The bruise on Jonah's cheek is faded to the color of a smashed blueberry, but he never cried so hard as when Pa whooped him for mouthin' off.

He asks, "Can I watch a cartoon?"

"Not today, we got work to do," I tell him.

Jonah sighs, takes a bite, and milk dribbles down his chin.

Outside the garage, Jonah folds in half and barfs up breakfast when I tell him 'bout Trigger. He cries so hard he starts wheezin' when he breathes, and I have to go get his medicine. He sucks on the inhaler, which calms him down a bit, but his chin won't stop movin', and some part of me wants to hold it shut.

Jonah got Ma's weak stomach too. When she and Pa used to fight, she'd wrap her arms 'round her belly like her guts were gonna fall out. And she'd fold up, just like Jonah is, and the sounds she'd make were like Jacoby's sheep giving birth.

At least she could cover her bruises with makeup. She didn't ever go nowhere anyway.

Jonah's sobbin'. Steam comes off his barf, and I tell him, I'm sorry but he needs to calm down.

"He didn't never do nothin' to nobody," Jonah says.

I tell him he needs to brush his teeth. The smell of the barf makes me think of what it tastes like, and it make me want to barf.

I tell him the cougar's like a monster in one of them books Ma used to read to him. It's just out there hungry and waitin', and sometimes it comes to take things. I tell him that's what life is, this monster with teeth rippin' stuff away from us.

He stops blubberin' just enough to look at me with big, wet eyes. "Did the monster take Ma?" He says.

I tell him no. But sometimes people get so beat up by the world they start rippin' stuff apart themselves just 'cause they know the monster's gonna do it anyway. Someday.

Jonah turns to go back inside. He whispers, "Goddamn it," but I don't hit him like Pa would. There's a lot I don't know, but I know he ain't just cryin' for Trigger.

3

When Jonah comes back out of the house, he's got Pa's huntin' rifle over his shoulder. The stock hangs down to behind his knee.

I ask him, "What the hell you doin' with that?"

Jonah's not cryin' anymore, but his eyes is all red, and he's got this look like when I pretended to flush his comic books down the toilet. I shouldn't of done it because those mean more to him than anything. Ma got 'em at a garage sale, and he's read 'em so many times the covers are all falling off the staples.

"In case we see the monster," he says.

Pa would be so mad if he saw Jonah with that gun, but Pa ain't here and if it makes Jonah feel better, I figure I won't say nothin' 'bout it.

When I open the side door of the garage, the smell's not as bad as it was, but there's still the stink of something dead in the air. The blood smell's mostly gone, but now the burnt meat stink of when the saw cut through Trigger is stronger. I yank the chain, and the light comes on, and the bulb swings back and forth over two duffels sittin' on the floor. Jonah won't notice, but the table saw is cleaner than it has been since Ma left, and the dirt on the floor is raked.

Jonah steps in behind me, wrinkles his nose. "Why's there two bags?"

"Trigger was a big dog," I tell him. I grab the straps of one and start to lift, but it's heavier than I thought it'd be. I test the other one, and it's a bit lighter, so I tell Jonah to take that one and to use both hands.

There's stuff movin' around in the bag. It shifts like carryin' a cooler full of beer after all the ice has melted. Heavy things movin' inside liquid.

Jonah can't quite carry his bag, he's more draggin' it than anything. The gun slaps against the back of his legs, and one of his shoelaces is untied. I hold up my hand for him to stop, then kneel down and tie it for him.

He smells like B.O., which is the first time I ever noticed it on him. He's still young, and sometimes he smells a bit ripe, but this is different. I bet he's getting pubes too. So maybe Pa is wrong, maybe Jonah isn't weak. Maybe he's just growin'.

We go out behind the house, me carryin' the heavier bag and Jonah pullin' his through the grass like it's a shitty sled. His face all serious and tight-lipped like that. He looks older, too. Pa always said brushin' up against Death ages the ones still livin'. Guess he was right.

My arms are burnin', so I drop the duffel and take a breather in the middle of the field. Jonah stops, too, puts his hands on his knees, and breathes heavy like a smoker.

The old dead tree is still a ways off, and that's where the field dips down into a valley, and then the forest begins after that. When you're down in that valley, no one can see you. That's where we buried the deer Pa hit with his truck. He said it was an elk, but we never saw no antlers, so maybe he got that part wrong. I think he'd been out drinkin' with Booker that night because it was so late, he had to wake me up, and it was morning by the time he finished tellin' me what happened.

I shake my arms out and lift the duffel back up. Jonah starts draggin' his again, pullin' a trail of flat grass behind him. When we get to the tree, I stop again. Breath stings in my chest, and I wish I thought to bring some water. Or shovels, for that matter.

Jonah reaches me and drops to the ground. The shirt under his armpits is all wet, and I ain't never seen that before either. Not on him. He looks down the hill to the valley floor. I see it, too. The mound where the deer is buried. Young grass grows over the top.

The ground is rocky down there. I 'member sparks flying when the shovel blade hit them, and Jonah and I takin' turns, but me gettin' pissed 'cause he's not as strong as me and the job had taken longer, so I did most the diggin'.

I look back across the field to the house, and there's somethin' dark and low to the ground runnin' at us.

My balls tighten up. I say, "Jonah, gun."

He looks up like he been caught with his pants down and looks where I'm lookin'. He struggles to get the rifle off his shoulder, and still, this thing is runnin' at us full speed, but the closer it gets, it don't look like no cougar.

This thing barks twice, and I know the sound 'cause I been hearin' it for years, and it's gotta be a ghost, or me wishing things was different than they are.

Jonah's got the gun held out, fightin' to the hold the barrel steady. It swings past me, and my stomach falls lower 'cause if he twitches at the wrong moment, he's gonna hit me.

The thing is close enough now to hear panting and Jonah is sayin' my name over and over, and then the thing is right on me and Trigger jumps up, puts his muddy paws all over my chest.

I get all dizzy because I ain't sure if time stopped or the world started spinnin' backwards, but sure as hell this dog is real. It barks again and I get down on my knees, rubbing his neck and head. He's covered in mud and some of his fur is all matted down with dark red stuff, dry and crusty.

Jonah drops the rifle on the ground, somethin' Pa would've given him a black eye for, and comes over.

"Is it him?" he asks.

Trigger didn't never have no collar, but the tip of his tail is gone from when Pa backed over it in the truck, and his one ear is almost the color of a blonde lady's hair. This dog has both them things.

I nod at Jonah, and he smiles so big and laughs. Trigger runs to him next, rubbing the mud and blood all over Jonah's clothes. Licking his face, nubby tail waggin' like he ain't never been so happy in his life.

But then the tail stops waggin' and Trigger puts his nose up in the air. Jonah keep rubbin' but the dog don't notice. Trigger puts his face to ground, waves it back and forth, leaves Jonah and walks like he's on the trail of somethin'.

He goes over to the Jonah's duffel and makes a whinin' sound like he does when he's gotta go outside to pee. Trigger paws at the bag and nips at the corner.

"Trigger, knock it off," I tell him.

But then I get that feelin' again. My balls shrink and I feel like I'm gonna have diarrhea.

Trigger bites at the bag then jumps back, moves forward and bites at it again. Shakes his head with the bag between his teeth until the fabric rips a little and some dark liquid comes dribblin' out.

Jonah grabs Trigger by the scruff and pulls him back, then lifts up the bag and drops it just as quick and backs away, shaking his head and saying no no no. He trips over a root of the dead tree and goes down on his ass. All the color leaves his face until it looks like the skin of that dead hog. All grey and lifeless and bled out.

He points at the bag and says somethin' but I don't hear it. I lift the bag up too and somethin' is pokin' out the through the hole. I know what it is, but my brain is slow to believe it, because I know what's in the bag. Pa told me. But this thing hangin' out is not what Pa said.

It's a hand. Pale skin like when you've been in the bath too long, no hair. Stained in that same black-red stuff that leaked out on the grass. I lift the bag up more and the stuff inside moves around. The butchered hog smell comes rushin' out and hits my throat. The rip gets wider and this dead person's hand flops out more, all five fingers. One finger shorter'n the others. There's a rippin' sound and the tear gets bigger and there's the trash bag in the duffel, torn open too, and staring up at me from inside is an open eyeball. I can't tell if it's on a face or just floatin' there in all the blood.

I let go the bag and it drops and makes a waterbed sound and a bunch a dark liquid comes splashin' out onto my jeans.

"Jesus, Travis," Jonah says. "What the hell is that?"

His mouth hangs open and his chin is shakin' and there's a big wet spot on the crotch of his jeans.

"It's Booker," I tell him, and I almost can't breathe when I say it, because of what it means.

"You sure?" Jonah says.

I hold up my hand and tap the ring finger. Jonah knows what I mean.

Jonah starts cryin' and I wish he'd stop. I can't think any thoughts.

Pa lied, and that's a cold knife slippin' between my ribs. My throat's closin' up and I'm seein' black. Oh Jesus, I just wanna lay down and be nowhere.

4

Jonah's just wailin' now, rockin' back and forth with his arms 'round his knees and he don't look so old anymore. He looks just like he did when he was small enough to fit inside the dresser drawer where he'd hide and fall asleep and make everyone lookin' for him sick with worry.

The sun's behind some clouds and I stare at it until my eyes go white and I see lights floatin'. When things clear I turn back to the house and there's someone coming 'cross the field. A big woman with curly hair piled on top her head. She looks kinda familiar but she's just a shape right now.

I go over and slap Jonah on the face. "Stop your blubberin' and get down there." Pointin' to the valley and the grass covered mound where we buried the deer. "Take the duffel."

Jonah looks up, sees the woman comin' closer. He grabs the duffel and drags it down the hillside, and all the sloshin' makes more blood come spillin' out. A long pink tube squeezes out past the eye and the hand, trails behind the bag like a tail. Trigger takes off running after Jonah.

The woman's voice calls out, "Howdy. What are you boys doing out here?"

I look back and Jonah is almost at the bottom of the hill. He doesn't notice that Booker's hand has come all the way out of the bag and sits there in the blood trail like a dead fish. The pink tube has come out too. My whole stomach clenches up like a fist and acid burns my throat. Good thing I didn't eat breakfast, or it'd be all over my shoes.

"Just buryin' our dog," I yell back to the woman.

She's closer now. Close enough to see she's wearin' an Eddie's Diner waitress uniform, and the name "Lena" is stitched on the breast pocket.

Her perfume smells like a grandma, but she don't look quite that old. Her eyelids is blue and the makeup on her cheeks cracks when she smiles. There's some wetness just under her nose. Her face is wide and the uniform fits pretty snug, shows the rolls of her arms, her belly.

She says. "Shouldn't you be in school?"

I glance back and see Jonah doing his best to drag the duffel behind the grass mound, but if the woman looks down there, it ain't gonna matter. A snail trail of blood with a dead man's hand and a piece of his guts. Trigger's runnin' in circles 'round that hand.

"No, ma'am," I say. "Me and my brother is sick. Dog died last night, and Pa told us to bury him."

The woman is close enough for me to hear the creak of her leather shoes. She stops and stares at me and her eyes are kind, but there's some worry in there too. She's got a handkerchief all bunched up in one hand and a purse hangin' from the other.

"Travis, isn't it?" she says. "Do you remember me?"

"No, ma'am," I say.

The woman wipes at her nose, says, "I'm not surprised, we haven't seen each other in a while, and I'm a little bigger than I used to be. I'm Lena Crenshaw, Booker's wife."

I feel like there's another person inside me, living in my stomach, and he's tryin' to push everything up out my throat.

She says, "Booker didn't come home last night and I'm getting kinda nervous. You haven't seen him, have you?"

I shake my head, but I can't speak, and I don't trust my legs no more. They're going all jelly. I suddenly have to pee real bad, and I got that bad taste in my throat like I wanna barf.

Lena takes a few steps to me. "Is your daddy home?"

I swallow and say, "No, ma'am. He's at work."

Lena opens her mouth, but she doesn't say nothin'. She looks at me like Ma used to when I'd got scraped up or fallen down.

"Oh sweetie," she says, and reaches out a hand like she wants to touch my face. "You're all covered in blood. What happened?"

I look behind me real quick, but I don't see Jonah. He must have run into the woods. I don't blame him. I see Trigger and I can't get any air. He's sniffin' at Booker's hand, and it takes all I got to not yell at him.

Lena comes so close her perfume's all I smell. My eyes is burnin' somethin' awful when she puts a hand on my arm.

"Come on," she says," let's go inside and get you cleaned up. I'll make you some food. You're all skin and bones. Your daddy ain't cookin' much these days, is he?"

Her foot moves into the blood on the grass. She feels it, looks down and sees the dark red liquid on her shoe.

"Travis, sweetie, what's all the blood from? Are you hurt?"

"I told you," I say, and hold one arm over my belly. I can't help it. "Our dog died."

Lena looks over my shoulder. "Where were you gonna bury him?"

Oh Jesus, my stomach. It hurts so much I hunch over. Tears are comin', I feel 'em.

Then Trigger barks and Lena's eyes go big. She walks past me to the edge of the hill. She's quiet as long as it takes me to stand up straight, then she's screaming and it's so loud and full of hurt that her voice breaks into big wheezy sobs like she can't breathe. I go to the edge all hunched over and look down and see the dog has Booker's hand hangin' out of his mouth and he's pawin' at the piece of guts like it's a red snake. Lena's whisperin' "Sweet Jesus, dear sweet God in heaven." She spins around and her face is pain and fear and anger and I see her eyes real clear and they look the same color as the gravel, and my stomach clenches again so tight I swear it's twisting itself into a knot, and Lena's shakin' her head and breathin' heavy like a dog that's chased somethin' and I smell her sweat now and her perfume makes my head hurt like allergies and she's sayin' somethin' about callin' the cops and she doesn't know what's going on but she's gonna find out and take us away from Pa and oh sweet Jesus what have you done, and I sink to the dirt and dry heave just like Jonah does, and then Lena puts a hand to her forehead and her skin is turnin' red, and she calls me a monster and she screams again and there's a thunder crack but it don't come from the sky, it comes from the hill, and a hole bursts open in Lena's chest and I feel a warm mist fall on my face, and her mouth opens and her eyes get big and she stumbles forward a step or two, and she goes down to her knees, looking at me at the whole time, and I see her lips movin' and I want to know what she's sayin' but I also don't because it's probably bad, and blood comes up over her lips and down her chin, and then she falls forward straight onto her face and her nose makes a snappin' sound, and from behind her comes Jonah holdin' the rifle, a little smoke still comin' from the barrel.

Jonah don't look like no killer. His lips and nose are movin' like he's tryin' not to cry. I get up and go over to him and he hands me the gun like its somethin' horrible he don't want to hold no more.

Lena's hands are grabbin' grass, and her thick legs are twitchin', tryin' to push herself forward. She scrapes her belly along the grass. Bubblin' sounds come from her mouth and she's moanin', but it's weak. She's draggin' a big trail of bright blood now and the moanin' drives me crazy, like a squeaky wheel on a shoppin' cart.

Jonah pushes into my leg, both his hands held together up by his heart, like prayin'. He sniffs against my jeans and says, "Can you make her stop? That sound is hurtin' in my head."

And Lena moans and gurgle breathes as she drags herself further into the field. I leave Jonah and walk over to her. I could take the blame when it all comes out, but that don't help Jonah none. He knows what he did, and he can't carry that all by hisself. Lena coughs and sprays blood on the grass and her moanin' has a wheeze in it, like a balloon leakin' air.

I raise up the rifle, look back at Jonah and tell him to cover his ears and close his eyes. He does as I say then I aim the gun and pull the trigger.

5

Jonah and I sit at the top of the hill. He chews his nails until they bleed and there's red smeared around his mouth. Trigger dropped the hand a while ago and now he's pawin' at the grass mound and whinin'.

"Are we thinkin' the same thing?" Jonah says.

"I figure we probably are," I tell him.

Jonah's chin is shakin' and his eyes are full of water.

"Can you say it?" he asks. "Please, I don't want to."

I breathe out as far as I can. "We're thinkin', if it wasn't Trigger in them duffels, that means Pa lied, and now we're wonderin' if it was really a deer in them duffels we buried down there." Noddin' at the green mound.

Jonah sniffs and nods.
"Stay here," I tell him.

He's sittin' in the same place, chewin' the nails on his other hand when I come back with the shovels. I hand him one and we go down the hill to the grass covered mound where we buried the deer. We don't say nothin'. We just stab the blades into the ground and dig.

6

Jonah digs until he can't dig no more. His arms is shakin' like he's cold, face all scrunched up tryin' not to cry but he's cryin' anyway. Quiet though. Wet muddy tracks from his eyes to his chin and he won't look at me.

I take his shovel, tell 'im to sit down and he does, shiverin' with his arms 'round his legs. I keep diggin', makin' a pile of dirt next to the pile I'm undoin'. I ain't ever had a flashback before, don't even know if that's what this is, but real quick like I'm not in Today, I'm in Awhile Back, diggin' this same hole and draggin' some duffel bags into the hole. Nothin' rippin' up my mind like right now. Just a deer that's gotta be put somewhere and a hole is as good a place as any. But that was Then, and this is Now, and some part of me knows things ain't ever gonna be like they was in Then.

A nasty smell, like the trash pile 'fore we burn it, sneaks up outta the hole and burns my nose. It's the smell of dead and old and turnin' back into earth. It hits my throat like when I accidentally shove my toothbrush too far back there. I cough and swallow a bubble that goes down to my stomach and pops, fills my mouth with the taste of burned up cereal.

I stab the ground again and the smell comes out more.

Jonah watches the shovel goin' in and out, and he's rockin' back and forth, his eyes big like if he blinks more tears'll come.

I go careful with the shove, feelin' close to somethin' even though I can't see nothin' yet. And sure enough, the blade hits somethin' that ain't dirt. The shovel sorta pushes back but it's not hard like a root. It has some give.

I scrape away some dirt and there's the blue canvas of Pa's gym bag, from when he used to box down at Rider's, and even though he stopped boxin' Pa still knows how to hit. And the sight of that bag makes my head go balloon and the hillside kind of wobbles.

The smell is so bad I breathe through my mouth, but don't help none 'cause now I taste it, and so does Jonah. His face goes the color of Booker's skin, and his cheeks puff out like he's gonna blow a bubble, but then his mouth opens, and barf comes pourin' out. It splashes on the ground between his knees, and 'fore he can move he brings up another mouthful on his shirt.

He starts cryin' again. Barf on his lips, his teeth.

There's a split in the wet and dirty fabric, but I know what color it used to be because it was still blue when I buried it. I take the pointy end of the shovel, use it tear open the bag a little more.

The smell that comes up outta the hole is worse than when we came across one of Jacoby's sheep that wandered into the woods and died. A rotten death smell that makes me never wanna eat anything that was ever livin' again. Thinkin', this is what we smell like when we're so gone that we ain't nothin' but the rotten soup of all the stuff we was made of.

I think I can hold it in, but when I see the flowers, I suck a breath and the smell hits the back of my throat, makes my stomach come rushin' up.

I drop the shovel, turn, and barf.

I kneel down and brush some dirt away from the hole in the bag. Little blue flowers on a yellow dress, the one Ma was wearin' when Pa said she run off. But the dress ain't yellow no more, and the flowers are changed from blue to rusty brown.

She's in there, whatever's left of her. My neck aches like I got the flu, and my hands is shakin' as bad as Jonah's. I put her here, and it don't seem to matter that she was dead when I did. Right now, looking at her dress, it matters that she ain't in a grave and with all the talk people do about the dead restin', I worried she ain't gonna have any peace.

I look over and Jonah's watchin' me, mouth hangin' open, eyes all big like I'm gonna tell him ain't nothin' but a deer in the hole, just like Pa said. And I wanna lie to him, but lyin' only ever got us where we are now, and that's a world of shit. So, I look right at 'im and nod once. When my eyes close, tears itch down my face, and it takes all I got to not bawl like a baby.

Jonah sucks in air and his chin moves like he wants to say somethin', and his eyes fill up and spill over.

Guilt just kinda covers me up like a blanket that's been left out in the cold, and I know I shouldn't feel it, but I do.

I get up and go over to Jonah. I touch his shoulder, and he keeps starin' at the mound.

"Don't look at her," I tell him.

As I walk back up the hill the whole earth slips sideways, like maybe I'll go tumblin' right off the edge. Past the torn-up bag and Trigger's back to snoutin' 'round in the mess. His teeth grab the black garbage bag inside and he shakes his head to get it loose. A hole tears and more of Booker comes spillin' out.

I go over to Trigger, and he drops a piece of somethin' and backs away, head down, takin' quick looks up at me with a face as happy as it is guilty. I swat him on the nose harder than I mean to and the way his tail drops makes me even sicker.

I yell, "No" and make like I'm gonna swat him again and Trigger jerks away, trots off, his tail dragging dark red on the grass behind him.

Jonah still sits down by the dug-up mound, cryin' himself to hiccups.

Trigger follows behind me, head down. He looks at the other duffel of Booker, looks at me, and keeps walkin'. Dark clouds have rolled in and there's a breeze rustlin' through the grass. Jacoby's sheep start bleatin' and it sounds like kids cryin', or maybe that's just Jonah. I look up at the sky and close my eyes, feel little drops of rain, and I wish another Noah's flood would come and just drown everything clean again.

Our house is a shadow in the distance. Pa's American flag snappin' in the breeze on the front porch, the ends all shredded.

I try not to look at her, but Lena Crenshaw's body keeps drawin' my eye. Flies are already buzzin' 'round her head.

That cold blanket get a little tighter 'cause I didn't do nothin' to Ma, but Lena's the way she is 'cause of me. At least Booker's already gone too, so he ain't have to miss her.

My toe kicks somethin' hard and I look down and see the rifle. I pick it up and use my shirt to wipe the whole thing down, like guys do in the movies to ruin their fingerprints.

There's a rumblin' in the sky and the hairs on my arm raise up a little. Trigger lies down next to me, puts his head on my shoe. My legs look like they're far below me, like my balloon head is floatin' up into the clouds. Between where I am and where Jonah is, there are three bodies on this land.

My thoughts move slow, like they do when Pa hits me, and I see things I ain't ever seen before, but I don't know what to do with them. Everything here should be hidden. Every-thing here is bad. It's death and murder, and it means none of this is gonna end good.

And the blood. Shit. There's blood all over the place. The whole trail of it that leads to Lena, and then every-thing splattered 'round her. Booker's just everywhere. Trigger was busy while we was diggin'. Speakin' of Trigger, the damn dog's fur is all crusty with blood and his tail's still thumpin' like he's glad about it. Muzzle wet and red, he looks like he been doing exactly what he's been doing. Rubbin' his nose in what's left of a guy chopped up.

It can't get clean. None of it.

Jonah comes up behind me, sniffin' and hiccupin', and I smell the barf on him. When I turn there's a big wet stain on the front of his pants and he smells like piss. His eyes look like they did the time he had pink eye, and snot drips 'round his mouth.

"You didn't look, did you?" I say.

Jonah shakes his head but he's cryin' again. He stands straight like he's tryin' to be tough but he ain't convinced himself.

"God damn it," I say, and his head falls a little. I want to scream and yell at him, but I can't blame him for lookin', and I ain't Pa.

I touch his shoulder and his whole body melts. He folds over and cries so hard he starts coughin'. I pull him close and hold him, body jerkin' like he's havin' a fit.

"I knew she wouldn't just up and leave us," Jonah says. "I knew it."

He goes down to the grass real slow and sits, legs goin' all Parkinson's. I sit next to him, and he stares at Lena Crenshaw's body, his eyes bigger than they should be. I don't tell 'im not to look 'cause it ain't nothin' he ain't already seen. And that hole in her back was him. If he wasn't older before, he sure as hell is now.

He picks a blade of grass, rips it into small pieces and lets 'em fall.

"Ma used to say to me at night, right before sleep, she'd say 'I'll love you forever.'" He looks at me. "You don't just say that and then leave."

I nod.

"Forever is forever," he says.

Lookin' at 'im, the way he is, I can barely remember the way he was. Somethin's changed, like time went real fast while we was out here in this field. Like maybe years went by instead of hours. I feel the cold blanket even tighter now, that guilt, but it's all mixed together with something else and I don't know what to call it. Somethin' missin', I guess. Like somethin' important inside us got blown apart today and it's scattered all over in pieces as small as the grass Jonah keeps tearin' up.

She's gone. For real. And it hits so hard, makes my hair itch like poison oak. If she'd run off, she'd be somewhere out there still livin', and we could hate her for leavin', hate Pa for makin' her leave. But this, there ain't words for this. She ain't out there, and wherever she is, she took that forever love with her.

Jonah sniff, hiccups. "I miss her more now," he says.

Forever.

Maybe forever is a lie just big enough to believe in. Makes us think we got more livin' ahead of us than we do behind us.

"This ain't our fault," I say. "You know that don't you?"

Jonah nods, but he don't look like he means it.

Trigger gets up and moves closer to Jonah, rubs crusty blood against his shirt. "What do we do?" Jonah says.

The cold I felt is gettin' warmer. I think of Pa comin' home and seein' all this, losin' his mind. I think of all that anger he got, and it makes me mad that he ain't ever let us feel what we felt. He always made his mad so much bigger than ours.

Three people, between us and them woods. Dead.

"We leave," I say. "We ain't got no choice."

Jonah nods slow, like he knew that's what I'd say.

"What about Pa?" he asks.

I think about Pa and see his face, and the cold gets warmer and warmer, and part of me wants to wait for 'im in the house. Be sittin' there in his chair with the rifle in my lap when he comes through the door. I'd say the perfect thing, somethin' I can't think of right now, but I'd say it and he'd look at me and see a man instead of a boy and his eyes would go all big with fear 'cause he knew what was comin'. Then I'd pull that trigger and watch his body hit the floor, and I'd watch the blood leakin' out of him and I'd know that blood is in me and Jonah, but we got lucky 'cause it's mixed with Ma and maybe that's makes us better. Maybe that means we got a chance.

"What about Pa?" Jonah asks again, and I look at him.

"He's gonna have to face whatever comes next all his own," I say.

I get up, give my hand to Jonah and help him up. Trigger trots over to the trail of Lena's blood, but I snap my fingers, and he comes to me. We go back across the field to our house, and the sky gets darker with clouds, and by the time we reach the house, the sky done ripped, and rain is fallin' hard.

7

We get inside, and Jonah looks around like it's a place he ain't ever been before—like it's a place we ain't supposed to be. All the lights is off, and the place is dark. The rain beats loud on the roof.

I tell Jonah to strip down and he does, stands there in the kitchen butt naked holdin' both hands over his privates. Ain't nothin' I ain't seen, but I don't make nothin' of it. I tell him to go upstairs and shower, and to take Trigger with, get 'im all cleaned off.

Skinny kid with rusty red stains on his hands, his arms, his face and neck, he shivers and asks, "Do we need to be careful?"

He lifts his hands up, shows 'em to me. He means the blood, the evidence, I guess you'd call it. And I see his weiner real quick, and like I thought, he's got some pubes. Pa never did understand Jonah. Not like Ma did, not like me.

Jonah puts his hands back and he reminds me of a foal what just falled out of the momma's backside, all weak and skinny and covered in gunk, shiverin' in the air of a world it ain't ever seen before.

"No," I say. "I don't think it matters."

Truth is, I been thinkin' 'bout it since I walked back up the hill. Our cops ain't the smartest bunch, but they ain't the dumbest neither. It wouldn't take long to get an idea about what happened out here. Maybe they'd figure out Pa didn't shoot Lena, but maybe they wouldn't.

"Get you and Trigger clean. Then start packin' up. Can't be too much."

Jonah nods and some tears run out his eyes. I know what he's thinkin', 'cause I'm thinkin' the same thing. So much we gotta leave behind. He can't take all his favorite toys, and I can't take my muscle car models.

It'll all be just another shovelful of dirt on Pa's grave inside my head.

Jonah turns and goes upstairs, Trigger followin' his skinny ass. Soon as they're gone, I go back outside, head to the garage. It don't take me long to find bits of blood and tiny little chunks of Booker on the floor under the saw. Pa tried to clean it, but he ain't ever been good at knowin' what other people see.

I dig through some shelves until I find the Army green rucksack Pa uses when he goes huntin'. He ain't never been in the Army though, I think he got it from some surplus store.

All sudden, my head goes light again, and the garage moves a bit. I don't know what to take. I dig through the box of campin' stuff, but I don't where we'll end up, if campin' is what we'll be doing. I grab some of the metal plates and cups, the little pot, some forks and spoons, and put 'em all in the sack. I grab two sleepin' bags, a tent, and a blue tarp, and take everythin' inside the house.

The shower's goin', and the pipes is clangin' in the walls. I can hear Jonah sobbin' from here. Rain hits the windows hard and sounds like BB's against the glass. Jonah can't carry as much as me, so I'll have to carry all the food and supplies. I go through the cupboards and grab the stuff that don't go bad. Cans of tuna, soup, crackers. There's a big ass bag of dog food, but ain't no way I'm carryin' that.

I shove everything in the pack and lift it up. The god-damn thing is heavy already, and I ain't even got my clothes in it.

"This is too heavy for me to carry," I say, out loud. And when I say it, it sounds like somethin' you read in a poem, somethin' that means more than one thing and the other thing it means makes my eyes burn 'cause it's true.

But I ain't got no choice in the matter. We gotta go and we need what's in the pack. I'll take less clothes, I guess.

Once Jonah's outta the shower I tell him to get his stuff together, then I take a shower so hot it makes my skin bright red and tingly. In my room, I put on clean clothes and pack up two pairs of jeans, a long-john shirt, a couple t-shirts, a sweater, and some socks and underwear. It ain't much, but it'll have to do.

I go into Jonah's room, and he's strugglin' to zip up his backpack it's so full. Trigger's lyin' on the bed wrapped in a towel, just watchin'. I lift the bag and hear all sorts of stuff clankin' around, so I open it up and the kid ain't packed nothin' but one shirt, one pair of pants, and a shit ton of toys.

"Jonah, you can't take all this shit. We gotta pack light."

Jonah starts cryin' again and it makes me mad, but I tell myself that's how Pa gets whenever Jonah's hurtin', and it makes the mad go away. I go through Jonah's closet and dresser, take out the clothes I think he'll need.

"Pack these first," I tell 'im. "Whatever room you got left over you can fill with toys. But remember, you gotta carry it. I got way more shit in my bag and I ain't gonna be helpin' you, alright?"

Jonah sniffs, starts doin' what I asked. I go to leave the room, turn around, and say, "We'll be back for it someday. It's for a little while, you know."

We ain't got no Zip-Loc bags, so I pull out a big sheet of tin foil, pour a bunch of dog food on it and wrap it up. I look outside and the rain has stopped, and the clouds have parted enough to see the sun is headed for the hills. Soon they'll turn red, and the sky'll go pink, and that's about the time Pa gets off work.

I open the fridge to see if there's anythin' worth takin' I missed. There's a couple cans of Pa's beer, and I think what the hell, and grab 'em. There's a couple slices of old pizza, and I figure that's good enough to get us somewhere, and wherever that is we'll figure somethin' else out then.

I yell for Jonah and he and Trigger come downstairs. Jonah walkin' all wobbly with the big ol' bag on his back. I make him take it off so he can put on his jacket, and the words I say when I do remind me of Ma. Jonah and I used to tease that half of what she said to us was wear a jacket and drink more water. Guess I'm the one gonna be tellin' him those things now, and Jesus does that sting more than I thought it would.

I tie one sleepin' bag to his backpack, and the other bag and tent on mine, then make Jonah sit down when I tell 'im what I aim to do. He watches my mouth, don't look into my eyes, and I can see them wheels turnin' in his head. He ain't nothin' but a kid but his moral compass always been true, and he knows what I'm sayin' is right.

He listens, then nods.

I say, "With any luck, they'll blame him for all of it. We can always say we ran 'cause we was afraid. Then, I guess it's just you and me, which ain't so bad. Better'n bein' alone anyway."

Jonah nods again, moves his eyes up to mine and his lips are so tight you can't even see 'em.

I go over to the phone on the wall, take it down and dial 911. A lady picks up real quick and asks what my emergency is. *Everything, right now, all of it*, I think. But what I say is, "Help us, please," and give our address, then hang up the phone.

We stand in the door, watch the hills light up, and then start walkin' 'cross the field. Jonah stops halfway, turns 'round, and looks at our house. I can't remember the last time I saw it like just a shadow with no lights on.

When Jonah turns back around, I expect him to be cryin', but he ain't. There's a time for leavin' things behind, and that time can't be argued with no matter how bad you wanna stay. Guess Jonah knows it as well as I do.

Lena's body is up ahead, and Jonah, he don't look, just stares straight ahead as we near the hill.

We stop at the edge and the woods is all stretched out in front of us, so far, I can't see the end of it. We gotta go down past Ma's grave again to reach the woods, and that's where Jonah's lookin'.

"Should we cover her up?" Jonah asks.

I heave the heavy pack up, and the stuff inside clangs and clatters.

"They need to see her," I say. "But it ain't her, you know that. Remember what they said in church, just a shell. The real us leaves when we die."

And standin' there where the ground goes down to the edge of the woods, I look left and right, and maybe 'cause of the shadows, I see somethin' I ain't ever noticed before. Little grassy hills down along the trees, so many of them in either direction. Little hills about the same size as the one Ma's in.

The pack suddenly weighs a thousand pounds, and I fall to my knees, breathin' like I ran the whole way here. Jonah asks if I'm okay, but I can't say nothin' back. Them mounds, they're covered in old grass, covered so much they just blend right into the grass around them.

Sirens echo 'cross the field. I turn and see lights flashin' on the road.

Jonah takes my hand, and I give it a squeeze, then struggle up to my feet, and we head down the hill, goin' as fast as we can into the dark of the trees.

THE GOLDEN RULE

When bad people need bad things done, it's me they come to. I don't do it myself, but the one who actually do it, no one see him.

The bell above door ring and in come some suit-man with squeaky shoes. He something big in company, my eyes see. He sweaty. Tie untied. Cigarette smell but yellow fingers, no. Scared smoker, he is.

He look around with big eyes. Shelves of things I collect since I come to this country. I buy, I sell. Most best expensive things in attic. I show if someone knows they there.

"I help you?" I say. I do American smile with much teeth. This suit-man, he no do smile back.

Suit-man smells like ciggy smoke and cologne. He look at me same way every suit-man look at me.

"I was told to come here," suit-man say.

I wave hand at many things I have. Power tools, not much rust. Televisions, guitars, rings, necklaces, videogames, guns. Suit-man look at frame hang on wall behind me.

Suit-man point and say, "What is that?"

Old wrench hung inside frame. Plaque that say my father name and day he born, day he die.

"Is it special?" suit-man ask.

I say, "Very special but not for sale."

"It just looks like a wrench." Suit-man scuff shoe on carpet. It worn and dirty. Stained.

"Everything just look like something." I tap glass countertop where I keep coins. "Best good top investment, right here."

Suit-man shakes head, sniffs. He pull suit jacket tight, stretch neck around. I know what he want, but I wait so he have to say it. He come over to counter and put hand on glass. Gold rings on fingers tap. Eighteen-karat yellow-gold with four diamonds on right-hand ring finger. Ring on pinky bigger, have red gem in center. He look in my eye. Many drops of sweat on forehead like suit-man ate spicy food.

"I need to know, is the place or not?" Suit-man say. His breath, much whiskey.

"Yes," I say, and do American smile again. "This is place."

Suit-man make long blink and breathe from nose. "Listen comrade, do you have something in here that solves problems?"

No more American smile I make. Home-country stare I give him. Stare so long forehead make more sweat.

"What problem you have?"

Suit-man's eyes look up at ceiling, at corners. "Are we being recorded?"

I shake head, and suit-man's face say he no believe me. But he wrong. I no record anything.

"We just talk about it in the open?" suit-man ask.

I hold out hands and do American smile. Nothing to hide here.

Suit-man lean in, put elbow on counter. He speak quiet like secret.

"You know Damon?" he say.

I nod.

"He sent me." Suit-man sniffs. "Said you could help me with something."

Man reach into suit pocket, pull out envelope, and put on counter. I don't open—not yet.

Mr. Damon send many suit-man. Mr. Damon know of box. He believe, and that make him careful. Next day, I walk to bank and look at account. Number always bigger. Someone from Mr. Damon make deposit for me. Every time.

I take out pad of pen and paper, set on counter.

"Write down name," I tell suit-man. "Write down how you want it to happen."

Suit-man's eyebrows lift surprise look. Make no-believe-me look. "Then what?" he ask.

"Then you put in box," I tell him.

Suit-man sniff and wipe nose. Finger make sparkle with snot. "That's it?"

I try do American smile, but it no feel right. "That's it. But you have to remember Golden Rule."

Eyes narrow, Suit-man say, "What does that have to do with this?"

"You remember rule?" I ask.

"Yeah, do to others and all that shit." Suit-man say.

"Remember when you write down how," I tell him.

Suit-man stare at me. Eyes be dark, distrusting. "Where is this box?"

I make head jerk to door that lead to cellar. "Down there."

I see bump under arm of suit jacket, smell odor of sweat.

"And after that?" Suit-man ask and pick up pen.

"You leave," I say. "I take care of rest."

"Just like that?" Suit-man shakes his head and starts to write. "Damon said I'd need to disappear for a while, let the dust settle before coming back."

"Yes, good to leave for days. Weeks maybe."

Mr. Damon ask me once where I find box. I tell him truth, and now he only one who knows. And because Mr. Damon believe, he no want to see box. He pay me to keep box secret.

Back in my country, I tell Mr. Damon, when I was child, my father was most best mechanic in city. There was no car he could not fix. One day, very bad man bring very nice car from Europe. Car cost much money. My father, he say, I no can fix this car. Bad man, he say, you fix or I burn down shop.

This bad man, he work for group of bad men. Very protected. Much fear. My father do best to fix car. Bad man take and drive away. Later in week, it break down on road. Bad man come back and tie my father to chair. He cut off each finger and shove in father's mouth until he no breathe. Bad man beat my father in head with wrench.

My mother come bring dinner and sees men. Bad man shoot mother and leave her to die.

Me, I'm just boy. I come to garage and find father with ten fingers stuck in mouth. Eyes bulge from head. Split skin around mouth, blood flow. Mother on floor in front of chair. Hole in forehead. Everything from head all over walls.

On floor next to mother is father's wrench, sticky with blood from where it beat him.

After parents in ground, I no can get job, so I go to old houses where people no live. I take things they leave, sell them. Not much money but enough.

Boy-me go to one house older than all the others. So old no more glass in windows. Big stones, some crashed to ground and stayed there for hundred years. There nothing but dust and broken bottles. I hope for one good thing, make time worth it. One thing to sell.

History-me find staircase lead to cellar, wood so rotted it dust apart with one step. I jump down into dark, hold flashlight between teeth. I stand on dirt floor, black dirt, wet and stinky. Air feel like blanket on face.

Bones there, in the dirt. Old bones, new bones. Some with piece of clothing, stiff to touch. All bones lie facing something in corner. Arms stretch at it, like worship. Dead worship.

Young me go to it, this thing. Flashlight become dim then no work. Some kind of box, maybe for travel long time ago, made of wood and leather and metal. Metal rusty and lock so old it look like something from dungeon.

Remember, this old country with old stories. We still believe in things we not see, because those things still live here. The stories not just stories. They are warnings. History. I look at bones. I look at box.

I say to box, "Hello."

I say, "I want nothing."

The box say nothing back, but I feel it—make swallow hard—shaking in throat. Shaking very fast. I touch lock and lock is broken, hanging. I think if box want to kill me, it don't matter if I touch or not. So, I touch box, and say "I have nothing, but I want nothing."

The box no kill me, but the shake in throat get harder. I take off lock and lift lid and look inside.

I see everything. Then nothing.

I wake up like from dream, and I'm on big ship. On ocean. The box in room but inside other box. New wood box.

I come to here. I open store. I sell things. Better things than I find in old country. I keep box in cellar, and I talk to it. I think it not talk back, but maybe me only not hearing. Something stay in box, live there, and want me to help. Box is reason I have store, so I say, "I will help you like you help me."

Suit-man finish writing on paper. He fold in half and hold out to me.

I say, "No. You put paper in box."

Eyes distrust, but I no smile no more. I wave suit-man behind counter and open door to cellar. Stairs lead into dark. Smell the dirt floor, the oldness.

"Light no work," I say.

Suit-man put hand to bump under jacket and say, "If you try anything, I will fuck you up."

"Box in corner," I tell suit-man. "It unlocked. You careful, lift lid, put paper inside. Then wait."

Hand still on gun-bump, suit-man say, "How long do I wait?"

"Not long."

Cold air that smells like dark comes up stairs. Suit-man wrinkle nose. Piece of paper in hand wet. Fingers itch to touch gun, but he not know what he scared of cannot be shot.

He sniff again and begin walk downstairs into cellar. He stop halfway down and look up.

"Leave the door open," suit-man say.

I do American three-oh with fingers. "A-Okay," I tell him.

He disappear into dark.

I wait until I hear creak of box open, then close door and lock it. I stand with back to door. Something happen down there every time like spark in air before storm. It come from under door and touch ankles like little bees. It hurt, but it also feel good like fingernails on skin.

I open envelope suit-man gave me. Envelope from Mr. Damon. Inside one piece of paper and one picture. I open the letter first and read.

Mr. Damon say it time to stop using box. There is talk on street about my shop, about me. Much danger if we continue. We knew this happen someday. Mr. Damon also say he found what he owe me, what he promised.

I look at picture. Mouth go dusty and head feel light. Scared like suit-man, I am.

Picture, no color. Photo of man on street in old country, walking, smoking. Older than history-me remember. Swallow feel like stones in throat.

It picture of bad man I not see since long time. He still live. Bad man who kill mother, kill father. I look for him, make telephone calls, but no one know. Mr. Damon say he ask for me. Mr. Damon found him.

I put picture back in envelope and wait.

I wait.

I wait until I hear scream. Awful bad man scream. It become gurgle, like choking on food. Spicy food, maybe. Then it stop. Storm feeling go away.

I unlock door and go downstairs into cellar. Box is closed, but dirt around box is blood wet. Suit-man lie on ground, half his face missing. Jaw torn off, some white teeth scatter on black dirt. Suit-man's eyes open so big. Gun lie next to open hand. He never fire shot.

Blood puddle in dirt move toward box. Flow through dirt and under box until disappear.

I get shovel and start to dig. Suit-man probably no see other dirt piles in corner. Other bad men. Other suit men. And somewhere in city is man whose name was on paper. Paper put into box. This man, probably other bad man, he lie dead with half his face gone. He die like it say on paper, like Suit-man die.

No one remember Golden Rule. I tell them all, but no one listen.

Sometimes I read newspaper and see story of horrible murder. No suspect. Just body torn apart and rotting. I never see what they write on paper, but when I read story I know. Head cut off. Guts pulled out. Balls ripped off. Bones broken, fingers shattered. Eyeballs plucked out.

But for every body there is another that no one know about. Buried here in cellar. Sent by Mr. Damon. I know what he's doing. Soon Mr. Damon will be one in power. I don't care. Everything gets settled in end.

After body buried, I go to box and touch lid. It warm after, always warm. Tomorrow, it go cold again.

"One more," I say to box. "Just one."

I go upstairs and take piece of paper, write down name and tell box what I want it to do. Only time I want anything from box. The name I write, it make stomach feel like vomit, but I smile when I write how. Think of this for such long time.

I fold paper and then take down frame with wrench. Undo back and take wrench out. Paper in one hand, wrench in other, I walk downstairs and go to box. I lift warm lid, look inside and see everything. It make brain hurt to see so much. I drop paper inside then walk back to middle of cellar. Fingers tighten around wrench. Soon, will smash face, my face. I will fall and wrench will keep smashing until head is nothing. But I know that across ocean in old country, very bad man will fall to ground with no face. Wherever he be, blood will cover walls. Police will not know what to say.

Sweat drip down into eyes and sting. My fingers tighten on wrench as the lid of box creak open and blue light shine comes out.

THE DEVIL ON THE STAND

1

When Carol Delaney's father committed suicide, it didn't come as a surprise. It was a long dark fall into a long dark night. It had been like watching him die from a slow disease, something that ate away at him over the course of months and years. She often woke up in the middle of the night thinking about him, wondering if his soul was floating somewhere in the room, watching over her. Sometimes, she would get up and try to draw him how she remembered him. But no matter how realistic her drawings were, there was always something they could never capture.

Carol was awake when the phone rang so loudly in the quiet room that the sound caused her entire body to jerk. Her hand shook as she batted the nightstand, searching. The sky was dark gray through a crack in the curtains. She found the phone and answered. It was the station manager.

"I can't get ahold of McAdams," his was voice a register higher than normal. "I need you to work today."

Without her glasses on, the shape of Henri Matisse, the cat curled at her feet, was a blur of white and gray. "What time is it?"

"I've been calling him since yesterday morning. He's never not called me back."

Carol could picture the skin on his cheeks turning red with blood blossom, the way they did whenever he was stressed, which was often. "The Jenkins trial, right?" She asked, even though she knew it was. The trial was major national news. You couldn't turn on the TV or open a newspaper without seeing it.

"It's closing arguments today. Can you work, yes or no?"

Carol knew why she woke up thinking of her father. He had died on this day, eight years earlier, and it rained on every single anniversary. She planned to visit the cemetery like she did every year, leave flowers at the headstone, and talk to him like she was leaving a voicemail that he would eventually get. Some people she knew were afraid of ghosts, but the idea that the dead were still close by, close enough to listen when we spoke, was comforting to her.

Carol made a humming noise as she thought. She could always go to the Catholic cemetery on the weekend. Maybe it wouldn't be raining then. So, she agreed to work, and the station manager ended the call without even thanking her. She got out of bed, feeling all fifty-four years in her knees, and pulled open the curtains. Low thunder-clouds hung over the city, a heavy rain beat at the window, and the sky looked like it was coming apart.

After she showered and did her hair, Carol stared at her own face in the mirror. She looked more like her mother with every passing year. Her mother was, at that moment, wasting away in a nursing home on the East Coast, and they hadn't spoken since Carol moved to Portland. She studied the wrinkles around her mouth, eyes, and gray hair, slowly turning silver. Her mother had always worn lots of makeup, bright, bold colors over thick foundation. Carol wore no makeup, she never had.

Carol ate a quick breakfast of oatmeal and raisins while standing at the kitchen counter. Half a dozen easels with unfinished paintings were scattered throughout the living room of her small apartment. Each was of a city street packed with people walking in every direction. Some streets were framed by skyscrapers, others led through quaint villages with brightly colored doors. None of the places in the paintings were real, they were images that came to Carol only when she was holding the brush. Places that existed inside her. And within each one of the paintings, hidden somewhere in the crowds, was a familiar face. Though she never meant to draw him, he always appeared. Sometimes, with the beard he had when she was young, occasionally clean-shaven as he was in later years, but always present. Standing at a shop window, looking over his shoulder at her as he walked.

The largest canvas was not a painting, not yet. It was only the pencil outline of Carol's father's head and face. An outline she had started and erased so many times that the white canvas was now smudged and discolored. But the face was there, traced in faint ghost lines. Carol tried to draw him as she last remembered him. Wrinkles that surrounded his eyes and deepened whenever he smiled. But it was the eyes she was never able to get right. No matter how much she concentrated, the drawing never looked like his eyes. They never looked alive.

Henri Matisse stretched on the floor in the glow of the television. On the screen, a reporter wearing a yellow raincoat stood in front of the courthouse, recapping the trial.

Rory Jenkins had been arrested and charged with murder, accused by his wife, Nadine, of throwing their nine-month-old son to the ground in a fit of anger. An act which fractured the boy's skull and killed him. The case seemed clear until Rory took the stand and told the jury that his wife was evil and it was she, not him, who had thrown their child. He said that she would sometimes put him in a spell and force him to do things he did not want to do.

Rory had a sharp nose, receding hairline, eyes that were too close together, and the sinewy body of a heroin addict. His wife, on the other hand, was beautiful and graceful. She had looked at her husband with sadness and sympathy as he told the courtroom about how nobody else could see her for what she really was.

Since video or photography was not allowed in the courtroom, the news showed some of Christopher McAdams' sketches—images of real moments made to look unreal. Carol could not help but criticize their composition and color as they flashed on the screen.

"Can you believe he outlines in permanent marker?" she said to Henri Matisse with a shake of her head. "Like he's drawing a cartoon."

She put her empty bowl in the sink and knelt next to the cat. She scratched his head and told him to be good. He purred and pushed himself against her hand.

The trial also gained national attention because Nadine Jenkins refused to place her hand on the Bible or say "so help me God" when being sworn in to testify. Through her attorney, Nadine requested to swear instead upon a law book, which she felt was more appropriate. Judge Irwin recessed for the day to consult with his colleagues before deciding to allow Nadine's unusual request the next day.

Carol gathered her sketchbook and leather case of pencils and put them into her bag. The pencil case was a gift from her father, who has been dead for over twenty years now, and the feel of its weight, the shift of the pencils inside, caused her to remember the day it was given to her. Something special to carry the only things in the world that made her feel truly at peace. The only things that covered up all of the noise. Her father gave it to her the day he left, and he also gave her the black leather Bible that he'd used for years, full of tattered pages and highlighted words. She wasn't crying, not then. That happened later at night when she was alone in bed. She asked him why he was moving out. He knelt so they were face to face. His eyes were glistening as he spoke, magnified.

"Your mother doesn't want me here anymore," he said. "But I'll always be close by."

A few days later, Carol overheard her mother telling a friend that her husband used to brutally beat her, a statement that Carol knew to be a lie. Over the next few months, Carol's mother repeated this lie to anyone who came into the house, but she always said it in hushed tones, like it was the truth. Carol's father was a successful attorney, and it was only a matter of time before the secret lie became well-known, and one by one, his wealthy clients started leaving him. No one wanted to be represented by a wife beater.

She left the TV on for Henri Matisse and put on her jacket. She blew the cat a kiss, touched her hand to the golden crucifix hanging on the wall, and opened the door.

The moment Carol stepped out of her apartment, Henri Matisse began hissing and snarling. She turned around to see the hair rise up on the cat's back, his claws gripping the carpet as his back arched.

She took a step back inside. "What is the matter with you?"

Henri Matisse continued hissing, staring at the television as the news showed another McAdams sketch: the one of Nadine Jenkins.

2

When Carol arrived at the courtroom it was already full of people, their voices the drone of an insect swarm. She took her seat in the jury box, then reached into her bag and took out a sketchpad and the leather case of colored pencils. The trial was not set to resume for another thirty minutes, but Carol liked to start with a sketch of Henri Matisse to warm up her hands. She took out a Coal Black pencil and a Warm Gray from the case and began to draw.

Although she had been sketching for the better part of twenty-five years, Carol had only taken over a colleague's work in the middle of a trial a handful of times. With only two sketch artists working in the city, you couldn't afford to work when the opportunity presented itself, especially when the trial was so high profile. She wondered if Christopher McAdams was sick, so sick that he couldn't even answer his phone. But she had seen him work sick before, looking half-dead as he sat slumped in his chair, hands moving over the paper as though they were the only part of him still alive.

As she drew, Carol thought of her father, a broken man, branded by an accusation he could not shake no matter how hard he tried. Eventually, he stopped trying, and then he died. He was found kneeling in the closet of his one-bedroom apartment, only eight miles away from the 4,000-square-foot home he'd been kicked out of. An off-white bed sheet was tied around his neck, the other end tied to the rod from which his clothes hung. He leaned into the tension of the sheet, allowing it to tighten around his throat until he couldn't breathe. And that's how he was found, his body suspended at an angle, defying gravity, halfway to the floor.

And that image of her father was what Carol drew, though she didn't mean to. His bulging eyes coursed with red veins. His purple tongue sticking out obscenely through his lips. The old ratty t-shirt he wore, the white flesh of his belly peeking out beneath the hem. Carol was in a trance as she drew, so she didn't realize what was coming out of her pencil until she drew the sheet. That's when she stopped, her eyes burning with tears, and scratched out the image with her black pencil. Scribbling over it all until it was invisible.

By the time Carol fished out some tissues from her bag and wiped her eyes, the jury had entered and taken their seats. Then, from behind the bench, a door opened. The bailiff raised his voice and told everyone to rise for the honorable Judge Andrew Irwin. The entire crowd stood as Judge Irwin walked into the courtroom, black robes flowing around his body in a way that made Carol think he was wrapped in shadows. His white hair stood in stark contrast to his clothing.

A few moments later, a thin man with haunted eyes, dressed in an orange jumpsuit, was led through a side entrance by two large police officers. The entire room seemed to inhale collectively, creating the sound of the wind's low howl as Rory Jenkins walked down the aisle to where his attorneys sat. This thin man did not look either of them in the eye. His gaunt face was expressionless. He sat slouched in his chair while looking at the Judge with narrowed eyes. Carol could feel the hatred radiating from the crowd at the back and the jury box. Several of the jury leaned forward as if their disgust became magnetic, drawing them closer.

Then the back door of the courtroom opened, and Nadine walked in with the two prosecutors. Carol watched as Nadine took her seat just behind the attorneys' table. She was even more beautiful in person, beautiful in a way that felt unnatural. Her face displayed just the right amount of pain without ever completely collapsing into the raw, ugly hurt that one must feel when they've lost a child. It was a poised face, but Carol could tell it took great effort to remain that way by her tight lips and clenched jaw.

When Carol began drawing Nadine, she started with the mouth. Beautiful full lips, slightly chapped. Her light brown hair didn't look dyed, and Carol liked this about her. Nadine's makeup was classy and not overdone.

Sometimes, Carol drew a person without looking down at the paper as her pencil moved. Her hand felt each motion, each distance, and she did this now as she stared at Nadine, almost mesmerized by her beauty. She continued drawing as Rory's attorney stood and delivered his closing argument.

The man spoke about how it was not his job to prove Rory's innocence but rather the job of the prosecutors to prove his guilt. And so far, no evidence had been presented that definitively substantiated the claim Rory killed the child. In fact, the only certainty was that a child had died, a loss shared by both parents, not just Nadine.

Black lines appeared on Carol's paper, curving, creating a shape.

The defense attorney came closer to the jury and looked each of them in the eye. "We may never know what really happened that night," he said, "but we cannot make this tragedy right by imprisoning an innocent man. A grieving father who has not yet been able to properly mourn."

The attorney walked the length of the jury box, keeping one hand in his pants pocket and holding out the other as though he were offering them something.

"Have we reached the point in our history in which an accusation, a story, is all that's necessary to convict a man? The prosecutor has presented you with one version of events. I've presented you with another. So, if you have any doubt whatsoever, you must choose to see him as innocent. Ask yourselves this, what is the greater crime, to imprison an innocent man or to let a guilty man go free?"

Carol found a Carmine Red pencil in her hand, though she did not remember reaching for it.

Some of the jurors shifted in their seats after the attorney finished speaking. One woman to Carol's right whispered the words "burn in hell" so quietly they seemed to come from nowhere.

As Rory's attorney sat back down, Carol looked at what she'd drawn. When she saw the picture, she took a sharp breath in and held it. She didn't understand. She blinked once, twice, rubbed her eyes, and looked at it again. The hand that held the pencil began shaking, leaving small red marks on the paper.

There was the table and the prosecutors, all sketched accurately. But seated behind the lawyers was not Nadine. Carol had drawn a deformed thing with coal-black skin she presumed was leathery over a body with stark ribs protruding from its torso. Gaunt arms led to hands with wickedly long fingers tipped with sharp points. The face was the true horror: lifeless and without any trace of human emotion, set in a triangular-shaped head. Two red points that she took for eyes stared at Carol.

She turned the sketch pad over on her lap and tried to calm her breathing. The real Nadine still looked human as one of the prosecutors, a woman in a black blazer, stood and approached the jury box, and Carol told herself she had gotten lost too far in her own thoughts and had drawn some horrible image from her subconscious.

The attorney in the black blazer began by making a list of all Rory Jenkins's failures as a husband, a father, a provider, and a human. He was lazy and self-centered, a sometimes verbally abusive drunk. His friends were lowlife drug users and thieves. Here was a man, the attorney said, who had no concept of what it meant to truly be alive. He ignored his family and his responsibilities, thinking of no one but himself. He continued to drink and use drugs, no matter how many times Nadine begged him to stop for the sake of their child. And now that child was dead, by his own hand.

Carol knew she should have been drawing the scene. Sketching the attorney as she stood so close to the jury box the group could smell her perfume. Her face was radiant as she spoke, almost glowing with righteous fervor.

Carol turned the pad over and meant to start sketching the prosecutor. But her attention had moved back to Nadine, sitting there poised and elegant, eyes glistening with tears as her attorney described the dead boy. Eyes that looked up and locked onto Carol's for just a second, but it was long enough for Carol to feel a shock in her nerves. Then Carol's hand started moving without her permission. The courtroom narrowed to a single point until all Carol could see was Nadine. And still, her hand kept moving. The attorney's voice came to her as though it was underwater, distant and garbled. She felt her hand tense and press the lead deeper into the paper, scratching back and forth in quick, violent motions.

All at once, the room came back into focus. The attorney had finished her closing argument, and Judge Irwin asked the jury to exit and begin deliberations. Carol sat where she was long after the twelve men and women stood and walked through the door, the sketch pad face down on her lap. She turned it over slowly, hoping desperately she would see something beautiful looking back at her, but Nadine was nowhere to be found on the paper. Instead, Carol had drawn the attorney, looking very much as she did while she spoke to the jury. Standing next to her, however, was the demonic figure, risen to its full height. One long arm lay at its side, and the other hand rested on the attorney's shoulder, its long claws reaching halfway down the woman's chest. Once again, its small red eyes were looking directly at Carol. Behind the creature, the courtroom was melting like wax. Every person and object, even the tables and walls, was dripping down into puddles on the floor. A cold sweat trickled down Carol's back and made her shiver. Even her hands were leaving wet smudges on the paper, smearing the drawing.

She needed fresh air, and she needed it now. Carol stuffed the pad into her bag and left the courtroom in a hurry. She ran outside without putting on her coat and inhaled the crisp air deeply. A light rain fell, and Carol lifted her face toward it, allowing the drops to land on her skin and in her hair.

A producer from Channel 12 News approached her, clipboard in hand, curly wire leading to an earpiece. Behind him stood a cameraman filming as people exited the building.

"Please tell me you have something we can use," the producer said. "Not like the stuff McAdams gave us yesterday."

Carol looked at him and shook her head. "I saw his sketches on the news this morning."

"Those were old. The stuff McAdams gave us yesterday, they were—"

The producer held one finger up while the other hand went to his ear. He spoke into a small microphone clipped to his raincoat. "Use some archive footage of the courtroom. I don't know, find an old case."

Carol backed away slowly as the producer continued talking to the person in his ear. The world around her felt changed somehow, hollow. She knew she was in the city, standing in front of the courthouse, but the people, the buildings, the rain—it all seemed fake in some way, and she could not name it. She wrapped her arms around herself and walked down the steps, away from the producer's voice, wondering what McAdams had seen, what he had drawn.

Carol Delaney looked at the red brick exterior of St. Mark's across the street. Though it had been years since she had stepped foot inside a church, Carol still believed there was an invisible world just behind the solid world.

Could it be, she wondered? Was she being allowed to see Nadine Jenkins for what she really was? Were her pencils drawing a truth that could not be seen? She remembered being a little girl in Mass and the priest saying that the devil was more of an idea than a person. A force from beyond our world that compelled human action in order to shape the future, to make something darker and far more sinister than the world the rest of us would have made on our own. As Carol stood staring at the golden cross across atop the building, she could not understand why she'd been given such a gift, but she knew it had to be for a reason.

Carol Delaney closed her eyes and began speaking to her father. "You said you'd always be close by," she whispered. "If that's true, tell me what to do."

She stood in the rain until her clothes were soaked through, but she kept her eyes closed so tight she could see little white fireworks exploding in the darkness. Then, a warmth spread through her as a memory came into her mind. An image materialized in her thoughts. An object, something she had forgotten that she owned. Something that had once belonged to her father.

Carol opened her eyes and blinked hard against the brightness. Then she started to jog, praying that a bus would be waiting at the stop to take her home.

When Carol reached her apartment, she was no longer cold. Her heart was beating too fast, too hard. Her breathing came out in ragged gasps as she turned the key in the lock and walked inside. Henri Matisse was lying in front of the sliding glass door that led to the small deck. He turned and looked at his owner as she walked inside.

Carol went to him and knelt, rubbing his head and neck with both hands. "It's going to be okay. I know what to do."

Then Carol rose and found what she was looking for. It wasn't hard to find. It had been in the same place for years.

3

The rain had grown heavier by the time Carol arrived back at the courthouse, and her clothes hung on her frame, wet and dripping. The steps were oddly empty except for the news cameras.

The producer caught sight of her and jerked his head toward the doors. "You better get in there—they're reconvening."

"Already?" Carol asked.

"Someone said it was the fastest deliberation in the history of the city."

Carol ran back inside and took her seat as the court filled back up. The energy in the room was electric, and the loud whispers of the crowd were tense with anticipation. Rory was already seated with his attorney, the left side of his mouth curled into an expression of disgust. Tattooed arms crossed over his chest. Nadine sat behind the prosecutors, her face calm, the skin at the corners of her eyes creased in a faint smile as if she already knew the verdict. Carol told herself that she would draw one more picture. She would draw Nadine and Rory side by side and see what was revealed.

As soon as she started sketching Nadine, the demonic face began to take shape. Carol wanted to stop, she couldn't bear to see those red eyes again, but her hand continued moving, and by the time she finished, Carol was sweating. The demon had moved even closer, standing now in front of the jury box, looking right at her. She immediately started drawing Rory on the other half of the page, starting with his eyes. Eyes that were deep set and surrounded by flesh so dark it looked bruised. Carol continued sketching furiously as the jurors came through the door and took their seats. Judge Irwin spoke, and the jury foreman rose, holding an envelope that he handed to the bailiff, who then gave it to the judge.

Carol's picture became clearer, and the Rory she saw on the page was not the smug, detached man sitting before her. Tears flowed from his eyes. His mouth was open in a howl of pain, but around him was a glow, something bright and pure. As she filled in the rest of his features—the creases in his forehead, the scar at the side of his mouth—she found herself drawing a scared and broken man. She was suddenly flooded with sympathy. She couldn't help it.

The foreman cleared his throat once, and the crowd hushed. He projected his voice out over the room, "We, the jury, find the defendant…"

Carol stood up so suddenly that her chair fell backward. She screamed at the top of her lungs, a sound so terrible that several jurors clamped their hands over their ears. Carol imagined what she must look like—a middle-aged woman with grey hair, soaking wet, wild eyes, and screaming at the top of her lungs. Every face turned in her direction as every mouth fell open in surprise. Judge Irwin nodded at the bailiff, who cautiously moved in her direction with one hand held out like one would approach a cornered animal.

Carol knew she could not allow herself to be tackled to the floor, handcuffed, and dragged from the courtroom like a lunatic. So, she did the only thing she could think of to do. She began convulsing. She made her entire body shake like she was being electrocuted. The open leather pencil case fell from her hand. A rainbow scattered on the floor as the pencils rolled away. Drool hung from her mouth, her eyes rolled back in her head, and then she fell to the ground and continued shaking, all the while screaming out.

The bailiff reached her and spoke soothingly, "Shhh," he said, "you're going to be okay." He took her cold hand in his warm hand and brushed wet hair away from her eyes. The feel of another person's skin on hers was so foreign that she stopped screaming for just a moment.

"You're going to be okay," the bailiff said again. "Let's get you to the hospital."

Then, she was lifted in the bailiff's strong arms. She was weightless for a few seconds, looking at the room sideways until he gently set her feet down on solid ground. She caught a glimpse of the Carmine Red pencil underneath the chair of juror number ten, a middle-aged man in a dark blue suit who looked at her with a mixture of pity and disgust. Carol's notebook lay open on the floor, the last image she had drawn face-up for anyone to see. Nadine, a devil. Rory, a wounded angel. That would be used against her when all was said and done, and she was sure of it.

Carol Delaney saw Judge Irwin's concerned face, and this made her aware that the entire courtroom was staring at her. Those whose mouths weren't covered by their hands, their chins hung, mouths agape, watched in suspense to see if she would have another fit.

Carol tried to straighten out her shirt and tuck it back in. The bailiff kept one hand on her back as she smoothed down her hair. He kept asking if she was okay, but her heart was pounding too hard to hear his words. She pointed at her bag, which lay on the floor next to her overturned chair. The bailiff picked it up and handed it to her. She smiled at him with gratitude, thinking, *there is goodness in the world if only it wasn't so hard to find.*

The bailiff put his other hand on Carol's arm as she took a tentative step, the entire courtroom silent except for the air being blown through the vents. She put a hand to her head and moaned once, softly, allowing herself to be led down the aisle toward the nearest exit, which was the door the jury had just come through. Judge Irwin's eyes followed Carol, as did everyone else's, and she felt their stares as if their vision had gravity, and she could feel the pressure of it on her skin. Now she knew how Rory felt when he'd entered the courtroom. So many people stabbing him with their thoughts, their eyes. So much psychic energy directed at one person, and her heart broke for him a little more.

They were nearing the bench when Carol looked at the bailiff's face, at his dark skin and kind eyes, and she felt sorry for what she was about to do. Sorry, too, that the bailiff may get in trouble.

In one swift motion, Carol twisted her arm and broke away from the bailiff, turning sideways and running toward the bar that separated the court from the gallery. Rory's attorneys stood as she approached, their mouths moving, but she couldn't hear anything they said. She was faintly aware of the bailiff calling her name, his arm reaching out to grab her.

Carol Delaney reached into her deep purse and took out her father's black leather Bible. The feel of it in her hand brought back forgotten memories, the feel and weight of it, the smell of it. She did not know what would happen when it touched Nadine's skin—whether she would simply suffer a broken nose or whether she would burst into flames. All she knew was that Nadine, or whatever she really was, had refused to touch a Bible when she was sworn in. And now Carol knew why. Rory was right about his wife. He was right about everything.

Carol kept running, eye to eye now, with Nadine, whose mouth was just beginning to twist into a sly and arrogant smile until she saw what was clenched in Carol's hands. Carol watched Nadine's face contort and her eyes became just two red circles.

Carol planted her feet, sensing the bailiff close behind her, and then, screaming with all the air inside her lungs, Carol Delaney said a quick prayer and swung the Bible with all her might straight at the woman's face.

The Bible slammed into something solid, and one strong arm wrapped around her shoulders pulled her backward. It was only then that she realized it was the bailiff's massive hand that stopped the book from hitting Nadine. The book lay on the floor, open, its fragile pages bent and folded over. The prosecutors were shielding Nadine, but Carol still saw her face, and the wounded look of surprise seemed so false it almost made Carol laugh.

Voices. The courtroom was filled with shouting voices—from the prosecutors, the defense attorneys, the crowd, and even some of the jury. The judge's gavel slammed down again and again.

The heels of Carol's shoes dragged along the floor as the bailiff carried her toward the door. She took a deep breath and screamed, "Make her touch it! Make her touch the Bible."

The gavel banged again and again. She heard the judge's voice yelling, "Order, order!"

"Put her hand on it," Carol screamed. "You'll see what she is!"

Every person in the room was in motion except Nadine. She stood perfectly, staring directly at Carol. The left side of her mouth lifted into a slight smile. Carol screamed again, but no words came out. Her body was moving through the doorway into another room. The door slammed closed and shut out all the chaos. Suddenly, she lost strength in all her muscles and stopped fighting the bailiff. She allowed herself to be carried. She tried to keep her eyes open, to stay connected to the waking world, but her vision narrowed until she slipped into unconsciousness.

4

Carol awoke briefly, her body jostling back and forth. Tight straps held her down. Was that a siren she heard? A man's face leaned over her, a stethoscope hanging around his neck.

"We're almost there," he said.

And Carol slipped away again.

When she awoke again, she was in a hospital room with an IV connected to her arm. The curtains were open, and rain tapped against the window.

Henri Matisse, she thought. *Someone needs to feed him.*

She felt dizzy and weak. A machine beeped beside the bed, and her limbs were so heavy that she could barely lift an arm to rub her dry eyes. She was covered in a scratchy, paper-thin hospital gown, and she hated to think that someone had taken all of her clothes off, had seen her naked, before putting this awful gown on her.

Carol wanted to cry and hold Henri Matisse to her chest, to feel his warmth and hear his purring. She stared out the window at the endless rain. She remembered what had happened, but now, she wasn't sure how much of it had really happened.

There was a soft knock at the door. Carol tried to speak, but her tongue was thick, swollen, and dry. She could only make a moaning sound.

The door opened, and the silhouette of a tall, thin man dressed in a suit came into the room. As he approached, the light from the window revealed a kind face. His hair was white and combed very carefully. He came around the side of Carol's bed and sat in the chair next to her. He reached out and took her hand in his.

He smiled. "Hello, Carol, I'm Lieutenant Marshall Atwater. It is wonderful to meet you."

He gave her hand a little squeeze. His eyes were pale and intense. He blinked less than she thought he should. In his other hand he held a manila folder. Atwater placed it on the bedside table and opened it. Carol's heart started beating harder. Inside were the drawings she'd made of Nadine, of the prosecutor, of Rory.

Atwater smiled. "I'd like to show you a photograph of someone. Someone you may even recognize." He reached into his jacket and took out a leather pencil case, the one Carol's father had given her. "And I'd like you to draw this person for me. Don't think too much about it, just draw what you see."

Atwater moved Carol's courtroom drawings. Several pages of blank white paper were underneath them, and a photograph on top. Carol recognized the man in the picture, had seen him on TV dozens of times, and even knew his voice.

Atwater handed her the pencil case. His eyes held hers. "Just draw what you see."

Carol couldn't explain why but felt compelled to do what he asked. She undid the zipper of the case, picked a color, and began to draw.

BOO!

1

I come downstairs, careful to avoid the creaky stair in the middle, and Mom is in the kitchen making faces again. Kissy face. Serious face. She's dressed in workout clothes. One hand moves her hair around, twists strands of it, and pulls a little at the neck of her shirt. She's got her phone up, so she can't see me when I come in.

"We have ghosts," I say.

Mom's whole body jerks as she yells. The phone falls out of her hand, and she juggles it a couple times before it hits the floor. There's a sound like dry pasta snapping in half.

"Jesus, Caleb!"

Mom picks up the phone, looks at the cracked screen, and makes a fist with her other hand. She closes her eyes and breathes out real loud. When she opens her eyes, she gives me a big smile, and it's kind of scary because it's not a real smile. Her hand is still a fist, and it's shaking a little bit.

"It's okay," Mom says. "I need a new one anyway. I was going to give this one to you when I did, but now it's broken."

"In the walls, I think," I tell her. "Bumping around, making noises."

Mom touches the phone screen, and it still lights up, but it looks like a bunch of puzzle pieces. She swipes a couple of times, tilts her head, and then looks at me.

"What are you talking about?" she says.

"Ghosts, I heard them last night," I say. "It started with the creaky stair. It made noise by itself."

She makes a Whatever face. "Ghosts?"

"I think there's two of them."

"Caleb, you're almost 11 years old, I don't want you worrying about ghosts."

Breakfast is already on the table: a bowl of yogurt with fruit and granola, plus a glass of green juice that looks like it came from a swamp. A spoon is next to the bowl, and there's a flower in a vase at the middle of the table.

I sit down and pick up the spoon. "Is dad home yet?"

Mom makes a Panic face and grabs the spoon from my hand. "Hold on," she says.

She pulls me out of the chair, puts the spoon back, and then holds up her phone. The bowl and juice are on the screen now, and there's a camera sound. Mom looks at the picture and smiles.

"Okay," she says. "You can eat now."

She never tells me what she's doing, but I know. Once, while she was in the shower, I looked at the app she's always on. So many pictures. Most of them her, but there's a lot of our food, the weather. She's checking that app like all the time. Trees. Our cat. If she hangs something on the wall, she's got to take a picture. She told me once she does it because she likes sharing things with people. So, tell me why she hides Skittles from me in her dresser?

She never posts pictures of me or Dad, though. She says there are things that don't need to be "out there."

Mom taps on the screen and says, "Your father is sleeping," without looking up.

Sometimes, I feel like I only see half her face, like the phone is some kind of comic book villain mask, like the Devastator.

Swipe, tap, swipe, swipe. "Mice, probably," she says, with Rolling Eyes face and sighs. "Your dad was supposed to set traps."

Another thing Dad *was supposed to do* but didn't. She's got a whole list of them. Like he didn't already have enough with working nights as a hospital security guard. Sleep all day, work all night. Sometimes, a whole week goes by, and I don't even see him one time. It doesn't usually bother me, but right now, it does.

Mom makes faces she doesn't mean to when she looks at the phone. Faces I don't think she'd like. But I think, maybe, that's her real face. Sometimes, it's a smile, but mostly, it looks like the way I feel when Toady and I buy packs of MagiQuest cards, and he gets one I want.

"School," Mom says. "Finish up breakfast and get ready."

I put my empty bowl in the sink and head upstairs, grabbing the railing and stretching one leg over the creaky step and onto the next one. In the hall I hear the ocean, but it's not real. It's coming from Dad's sound machine that he uses to block out any noise. So, he can sleep.

I stand in front of the closed bedroom door and listen. I know he's in there, but I can't hear him.

2

Toady's name is actually Torrey, a girl's name. He used to get made fun of a lot before we started calling him Toady. His mom is from one of those Russian countries, and she talks with an accent. I was over at his house once, and we were playing outside. It started getting dark, and we heard his mom yelling, "Toady, Toady, time to kem een ford suppah."

I don't think I've called him Torrey since.

It'd be a mean nickname if he was fat, but he's super skinny with black hair and skin that just burns in the summer.

We're in the same class and we used to sit by each other, but Mrs. Grayson moved us apart because we wouldn't stop laughing. When the lunch bell rings, we go outside and sit by ourselves at the rusty table with the peeling paint. He takes out his MagiQuest cards, and I take out mine. Sometimes, we trade, but today, I don't want to.

Toady pulls a sandwich out of his lunch box and makes a Yuck face. "I wish I had a peanut allergy," he says. "I tell Mom I hate PB & J, but she says it's so American."

I hand him the sandwich my Mom made: organic turkey breast with cheddar, sprouts, and cucumber. There's probably a picture of it online. Toady gives me his sandwich, and I start eating..

I'm getting sick of PB and J myself with how much we trade.

"I think our house is haunted," I tell him.

Toady stops chewing. Sprouts hang out of his mouth.

"What? Like haunted, haunted? Like ghosts haunted?"

"Noises in the walls," I say. "Moaning, whispers, a kind of knocking sound."

Toady puts down the sandwich. "When did you figure this out?"

The sandwich he gave me is all smashed in the bag and bleeding grape jelly. I've never liked grape. "I don't know," I say. "Couple weeks ago, maybe."

Toady makes a Big Eyes face. "Couple weeks ago? Why am I just now finding out about this?"

Peanut butter gets all over my fingers when I take the sandwich out.

"I wasn't sure. But then last night I heard them again and I don't know what else it could be."

A group of girls walks over and sits at the table close to us. They talk nonstop and fast. I don't know how any of them keep up with what they're saying. We mostly stay away from them, but Mckenzie is in my class, and she's super nice. And she smells nice.

And her hair is pretty. And her handwriting is really, really good. It's like clouds.

Toady drops his sandwich, leans forward, and whispers, "Were you scared? Be honest. Were they whispering murdery things?"

"Not really," I lied.

"Come on," Toady says, "even the guys on the ghost hunting shows get scared."

"Ghost hunting?" I say.

Toady slaps the table and makes our cards jump. "God, I wish it was the weekend so I could stay over at your house."

Mckenzie looks over, sees me, and smiles. It makes my stomach hurt a little, and I smile back. Then I wave like an idiot.

"You've got jelly on your face," Toady says.

I scramble to wipe it off while Toady keeps eating his sandwich, and now the other girls are looking over at me and making Crying Laughing faces. The sound makes my face feel all red. All of them laugh except Mckenzie. Her smile is so nice. I don't even know her and her smile just makes me think she's a good person.

"You know what you need to do, don't you?" Toady says. "You have to document it, that's what they do on the shows. Recording the noises and everything would be awesome, but it doesn't prove anything because anyone could make noises."

His fingers move aside a few of MagiQuest cards until he sees the one he wants and picks it up. He turns it and shows it to me. A thing floating in the air dressed in a torn sheet. There's a crown on the head, and skeleton arms poke out of the sheet. There aren't any eyes, but the sheet is all wrinkled, making it look like he's angry. Smoke and stuff are behind him. He's got a glass jar in his bone hand where he keeps souls.

That card has always creeped me out.

Toady smiles. "But a picture is even better."

3

When I get home, Mom is at the kitchen table with a small white box opened up. She has a phone in her hands, but the phone with the cracked screen is on the table.

She says, "Hey, sweetie, how was your day?" But she doesn't look at me, she just points to a plate with celery and peanut butter on it. More peanut butter, great.

"Come here," she says and finally looks up. I go over and she wraps an arm around my shoulder. She smells like hair dye and shampoo. I see us on the screen of her new phone.

Mom flips her hair a little, does a Heart Eyes smile, and snaps a picture.

"Oh my god," she says, dropping her arm, "this camera is so much better."

I sit down and take a bite of celery. I've never liked celery because it tastes like grass-flavored water and leaves those fibers between my teeth.

"Where's Dad?" I ask.

Mom tilts her head and smiles. The phone makes a camera noise, and she looks at a picture of herself looking exactly like she does right now.

"Someone called in sick at work," she says. "He had to go in early, but he'll be home a little earlier too."

She puts down the new phone long enough to slide the old one over toward me.

"You can have this one now," she says and makes a serious One Eyebrow Up face. "But no internet, okay? Not yet, you're still too young. But you can play some games, use the camera."

I thank her, but I don't touch the phone. My reflection is split in the cracked glass in this really creepy way.

4

Later, in my room, I turned the phone on and opened the photos. Everything that Mom took is gone. I swipe through the apps, and all the stuff she uses has been erased, too. As I swipe back, my thumb catches on a crack and slices open. It doesn't really hurt, but blood smears across the screen, and I suck the cut until my mouth tastes like metal. I turn the phone off, and there's my reflection again, except this time, there's blood on my face.

My face. I have a camera now. I can take pictures of ghosts.

I wake up to the metal sound of keys hitting the kitchen floor and Dad whisper-yelling, "Shit." The clock numbers say I have to get up for school soon, but it's still dark, so I pull up the covers and stay in bed.

And I listen.

When Dad comes up the stairs, the house moves a little. These little vibrations go through the walls and floor, making my bed shiver. The vibrations are soft and quiet, which means Dad is walking in his socks. I listen for the creaky step, but Dad always skips that one. When he goes to work and when he comes home, he makes a long step over it so that it won't wake me up.

Mom doesn't do that. But Dad never forgets.

I get out of bed and open my door a crack. I whisper Dad's name as he reaches the top of the stairs.

He sees me, comes over, and gives me a hug. "Hey, dude, can't sleep?"

He closes my bedroom door, and it barely makes a sound. Dad is big and strong but does everything gentle. I know he could break lots of things if he wanted, but he doesn't, and somehow, that makes me think he's even stronger.

I shake my head and ask how the hospital was. When you're a security guard, you've got all kinds of crazy stories. Some are sad, and he doesn't tell me those ones unless they really bothered him.

"Slow night," Dad says, one hand on my back. "I did see a raccoon, though."

"Serious?"

"Serious. He was digging through one of the dumpsters with those little hands." He holds up a hand and wiggles his fingers.

"Did he find anything good?"

Dad pulls my covers back and pats the pillow. I lay down, and he covers me back up.

"Not much food," he says, "but it did find a few old patient gowns that it dragged off."

"Why the gowns?"

Dad keeps rubbing my back, and it makes me want to sleep.

"Probably for its nest."

"Raccoons build nests?"

"Just like birds," he says. "I'll tell you all about it this weekend, okay? For now, try and get some sleep."

I want to ask him, but I don't want to ask him…. You know what I mean. I feel a little nervous about it, but I won't be able to sleep if I don't. Dad kisses my forehead. "Sure missed you today, dude."

I wait until he's almost at the door. "Hey, Dad?"

He turns around.

"Can I ask you something?"

"Of course."

"Do you think ghosts are real?"

He laughs a little. "That's a big question." He comes back to the bed and sits on the edge. "Why do you ask?"

"I think I hear them sometimes, at night. Ghosts in the walls."

Dad goes quiet. His breathing changes. "You sure they're ghosts?"

"Pretty sure. I don't know what else they could be. Mom got a new phone, so she gave me her old one, and Toady, I mean Torrey, says I should try and get a picture of one. But you know Toady."

Dad sees the phone charging on the nightstand. He picks it up and runs his thumb over the cracks. "Toady's absolutely right. Next time you hear those ghosts, especially if I'm not here, you try and get a picture and send it to me right away."

He pauses, still holding the phone, his thumb still moving on the cracked screen. He turns to me and says, "Then we'll sell it and become millionaires.

I smile in the dark, and I know Dad is smiling, too.

5

At school, Toady shows me how to use the camera even though I already know how. He thinks because I've never owned a phone, I've never used my Mom's, or my Dad's, or their tablets. Just because he's had a cellphone since he was eight. And the one he has now is super nice. Yeah, Toady, we all know your parents are rich.

He pinches his fingers on the screen and spreads them apart to zoom.

"Then tap the screen to make it focus," he says. "You don't want a blurry picture of a ghost. Those are everywhere. You need it to be clear."

He shows me how to make the camera lighter or darker, and I didn't know that but act like I did.

There's something I've been thinking of since I first heard the noises, and Toady is the only person I could ask. But still, it feels like a stupid question, even though it's not.

I cough once. "Uh, Toad, do you think ghosts really wear sheets?"

Toady lowers the phone and looks at me. He's got these black eyebrows, thick like that kind of caterpillar, and they go up.

"I don't know," he says. "I've always wondered that too."

He goes back to the phone and says, "You don't have any games on here."

"I think it's because of the old days," I tell him. "When people used to be just covered up in cloth when they got buried."

Toady makes a fart sound with his lips. "That means that zombies would be covered in sheets, not ghosts. Ghosts are spirits, dipshit. And they usually just want a living person to get out of their house or solve their murder."

Then he smiles and hands me the phone. "Guess we'll find out for sure when Caleb, fearless hunter of ghosts, snaps a pic."

I laugh and take the phone, but something else has been bothering me, and I don't think it's something I can say to Toady. I don't know for sure if he really believes or if he's just going along with me because it's fun.

But I believe. No, it's more than that. I know ghosts are real. Mom, dead asleep, Dad at work, and people are moving around in our house. People I can't see.

I'm scared.

I don't know why, and I don't even know what a ghost could do to me. But I'm still scared.

6

I fall asleep with the phone under my pillow, all charged up. I kind of hope I don't wake up. I kind of hope that it's just another night.

Something jerks me out of a dream, and I lie there breathing like I just ran the track, staring into the dark. The red numbers on my clock glow, but they're all blurry. There it is again. A sound that makes me think of those pirate movies and the sound the ship makes in a storm. Wood, bending. Creaking. The stair. Something is coming up the stairs.

The house vibrates like it did when Dad came home but moves differently. My room feels colder as something goes past my room. My hand reaches under my pillow and comes out with the phone.

I wait, holding the phone to my chest and feeling like what a kid with asthma feels like. Like I can't breathe. Like the air won't go where it's supposed to.

Toady said they're only spirits. Maybe they want us to go.

I wait for the other one. There's always been two, but I only heard and felt the one. And just when I'm getting out of bed, I hear voices coming through the wall. A man and an old woman, I think. It's hard to tell.

They're whispering, and the old woman is laughing. Then their voices don't sound like words anymore. Small little moans, like a dog that wants to go outside. Vibrations move through my feet. Cold feet on wood floors, and something is making them shake.

I open the door and step out into the hall. The sounds are a little clearer out here, but not much. I keep going, telling myself not to be afraid.

The moaning gets louder the closer I get to Mom and Dad's room. Something is moving around in there, and it makes a sound like when I get into bed. A creak, but not like the stairs. Different. The voices are all muffled and making sounds together, and I know that it's now or never, so I open the door and go inside.

There's enough light coming from the window to see the blankets on the bed don't look right. They're up high like something is underneath. A face looks at me from the pillow—a face that looks as scared as I feel. Its eyes are huge, its mouth is open all big, and it knows my name. It screams the word in a voice that's all scratchy and hurts my ears, and I can't get any air. The blanket falls, and there's a white sheet underneath, and the sheet goes up, rises, and there's a shape under it moving, and the face on the pillow hasn't stopped screaming. The thing under the sheet reaches out, and the sheet falls away, and it's the ghost—not see-through like I thought a ghost would be. It just looks like a man, all skin and stuff.

I hold up the phone, push the camera button, and say, "Boo!"

I snap a picture and the flash lights up the whole room and makes everything frozen like lightning. My hands shake as I push the arrow button and pick Dad's name. I push another arrow, and the phone makes a sound like something whooshing out of it. I don't know what will happen next, but if I die, at least Dad will know how it happened.

The face on the pillow twists as it keeps screaming my name. So I start screaming, too.

A SHARP BLACK LINE

If you find this, don't come looking for me. Everyone who searches for the missing goes missing themselves. Maybe if I'd been honest from the start, we wouldn't be here. Maybe if I wasn't so afraid of Luke learning what I already knew.

I was his age when I learned what all of us in West Linn know, and I never forgot. None of us ever do. But somehow, every year, we find ourselves standing in the graveyard, watching as another empty box is lowered into the ground.

Yesterday evening, Terri was at dance practice with our daughter, Elsa, and Luke went over to a friend's house after school. He was supposed to be home before dark. I should have waited up for him. Instead, I drank too much wine and fell asleep in front of the TV. When I woke up, it was night, and rain pounded at the windows. Thunder rattled the glass.

I went upstairs, and Luke's bedroom door was closed. I thought he was asleep. We didn't figure out until the morning that his bed hadn't been slept in, and he never came home.

I called his friend, and he told me that Luke had left just after 5 pm. Luke told his friend he wanted to take the river path because of the storm. He wanted to see if the stories about the island were true.

I always told Luke to never go down to the river during a storm. But I never told him the real reason. I said it was undercurrents and debris, everything except the truth.

I should have explained everything to him, but that's the thing about guilt, isn't it? It makes truth shameful when it should set you free.

Terri stood in the kitchen, wearing a bathrobe over her pajamas. The skin under her eyes was dark and swollen. Elsa sat in the living room, eating cereal while watching cartoons. Her head had jerked when Terri threw her coffee mug at the wall. The shattered pieces shot across the kitchen. Coffee sprayed up against the ceiling. Elsa turned around and heard her mother screaming, and then the volume went up on the TV.

Terri's voice was hoarse from crying. Her chest moved in and out fast, and when she spoke, it sounded like she was out of breath.

"Find him," she told me. "And don't come back here without our son."

I didn't respond. She knew what she was saying, what she was asking.

I went into the living room, kissed Elsa on the head, and told her I loved her. Then, I grabbed my coat and keys and headed out the door.

Terri, if you're reading this, I'm sorry. I should have said that before I left.

I got in the shitty Camry—trunk still full of boxes of business cards and pens from the realtor job that never took off—and tore out of the driveway.

I pulled into a gas station and bought a pack of cigarettes even though I hadn't smoked since Luke was born. I also bought a cheap bottle of wine and grabbed an empty soda cup.

Since I didn't have a corkscrew to open the wine, I found a rock, carefully broke the neck of the bottle, and poured the wine out of the jagged glass into the soda cup. Then I hit the road again, the smoke and wine making my head feel like a balloon barely attached to my shoulders.

The sky lowers when I pull onto Willamette Drive. Thick grey clouds and hazy air. Heavy rain beats against the windshield so hard the wipers can't keep up.

I head onto Riverview Drive. Last time I was on this road, I was riding a bike. Huffy BMX with flame decals on the frame. I'd ride by all the rich houses on the riverfront and imagine what it would be like to live in one.

I turn on the radio and tune into a local station. The weather report says the storm is expected to last all day. I take a drink of wine and try to fight back the tears burning in my eyes.

I drive past the gas station on the corner with the paint-peeled siding and sun-faded beer signs in the windows. I used to come here and buy cigarettes and smoke them under the overpass with my friends. I haven't seen any of them since we graduated.

I turn right past the gas station and head down a residential street. A poster for a "missing child" is stapled to a power pole. You can't read any of it because the rain has bled all the ink.

I take another drink of wine and pull into the parking lot of McLean House, an old plantation home that was built in the 1920s. No one lives here now. It's just a historical landmark, used for weddings and graduation parties.

My dad used to talk to me before the summer Jackie disappeared. He taught me things I still remember. He said, "If things go wrong, if you lose something important, go back to the place you last had it."

A path leads from McLean House through the woods, a yellow path of dead leaves and moss. The raindrops falling through the trees sound like fingernails tapping on a window. I light a cigarette and walk the path.

I tell myself the weakness behind my knees is because I haven't eaten. But it's more than that. The last time I walked through these woods was with John Shimura, the summer between junior high and school. And we were looking for his little sister. She'd been missing since the night before.

If you're me, you go back to the place where you last had it. Something inside that made you believe the world was good, that you had some control over your life. Every person you see on the streets wrapped in sleeping bags, pushing shopping carts full of garbage, muttering to no one, and looking through everything. I think they all lost it, too. The Light. The Way. I don't know what to call it, but when it's gone, nothing goes right.

It was raining, just like it is now, the morning my dad woke me. "Aaron," he whispered, "get out of bed."

My eyes adjusted slowly to the grey morning light.

"Whatever it is, I didn't do it," I said, still shaking off a bad dream.

"Get dressed and come downstairs."

I did what he asked, and when I came into the kitchen, I saw Mom seated at the table. Her eyes were red. She held a phone to her ear and nodded at whatever the other person said. She traced one finger around the rim of her coffee cup.

"They're about to head out the door."

Dad had peanut butter and jelly jars and pieces of white bread scattered across the counter.

He looked up and pointed at my feet with the jelly-covered knife. "You'll need rain boots. And get a warm jacket."

"What's going on?"

Mom hung up the phone and said to Dad. "Carter came back a few hours ago. He was banging on the door of a house near the river. People called the cops, said he was soaking wet and covered in mud."

"That's great," I said.

But my parents ignored me. Mom stood up and went to the hall closet. Dad put the sandwiches together, put them into the now-empty bread bag, and twisted the top.

He sighed and put both his hands on the counter. "Jackie Shimura went missing after soccer practice last night," he said. "Her friends said she went into the woods to take the river path but never made it home."

It felt like the ribs in my chest moved apart to make room for my lungs, which suddenly felt enormous. "Are we going to look for her?" I asked.

Dad poured some coffee into a thermos. "Her father's trying to get as many people to help as he can. Cops are already out there."

John and Jackie's parents had come to America from Japan and started a restaurant. Their dad still spoke with an accent. I didn't know John all that well, but I saw him in school every day.

Mom came back carrying my boots and a jacket and hat. She leaned over a little, so we were eye-to-eye. Her hair was still bed-messy, and she didn't have any make-up on. She put one hand on my shoulder and squeezed.

"You be kind to John," she said. "Stay close to him at all times and be careful."

Her eyes shimmered, and a tear slipped out, ran around her tight lips, and down her chin. She got this same look the week before when Carter Greenblatt went missing. The look that said she was thinking of what the parents were going through and how horrible it would feel to be looking for a child you knew probably wouldn't be found.

"Promise me," she said and squeezed harder. "Promise you'll stay close to John."

"I promise," I said.

Dad and I left the house and got in his truck. Mom stood in the open doorway, one hand on her heart, watching as we pulled away. We drove to Mary S. Young Park, a huge, forested area with multiple paths that lead down to the river. A bunch of other cars and trucks were already there, including a cop car. A group of men stood around in a circle. They all drank coffee, a few of them smoked cigarettes. The parking lot was covered in dead tree branches broken off by the storm the night before.

I recognized John's dad because I met him once when we ate dinner at his restaurant. He looked older than I remembered, smaller too like he'd shrunk and put on another man's clothes. The raincoat he wore came down to his knees. He walked around the men handing out flyers with Jackie's picture printed on them. He had this desperate look, and his movements were quick and jerky like he had been up all night and was functioning on nothing but nerves and coffee.

He handed a flyer to me and Dad, and raindrops fell on Jackie's school picture, making the ink bleed all down the page. Beneath the picture, it said she had been wearing a pink knit hat and a Portland Thorns scarf the last time she was seen.

The cop divided everyone into pairs and gave a quick speech about being safe. He showed us a laminated map and sections of the woods outlined in different colored markers. Each group was given an area to search.

John and I were paired together, and it wasn't until years later I wondered why we didn't go off with our dads. I think it's probably because if John's dad were to find his daughter, he'd need someone stronger and older than his own kid to lean on. Besides, John and I were teenagers, and I spent a lot of time in the woods with my friends.

Dad handed me his Swiss Army knife before we split and started our search.

"Just in case," he said. "Keep your eyes open, and do not let John out of your sight."

I promised him like I promised Mom.

The whole group went their separate ways, and John and I headed off into the forest. The rain fell harder. The ground was slick and muddy. John didn't say anything as we walked the path. His raincoat was the same one he'd been wearing for the last few years, and his belly pushed it out.

John wasn't fat, but he was chubby and breathed heavily as we made our way down the steep, slippery path.

"I'm sorry about Jackie," I said to break the silence.

John nodded.

"I'm sure she's fine," I said.

John stopped and looked at me with the same look his dad had. It was strange to see that on such a young face.

"Are you still drawing robots?" I asked, knowing full well he was. It was all he did during breaks at school, sitting off by himself to draw. The other kids talked about him, made fun of him. I never did, but I never said anything to stop it, either.

John unzipped his jacket, took out a small yellow notepad, and showed it to me. The drawing was really good, an animal of some kind that looked made out of metal.

"It's a dog," John said. "It's got GPS and a halogen lamp on its head. There's water, food, medicine, and a blanket in that pack on its back."

A raindrop fell right onto the drawing of the backpack. The ink lifted and spread in a blue blotch. I leaned over to protect it.

"When someone goes missing, instead of people, you send out an army of these," John said. "They can search all night, and they don't get tired."

Voices called in the distance, shouting Jackie's name. According to the map the cop showed us, we were supposed to go left where the path split and search the little valley where a creek ran. But John pointed straight ahead, away from our search area.

"I think she probably went down there," he said. He didn't have a hood on, and his wet hair hung down his forehead. "She kept talking about wanting to look for Carter. He was in her class. I told her not to because of the island that appears in the river whenever there's a storm.

John closed the notebook. Raindrops splattered onto the back of it, leaving dark stains.

"Todd said something on the island takes the kids."

He bit his lip, put the notepad back into his jacket, and wiped at his eyes. "I never should have told her that."

Every kid in town knew that story, and even though we didn't believe it, we never went down to the river during a storm.

"It's just a story," I said. "You knew it wasn't true when you told her."

He started to nod, to agree with me, but he stopped. "She snuck down there a few times after practice. I saw the mud on her shoes. She made me promise not to tell. Said she couldn't stop thinking about Carter's mom and dad. She just wanted to find him. Bring him back."

I shrugged. "Alright, let's go there. We don't find anything, we can always come back and search where we're supposed to."

I left the path first and went into the thick woods. The ground sloped, but it was hard to see because of all the shrubs and ferns. I turned back and saw John coming after me, breathing heavily as he struggled to keep his balance.

More voices shouted Jackie's name, and the word echoed from other voices to our left. After we'd hiked for a while, I heard something like white noise on a sound machine. I held up my hand, and we stopped to listen. There was music to the sound now.

Water.

We kept going until we reached the shoreline of the river, a rocky beach. The brown water moved fast and carried logs and debris in a swirl of foam. I knew if Jackie fell in, there was no way she would survive. John seemed to have the same thought because he stood at the water's edge, hands on his head. His eyes were all red, but I couldn't tell if he was crying because of the rain.

Where John stood then is where I stand now. It's hard to believe how much time has passed. How much has gone wrong. The normally blue water of the river is churned up into the color of coffee and cream. A rolling wall of mist comes around the bend. I stand and wait.

That day, as we looked for Jackie, John and I didn't see the mist roll in. It was already there. So thick you couldn't see the other side of the river. You couldn't even see halfway across the water.

We watched the mist drift past us, hovering just above the river. Then something moved inside that silver wall, a dark triangle shape that came closer and finally broke through. I thought it was a piece of a house at first, something that had broken off upriver, but what bumped into shore was the wreckage of a little rowboat.

The wood was all rotted black and covered in algae. Water-warped and weather-worn. There were large holes in the bottom where you could see the river, and water sloshed around in the hull. There was no way it should still float. It looked like it had just risen off the river bottom, mud still clinging to its sides to come ashore for us to find.

I was about to tell John we should move on and keep looking, but his face went slack and then pale, and he pointed into the boat while his mouth moved without making any sound. I followed his finger and saw it.

A pink knit hat. It looked perfectly dry.

Before I could try and stop him, John climbed into the rowboat and picked up the hat. He held it to his nose. Whatever he smelled told him it was Jackie's. I climbed in after him, but I didn't know what to do. Drag him out, maybe. And as soon as my foot touched the soft wet wood, the boat lurched backward into the river. John screamed and clutched the hat tighter. My hands gripped the sides just in case the thing came apart.

Water rushed around us, but the boat moved against the current, almost like it was on a track, like those rides at Disneyland. It rocked back and forth but never strayed from its path.

John fell on his ass. His voice squeaked, "Are you doing this?"

"Hold onto something," I told him. "If this thing breaks, grab one of the boards."

But it wasn't going to break apart. I don't know how I knew that, but I did. Maybe it was because I saw that dark shape looming up ahead in the fog. Maybe it was because the boat was headed straight for it.

A log rushed toward us and slammed into the side of the rowboat, knocking John over again. The boat shuddered but kept on going, plowing along through the water. John closed his eyes, mouth making words I couldn't hear. I wondered who he was praying to.

The shape became more defined as the boat brought us closer. John opened his eyes, saw it, and his mouth fell open. I hoped it was a rescue boat, but I knew better.

The rowboat scraped up along the rocky shore of a small island. Small enough to walk across before you could count to a hundred.

John held the pink hat in both hands. "This shouldn't be here. It doesn't exist." His eyes were so wide that all the white made his irises look small.

I didn't know what to say. Because it did exist, and we were on it.

"I'm not leaving this boat." John's voice shook like he was trying hard not to cry.

With my hands still gripping the edges, I tried to move the boat, but it was stuck like it had cemented itself to the shore.

"I don't think we have a choice," I said.

John opened his mouth to say something else when a flurry of color caught his eye. A flutter of red and white, tassels moving with the wind. A Portland Thorns scarf caught in the rocks just up on the island. The scarf Jackie was wearing when she disappeared.

John went silent, climbed out of the rowboat, and clambered up the shore on all fours. I followed him. I expected the rocks to feel different, but they were just normal rocks, slick and covered in muck.

John already had the scarf in hand by the time I reached him.

"How am I going to tell my dad?" He asked, chin shaking.

"Maybe she's still here."

The wind blew even stronger, and some mist swirled away from the island's center. But the mist didn't leave, it got sucked backward and spun like a tornado around a small structure made of rotting wood. A shack.

I looked up, but I couldn't even see the sky, and for a moment, I believed there was no sky, just an endless gray, water-soaked atmosphere all the way in space.

Then the door of the shack flew open and banged against the wall with a crash. A figure wearing a tattered black dress stood just inside. Tangles of long, wet hair hung around a skeletal face I could barely see in the shadows. The eyes stared out from that gaunt face, and I felt like ice water had suddenly flooded my veins. It made my chest hurt to look at her because I was sure it was female.

My hand reached into my pocket, and I took out the knife my dad had given me. I flicked open the blade and held it out.

John started crying. He was on his knees, holding the hat and the scarf, staring at the woman in the shack and blubbering like a baby. His fear paralyzed him, but mine was gasoline. I turned and took off, running back toward the rowboat. If it didn't move when I jumped in, I'd dive into the water and swim for it.

I slipped on a rock near the shore and almost went down, but I kept going until I reached the boat and jumped in. It started slipping slowly back into the river when I felt a hand grab the back of my coat. I turned to see John sprawled on the ground, one hand still holding his sister's hat and scarf, the other hand gripping the edge of my raincoat.

I couldn't see the shack anymore. The mist had stopped spinning and spread out over the island again, enveloping it.

"John," I yelled above the wind, "let go!"

"Don't leave me here," he said. "Don't let her take me!"

The mist came rolling toward the shore, toward John's feet.

"Let go," I screamed.

I tried to pull my coat, but John's grip was so strong that I almost lost my balance. John hadn't moved to get up, so I took the Swiss Army knife and ran the edge of the blade over his hand. The skin split open, and blood came leaking out of the wound.

He yelled once and pulled his hand back just as the mist curled around his ankles. The smell of rotting fish and seaweed. Two corpse-like hands, covered in patches of decomposed skin, reached out of the mist and grabbed his legs. I glimpsed a face in the mist, its eyes locked onto mine.

John's eyes went all wide and his face lost color. His mouth opened so I could see his back teeth, but no sound came out. Then he was yanked backward into the mist, his chin bashing on the rocks, his bloody hand leaving a trail. The mist came curling to the water's edge and stopped. I yelled John's name, but only the wind responded. The little rowboat that shouldn't have floated left the shore and took me back out into the river.

I curled up in the bottom and let it carry me. Part of me hoped it would sink, take me to the river bottom, where the mud would settle over my body and bury me. My stomach clenched so tight I thought it would never come undone.

Waves shook the boat, but it kept on moving until it bumped into the rocks of the shoreline. I got out, still holding the knife with John's blood on it, and staggered to the tree line. I sat down on the wet ground and watched as the dark shape of the island dissolved in the fog.

Then I heard a voice, a little girl crying. Some of the mist had come up and touched the beach, and as it drifted backward, I saw a figure standing there by the river's edge.

I scrambled up and ran down to her. Her thin arms were folded over her chest, and she shivered, teeth clacking together. She let out a little whimper between each shaking breath. I took off my coat and wrapped it around her shoulders, then knelt and looked into her eyes. They were wide and white, and they stared at me with uncertainty, like she wasn't sure if I was real.

I rubbed her arms to make her warm and said, "Jackie, it's okay. You're back now."

Her eyes focused on me, and she said, "Are you sure?"

I opened my mouth to say something reassuring, but nothing came out. I took her hand and led her back into the woods, where her dad waited. I'll never forget the look on his face when he saw his daughter as if she'd came back from the dead and held her to his chest so tight I thought he might suffocate her. Then he looked at me, looked beyond me, and when he didn't see his son, he closed his eyes and began to cry.

I don't know why I cut him. There are a thousand other things I could have done, but in that last moment, I caused him pain instead of trying to help. I've never let go of that, because I feel like that island showed me something about myself, something dark. It was my choice and I drew a sharp black line between who I was and who I would become.

I can't remember my dad and I having another real conversation after that summer. Sometimes, he would look up and see me, and his body would shudder a little like he was surprised I still lived in the house. Then, without saying a word, he'd leave the room. Sometimes, I would catch Mom looking at me, and there was fear on her face. Not love, not pride, just fear.

I first got arrested at thirteen for beating up a kid I went to school with, just to prove nothing could touch me. I dropped out of college because I was too high to make it to most of my classes. I got arrested again for getting into a fight with an ex-girlfriend's new boyfriend. Alcohol became a constant companion, and to this day, I still drink on the sly. Not a day has gone by when I haven't secretly had some booze. Terri, if you're reading this, I'm sorry. I just never could kick it.

That day on the island, I was shown a version of myself, an outline I grew to fill in. And that person has ruined everything good in my life. One mistake after the other. Now it leads to this....

So here I am, back where it all went wrong. Standing on the same shore where we saw that little boat coming out of the fog.

All this time, I've been waiting for things to be made right. But nothing happens on its own, and maybe that's what I forgot. You have to make things right. It takes effort and, sometimes, sacrifice. I don't care what happens to me. I just want Luke to come back, to appear on that foggy shoreline like Jackie did.

I hope I disappear and you never see me again.

Raindrops fall onto this letter, making the ink bleed just like it did on John's drawing.

Don't come looking for me. Please.

Today feels just like that day. A light rain falls, and mist rolls in from around the bend, covering the river. There's a little crackle in the air like lightning will strike, and I squint into the mist. My heart flutters like a bat trapped in my chest, and I see something dark floating in the water, something moving in the fog. A small, rotted boat and it's slowly coming toward me.

CHARWOOD

The forest had caught fire just six days earlier. Heavy smoke still hung over most of the town, plunging it into a state of permanent dusk. All the green burned away, leaving just the black skeletons of trees. Thick gray smoke drifted between the bare branches, making it look like a floating dead forest. At night, you could see places on the ground where embers still glowed an orange pulsing light that was strangely beautiful.

Kayla Jensen was awakened by a blinding flash of red light that filled her entire room the night it happened. By the time she got out of bed and ran to the window, the light was gone, but the entire forest was engulfed in flames. Her foster parents told her to stay away from the woods. It was too dangerous. But every night since the fire, she took their dog, Phineas, out for a walk, and they ended up at the blackened edge of the forest. There was something mesmerizing about it.

It wasn't Kayla's chore to walk Phineas—it was her foster brother Santiago's job. Hers was to unload the dishwasher and fold laundry. But since Santiago was only eight, and the dark still scared him sometimes, Kayla traded chores with him.

Being alone was the only time she felt safe.

As soon as school let out, Kayla took a detour to the woods on her way to Marty Collins's house. The smoke still hung like a silver curtain. Dark tree shapes materialized and disappeared as the smoke moved with the breeze. It burned her eyes to look for too long, but she couldn't look away. She stared until tears started running down her face, and then she continued walking, that campfire smell clinging to her clothes.

Stupid, asshole kids smoking marijuana in the woods, some of the adults said. But as they hung out in his room, Marty swore he saw a bolt of lightning tear through the sky and slam down somewhere in the center of all those trees. Kayla was inclined to believe him. He was a nerd, for one thing, always had been. When he wasn't playing online video games with his nerd friends, Marty was writing his own fantasy novel, complete with wizards and dragons and black magic.

Marty Collins never tried to impress anyone. He knew what he was and didn't care what anyone else thought, which was why Kayla liked him. She envied him in some respects. She wished she had something that meant as much to her as his fantasies meant to him.

Marty also said the lightning was weird. Not whitish-blue like you normally see. It flashed bright red, he told her, like the brake lights on a car. One bolt, boom, and then the trees were burning. Sirens howled all over town as fire trucks rushed to the scene.

"I saw the red light, too," Kayla said. "I thought I imagined it."

Marty laughed. "Freaky shit." His eyes were magnified behind thick glasses as he looked at the coffee-with-cream-colored skin of her arms, the tight sun-bleached curls on her head,

"Hold on a sec," he said. A message bubble popped up on his computer screen and he typed a quick response, hit send. Colorful posters covered his bedroom walls depicting the same type of world as his game: Elvish babes shooting flaming arrows, muscular knights in dented armor, wizards in long flowing robes, dwarfs with braided beards, and, of course, a dragon spewing flames at the heroes.

Marty went over to the window and pointed toward the woods. The ghostly silhouettes of trees hovered in the smoke.

"The lightning came down right over there," he said. "No thunder though. It was super bright—lit up my whole room in red for a few seconds."

Kayla stood next to him, resisting the urge to smooth down the cowlick on the back of his head.

"Do you think it will ever grow back?" she asked him.

Marty shrugged. "I don't know. I think the fire killed everything."

"All those animals," Kayla said.

"I'm sure most of them got away," Marty said, then he pointed down the street. "I've seen like five or six deer eating flowers from people's yards. They'll find somewhere new."

A chime sounded from the computer. Marty went over, typed another message and then asked, "Any word on the adoption?"

Kayla shook her head, feeling the blood rush to her face. She appreciated that Marty wasn't afraid to ask questions like that, and she was grateful he didn't treat her differently just because she didn't have a typical family. But it also made her nervous because she always felt so close to saying things she shouldn't say. Words she needs someone to hear.

"Courts, you know?" She said. "They take forever."

"And you have no say in the matter?" Marty asked.

Kayla shook her head, feeling a pressure build up in her chest. *No say in the matter. No choice.*

"Not until I'm fourteen," she said.

Marty nodded like he understood. "Sucks being twelve," he said, still looking at his computer. Kayla found herself standing in front of his bookshelf like she usually did when she came to visit.

Marty appeared beside her, smelling faintly of the corndog he'd eaten for lunch. "What'll be it today, miss?" he asked with a flourish of his hand. "Witchcraft, wizardry, mysterious societies, murder?"

Kayla unzipped her backpack and took out a hardcover book called *The Goblin's Lair* and handed it to him. Marty put it back on the shelf. "What did you think?"

Kayla wrinkled her nose, "Not my style," she said. "They all seem the same to me."

Marty placed a hand over his heart and staggered backward. "Blasphemy!" he said. "Heresy!"

"I want something scary," she told him, running a finger along the spines. "Something really creepy."

"Ah," Marty said, tapping his fingertips together. "The lady doth wish to be frightened. I have just the book."

Despite his room's general chaos and clutter, Marty's bookshelves were arranged alphabetically by genre and author. It was obvious he took great pride in his modest collection of books in which nothing normal ever happened.

He found the book he was looking for, pulled it out, and handed it to her.

"*Depth Charge*," she read aloud. "Is it good?"

"That book got me a C on the history test," Marty said. "I stayed up half the night reading and then the other half afraid to go to sleep. So yeah, it's good."

Kayla thanked him and put the book in her backpack. "I should get going," she said. "Before... you know."

"Before the troll under the bridge gets angry," Marty said, his eyes turning a little sad.

"Yeah," Kayla smiled. "The troll."

Marty walked her downstairs to the front door. "You can text me later if you're up," he said. "I mean, if the book gives you the willies. I've got a campaign tonight, so I'll be up late."

"We'll see," she said. "I don't scare easy."

Marty rubbed his hands together nervously. "Hey, I don't know exactly what you're going through, but if you need to talk—"

Kayla patted his arm, "Thanks, Marty."

"I mean it," he said, trying to stop the tremor in his voice. "I just want you to know that you're bright....and alive."

Bright and alive? He thought. *You idiot.*

Kayla gave him a soft smile and walked away, waving at him over her shoulder. Marty stood in the doorway watching until she was out of sight, thinking she would be a badass elf.

Kayla walked at a regular pace until she couldn't see Marty's house any longer, and then she started walking faster to make up for lost time. Rhonda didn't really care what time she came home as long as it was before Peter got off work. If Kayla wasn't there when he walked through the door, he'd want to know where she was, who she was with, how many of them were boys, and how old they were.

"You know it's because he cares," Rhonda told her once. "I was a twelve-year-old girl, so I understand. He doesn't. He just worries about you, that's all."

Thankfully, he wasn't there when she got to the house.

Even though Kayla had lived there with Santiago and the baby, Henry, for almost six months, it still didn't feel like her home. The adults weren't actually her parents, and the two other kids weren't her brothers but foster kids, too. She told Marty it was like a puzzle family. Something thrown together, even though none of them belonged together. This was her third foster family, and Kayla was starting to get used to the idea that she'd be shuffled around until she was old enough to make it on her own. And she dreamed of that constantly. There was nothing in the world she wanted more.

But all that changed last month when Peter and Rhonda announced they wanted to adopt her. Make her officially their daughter. She smiled and let them believe they saw tears of happiness.

After the conversation, Kayla went straight to the upstairs bathroom and threw up as quietly as she could.

When Kayla walked through the door, the two boys were in the living room, sitting in the blue glow of the TV, toys scattered all around them. She found Rhonda in the kitchen dishing lasagna onto paper plates. She was dressed in her blue scrubs and would be heading off to work at the hospital as soon as Peter arrived.

Rhonda gave her a quick peck on the cheek. "How was school?" she asked, handing Kayla a plate.

"Fine."

"Just fine?"

Kayla shrugged, "It's sort of the same thing every day. You know, like that one movie."

Rhonda took a bite and nodded, her eyes narrowing. "Everything okay?"

Kayla took a bite as well, even though she wasn't hungry. Rhonda was sweet, a born mother who couldn't have any kids of her own. She probably had no idea what kind of monster she was married to.

Kayla was about to say something, anything, when they both heard Peter's car engine. Rhonda glanced at her watch, "Oh, gotta run. Love you, sweetie. Be a good girl and help your dad with the boys, okay?"

Kayla nodded and tried to smile, thinking, *he's not my dad.*

Peter Hughes came inside, still dressed in his suit, tie loosened, and kissed Rhonda as she rushed out the door. He gave Kayla a side hug, and she smelled the lingering cologne he had put on in the morning after working out at the gym. A smell that made her nauseous. He dished up a plate, smiled at her, and then went into the living room to see the boys.

Like a normal family.

They all sat on the couch and watched a gameshow on TV. Peter held Henry and made baby noises at him. He helped Santiago with his math homework and told Kayla about a beautiful house he had just put on the market.

"You'd love it," he said. "It's like a castle. There's a massive library with two levels, and it's got a ladder so you can reach the high books. Absolutely beautiful."

"Does it have a pool?" Kayla asked. She knew that talking was better than not talking. If she didn't say anything, he would bring up her silence later and demand she explain it.

"A pool? Oh yeah, it's got a huge pool in the backyard with a waterfall and everything." He said. "I should take you by to see it this weekend."

"That would be fun," she said, making her voice sound excited.

After dinner, she got Henry ready for bed while Peter helped Santiago. When it was all said and done, Peter took off his shoes and sat on the couch with a glass of whiskey. His shirt was untucked and stained with lasagna sauce. The glow of the TV made his skin look pale and loose. Dark circles appeared under his eyes that Kayla couldn't see before, the pupils glistening like two black stones.

When she announced she was going to bed, Peter looked at her with glossy eyes and tapped one finger on his cheek. She leaned in to give him the kiss, and Peter reached out a hand and caressed her cheek. His cold fingers brushed hair away from her eyes, and she felt like insects were crawling up her arms. She bit her cheek to stop herself from shivering.

"Thanks for your help tonight," Peter whispered in her ear. "You're an amazing girl, Kayla. Truly. Don't ever forget how special you are." Then he smiled. "Sleep tight."

She lay awake in the dark, listening to the second hand on the clock. Her heartbeat quickened when she heard Peter's weight on the stairs and felt the house shift ever so slightly as he ascended. She tried to calm her breathing, but it kept rushing in and out of her faster and faster. The tick grew so loud in her ears that it sounded like an ax chopping wood. She focused on that sound and pulled it inside her until she could hear nothing else.

Soft vibrations moved through the floor as Peter reached the top of the stairs. She heard him sigh. His breath would smell like whiskey—it always did—a smell that made Kayla think of flammable things.

Her heart grew bigger and wider, and every beat was uncomfortable, like it was taking up too much space inside her chest. Then the band of light under her door darkened, and she held her breath, her tears, dreading the moment the door would creak open and Peter would walk into the room.

The next day, Kayla moved through the halls of her school with heavy steps, as though she were sleepwalking. She hardly spoke, avoiding everyone she knew, especially Marty. Time seemed to run at half-speed in the space she occupied while running double around her. Bodies rushed past, their voices high-pitched and sped up. The kids she saw were objects of matter and substance, but Kayla herself felt emptied out, hollow.

By the time she reached her third-period History class, the door was closed, and class had already started. She stared at the solid wood of the door and wondered if she would be able to simply walk through it.

When she got home, Kayla drank a glass of milk and stared at her homework for an hour before deciding to take Phineas for a walk. She said goodbye to Rhonda, who was busy feeding Henry, and left the house.

Without thinking about it or even deciding to do it, Kayla found herself standing at the edge of the grass field that lay between her and those charred skeleton trees. The smoke seemed to stay inside the woods for the most part, so thick you couldn't even see into it.

Phineas pulled at the leash as Kayla began walking across the grass.

"Come on, boy," she said, tugging gently. "Just a quick peek, I promise."

The closer she got, the more Kayla found the burned woods fascinating. The smoke appeared to expand and contract, almost as if it were the skin of something living, something breathing. Phineas' tail fell between his legs, and a low growl came from his throat.

A massive wall of silver smoke hovered before her, its tendrils twisting and undulating in an unfelt breeze. It was like something from one of Marty's books. A mystical place that harbored a dragon or a witch.

Some of the smoke hung in the air like a thin blanket, while other, darker pieces of it were in constant motion. Long fingers that caressed the trees, moving back and forth, up and down, putting Kayla in a sort of trance.

She hadn't blinked for a long time when a sound came from the woods—a loud crack like a tree snapping in half. Phineas' ears shot up, then he bolted, yanking the leash right out of Kayla's hand. He skirted right then left and ran straight into the woods.

She called after him. "Phineas, stop, come back!"

The dog kept on running until he disappeared into the vapor, Kayla's voice echoing after him.

"Shit," Kayla said. "Stupid dog. You don't run into danger, you run away from it."

She could not go home without the dog, especially since he had run into the one place Peter and Rhonda had told her to stay away from.

"Shit," she said again.

As much as she hated to admit it, she didn't have much of a choice. Kayla wrapped the leash around her wrist, took a deep breath, and walked into the woods, tentacles of smoke swirling around her until someone standing on the outside never would have known she was even there.

The first thing Kayla noticed was the silence. But it was a heavy sort of silence, the quiet of a place that used to be alive with motion and noise. As soon as her foot crossed from grass to charred ground, an immediate pressure squeezed the back of her neck, like someone, or something, was watching her. It was the same feeling she got at the dinner table with Peter or when a group of boys stared at her as she walked past them at school. The feeling moved up into her hairline, making her shiver.

"Phineas?" she called out, then stopped walking and listened, but she didn't hear anything that sounded like the dog. There was only a soft sigh as the smoke moved around her.

Kayla called for the dog again, and she didn't like the desperation creeping into her voice. She walked further into the haze, eyes burning and watering. She called again, as loud as she could, and the effort made her cough so hard that her gag reflex was triggered. She doubled over and hacked a dry, shallow cough.

Kayla thought the smoke might be less oppressive closer to the ground, so she lay down with her cheek on the burnt remnants of leaves and pine needles. It was only a little better, but enough to calm her breathing and settle her spasming throat.

She looked around, trying to figure out which direction she was coming from, but the edge of the woods was gone. She had no idea which way would take her to fresh air and which would take her deeper into the ghostly forest. Small patches of orange light were scattered on the ground, glowing embers that pulsed like a slow heartbeat.

Tears burned her eyes, and it wasn't just the smoke. It was everything, all of it wrapped up together in a knot she couldn't undo.

No matter how much she pretended or hid behind those barricades she'd built, she wasn't okay. Every night, she went back to a home where she didn't belong, to be with people she didn't share blood with. And every single night, something was stolen from her, something vital that was being taken in pieces. At first, she thought she didn't need whatever it was or that the flow could be staunched over time. But now she knew, lying on the ground in the woods, that it was the line between being a child and being an adult. Peter Hughes dragged her over that border before she was ready, which made her furious because that was a line you couldn't cross over again. It happened once, and then you were on the other side.

With that realization, the walls cracked inside her. All of the shame she'd hidden away flooded into her heart. Kayla saw her future stretched out before her like a line. There she was at the end of it, just like her mom. Bone thin, paper skin mottled with dark spots and scars. Eyes half-closed all the time, stumbling around the apartment and speaking to people who weren't there. Itching, scratching, pulling out her hair. An animated corpse that forgot every basic function of living. Forgot she even had a daughter or a job. Forgot to bathe and eat and shop for groceries. Nothing mattered more to her than those needles and those men who gave them to her.

Something soft and cold ran over Kayla's back, down her legs. She rolled over and looked up into the silver fog above her. No sky, no sunlight, just the iridescent particles of ash that floated within the smoke. But it no longer moved like smoke. It twisted and swirled against the breeze, forming into a shape. It created a sort of vortex, pulling ribbons of vapor into itself, growing in size until it towered above her, as tall as a man. The embers around her glowed brighter, pulsing red as if in warning.

A small voice inside her said, *Run*! But another voice, this one much stronger, said, *If you run now, you'll never stop.*

Kayla crawled backward away from the spinning cloud until her hands hit the hard, chalky remains of a tree branch. The smoke continued to shape itself. A head emerged, then two arms, then two legs. It stood separate from the smoke around it but still connected to the mist that floated above the ground.

The shape was specific, defined, and it was familiar to Kayla in some way she couldn't quite name. Two dark circles opened in the center of the head, as black as the burned wood of the trees, and stared at her. As Kayla stared back in horror, she sensed some form of intelligence radiating from those eyes. They knew her.

The smoke was silent as it swirled around the figure, then it stopped, and Kayla knew why she recognized the shape. It was the same shadow that fell on the floor of her room at night, the same silhouette that stood in her open doorway.

She wanted to scream, but the smoke was suffocating. Fear pounded in her temples. She swallowed hard and tried to control her breathing.

The creature had a voice, but it wasn't audible, it was more of a vibration that carried thought. It sank into Kayla's mind, slipped past all her barriers, and went straight for the dark parts she had tried so hard to keep buried. Whispering them until they filled her head.

Kayla clamped her hands over her ears, but it did nothing to muffle the sound. The smoke figure stood there, watching. The dead black eyes pulsing with dark light.

She finally found the breath to scream so she could drown out those horrible whispers. *Lies, all lies*, she told herself. *I am not worthless.*

Kayla's hands scraped through dirt and debris as she scrambled backward. The smoke figure floated closer with every inch she backed away. The mist at the bottom of the smoke figure's legs began to twist around Kayla's feet. There was a tightening on her ankles as tendrils of smoke gripped her, pulling her closer.

"No," she screamed. "I don't belong to you!"

The creature tilted its head at the sound of her voice, leaning in. Its black eyes had no emotion, but the longer Kayla stared into them, the worse she felt, as if every bad thing she'd ever thought about herself was swirling in them.

It leaned in, the smoke growing darker until it was almost as black as the eyes. An arm lifted, and the misty shape of a hand reached for her face. She tried again to break free, but the smoke around her ankles squeezed so hard she thought her bones might break. Long, thin claws extended and caressed her cheek.

"Leave me alone!"

The creature's head moved back a little at the force of her shouting, and then the body began to swirl again, gathering smoke from around the trees, and Kayla knew something bad was about to happen. Just like she knew when she lay in bed at night, wanting to fall asleep but knowing that her nightmares came first while she was still awake.

Her fingers scratched in the dirt until she felt something hard and round. Out of the silver mist, she lifted a charred black tree branch, thick at the base and broken off in a sharp point at the end.

Kayla thought of the posters in Marty's room, those colorful illustrations of warriors locked in battle. The branch felt like a weapon in her hand, a sword. She wasn't powerless. If this thing wanted to kill her, tear her apart, absorb her, it would have to fight for it because she wasn't going quietly. She'd had enough of lying in the dark, shedding silent tears while a monster robbed her of things she doubted she could get back.

Kayla rose to her feet, standing as tall as she could, wielding the tree branch high above her head.

"I am more than you'll ever be," she said to the smoke. "I am bright and alive, but you'll always be dark and empty."

The creature straightened to its full height, eyes flashing with dark light. Kayla felt anger pouring out of the smoke, trying to wrap itself around her. As the creature moved forward, Kayla saw something glint in the center of its chest. She squinted into the rush of smoke that burned her eyes and saw what looked like a polished black stone the size of her fist again.

Ash gathered around the creature as it advanced, ready to envelop her in its dark swirls of smoke and hatred. Red embers glowed angrily on the ground behind it.

"You don't make me," she screamed into the smoke and debris. "I make me."

Then she raised the branch, aiming for the creature's chest, and stabbed the jagged point into the black stone with all her strength.

There was no roar of pain. The dark eyes widened and looked into hers, their brightness dimming, and as they did, the whispering in her head hushed. The smoke began to fall off the creature in shredded tatters, dispersing back into the air. The shape melted until it looked nothing like a man, and then it was gone.

Kayla fell to her knees, a sudden flood of emotion welling up inside her. She laid down her sword and wept into her soot-covered hands, smearing her face with black fingerprints.

She knelt there for a long time in the stillness of the smoky forest until she felt something wet brush up against her arm. She opened her eyes to see Phineas nuzzling into her with concern, covering her with his body. Kayla wrapped both arms around his neck and hugged him, burying her face in his warm fur.

The sky was dark by the time they walked out of the woods. The streetlamps were nothing but blurry orbs of light suspended in the air. Kayla felt a stab of dread as she imagined walking into the house and dealing with Peter's interrogation. But the feeling quickly passed. He was nothing more than a monster, and monsters, she'd learned, could be defeated.

Kayla lifted her head a little higher and walked toward home with determined steps.

The cool night air felt good on her face, and she took in deep breaths to clear away the smell of smoke and ash. For the first time in a long time, she felt like a weight, something she hadn't even fully realized was there, lifted. She didn't know if any of it was real, but it felt real, and that was enough for now.

When she and Phineas turned onto their street, Kayla saw red and orange lights flashing up ahead. At first, she couldn't tell where they were coming from, but as they came closer, she realized the lights were flashing atop an ambulance parked in the driveway of her house.

Her stomach dropped. She gripped Phineas' leash and ran toward the house, praying to God that Santiago and Henry were okay. She even prayed for Rhonda—the woman was always kind to her.

When she was only one house away, the door of her house opened, and two paramedics came walking out, carefully rolling a stretcher. A white sheet covered the shape of a body. A voice wailed from inside. Screaming, crying.

The stretcher was set down gently and wheeled to the ambulance while two other paramedics remained just inside, trying to comfort Rhonda. She wore her blue scrubs, face buried in her hands, shoulders shaking as she sobbed.

When Rhonda looked up and saw Kayla standing there in shock, she ran out of the house and took her foster daughter into her arms.

"He's dead, Kayla. Oh God, he's dead!"

Kayla swallowed hard, bracing herself for the worst. But then, from over Rhonda's shoulder, Kayla saw Santiago and Henry just inside. A paramedic knelt next to them, one hand on the oldest boy's arm.

"Peter?" Kayla whispered.

"He had a heart attack," Rhonda cried. "I called 911 and started CPR, but he was gone before they got here."

Tears started running down Kayla's face, but she didn't feel them. She stared at the motionless shape under the sheet as it was loaded onto the ambulance. She felt something, but she wasn't sure what it was. Relief, maybe, but something else too, something she didn't yet have words for.

As Rhonda held her tighter, Kayla had a glimpse of the future—the four of them—her, Rhonda, Santiago, and Henry—all living together, all happy. And that future was brighter than all the darkness that lay behind her.

CRATE 42

The bodies of the two pilots and the archaeologist had washed ashore, along with some of the wreckage. Beckett stood on the sand under the hot sun, holding his hands over his eyes and watching as the bodies moved lifelessly with each wave. Capo was still way out there, floating face down near a burning oil slick. Pieces of the plane were scattered up and down the shoreline, but Beckett didn't see what he was looking for. He didn't see the crate. He hoped to God it sunk to the bottom of the ocean, where it belonged.

Beckett hadn't felt right since he first laid eyes on the crate while he and Capo were loading it onto the plane. That crate was just one of sixty-seven full of ancient Sumerian artifacts discovered by Dr. Antonio Franelli, a Vatican archaeologist who watched nervously as the two men loaded the cargo bay. Franelli also happened to be a priest, and he stood sweating in his collar on the tarmac with a clipboard in hand, checking off each crate as it disappeared inside the plane.

There was one crate, though, crate 42, with two long poles attached to either side.

"Don't touch it," Dr. Franelli said, sweat glistening on his upper lip. "Whatever you do, you must not touch the crate. This is very important. Use only the poles."

Beckett and Capo followed his instruction, lifting the small but heavy crate by the poles and carrying it on board. But once they set it down, Beckett put both hands on the crate to push it into a tight space. When his gloved hand touched the wood, Beckett felt like a bomb went off in his brain.

His body slumped to the ground, and although his eyes closed to the outer world, they opened up to another. He saw a future world, dark and empty. There were no humans, no animals of any kind. Skyscrapers and buildings were nothing but rubble. A thick smoke hung over everything. Dark clouds hid the sun, and the landscape was covered in shadow. But these shadows moved. They sensed him watching and approached, reaching out with shadowy hands and fingers. Deep within the darkness of the shadows was a presence. A faint yellow light glowed there, and a voice spoke inside Beckett's head in a harsh whisper.

As in the very beginning, it shall be at the end. We have been here since before Time had a name, and we will be here when Time no longer has meaning.

Beckett stood and watched the oil fire for a few more minutes before turning around to survey the island. It was small, he could tell that much. Looking down the shore, he saw the curve of the land, and he suspected he could probably walk the entire length in just a couple of hours. To his left was a small scattering of rocks, which he thought might be helpful when the tide came in—good for trapping fish.

Behind him was a green wall of foliage. Tall trees and broad-leafed plants obscured any view into the jungle beyond. Beckett closed his eyes and let his other senses *see* the island. He heard the call of birds, a distant sound that reminded him of women screaming.

A breeze blew from the inner part of the island. A cold and dead breeze that carried the faint odor of something rotting. He didn't like not knowing what lay beyond the green wall, but he had to collect supplies before the ocean took them back again. Beckett removed his shoes and ran to the shore, scavenging what he could and dragging it back up to the dry sand. The bodies he left alone. Night would be coming soon, and he didn't want to waste energy trying to bury them before they began to rot.

On the plane, Franelli had told him the artifacts would be taken to a museum in America where they could be translated and studied. But as the archaeologist spoke, Beckett heard another voice, the voice from the shadow saying, *We will start over from the ground up. We will grind your bones to powder and walk in the dust of your memories.*

The last thing that Beckett remembered was that the engine outside his window caught fire, his heart leaping up into his throat, and the look on Capo's face was pure terror as the plane began its trembling descent into the ocean.

Beckett sat surrounded by the few things he was able to salvage. They had not been carrying much food, and he was doubtful that enough wreckage would wash ashore for him to build a shelter. He felt he needed to walk around the island and know what it had to offer.

Somehow, it seemed right to him that he should be the one to survive the crash. He should be the one to know the crate had been sent to a watery grave—after all, he was the only one to whom the crate had spoken.

Beckett began his trek around the island, staying outside the jungle and the coldness that lay within. The water of the ocean was very clear, and he could see fish darting about. This gave him hope that he might survive long enough to be rescued, although he did not entertain such thoughts for long. He should have died in the crash, but he didn't. Whatever came after that, he would accept it as his fate.

When Beckett reached the rocks, he felt a sudden pain in his chest, and the skin on his arms went pinpricked and numb. As he walked around the largest rock, he saw it. Washed ashore not twenty yards ahead, completely intact, with the wooden poles still attached, was crate 42. And the shadow voice spoke.

HOW WE LEARN

Kylie grabs my hand, and we run away from the burning house. We run until a car comes, and we slow down until it passes, then start running again. She squeezes so tight my bones scrape together, and her breath is the dog panting in my ear at night. The big, brown dog we had in that first apartment when we were too young to make memories. But I remember.

We run, and the heavy backpack slams against me with each step.

My breath is hot against my face, and it feels like I'm suffocating. I used to want to take the mask off, but I'm used to it now. It's not really a surgical mask like you'd get in the hospital. I used to wear those, but they got all stained and gross and fell apart really easily, so Kylie got some fabric and sewed me new ones. I wanted cool patterns, but Kylie said they'd make people stare, and patterns are things people remember. So, I have just enough black ones for every day of the week.

Breathe in and out through your mouth, Kylie says in my head. Kylie speaks for me. Always has. We found out pretty quick that it's best if

I keep my mouth shut. She always knows what I'm thinking anyway. It's been so long—I've forgotten what my voice even sounds like. Maybe I don't know how to talk anymore.

Kylie says we smell like a campfire, even though neither of us has ever been camping. But she's probably right. She usually is.

I turn around and see the house and feel all bad inside. It's not the first time, but this one is worse. We liked that foster family until we didn't. There's a big orange glow in the sky around the house. Smoke, too, but we can't see that because the low clouds are grey like the smoke. We hear sirens, woo-wooing, not that far away.

Kylie's sticky hand squeezes mine, and we walk faster.

It's I-can-see-Kylie's-breath cold, and her lips are kind of pale, but the surgical mask I wear keeps my warm breath in my face, which is annoying when I've got the burps.

When we moved in with the Pryors, Kylie said we needed a backpack ready to go, just in case. She gets these signals sometimes, but they're not always clear, so Kylie says it's best to be careful.

A siren wails and gets closer. Kylie puts her hands over her ears to block the sound. Those high-pitched sounds have always bothered her. We're just past the park when a car comes tearing around the corner, blue and red flashing us blind. Kylie drops her hands and starts skipping, like just another beautiful night.

The cop car goes by, and Kylie covers her ears again.

She grabs my hand and starts jogging.

"We're still too close," she tells me.

I hate sirens for a different reason. They make me think of Mom and Dad and our apartment. Maybe Kylie hates them for the same reason.

We go around the park, but we don't go in. I run my hand along the cold chain link fence until my fingers go numb, and Kylie pulls my hand away, says the sound bothers her.

I say *sorry* in my head, and she says, "It's okay."

We keep going until we get to the edge of town. There aren't as many clouds here, and the sky is clear. There are some streetlights on the other side of the train tracks, and they look all fuzzy, like when you first wake up.

Kylie tells me we'll have to change schools again, like I don't know.

In my head I say, *let's just skip the rest of junior high and go straight to high school.*

Kylie says, "If we're skipping the rest of junior high, why go back at all?"

I think, because it's something normal. But I don't say it in my head. Kylie taught me how to say things in my head, but I learned all on my own how to be quiet.

I can't hear thoughts like Kylie can. All I can hear is her. But sometimes I know things, and I don't why I know them. Like I know there will be a brown truck somewhere soon and we'll go for a ride in it.

No more families, I say.

No more families, Kylie says back. *Just us.*

There are pieces of thin metal sewn into my masks, like what a tape measure is made out of, but they don't roll up. Sometimes they push into my face and bruise my chin if I'm not careful.

We come to a strip mall with a little store where we buy candy. Next door, there's a Chinese restaurant with windows full of neon signs. The smell of food makes me hungry.

A couple comes out of the restaurant and stares at us. Maybe because we look too young to be out on our own, or maybe because we're holding hands. I don't give a shit.

Kylie squeezes once and nods toward the store. An old guy comes out carrying a plastic bag. He's white-hair old. Bald on top with bedhead everywhere else. He sees us and stops. He looks both ways like he's going to cross the street, then he comes over to us. He's dressed in a nice grey suit that looks a little big on him.

He smiles with teeth that are big and white and fake.

"Lost your way?" he asks us, and even though he still smiles, his eyes look sad. But a lot of old people's eyes look like that all the time.

Kylie keeps my hand in hers. She'll squeeze once if we're good, twice if she reads something bad.

"We need a ride," Kylie says, and makes her voice sound kind of froggy, like she's been crying.

"Oh, sweetie," the old man says. "I don't drive anymore. Otherwise, I'd take you wherever you need to go. Is everything okay?"

Kylie starts to say something, stops, takes a shaky breath, and says, "Our dad got drunk and hit my brother. I think he hurt our step-mom too, and we just want to get home to where our real mom lives."

The old man sets his bag down and leans over. His eyes clench tight when he does. Both hands on his bony knees, he looks into our faces.

"Have you called the cops?" he asks.

"Our stepdad is a cop," Kylie says, and it sounds kind of whiny but also kind of real.

The old man nods. "I see." Then he looks at me, at my mask. "Is he sick?"

Kylie squeezes my hand once. "He's got bad asthma. The air, you know?"

There's another siren getting closer. It gets so loud I can't think for a second, and the old man straightens up and watches as a cop car tears down the road behind us.

After it's gone, he looks back at us. "Listen," he says, and his voice is every nice old man in the movies. "There's nothing I can do but cheer you on. You understand?"

Kylie squeezes my hand once. Hard.

The old man says, "We're always watching, but things have to play out. You know that by now, don't you? Some want you to fail, some want you to succeed. Me, I want to see the world gets whatever it has coming."

The old man picks up his bag, and through the plastic, I see milk, crackers, and that gross pink stomach medicine.

"Bad people will be looking for you," he says.

Kylie swallows, and I hear it.

"How will we know when they're bad?" she asks.

The old man leans forward again, and his breath is cherry cough drops. "When they want something from you that you don't want to give them."

He reaches out a skeleton hand, all blue veins and swollen knuckles, like he wants to touch my arm. But he pulls back. "Take care of each other." Then, he turns and walks around the strip mall, off into the dark where there's no path and no houses and no light.

We keep walking toward the train tracks, going from streetlight to streetlight. I look over at Kylie and think how much we look like Mom and Dad—not the way we remember them, but how they were at our age.

A couple older kids are up ahead. Older because of how they walk like they're not scared. They both have hoodies on and backpacks, and one carries a skateboard. They walk under the fuzzy lights and pass a cigarette back and forth.

We're closer now but I don't really watch them. I watch Kylie. She grabs my hand, holds onto it. My skin is all warm and sweaty, but Kylie's is cold.

Close enough I can smell the smoke that's even worse than a burning apartment, these guys stop and the one with a baseball hat on under his hood jerks his head at us.

He says, "You on your way home?"

"What does it matter?" Kylie says.

This guy laughs and moves around a little like a rapper in those videos Janice wouldn't let us watch.

Kylie gives my hand one squeeze.

"Hey," Hat Guy says. "How old are you?"

And I know he's not talking to me.

Kylie sighs. "Again, what does it matter?"

Hat Guy slaps his friend, who is moving kind of funny like he has to pee, and they start walking next to us.

"You don't have to be a bitch," Hat Guy says.

"And you don't have to be a dick," Kylie says.

Hat Guy jogs ahead, skateboard under his arm. A picture of zombies crawling out of a graveyard scratched up on the bottom of it.

Kylie and me, we don't stop, we just move around him and keep walking, but Hat Guy reaches out and grabs onto Kylie's jacket and tugs. It pulls her back, but she still grips my hand and squeezes once. Even the squeeze doesn't stop the hot feeling in my chest that makes me want to drink a bunch of water, but it never helps. Like the heartburn Chris used to take medicine for. He always wanted us to call him "Dad," but we never could.

We turn around to face this guy.

"I'm just trying to have a conversation, is all," he says.

Kylie's eyebrows go up. "I don't want to talk."

Hat Guy's friend looks up and down the tracks and itches at his pockets. He says, "I don't want to be here."

Hat Guy ignores Twitchy and looks at me. His eyes stay on my mask for a while before moving to my eyes.

"What's with Batman?" he says.

Kylie puts all her weight on one leg and leans like she does when she's irritated.

She says, "Batman's mask didn't cover his mouth, asshole."

Hat Guy blinks once, makes a face, and shivers a little like he doesn't care. "So why is he protecting his identity?"

Kylie shoves her free hand into her jacket pocket. I can't see it, but I bet she's cracking every knuckle.

"It's not to protect himself," she says. "It's to protect you."

Hat Guy laughs again, but it doesn't sound real. Then his face gets all serious. "From what?" he says. "Something contagious?"

"Oh yeah," Kylie says, her face as serious as Hat Guy's. "Super contagious. It's so rare that scientists think only a couple of people have ever had it." She makes a circle around her stomach with one hand. "It starts in the guts and eats everything it can, then it moves to tissue and eats that up. Makes him feel like he's on fire inside."

Her hand moves up her chest, "It burns up through him and infects the heart so that all the blood going through him feels like it's a million degrees."

Kylie moves back to her other foot, and her eyebrows go up.

Hat Guy shakes his head, trying to smile. "Nah, that ain't true." He jerks his head at Twitchy. "It ain't true, man."

Twitchy walks with a limp, drags one leg down the fence line a bit, then turns around and comes back. He's talking, but I can't understand him.

"We just escaped from a research facility down the road," Kylie jerks her head toward the sirens and the smoke. Then she looks at me. "He's never been outside, never even felt sunshine." Kylie looks at the ground, and her hand grows warmer—or maybe it's my hand warming hers. "He doesn't have much time left. So, I thought, let him die in open air."

Hat Guy's eyes go small. He goes back a step and points a finger at me. "You saying he could infect me?"

"I'm saying we all die someday," Kylie says. "And he's almost there. From what I've read, when you've got this disease, it's beautiful when it happens. Your body just explodes into a bunch of sparks, but the sparks are really spores, and they travel on the air and can move through your skin. Then pretty soon everyone has it, and everyone dies, and the world starts over from scratch."

Kylie lowers her voice. "And all that's left is your skeleton, but the cool thing is, it's bright orange and glows at night."

Right on cue, I cough a big nasty hack, and Hat Guy jumps like I just shot a gun.

Kylie's eyes narrow as she tilts her head a little. She gets this look sometimes when she "knows" something when it shows up inside her mind like a thought that doesn't belong to her. She looks at Hat Guy like that now.

Kylie says, "The way things are going for you, I don't think it'll be beautiful when you die." She puts a finger to her forehead. "Maybe a bullet hole here," the finger moves to her side, "or a knife here. Or maybe you'll just be lying by the tracks with foam coming out of your mouth."

She takes my hand again and squeezes once as Hat Guy backs away from us. He shakes his head.

Kylie says, "People always think the stupid shit they do is changing the world. Stop this, do that, save this, get rid of that. And none of it matters."

She points at me now. "What's in him right now, that's the world-changing stuff. The stuff you can't stop from happening."

"I had a dream like this," Twitch says with a laugh.

"So did I," Kylie says as she pulls me along, walking past them. "In it, you, me, and everyone else on Earth were just a bunch of glowing skeletons."

After we've walked until we can't see them, Kylie lets go of my hand, moves behind me, and pulls a water bottle from my backpack. She takes a long drink then gives it to me. I pull the mask just off to the side a little and keep my lips tight when I drink. Kylie turns away when I do.

I replace the cap. *They weren't bad?*

"No, not bad," Kylie says. "Just lost. Confused."

Do you know where we're going?

Kylie shrugs and takes another drink. The water bottle is one of those metal ones. It has to be. She puts the bottle in the backpack and takes a deep breath.

"Wherever we end up can't be normal," she says. "We've tried normal. It doesn't work."

We're on the tracks now, walking right down the middle. I wonder if we'll hop a train at the depot and ride it as far as we can. The tracks are just these long, straight lines stretching into the dark ahead. Maybe going into the dark isn't so bad as long as you know there's a path, a place you're going to.

"I'm thinking Vegas," Kylie says, and I can't see her face anymore because there aren't any streetlights. "We could make a ton of money doing a show, and everyone would believe we're magicians or something."

I start laughing with my mouth shut, but Kylie can tell because it sounds like I have hiccups. She punches my arm, and not light either.

"I'm serious," she says. "We could save up a bunch of money and buy a big house that we'd never have to leave. Who were those guys with the tigers?"

Siegfried and Roy, I tell her.

Kylie says, "Right, them. They were rich."

We both feel it at the same time and stop. The metal vibrates under our feet and puts off a weird kind of hum, like the tracks are singing a one-note song.

"Time to move," Kylie says and takes my hand.

They call it a train "whistle" but it sounds more like an alarm, and it goes off in the distance. I turn and see a big round light way off in the dark. The tracks vibrate harder and make my feet go numb.

Kylie pulls me off the tracks, and we stand in the gravel as the train roars by. Boxcars speed past us, some painted with graffiti— words that aren't really words.

"I know you want to," Kylie says, her hair blowing back from the wind of the train, "but we can't jump on. It's going too fast."

And there it is. A brown truck parked in a circle of light just by the depot, its exhaust puffing out the tailpipe. It's an older one, with no extra cab or anything, and the brown paint is all scratched up.

I point. *I saw that earlier, just a quick flash. But I saw us in it, going somewhere.*

Kylie closes her eyes, but they're pointed at that truck. She stands still, then opens her eyes and shakes her head.

"You sure that's the same truck?" she asks.

I say, *Back light is broken.*

And it is. Shattered. I saw that, too, but I don't know why.

Kylie takes my hand, and we walk toward it, both of us tired and scraping our shoes along the gravel.

The driver's side door opens when we get close, and a man gets out. He reminds me a little of Superman—Christopher Reeve, not the other ones. His hair is a bit grey by his ears, and there are wrinkles around his eyes when he squints into the dark behind us, looking for something or someone. Then his mouth opens, and his eyes get big.

He says, "Oh my gosh, you weren't up there, were you? When the train went by?"

Kylie stares at the man, squeezes my hand once, and starts to say something.

"Do you know how dangerous that is?" the man says. "What are you doing out here?"

Kylie makes her face look like she does when she's in trouble and about to cry to get out of it.

"We ran," she says. "Our foster dad is really angry, and we need to get away from him."

This Christopher Reeve guy kneels right in front of us and takes Kylie's free hand in his. His eyes make my head go all fuzzy, and I see the small wrinkles around his eyes from smiling. But right now, he looks so worried that it makes me worried for us.

He says, "You're safe now, darling. Don't you worry, okay?"

He takes my free hand, too, and his hands are cold, even though he had been sitting in a running truck. "Listen, I can't leave you guys here alone, it wouldn't be right. Are you hungry? Let's go get some food, and we'll talk about what to do."

The man lets go of our hands and stands up. He's tall, too, like Superman. His shirt sticks out a little at the stomach, but his shoulders and arms are still strong. He starts walking, but Kylie doesn't move, and neither do I because I'm waiting for her. The man notices, stops, and turns around.

"I'm Dave, by the way," he says. "I have one daughter, but I'm divorced, so I live alone with a cat my little girl named Ricochet. We call him Ricky for short. I work here at the depot, and I was watching to make sure the train had the right number of boxcars."

Kylie squeezes my hand. One time.

Dave says, "Alright, guys, hop in, and we'll get somewhere warm." Kylie says "thank you" in a quiet voice and we go to the passenger side while Dave gets behind the wheel. Kylie opens the door and slides across the bucket seat until she's next to Dave. I get in after her and close the door.

Dave cranks the heat, and I feel it pushing against my frozen toes.

"Do you guys like hamburgers?" he asks.

My stomach goes tight thinking of food, and I nod once.

"He's got the flu," Kylie says. "Doesn't want to give it to anyone else."

But Dave doesn't drive, he just sits there looking out the window with an elbow resting on the seat back. One hand scratches at the stubble on his chin.

"Are you guys really running from your foster dad?" Dave asks.

Kylie is holding my other hand now. One squeeze.

She starts crying, and it's so real I think it might be. "I swear he's going to kill us someday."

Dave's eyes flicker to her and back out the windshield. "Am I going to get in trouble for taking you out to burgers and not taking you to the police?"

"Our foster dad is a cop," Kylie says. "That's the last place we want to go. Our mom lives in Eugene. We can call her to come get us. I'm sure she'd give you some money."

Dave breathes out and it lasts a long time. It's like he's deflating. He puts both arms on the steering wheel and puts his head down. We listen to him breathe, and it gets heavier, louder.

I can't see his face, but I hear his voice. "Listen, if I'm going to do something for you, I need you to do something for me. It's only fair."

When he lifts his head up, he looks nothing like Superman. His eyes are cold now, and maybe even dead in some inside way.

"We keep this between us," Dave says, dropping one hand to Kylie's leg. "Just between friends, okay? I help you, you help me. Sound like a deal?"

Kylie squeezes my hand twice, hard. I throw open the door and wrap both arms around her waist and pull her over my body. She makes a little sound as she tumbles out into the gravel. She gets to one knee and slams the door shut, and then I look into the surprised dead eyes of the man and tear off my mask.

When I open my mouth, the inside of the truck turns as bright as daylight, and I close my eyes and see black spots. Like staring at the sun, Kylie told me once. The man opens his mouth, too, and screams. It starts low but gets higher. It's a horrible sound, and I hate it. His hands go to his face, but it's too late. The skin is already coming off under his fingers, making him look like a candle melting down to nothing.

Everything the light touches starts to glow. The dash-board, the steering wheel, the guy's shirt, the fabric on the seats, even the glass behind him. It glows like the brightest lightbulb, and the guy keeps screaming and it sounds so much worse now. There's wet in his voice. His fingernails claw at his face and pull away strips of bright flesh. What's underneath pulses yellow-white.

Then his shirt disappears, and his pants. They don't burn, but they get consumed, I guess. They turn into this glowing dust that spins around the cab of the truck, like pollen that's on fire. The guy keeps screaming, but the light takes over, and the sound isn't a voice anymore. It's a hum, but not one you've ever heard. You feel it more than hear it, and it sings in your chest. Kylie says it's the sound the universe made when it was born.

The guy's whole body goes bright white, then explodes into a billion particles that float. They settle all over the truck until it's just snow under sunrise. It makes me think of mountains, and I feel calm in a way that's scary because I know what it means.

The mask in my hand, I don't want to wear it anymore. But I shake the glowing dust off and put it back over my mouth, pulling the straps behind my ears.

Kylie opens the door, grabs my arm, and pulls me out of the truck. All that dust still glows. It pulses with each beat of my heart. Like it's part of me.

Kylie hands me the bottle of water. I'm always thirsty after, like a man lost in the desert thirsty. I drink the whole thing, but it's not enough. Kylie has already taken the can of starter fluid and cigarette lighter out of the backpack. I sit down on the ground, coughing, and light shoots out from around the mask every time I do.

Kylie comes over and kneels in front of me. She puts one hand on my shoulder and leans in until our foreheads touch. Her skin is so cool and soothing. Mine is a fever.

I'm sorry. I'm so sorry. I wipe my eyes, but they keep burning. *I'm sorry. I saw the truck earlier. I thought he was good.*

"Thank you," Kylie says and sniffs. "He was bad. Really bad."

I look into her eyes, all big and wet and scared. If I asked, she'd say she wasn't scared, but she's never been able to hide it from me.

How do we know? Next time, before it gets to this?

Kylie's lips are tight like she's going to kiss something, and her shoulders are bunched up.

"We figure it out as we go," she says. "This is how we learn."

She stands with the starter fluid in one hand and the lighter in the other. "Remember what Dad used to tell us?"

She blinks quick and hard when she says the word "Dad" and it makes my eyes water.

I nod.

"We make the road by walking," she says.

We've said it to each other thousands of times. We didn't use to know what it meant, but we do now. It means there's not always a path, and even when there is, sometimes it's wrong. You have to go the way you think is right, even if no one has ever been there before. And you make the road. You scrape and claw and tear and crawl and hack and burn. You run until you find the place you're supposed to be.

We make the road by walking.

My sister sets down the can and lighter and kneels in front of me. She gently unhooks the mask straps from my ears and takes the mask off. She puts her hands on my face and looks at me. My true face. My mouth and lips. Parts of me that have no use and no one ever sees. But Kylie sees and smiles at me, and it's sad, and it's Mom's smile. The way Mom looked at me before she turned into light. There was pain in Mom's smile, too, but her eyes told me it wasn't my fault—even though it was.

Kylie walks over to the truck's open door, points the nozzle inside, flicks the lighter to a flame, and torches everything.

WARLOCK

As a travel writer, people often ask me, "Where is the most beautiful place you've ever been?" I always answer the same: Beauty is easy to find, peace is much harder. And I want that now more than anything—somewhere peaceful. Somewhere I can sleep because I haven't slept a full night in three years.

Only a few months after my wife died, a magazine asked me to write a feature piece about towns on the Oregon coast. I accepted the assignment just to have something to occupy my mind and to give my ten-year-old son Colin and me some much-needed time away from the city. So, we packed up our station wagon and drove up the 101 from San Francisco to Gold Beach. After one night, it was on to Port Orford and then Cape Blanco.

Four days into our journey, we arrived in Bandon, Oregon. Three blocks of wood-shingled buildings and shops that sold trinkets make up the old town. One store sold nothing but Christmas decorations all year round. All the tinsel and holly looked grotesque against the weather-beaten wood.

We rented a small cottage near the beach, and I took Colin down to the ocean on that first day. We wandered through the rocks and found tide pools full of crabs and sea anemones. He clomped around in his rain boots with pictures of robots on them, his too-big coat dipping into the water whenever he'd squat down to take a closer look at something. Wind-blown curls, red cheeks. His bright blue eyes were so wide and curious. But there was sadness in those eyes now. He always believed the world was a beautiful piece of machinery and wanted to know how it all worked. Then he learned that people sometimes got caught in the machine and ripped apart by the gears.

As I knelt next to my son and explained how the gravity of the moon controlled the tides, I looked into his face, and it saddened me that I couldn't find the boy he'd been before his mom died. That other boy was so playful, always laughing, but someone much more serious had taken his place. Someone tainted by death. I saw Elle in his face, in how he squinted his eyes when thinking. He always worried about the poor, the unfortunate, and the homeless. Every Christmas, we had to convince him to keep the money his grandparents gave him. Keep him from giving it away.

A flash of anger hit me. Anger at Elle for leaving us. Anger at the world for taking her away.

"I read that dolphins might be as smart as humans," Colin said, without looking up from a small red crab that scuttled away from him.

I reached down and picked up a sand dollar. It fell apart in the palm of my hand.

"They talk to each other," Colin said. "But we can't understand them. One book said they even have names for each other."

I brushed the dust off my hand, then hoisted Colin up as a wave rushed in between the rocks, filling the pools with more water.

"Is that why we don't eat them?" he asked. I held his small body in my arms, his mouth inches from my face. Particles of sand clung to his skin. Everything about him so brand new.

"I don't think they taste very good," I said.

Colin squinted into the gray light of the sky. "I think it's because they're smart."

Something moved at the edge of my vision, and I turned to see a tall figure with a haggard face and wild white hair walking toward us with slow steps. He wore a wrinkled black suit that looked slept in and a black wool overcoat that engulfed his thin frame. The sleeves hung down past his hands. We were alone on the beach, no one but us and this lone figure dressed in black.

Something about the man made me feel protective of Colin in a way I can't explain. Nothing more than an old man out for a walk, but my heart beat faster. I took Colin's hand and told him we'd walk further down to look for pieces of driftwood to take home. As we made our way out of the rocks, I turned around to look at the man again, but he was gone. I've wondered if I only imagined this part, but I swear there were no footprints on the beach. Nothing at all to mark he'd ever been there.

The midday sky grew overcast as we walked back to the cottage. A dark wall appeared on the horizon. Rain was coming.

We drove to Old Town Bandon and ate dinner at a seafood place famous for its clam chowder. I tried to jot down some notes for my story, but I couldn't stop thinking about the old man who seemed to disappear without a trace. Pressure started at my temples and spread until it gripped the top of my skull. Another headache. They started right after Elle died, and I had one almost every day.

Thunder cracked when we walked outside, followed by a heavy rain that fell fast and hard. We were soaked even before we made it under the awning of a shop. Colin stood there smiling, his curly hair wet and plastered to his forehead. As we huddled together, we heard a voice shouting into the storm.

"Standing at the edge," the voice yelled. "Always there, always watching. Standing at the edge."

Then we saw him, a man covered in trash bags, stumbling down the center of the street. He passed by, but he didn't notice us. His eyes looked at the sky, moving back and forth as though searching for something. Long, greasy covered half of his face, and the rest was hidden beneath a scraggly beard.

After the man turned a corner and disappeared from view, Colin said, "Dad, we should have given him some money."

Your mom would have said the same thing, I thought. But I didn't say it, and now I wish I had.

I don't know how long we stood there before I turned around and looked through the shop window. I found myself staring directly into the empty eyes of a bleached white ram's skull. I took a step backward, startled, into the rain.

The shelves in the shop window were covered with an assortment of antique oddities—a spinning wheel, a typewriter, a steamer trunk, and a lamp with a multicolored glass shade. Colin pulled on my hand and pointed across the street to a brightly lit shop that sold toys and kites.

"You can go look," I told Colin, "but be very careful. I'll be just inside here," nodding to the window. In every town we'd been to, I picked a unique shop to highlight for the story. Local color. And this place was as unique as any I'd seen so far.

I watched Colin run across the street before opening the shop door and stepped inside. A dusty smell hit me—old books, stale air. My shoes squeaked on the dark wooden floor. A few old lamps cast small halos of orange light, leaving much of the room in shadow.

A noise came from somewhere near the back. A footstep, a creak. I moved a little closer and took a sharp breath in when I saw the ghostly shape of a woman hovering in the dark.

She wore a Victorian dress the color of dried blood, the collar buttoned to her neck, and her silver hair was done up in a way I'd only ever seen in sepia-toned photographs.

Her face tilted as she looked at me over the glasses perched on the end of her nose. "You are welcome to look around as long as you like," she said, with a voice that was husky and aged.

"Are you the owner?" I asked, taking out my pen and notebook on instinct.

She came over to me, moving a thick book to one hand so she could extend the other. Her skin was soft but cold and thin. It shifted beneath my fingertips. A musty smell radiated from her, probably the old dress.

Her eyes squinted as she looked me over. "Are you a seeker or a wanderer?"

"I'm just curious how a shop like this stays open," I said.

The woman's eyebrows went up. "There are always enough seekers. Those who are meant to always find their way here."

Shelves lined with glass jars filled with liquids and powders covered the right wall. One held the twisted claw of a bird.

The woman's eyes followed me as I looked around the shop. I was about to thank her and leave when the bell above the door rang and someone came inside. The entire room went cold as soon as I heard his footsteps on the wooden floor. My head started to ache even worse, like talons digging into my skull. I spun around to see the man from the beach. Rainwater dripped from the shoulders of his black coat. He didn't look at me.

The old woman said, "Good evening," as she stepped behind the counter, but the man did not reply. He didn't even nod. History lined the man's face. Long, deep wrinkles curved around his mouth and lined his forehead. The white hair was bright and wild, and his cloudy eyes opened too wide.

The woman handed him a small glass vial half-full with a reddish-brown powder. The old man held it up close to his wide eyes and shook it gently. His wet hand smeared the writing on the label. He took some wrinkled bills from his coat pocket, set them on the counter, and then walked back to the door. Our eyes met, and I've never been so certain in my life that someone could see straight through me. Time slowed as the old man walked past. His eyes held mine. He did not blink once. Then the bell above the door rang, and the old man walked out, but there was a stabbing pain in my head that hadn't been there before.

I stood staring at the door when I felt a cool hand on my forehead. The woman had come over and looked at me with concern as she pressed the back of her hand onto my skin. She closed her eyes and tilted her head as if listening through her fingers.

"You have a fever," she said, opening her eyes.

She led me to a chair near the back of the store, then busied herself by pulling down five separate glass jars and tipping small amounts of whatever was inside into a glass of water. She stirred it all together with a pipette, which she removed and dipped on her tongue. She nodded once and handed me the glass.

"Drink it," she said.

I took a small sip. It tasted bitter and earthy.

"I need to get back to my son," I told her.

"Colin is fine," she said. "Drink up."

My pulse pounded through my ears. The talons gripped my skull even tighter.

The woman crossed her arms and leaned against a column as she watched me drink. "All of it," she said. "Stir it a bit when it gets to the bottom. Make sure you get all the powder."

I did as she told me, and as soon as I'd swallowed the last of it, the pain in my head went away. She took a step closer and felt my forehead again.

"Thank you, ma'am," I said.

"Charis," she replied.

"Are you Greek?" I asked.

"You know this word, Charis?"

I nodded. "Grace."

"Sometimes things are named not for what they are, but for what others wish they could be." She knelt and took my hands in hers. Blue veins and bony knuckles. "How many times have you seen him?" she asked, her face serious, eyes narrowed.

My hands tightened around the glass. "This was the second."

Charis closed her eyes and let out a slow exhale. "There is something between you," she said. "The world turned and brought you together twice."

"Coincidence," I said.

She smiled with closed lips. "So certain about that which you know nothing. He is a dangerous man. Be cautious."

"You know him?" I asked.

"I know what he is," she said, "and that's all anyone can know."

"What is he?"

Her eyes flickered from my face. She took the glass and stood, groaning a little as she did. She looked down at me, and her eyes glistened. The years showed in the lines on her face, in the marks and liver spots on her hands.

"Let me tell you a story," she said. "There was once a young family, a father, a mother, and a small boy. One day, the father became very sick. This illness lasted for weeks and did not get any better. The mother took him to the city to see the best doctors, but none of the tests could show what was wrong with him."

Charis still held the glass as she paced in front of my chair, turning it in slow circles.

"Over time, the father grew sicker, to the point of death. He could no longer eat, and his body slowly wasted away. The mother was told to keep him comfortable until the end came. Then, one day a man came to their home, dressed in a black suit and black coat, his hair as white as the fleece of a lamb. He said, 'All you have to do is ask.' The mother asked what it would cost for this help, and the man replied, 'I don't yet know what the cost will be, but I can promise it will be more than you expect, and it will not be me who collects what is owed. If you want my help, all you have to do is ask.' The mother had to think for only a moment. 'Please, help my husband,' she said. For the mother thought that no matter how much money was demanded, she would go into debt for the rest of her life if it meant her husband could live."

The lights in the shop flickered as thunder rattled the windows. Charis stopped speaking and looked over at the lamp as it turned on and off.

"So, she invited the man inside and took him to the father's room. He was so sick that he could not even open his eyes or speak.

The man asked the mother to step back, then took out a bag containing a male goat's ashes. He licked his finger, dipped it into the ashes, and drew a symbol on the father's forehead. A symbol I will neither describe nor name. Then, the man stood with his arms stretched out over the father and spoke in a language the mother had never heard. As the man spoke, other voices seemed to join him in chanting the words until it sounded like an invisible crowd had gathered. When the man finished, color returned to the father's cheeks almost immediately. He sat up and saw his wife looking at him with tears in her eyes. She threw herself at the feet of the man in the coat, who looked down at her with pity and some sadness. He departed without speaking another word. Months passed and the father was healthier than ever. The family was so grateful they treated every single day as though it were something precious and rare, which it is. But then, one night, the boy awoke screaming. The father found the boy sitting up in bed, staring straight ahead. The father took the boy in his arms and felt the small body tremble in his embrace. The boy pointed to the foot of his bed. 'A man was standing there,' he said. 'A man in a black hood and robe. I could not see his face. I could only see his hands and long fingers, skin as white as teeth.' The father comforted the boy and told him it was nothing more than a dream and to go back to sleep. The dream troubled the father, but he did not think much of it until the next night when the boy awoke screaming again. Again, he said that the hooded figure with the long white fingers had stood at the foot of his bed, watching him. On the third night of this, the boy started screaming in the dark, and it made a different sound than before. The father ran into the boy's room, and his son was writing in agony, crying out in pain. He said his bones were on fire. The father put his hand on the boy's shoulder, and the bone collapsed. The boy screamed even louder. He twisted and contorted, and every time he did, the father heard bones snapping. The mother came into the room and tried to comfort the boy. She stroked his face and was horrified when the bone around his eye caved in. The father called an ambulance, and by the time the paramedics arrived, the boy had passed out from the pain and exhaustion. When they tried to place him on the gurney, the paramedics discovered that nearly every single bone in the boy's body was shattered. They had never seen anything like it. They told the parents if he was not dead yet, he would be within hours. They decided to keep him at home and let him pass to the other side in peace. Both parents fell asleep beside their son, afraid to touch him. When the sun rose on the next day, the boy sat up and got out of bed. He was whole again and in no pain."

Charis sat in the chair next to me, her face crisscrossed with shadows. Her arthritic hands folded together as if in prayer.

"It never stopped, you see. Years went by, and this young boy awoke screaming every night. He would see that same figure standing at the foot of his bed. Every night, his bones would shatter, and his body would lose shape. He endured this torture for years. Eventually, the boy's mind fractured as well, but he was no longer a boy—he was a man."

"Is he still alive?" I asked.

Charis's eyes quivered with moisture. "You saw him earlier," she said, nodding toward the window. "Covered in trash bags, wandering the town, searching for something that can't be found."

My memory flashed back to the homeless man we'd seen, speaking his fractured prophecies to the dark.

"That man has this kind of power?" I asked, part of me waiting for her to smile and tell me it was all a joke.

"There is a story," Charis said, "that he once brought a man back to life. The man wasn't the same as before, but he was no longer dead."

I tried to laugh, but the sound came out all wrong.

"You ask yourself, how could this be?" Charis said, her face closer to mine. Her breath smelled of herbal tea and mint. "But these things have happened for millennia. This is nothing new."

Through the front windows, I saw Colin leave the toy store and run back across the street, head low against the rain. I stood up quickly, thanked the old woman for her time, and left the shop without looking back. I didn't want my son to step foot in that place. The old woman was harmless, but I didn't want my son to even breathe the air of a world in which all of the things she told me about were possible.

We should have left following day for Winchester Bay. We would have, too, if the rain hadn't stopped and the sun hadn't peeked through the clouds. The ocean water sparkled. The sand was golden and glowing. A light breeze blew, and kites floated in the distance. Multicolored diamond shapes drifting across the sky.

Colin stood at the window with his hands against the glass, looking down at the beach with excitement. "Can I go for a swim, Dad?" he asked. "Please?"

I wanted to just get on the road and leave the man, the old woman, the strange antique shop, all of it, but then I imagined what Colin's mother would have said.

Let him go swimming.

A morning like that should feel different, and looking back, it did. Something was off, but I couldn't tell what it was then. A small voice in my head told me we should leave, but I didn't listen. I couldn't say no when I looked at Colin's face, bright eyes, and hopeful smile.

He jumped up and down and gave me a hug when I told him to get changed. He ran into his room to put on his swim trunks.

"Only for an hour," I told him.

Colin and I walked down the sandy pathway to the beach. I laid our towels near some large rocks and sat with my bare feet in the sand while he ran straight into the water without even testing the temperature. He shrieked as it hit his legs and rose up to his waist. He turned and waved at me, smiling with chattering teeth.

I wasn't worried then, not yet. The waves were still gentle, and Colin has always been a strong swimmer. I stood up to yell for him to stay close to shore but stopped myself. At ten, the boy already knew not to go too far out. I sat back down as he threw himself into the small, white-tipped waves that rolled in.

Colin shouted for me to join him in the water. I smiled and shook my head no. A wave hit his back and knocked him over. I sat up straighter and stared where he'd gone under, and within a few heartbeats, he popped back up, his laughter carried on the breeze.

I looked at my watch, thinking of the time needed to pack up our stuff and drive north, but I told myself to relax and let Colin have fun. I didn't take my eyes off him as he played until dark clouds started to drift over across the sun. The beach, the ocean, the horizon, all of it turned gray. Something moved to my right. I glanced over and thought I saw a person's shadow stretch out on the sand. A thin figure with long fingers. I blinked, and the shadow was gone.

When I turned back, Colin was gone too. Just an empty space in the water where he should have been. The waves kept rolling in, but Colin was nowhere.

I walked down to the wet sand, wondering if he'd gone under on purpose and hadn't yet come up for air. My heartbeat grew inside me, became bigger, wider. It pulsed in my throat and made each breath tighter. I screamed his name at the ocean so loud my voice went hoarse. My heart slipped as I ran toward the water. I screamed Colin's name again—thinking, *I can't lose you too, I can't lose you*—and a bomb went off inside my head. A burst of liquid fire filled my senses and erased every single thought. Pain flooded my skull.

My body pitched forward, and my arms wouldn't move to brace me as I fell. My head hit the sand hard, and every muscle on the left side of my face sagged. I tried to speak, but only drool came out. The ocean waves sounded distant, distorted. Memories appeared in my mind and evaporated. Thoughts tumbled around, none of them making any sense.

I'm having a stroke, I thought.

My vision grew cloudy, blurring the ocean and the sky, but I saw Colin come out from behind one of the large rocks.

Thank God he's okay.

"Dad?" he said, his voice shaking with fear. "Dad, are you all right?"

I tried to tell him to call 911, and all I heard was my own voice moaning.

Colin knelt next to me. "I'm sorry," he said, touching my shoulder. "I was just hiding, I didn't mean to scare you, Dad. I'm so sorry!"

I tried to speak again. I knew the words I was trying to say, but they sounded like nothing, and Colin started to cry. He dug through my pockets to find my phone, and when he finally did, he cried even harder. The screen was shattered from the fall.

Colin's face was a trembling picture. The ocean and sky behind him jerked in rhythm as my eyes spasmed. I wanted nothing more than to close them, but I couldn't look away from my son's face, from his fearful eyes.

"Dad, please don't go," he sobbed. "Don't leave me alone."

The skin on my arms started to tingle like I'd touched something electric just as a long, dark shadow fell over us. Colin inhaled and held his breath as he looked up. I started to scream for help, but the words never even left my mouth because the shadow belonged to the man in the black coat. He stood there, shoulders hunched, head down, and stared at my son, his eyes both evil and sad at the same time. Wrinkles within wrinkles formed around his eyes and on his forehead. His white hair moved with the wind.

In my head, I screamed, *No, Colin, no! Run!* But I couldn't make a sound.

The man held out one hand to Colin, palm up, and said, "All you have to do is ask."

LION'S DEN

*** Norman Pinker was arrested on October 2 for involuntary manslaughter and taken to the Clearfield County jail. The following is a transcript from Mr. Pinker's "interrogation." Included are the notes of Detective Charles Brennan, who observed the following from behind the two-way mirror. ***

An officer brings Mr. Pinker into the interrogation room and removes the handcuffs. He wears stained jeans and a thermal shirt covered with cigarette burns. Over the thermal, he wears an unbuttoned red flannel. His shoes leave muddy footprints on the floor. He shuffles to the chair and sits down, puts both elbows on the table, and rubs at his scalp. His hair is completely grey and messy. Looks like he hasn't shaved in a while.

Pinker speaks to the officer in a voice low and hoarse. He says, "I'm sorry about your wife's death. Next few years gonna be hard on you and the kids."

The officer's eyes open wide. He takes a step back, shaking his head. His mouth opens and closes, but he doesn't say anything.

"Hell of a thing," Pinker says. "Going so young like that."

The officer finally turns around and leaves the interrogation room, closing the door behind him. A moment later, he enters the room I'm in, and tears are running down his face.

"He can't be right, can he?" the officer says. "Please tell me he's crazy."

I ask what the officer means.

"What he said about my wife," he sobs. "She's not dead yet... she's been diagnosed with ovarian cancer, but the doctors say her chances are good." He nods to the window as tears drip from his chin. "He's crazy, right?"

I gather the file and my notepad, and I'm about to enter the room when Mr. Pinker's head lifts up. He turns around and looks at the door. He nods a little, and his eyes move from the door to the chair across the table as if watching an invisible person enter the room. He sighs, cracks his knuckles, and begins speaking.

Whattya wanna know? That asshole who arrested me, I already told him what happened. But I guess I can tell it again. My memory's not so good these days, but maybe that don't change anything, right? What's done is done and all that.

Goddamn kids drivin' a million miles an hour around that bend like they ain't never gonna die. When I hear them engines roaring, it sets my ticker to fightin' against the pacemaker I got back when Celia was alive. Doug too, for that matter.

'Course I never meant for what happened to happen. I'm no monster. But sometimes the world feels like one. A monster, I mean. A big, noisy, slobbering monster out to eat everything you love. To tell the truth, I think it all started with the noise. Them cars these days sound like a hundred chainsaws all going at once. Can't stand the sound. Makes me think of choppers. You know that sound? Nah, you ain't never been in the service, have you? Didn't think so.

It don't matter what kinda car these little assholes have. They drive it like they in a NASCAR race. Pisses me off somethin' fierce, it does. Ignore the goddamn sign with the big ol' numbers printed on it so big you'd hafta to be blind to not see it. Ignore the fact the road turns so quick you can't see what's 'round the corner.

I always been afraid of cars. They're too big, and they move too fast. I tried to teach Doug that fear, but he wouldn't listen and look where that got him.

You know the bend I'm talkin' about? You know where I live, dontcha? Well, up there on Bishop Creek, just past my dirt driveway the road turns pretty sharp up there. Tell the truth, you should find the fuckin' asshole who designed the road and arrest him. Who'd make a road do that? I'll tell you. A drug addict, that's who. Someone high out of their mind and doesn't give a shit.

Good 'nuff for government work, ain't that the sayin'? Yeah, well. It ain't good enough. Doug wasn't the first, sure you know that. But I thought maybe he'd be the last. Guess I was wrong on that.

Like I said, my memory ain't worth shit these days. Not only got a bad ticker, my brain's fried too. I was in Nam—did I tell you that already? No? Well, I was. Came back home with a heroin habit that I kicked and a drinking habit that I didn't.

Mr. Pinker pats his pockets for cigarettes, apparently forgetting these were taken when he was booked.

Can I smoke in here? No? Can't fucking smoke anywhere anymore. You can eat all the poisonous shit you want, but people look at you like a goddamn psycho if you light up a ciggy.

Anyway, Doug was the second-best thing that ever happened to me. His momma being the first. God took her early though, but I don't blame him. Nam does that to a person. Gives you perspective on death. Doug died on that road, you know that right? Goin' 'round that same bend. And yes, that's why I'm afraid of it. Don't need no head shrinker to figure that out.

I ask myself all the time, why didn't I see that one comin'? Something like that should set off some psychic warning bells, you know? But I didn't see a goddamn thing.

Pinker takes a deep breath, puts his hands on the table. Spreads his fingers out.

I heard it happen though. I ran outside and see his car off the road, up on two wheels. The front end all folded up like an accordion. All that blood, that was my boy's blood. My Doug. All twisted and broken in that crushed car. Right outta college, he was. And good lookin', too. What a waste of a life. All that possibility bottled up in somethin' so fragile. Just like Nam, man. All those kids, so many of 'em woulda gone on to do great things. Instead, they busy dyin' in the swamp of some fucked up country they couldn't give two shits about. Man, losin' Doug fucked me up bad. Celia was already gone, now my son is gone, too. What I got to keep on goin'? Fuckin' whiskey and cigarettes and that's 'bout all.

Pinker goes silent, stares at the table, picks at the skin around his fingernails. He wipes at one eye and swallows.

Look what you did. You done got me goin'. Now what was the question? Yeah, yeah, the road. You mean the corner, the bend in the road, not the road itself.

That stretch a road always been bad, long as I can remember. Knew it when I bought the house. I had this movie play in my head that told me something bad was gonna happen there. And how couldn't it? It's a blind corner. Can't nobody see nothin'. Tight too.

What do I mean by the movie in my head? Shit. How much time you got?

I already told you I was in Nam. What I ain't told you is that I saved a buncha lives over there 'cause of a movie in my head. Not a movie like from start to finish. More like flashes of one, scenes I guess you'd call 'em. Thought I was dreaming at first, but I wasn't sleepin'. It's like I stepped off the world and into a movie screen. What's in front of me is light, but all around me is this dark. I'm looking at a place different than where my body is. Which I know makes no goddamn sense, but there ain't no other way to put it.

What'd I see? Well, I seen a tunnel in my mind, sweaty VC bastards crawling through the mud and popping up at a spot just outside our camp. Coming up out of the ground like a buncha goddamn ants. So, I see the movie and then get this cold feelin' all over my skin. It's fear, but not the kind you make up. The real kind. And over there you learn to tell the difference.

So, I tell my C.O. we gotta go check this area out. He asks why, and I just tell him I got a bad feelin' is all. But the C.O. won't let it go. Says, "Convince me." I tell him, "If we sit by that spot and no Charlies come up, he can have the naked picture of my lady that she sent me." That's good enough for him, so we take a few guys and go sit.

It don't take long before the ground moves and opens up like a trap door, and what comes out, but a helmet attached to the head of some fucker unlucky enough to tunnel up right in front of us. We blow away the ones that come out, and the rest get firebombed into hell.

That was the first time, but it wasn't the last. Figured out if I concentrated hard enough, I could put myself into the movie, take a look around and see what's what. The C.O. started showing me pictures of places and asking if all was clear. Sometimes it was, sometimes it wasn't. It scared me some at first, but it kept me outta the shit, so I didn't mind too much.

But I tell you, every time I went into the movie, remember how I said it was dark all around me except for in front? Well, I swear to God something else was in there, in the dark with me. I heard breathing. Just normal breathing, but coming out of a tar black mind movie, ain't nothing sound normal. Sometimes I could hear it walking. Sometimes watching me. Felt it like a spider up my neck.

Well, that C.O. musta told someone about what I could do, because next thing I know I'm being put on a plane and sent to the mighty state of West Virgina. They drive me out to the woods, to this wooden box they call the Rectangle, on account that's all it is. Plus, it's a joke. The Pentagon? The Rectangle? Never mind.

And that's where I meet Marshall Atwater. He's a lieutenant but doesn't want anyone to call him that. Just Marshall, or Atwater. A serious man who knows things. I've learned the people who want you to think they're smart are usually pretty dumb. It's the ones that don't say much, they're the ones that got the information. Skip was like that. Quiet mosta the time. But when he talked, you realized he's got more pieces of the puzzle than you'll ever have.

There was five of us at the Rectangle, all men, and every one of us had been found by Atwater because of our mind movies. We all called it by a different name, but it meant the same thing. We saw what was happening in other places, places where we weren't. Impossible, I know. But I also thought those naked beaches were a myth until I had three days leave in Thailand, so there you go.

This other guy there, name of Jamie Fuller, he always called it "Finding." Atwater called it "Looking," but Jamie said, "I don't go into that place to look, I go to find." And right he was.

The Rectangle was just one long poorly built shithouse. One end was all bedrooms and bathrooms, and the other end was made into these dark little cubicles. That was where we spent most our time. Atwater'd show us a picture of somewhere, tell us to focus and go take a look. Then he'd put us in one of those closets and we'd dive into the movie. Sometimes you couldn't really control when you came out of it, but sometimes you could. I don't know why, but every once in a while, I'd be looking and some-thing would pop in my brain, and all of a sudden, I'm sprawled out on the floor with the shakes.

It was harder on some of the other guys. Fuller for one. He saw something bad in the dark too, only it wasn't after him, it was after his brother. He'd come out of the movie screaming and crying. Some of the other guys too. Roger Meharry wouldn't tell us what he saw. Don't know if he could even if he wanted to. He got a little crazier each time he came out.

Afterward Atwater would sit with us, one on one and record what we told him.

Most of the pictures were of Vietnam, some of Russia and China. Sometimes Cuba. Sometimes other places, really old places with ruined temples and jungle all around. God knows what they were looking for there. But I will say, that's where the stranger in the dark felt the strongest. Felt like he was right fuckin' next to me in those places.

Yeah, yeah, yeah. Bullshit, I know. It's all impossible. The fuck I care what you believe or not? It's my life you piss-ant. Can't tell me what happened and what didn't.

Well, funding ran out, I guess. Or maybe we got used up. Stopped being able to find whatever they were looking for. I don't know. It started with Roger. He was just a broken piece of machinery by the time they sent him back to wherever he came from.

It took a little while for the rest of us to figure out how much the CIA was relyin' on our intel. I thought he was just giving 'em info, but no, they was makin' plans, movin' people around based on what we saw. But we weren't perfect, and this gift, if that's what it is, isn't somethin' you can control. It's got a sick sense of humor, fucks with you when it wants to.

Pinker closes his eyes, shakes his head a few times and resumes looking at the empty chair.

First time I got things wrong, people died.

We had spies in East Berlin, and I saw some Stasi gathered in an old cemetery, sitting around smoking. I could hear what they were sayin', talkin' about our guys. I relayed the information, and someone passed it along, but when our guys got to the cemetery no one was there. They went back to the hotel and those Stasi fuckers were there waitin' and killed 'em all. Each and every one of 'em.

I told Atwater I could try to find the bodies if he wanted, but he said, no. I went looking anyway. I saw the Stasi in the cemetery just like they'd been the first time. But it was déjà vu, the things they were sayin', the way they were sittin'. Those bastards went to the cemetery after they killed our guys. They each got rid of one body. One was cut up into pieces and fed to alley dogs. Another got dumped in the river. Another one got buried in cement at a construction site, and the last… well, the last one was given to some psycho doctor, a leftover Nazi from the war. The doctor did experiments I guess with the body, the tissue.

I still get torn up about it sometimes. Wonder how much pain they felt. Hell of a thing to live with, knowing that your mistake fucked up a buncha families for good.

That's when I figured it out. Maybe it was all the pictures they showed me that got the wires crossed, but I was seein' movies from the future. Not far, mind you, but far enough to not be the now. Those Stasi fuckers, when I saw 'em it was a movie that had happened yet. You get it?

Man, after that I didn't trust myself. I couldn't tell what I was looking at. Past, Present, Future, fucking end of the world. How's I supposed to know? I'm a simple man—you show me a thing, tell me what it is, and I'll accept it. Show movies of things that haven't really happened, well shit, how do you know when you're looking at the now?

I still got the guilts, you know? Still feel horrible 'bout those CIA boys. I keep tellin' myself there's no way I coulda known the movies changed, and that's the truth, but it don't do a goddamn thing to change how I feel.

Started happening to some of the other guys too. Jamie though, Jamie took off before the rest of us. Went to find his brother. Kept seeing his death when he went to the other side. Kept seeing that thing loomin' over him.

Shit man, we was all broken by the end of it. Some of us more than others.

Then the plug got pulled on the program, and we all had to leave the Rectangle. Atwater included. I told myself I wouldn't go back into that place never again. Wasn't no need. I just wanted to live in a world I could feel.

Oh, every once in a while, I'd slip in, take a look around. But I never stayed long. One time it was because I thought my old lady was cheatin' on me. Went into the movie, saw her fuckin' some guy, so I kicked her out. Come to find out she hadn't done it yet. But when I kicked her ass to the street she went to a bar, met this guy and went back to his place. That's what I saw in the movie. Fuckin' dummy I was. Messin' up everything 'cause I couldn't leave well enough alone.

And that was the end of that. Until I moved into the house by the bend in the road. Killer Corner, I call it. But that's no joke. Not long after I moved in, I started getting this bad feeling. Pains in my chest, headaches, bad shits, you name it. My body was a mess. Don't know why I went into the movies, but I did. Thought maybe the universe was tryin' to tell me something.

I go in my bedroom, close the curtains, shut out the lights, and in I go. What do I see? A fuckin' car crash 'round that bend. Bad one too. A blue car with rusted fenders, just like Doug's. Blood sprayed all over the broken windshield. Little sparkly pieces of glass scattered on the road. And the car, Jesus man, the car is just crunched like a beer can. Ain't no way in hell anyone survived that. So, I run outside and took a look, but everything's clear.

Fuckin' future movie, that's what it is. Universe, God, whatever, is tellin' me something bad's about to happen. Right outside my front door.

I decide ain't nobody else gonna get killed there. Not while I'm livin'. That's when I put up the big ol' sign. Handmade and hand painted. Drove the post into the ground and hung it myself. Yeah, you know what I'm talkin' about. That's when you guys sent the cop. He come out in his cruiser and his spiffy uniform, actin' like his shit don't stink, sayin' "You can't have that up. It's too big, too ugly." And I tell him to go fuck himself and his momma 'cause it ain't comin' down. If the county won't put up a sign, and you know damn well what I mean—a sign that works, that people actually see—then I'll do it myself. And I did.

Slow Down. That's all it said, and some asshole com-plains and here you come. I called how many times, said that bend ain't safe and no one does shit! One nosy housewife makes a call and oh boy, the cops are on the case.

At this point he stops talking, buries his face in his hands. His shoulders shake and sniffing can be heard on the audio.

The sign shoulda stayed up, I won't change my mind on that. But I shouldn't a done what I did. Don't know what I was thinkin' honestly. Fear does that, you know? You ever get so afraid of something that hasn't happened yet that you actually make it happen?

Speed bumps, that's what I was thinkin'. The bend wouldn't be so bad if people drove slower. The rocks I put on the road, those I gathered from the creek behind my house. Hauled 'em up in a rusty wheelbarrow and dumped 'em on the asphalt. Thought drivers would see 'em, slow down and just go over 'em nice and easy. Guess I didn't think about the dark. But then that's always been my problem, trustin' what I see. Always forgettin' in the dark, there's things you can't see.

Yeah, you a smart one, uh? Already done figured it out. This thing, whatever it is, these mind-movies, they're a lion in the circus. Sure, the big ol' cat is trained, but at the end of the day it's a wild and deadly fuckin' animal, isn't it? It open its mouth, you put your head inside and trust it ain't gonna bite your goddamn head off with them big ass teeth. But you don't know, do you? And then one day you don't even know if your head is in the mouth or not. It all looks the same.

That's what happened, if I'm honest. I started seein' the movies even when I wasn't tryin'. They just played in my eyes, and I went about my business. Most days it didn't matter. I was all alone, you know? Who the fuck cares if I think it's yesterday, today, or a month from now? My days all look the same anyway. Wander 'round the house, smoke, try not to drink until that judge show comes on TV, miss my wife, think about my son, smoke some more, struggle to piss, drink some more, and then go to bed. Not an exciting existence.

Yeah, I do. I do believe I've spent entire days lost in the mind movies. Days I lived that weren't even here yet. Like living two lifetimes.

Right, the rocks. They wasn't real big ones. Big enough to give one of those sissy cars a good bump, maybe a flat tire if they was going too fast. Scare 'em good so they'd be more careful next time. Honest to God, I thought it would help. I thought people would see them rocks and slow down. Never really considered someone wouldn't see them.

When I heard them tires screech and all the metal crunch up, I thought it was a mind movie, I really did. But I went outside anyway. Fuckin' worst thing I ever seen. Worse than Nam because you shouldn't see that kind of carnage at home.

Pourin' rain, just dumpin' from the sky. I run out there and I'm tryin' not to throw up when I see all that blood, when I see lines opened up in his face where the glass cut him. He's still awake....

He puts his head down, starts crying again. Harder this time.

The door was pretty crushed, but I manage to get it open, and I just about fall over when he turns to look at me. I know his eyes, my Doug's eyes, lookin' at me through all that pain. But I know it's not him. It's just the other part of my brain, the part that has its own memories. Because I know Doug is already dead, has been for years. But here he is, and it hurts so bad, even though I know it isn't him. It's someone's son.

I feel sick seein' him like that. My guts are just burnin'. His voice moans and it's nails diggin' into my ears. He coughs. Blood sprays all over the steering wheel, drips down his chin. His cheek, Jesus, the skin mouths up as he tries to speak, and I see teeth through the hole. There's a cut, here, across the forehead. I see bright white skull in all that wet red. I can't help it, I turn and run. Try to hold the vomit in, but I can't. Look, it's still dried on my shirt. No wonder I smell so bad. I went inside the house, called 911. Now here I am. That's it.

I fucked up. I know I did, ain't nothing else to tell. I know ain't leavin' here. Got no one to post bail, and I killed someone's boy. I wish I could tell the parents I'm sorry. I know what they're gonna go through.

Alright, I'm tired and I'm done. Got any other questions? No. Good.

I just want to sleep. I don't even give a shit if it's a mind movie I see when I close my eyes. Sometimes things are better there, mostly worse, but sometimes a little better is worth it.

Pinker stops talking at this point. His eyes move from the chair across the table, then move over the room and to the door, as if he's watching someone get up and leave. He wipes the tears away and lets out a long sigh.

I've called the psychologist. She should be here soon.

There are obvious holes in his story, things he claims he doesn't remember. But I do believe he is convinced by these delusions. I did come out to his house about the sign he put up. But more than that, the complaint was about him running into the road, waving his hands and shouting at drivers to slow down. He almost got hit more than once.

And Doug, his son, didn't die years ago. He was alive until earlier today. I got called to drag Pinker off the road so many times, that I got in contact with Doug and asked him to come out and check on his dad, see if maybe he needed to be a care facility. In the interview, he mentions the rocks that Pinker put on the road only once. The truth is, a cleaning crew removed those, but he did it again, and this time they were bigger. I didn't know that when I called Doug.

The Chief asked me why I didn't go into the room, why I let him just ramble on. Anyone reading this report won't believe me, but this is the truth: I had a list of questions written down on my notepad. Pinker answered them all in order. It was like he was talking to me even though I wasn't there. I don't know what that means if anything, but I can't get it out of my head.

The guilt that Pinker feels... I feel it too. If I hadn't called Doug, he would still be alive. Sometimes, I wonder if the world we live in is the mouth of a lion. It's dark all the time, and we're just waiting for the teeth to fall.

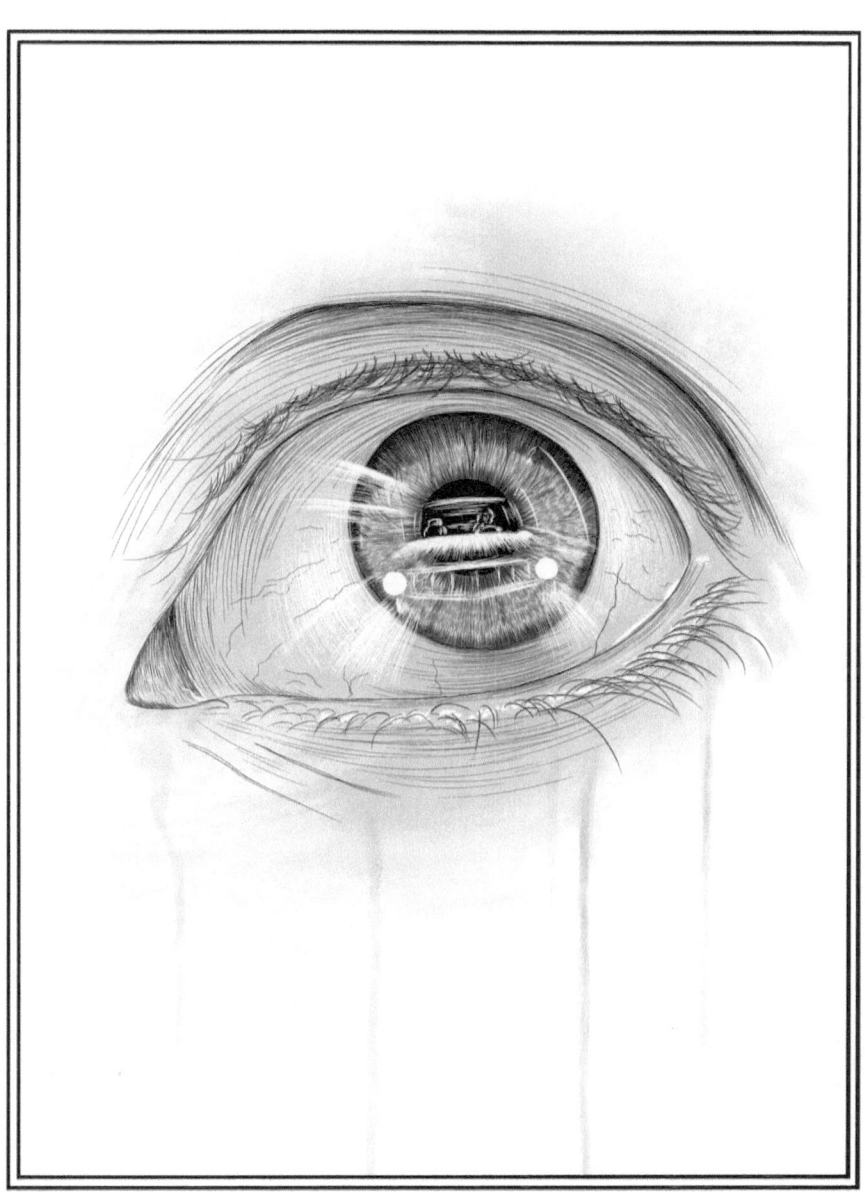

DEEP DOWN

Voicemail: 10/19/20__@ 3:36 PM

Sydney, pick up. We need to talk. There's something… something you need to know.

Voicemail: 10/19/20__@ 3:37 PM

Syd, me again. Come on, babe. Pick up the phone. I'm gonna call back in two minutes. I know you're mad and confused and all that, but this is important.

Voicemail: 10/19/20__@ 3:39 PM

Goddamn it. Okay, either you're not answering because you can't or you don't want to. But please listen to me very carefully. I need you to stay away from the house. Go somewhere, a friend's, wherever. Just don't go home. I'm not trying to scare you, but you should probably be scared. I need you to trust me, please. If you ever believed that I wanted the best for you, as soon as you hear this, go somewhere safe and stay there.

Voicemail: 10/19/20__@ 3:41 PM

Look, if you won't talk to me, then the best I can hope is that you'll listen to these messages. So, I'll try and get out as much as I can. I'm driving right now—you can probably hear the road in the background. I'm on my way home.

[Silence. Breathing.]

I don't know what to say. I guess I'll just start where it all started.

Voicemail: 10/19/20__ @ 3:43 PM

Okay, so this is all the stuff I never told you. Some of it you know, most of it you don't.

Listen, I promise you that what it wants is not what I want. Not really. Not deep down. But I think there are parts of us even deeper than the Deep Down. Parts we can't know or see.

That's what Santi called it, the Deep Down. And he knew more about this stuff than I do.

It started with pins and needles. This was right after the crash when I came home from the hospital. Remember that first night home when I screamed and woke you up? I told you my arm hurt, and you gave me some pain meds. You said the doctor told you the incisions and grafts would hurt for a long time. You ran your fingers over my sweaty forehead until the meds turned all my thoughts to dust. I fell asleep and dreamed I still had an arm.

When I told you my arm hurt, you thought I meant the part just above my elbow, wrapped in bloody gauze. But that's not where I felt the needles.

You told me you loved me, and nothing would ever change that. You said I'm alive, and that's all that matters. You told me tragedy puts things into perspective.

If you could've seen your face. God, you hadn't looked at me like that since forever. Since—

Voicemail: 10/19/20__ @ 3:49 PM

Syd, me again. It's not easy driving one-handed. At least I don't have a manual anymore. It'd be a bitch to shift and steer. Which reminds me, I never told you where I was driving to when the accident happened. Not the truth anyway.

So, the pins and needles. That's where it started, but not where it ended. And what was I saying? Right, the way you looked at me. Like you didn't want anything bad to happen to me.

It was the day the doctor took the bandages off and had me stand in front of a mirror so I could see the puckered skin of the stump. The folded flesh like a pair of old lady lips stapled together.

You inhaled and shook a little, but I never heard you breathe out.

The doctor said it was healing well. I laughed, and you started crying. I didn't even think then that it might not be for me.

We didn't say much of anything on the way home, and my arm hurt even worse. But not where it should.

Later that night in bed, you fell asleep, and your legs kicked at the blankets. I stayed awake, staring at the ceiling and trying to turn off all those needles. I don't know if you'd call it meditating, but I concentrated on that weird electricity below the stump, where my forearm used to be. You made a little humming noise and moved your head against the pillow, kind of rubbing it.

You said, "That feels nice," and I thought you were having a dream. A dream about him.

I rolled away, and you said, "Don't stop," and moved closer. I was at the edge of the bed, just burning up inside. I took another pain pill and stared at the ceiling fan until my brain turned off.

When I woke up, it was morning, and you weren't in bed. I started to get up and saw a dead mouse on the sheet, but there were no legs or tail. I touched it with my good hand, and it was just hair. I picked some of it up and smelled your shampoo.

Your hair.

The place where it was on the sheet, a handful of your black hair pulled out of your head, it was lying right where my hand left hand would have been if I still had a left hand.

Voicemail: 10/19/20__ @ 3:54 PM

So, the day I lost the arm. I always told you I couldn't remember it very well. But that was a lie. I remember everything up to the accident perfectly.

That morning, I came downstairs, and you had breakfast ready. You wouldn't stop filling up my coffee and adding more bacon to my plate. You paced around, wiping the countertops even though they were clean. You told me to sit, but you stayed standing.

You asked about my day, and I said I had to give a bid on pouring a driveway at some rich guy's newly built house. I asked if you wanted to have lunch afterward, and you wouldn't look at me. The skin on your neck turned blotchy and red, and you said you had to be at an open house. Someone was coming by for the second time, and you thought he might make an offer soon.

I never would have done what I did if anything about you seemed normal that day. Santi would say some of the threads in the Deep Down were humming away. He says all these invisible threads connect to what we do and say, and sometimes they intersect. It's what déjà vu is all about. Anyway....

Honestly, the way you acted reminded me of when your parents would come to visit, and those are the only people I've ever seen you afraid of. That's what you were like. Nervous and scared.

I asked if you were okay, and you tried to smile, but it just looked like you were in pain.

Hold on... phone battery's dying.

Voicemail: 10/19/20__@ 3:56 PM

I never went to the bid. You didn't know that, did you I passed it off to Kyle, and I called your office instead and asked Bethany where the open house was, and she said you didn't have one. So, I asked for all your listings and spent the whole morning driving from house to house, looking for your car. And I found it. But there was no "open house" sign in the yard. There was also another car in the driveway next to yours, a nice one. More than I could afford.

I parked the truck a few houses down and waited.

Something else I never told you, but you probably already knew… I had started smoking again a few weeks earlier. Not a lot, maybe two or three a day. Waiting in the truck, I must have chain-smoked half a pack.

I told myself I was being paranoid. That just because there was no sign didn't mean anything. But no sign was a sign. I knew it as much as you did. When the front door finally opened, and he walked out, I swear to God I stopped breathing. Could he be any more different from me? The suit, the hair, the shoes, the car, the way he walked.

First thing I noticed was the tie in his pants pocket, blue, hanging out like a dog's tongue. And then you were right behind him, one hand on the door frame, the other on the door. No jacket, just a skirt and blouse. Shoes off, no hose on your legs. You were wearing hose when you left our house.

This rich guy turns around and puts one hand on your neck. You smile at him so sweetly and lean into his kiss. I watched you as he walked back to his car. If you'd just looked up, you'd have seen me. I wasn't hiding, Sydney. Not from you. I was always right there in plain sight. You just chose not to see me.

When this guy pulled out of the driveway, I don't know why I followed him instead of going to talk to you. Guess I didn't want to see you right then. If I'm honest, I wanted to see this guy up close and scare the shit out of him. I wanted to maybe take a tire iron to the windows of his car and scream at him to stay the hell away from you.

I don't know. In the Deep Down, I couldn't quite believe this was happening and I needed to know it was real.

So, I followed him. And that's when the accident happened.

Voicemail: 10/19/20__ @ 4:01 PM

God, I sure hope you're getting these. You don't need to call, just text me you're somewhere safe. That's all I'm asking. Just one text.

[Road noise. A sigh]

Yeah, so your boyfriend's driving fast. That fancy car's just tearing down the road, and I'm having trouble keeping up with him. Asshole makes a quick right turn at an intersection without using his blinker. I make the turn to follow him without even seeing the red light. Suddenly, my windshield is filled with a semi barreling through the intersection. Big massive grill and headlights. The face of the driver, his eyes and mouth wide open. My arm, hanging out the window and holding a cigarette, catches fire. There's the sound of metal and glass being crushed, and then I wake up in the hospital with an emptiness where my arm used to be.

Voicemail: 10/19/20__ @ 4:10 PM

I can't explain what it felt like. Kind of like when your leg goes to sleep, but not really like that at all. That feeling of something being there, but something I couldn't see. Remember when we decided I should sleep in the extra room? Well, there's more to that, too.

I slept on my right side, all the way to the edge of the bed. The pain meds had kicked in, and I was gone, dreaming something awful. The sound of a crash and glass breaking woke me up. Woke you up, too. Then, the feeling of something held in my missing fingers, scratching.

I turned on the light, got up, and almost stepped on a broken picture frame. The picture of us on vacation in Mexico. The picture that was on my nightstand. I told you I must have accidentally knocked it off, but it had been on the other side of the lamp, against the wall. I would have had to reach out and grab it and throw it on the ground. But the thing is, when I woke up, I was still on my right side. My left arm could have reached...

You offered to help clean up, but I wouldn't let you because of the picture. Your smiling face was all slashed up, nothing but tatters. My side of the picture wasn't touched.

I ripped the picture apart and threw it in the trash.

The next night, you said I kept hitting you in my sleep, in the back of the head. The day after that, I saw you getting dressed—you had red scratches all along your back. That was when I suggested I sleep in the other room.

Voicemail: 10/19/20__ @ 4:19 PM

Okay, Sydney. I'll just keep talking. I sent you another text, please let me know you got it. Get somewhere safe, that's all I'm asking. You don't have to tell me where you are. I don't even want to know.

Here's something else I never told you. I sleepwalked into your room that first night we were in separate beds. I know because that's where I woke up, standing over you. When my eyes opened there was a kitchen knife hovering in the air right in front of me. Just floating there, the red numbers from your clock reflecting on the blade. I blinked, and the knife fell straight to the floor, stuck in the wood, point down. You stirred a little and turned over, and I could barely breathe. I took the knife back to the kitchen and stayed up the rest of the night, trying to think of a way to stay locked in my room.

Shit, hold on. Cop just flipped on the lights. Goddamn it, he's pulling me over. I'll call back.

Voicemail: 10/19/20__ @ 4:43 PM

That cop took one look at my arm and just gave me a warning. I swear, I'm coming as fast as I can.

Listen, Syd, just one text. Please. I'm getting a little nervous here.

So, when I told my physical therapist about the phantom pain, she said maybe meeting other people with missing limbs might help me accept mine. She said it could be a psychological thing. A reaction to the loss.

I saw Santi as soon as I got to the park where the group met. He stood at the edge of the crowd, a crowd full of men and women with missing arms and legs and hands and fingers. Some wore prosthetics, others didn't. Some were in wheelchairs or using crutches. I noticed Santi because he was missing an arm, too. The right one. He watched me for a while before coming over to introduce himself.

The first thing he said was, "You still feel it don't you?"

He nodded at the place where my left arm would have been.

"You keep scratching it," he said with a smile. He glanced down at the folded and stapled sleeve of his flannel shirt. "I used to feel it too."

Sergeant Santiago Bibiano. Served in Iraq and Afghanistan. Lost his arm when an IED blew up under the truck he was driving.

And that was it. He never told me about his time in the military. We ate hot dogs and drank beer, and all he did was ask questions about me.

Short guy, kind of stocky. Not what you'd expect a solider to look like, but you could tell he was from the way he stood perfectly straight, and his eyes moved around the picnic, from person to person, watching for something.

He asked about you, Sydney, about how I lost the arm. Maybe it was the beer, or maybe it was the fact that Santi seemed to care about what happened. I told him everything. You, the guy in the car. Everything. I even told him about the weird shit that had been happening. I expected him to laugh it off and blame it on something "inside" like the therapist did. But that's when his eyes stopped looking around at everyone else and focused right on mine.

"You do feel it," he told me. "In the Deep Down, that arm is still there. Still wanting something."

I laughed at first, but his face was solider serious.

I asked what the Deep Down was.

Santi said, "It's the place where everything really happens. All the invisible wiring of the universe, you know? The stuff that makes it operate."

That's when he told me about the threads. Like guitar strings, he said, that connects everything to everything else. They hum with every action, every choice, every thought. They shiver and vibrate and make other strings do the same thing. It's what coincidence and déjà vu and past-life experiences are all about. Nothing is random. It's all because of these threads.

I know, I know, it all sounds like a bunch of bullshit. But I had no doubt after Santi showed me why he knew all this. It's all true.

There's a gas station up here. I gotta pull over for a minute and fill up.

Voicemail: 10/19/20__ @ 5:07 PM

Santi told me the pain used to be so bad pills wouldn't even touch it. So, he started shooting heroin, but that just lost him his wife and kids, and the pain was still there. It wasn't until he met Dr. Caufield that he got the phantom arm removed.

I asked him, "How do you cut off something that isn't there?"

This was over beers at The Black Door. Remember that night I told you I was meeting a friend for drinks?

Santi drank the last of his beer and pointed at the empty glass. "Where is it?" he said.

I told him it was gone. He drank it all.

He shook his head. "It's inside me, now. You can't see it, but it's still there. Everything goes somewhere else. Nothing is ever really gone."

He talked about ghosts and premonitions, prophesies of the future. Threads, he said. Threads humming away, singing a song of everything that's ever happened and ever will.

I rubbed the stump of my arm. My fingers touched the puckered flesh through my shirt.

"You don't have to believe in anything," Santi told me. "It's still happening whether you believe it or not."

Then he leaned forward, lowered his voice, and told me exactly why my phantom arm wanted to hurt you.

"The arm remembers," Santi said.

He asked me what was the last thought I had before the accident. Before my left arm got torn from my body.

It makes me sick to admit it, Sydney, but we can't control our thoughts. As I chased after that guy in the fancy car, I remember how bad I wanted to hit him, to punch his face into a bloody mess. Then I saw your face, you kissing him. And I wanted to hurt you like you hurt me. I never would, you know that. In nine years of marriage, I've only screamed at you one time. One. But after seeing you with him, I wanted you to hurt.

Look, you know I've always protected you, and that's what I'm trying to do now.

Voicemail: 10/19/20__@5:10 PM

Hey Bob, I assume you didn't answer 'cause you saw my number. Look, man, I know you don't like me, and you think I'm a fuck up and that Sydney is too good for me. You're right about all of it, okay? But I need you to call her. I've been trying for the last two hours, and she won't answer. Please, tell her to stay away from our house. Please, Bob. I'm begging you. This is for her own good. Tell her to get somewhere safe. I don't want your daughter to get hurt.

Voicemail: 10/19/20__ @ 5:11 PM

Hey, me again. So, the surgery. Santi said it was experimental, and he didn't know if Dr. Caufield could see me because he's an Army doctor. But Santi said he'd ask. He told me he had the procedure at a facility out in the desert. It's not really a base or anything, just a shabby-looking building that the government owns in the middle of nowhere. But inside is some of the most advanced equipment ever that's been developed. All to make soldiers that can't be killed, Santi said.

The bid in Bend I told you about… that was a lie. Santi talked to Dr. Caufield, and he said he'd try to help me. I picked Santi up, and we drove east into the desert. He told me not to be scared the whole time and that it didn't hurt much. Not like a regular surgery. He said, you feel it, but only in the Deep Down.

It was dark when we made it to the building, and Santi was right, it didn't look like anything. Cement blocks painted white, no windows, a flat roof, and one scratched-up metal door. There were a couple cars parked outside, covered in dirt like they'd been for a while. We went inside, and the lobby, I guess you'd call it, had just a rug and an elevator. There was nowhere else you could go but down. Deep down.

Voicemail: 10/19/20__ @ 5:21 PM

As we rode the elevator, the air got colder and colder until I couldn't stop shivering, and my arm was covered in goosebumps. When the doors opened, we stood in a huge space that looked like a hospital from a sci-fi TV show. The floors were slick concrete, and every surface was stainless steel, reflecting lights and numbers from computer screens that hung everywhere.

People in blue jumpsuits, wearing masks and booties and goggles, and carrying tablets, moved around the place checking on pieces of expensive-looking equipment. None of them paid attention to us, and I couldn't figure out where they came from because there were just those few cars parked outside. Santi said they probably lived there and that the facility was five football fields long.

He walked me down a long room with empty beds lining either side. Machines hung from the ceiling, sleek boxes with touchscreens and hoses coming out of them. Other machines on wheels stood near the beds, and more hoses and tubes ran out of them onto the empty beds.

A blue jumpsuit person stood near each bed, monitoring the equipment and tapping on a tablet. I started to ask Santi what they were doing, but he shook his head and led me to the far end of the room. He knocked twice on a door, then opened it. A man in a white coat sat behind a desk, staring at a computer screen. He didn't look up when we came in, he just lifted a hand and pointed at two chairs against the wall.

Santi and I sat down and waited. There was nothing in the office, Sydney. No books, no diplomas on the walls. Just a desk and a computer and a few chairs. The man's eyes stared at the monitor without blinking. He looked about my dad's age, minus the smoking wrinkles and beer belly.

When the man in the white coat stood up, he came over and knelt in front of me. The badge hanging from his pocket said "Dr. Caufield." He held something in his hand, like those sunglasses people clip onto their prescription glasses. He put them over his eyes and the lenses swirled with multiple colors, like an oil leak on asphalt.

He stared where my arm used to be and his fingers gently touched the air, like he could see it.

Dr. Caufield took off the lenses and looked at me. He said, "How bad is the pain?"

I told him that sometimes it hurt so much I couldn't think about anything else.

I swear to God, he smiled a little.

He said, "I can help you with this. Just like I helped Santi."

He said, "There is one condition, though. You have to let me keep it when we're done."

I laughed and looked at Santi, but he wasn't smiling.

I said, sure, why not? Keep the thing I can't see? Go for it.

Then Dr. Caufield stood and asked me to step outside for a minute so he could talk to Santi. The door closed behind me, and I was back in that long room with all the empty beds. The machines hummed and beeped. The hoses hissed what I guessed was oxygen, but they all led to nowhere, and none of the blue jumpsuit people would look at me.

Voicemail: 10/19/20__ @ 5:37 PM

It's starting to get dark, and I just passed Hood River. I'm coming straight home, but God I hope you're not there. Please don't ignore these messages. Listen to them. Read my texts. Again, I'm begging you to just let me know you got somewhere safe.

Okay, where was I? Right, the blue jumpsuit people. I didn't notice this before, but the goggles they wore had the same weird lenses that the doctor had. One of them, a woman, I think, put two fingers just over a bed and lifted a wrist to look at her watch. Like she was taking a pulse.

These steel doors opened, and four people came in, pushing another bed into the room. There was something on the bed, and I knew what it was, but my mind didn't believe it because it didn't make any sense. A man's bare chest and arms. No head. No legs. Nothing below the waist, nothing above the shoulders.

They wheeled this bed against the wall, all talking in muffled voices.

I thought, okay, an organ donor. They're keeping all the organs going so they can put them in someone else. That has to be it. But my breathing told me I didn't believe it.

This thing on the bed, the chest, it moved and sat up. It looked like it was just floating there because there was nothing to hold it up. Just this torso and arms, sitting on the edge of the bed like it had legs, but there weren't any legs. The blue jumpsuit people talked to it, and it raised an arm and moved the fingers.

I got so dizzy I had to lean against the wall.

One blue jumpsuit held onto the thing's arm and helped it... stand, I guess. The torso rose off the bed and hovered in the air. The blue jumpsuits surrounded the thing and followed it as it started moving, floating down the room. Headless. Legless. It moved back and forth a little, like walking, like legs I couldn't see were attached to it.

I thought I was going to pass out.

When Santi and Dr. Caufield came out, I tried to say something, to ask what I saw, but I couldn't get the words out. They led me to another room, which looked almost exactly like where I'd been before, right after the accident. A single gurney at the center, three big round lights hanging from the ceiling and pointing right at it. Computer screens and monitors, a ventilator, and a team of people all dressed in white surgical gowns.

Dr. Caufield leaned in and whispered, "You'll need to sign a few forms giving me permission to perform the operation. One document prevents you from discussing anything you see in this place. Understood?"

I said yes and signed the papers on the clipboard he handed me. One of the nurses took me to the gurney and had me lie down, and that was when I saw the other gurney against the far wall. An empty gurney being monitored by two blue jumpsuit people.

I asked about anesthesia, but Dr. Caufield said I wouldn't need any. Whatever pain I felt would be nothing compared to what I felt most of the time, anyway. He snapped on some gloves and picked up a remote control, aimed it above his head, and this pole lowered down with something that looked like high-tech binoculars attached to it. He said, "Besides, you have to be awake for the procedure, it's the only way it works."

A nurse told me to take off my shirt. Then she put a few electrodes on my chest while another nurse handed the doctor a scalpel with a blade that swirled with color like his lenses. A third nurse strapped down my right arm and the stump of my left.

Dr. Caufield whispered, "Try to remain calm."

He pulled the binoculars closer, pointed them at my left arm, where it used to be, and looked through them as he moved the blade closer.

Four people hovered around me, and all I could see were their eyes. Santi stood near the door, watching.

"There it is," Dr. Caufield said. "Be as still as you can."

He brought the scalpel down next to the folded-up skin of my missing arm. A blast of heat shot down into fingers that weren't there. I felt the hand opening and closing. My legs thrashed against the gurney. Two of the nurses appeared and held them down. There was no pain anywhere else, just in that phantom arm.

The scalpel cut through invisible flesh and muscle, and it burned like a tattoo gun that's been set on fire. The surgical cap Dr. Caufield wore turned dark with sweat as his scalpel hit bone—bone only he could see—and he breathed heavier as he sliced through the air. I screamed so loud one of the nurses covered my mouth with a gloved hand.

Her eyes looked into mine, and she said—

Voicemail: 10/19/20__ @ 6:04 PM

It's completely dark now. The city is closer. Traffic is getting worse.

Once Dr. Caufield finished cutting, he pushed away the binocular machine and put on a pair of swirling goggles. He reached down, slid his hands along the gurney where the phantom arm would have been and lifted gently as though he was picking it up. He held his arms out and crossed the room to the other gurney. A nurse patted my forehead with a wet washcloth and told me I'd done well. She offered me pain meds. I didn't need them, though, the pain was gone.

I looked to Santi, but he was watching the doctor as he set my invisible arm down on the empty gurney, and a nurse handed him some forceps and thread that sparkled under the bright lights.

Shit....

Looks like an accident up ahead.

Voicemail: 10/19/20__ @ 6:10 PM

I'm stuck in a line of cars. Police lights are flashing.

Okay, listen…everything that happened next happened fast, and I've been going ever since. It won't make any sense, but it's the truth, as I saw it. This is what I know.

As soon as Dr. Caufield stopped with the thread, he cut the string with his special scalpel, but then the knife left his hand and floated in the air. He tried to back up but the front of his gown bunched up, like someone grabbed it. He got yanked forward and the scalpel flew up into his neck. He fell to his knees, both hands wrapped around his throat, blood spraying between his fingers, splashing the wall. One of the nurses, her body was pushed into a metal storage unit full of supplies.

Santi rushed over to her and yanked the goggles from her face just as the other door out of the operating room opened and closed on its own.

The other nurses tried to help Dr. Caufield as he thrashed around on the ground, blood gurgling from the hole in his throat.

Santi took something out of his pocket that looked like a taser. He motioned to the two blue jumpsuit people, who rushed out of the room.

I got up, tore off the electrodes, and put my shirt back on. The nurses were busy with Caufield, so I followed after Santi. I went through the door and came into a long hallway. Voices screamed, echoing off the walls. I ran down the hall as the sound of breaking glass and clanging metal came from another room at the far end.

I stopped at the door and looked through the round window into the room. The body of a blue jumpsuit person went skidding across the floor, leaving a trail of dark blood. The other jumpsuit was impaled on an IV pole, legs still twitching. And Santi... Santi was kneeling at the center of the room, his other arm barely attached to his body. Blood poured from the open wound. Caufield's scalpel floated in the air right in front of Santi's head.

I pushed the door open and yelled, "Hey!"

The scalpel twisted like whatever held it turned to look at me. I said, "Enough."

The scalpel turned away from me and moved toward another door. But before it left, it pointed at some metal containers against a wall in the flickering shadows.

I went over to Santi just as he fell to the floor. Thin strands of flesh and tendon were all that connected his arm to his shoulder. His face had gone the color of dried concrete.

"Your piece was the last," he whispered. "The threads are still humming, and the arm still remembers. Hurry…"

His body went still. I picked up the black box with the prongs he had dropped and went over to the metal containers the scalpel had pointed at.

The air cooled as I got closer. The lights sparked, blinking on and off, and I saw the containers were full of ice glowing with this purplish light. Both of them. Inside the first was a man's head. Just the head. Eyes closed, spinal cord still attached. It looked fake, like one of those props in the movie magazines I read as a kid. The other container held a torso—no arms, no legs, no head—just a half-person on a bed of ice.

I went back over to Santi, took his goggles, and ran all the way to the elevator.

He said my piece was the last, and it still remembered. And I knew exactly where it was going.

Voicemail: 10/19/20__ @ 6:38 PM

The traffic cleared up past the accident, and I'm almost there. Please, Sydney… please just pick up the goddamn phone!

Voicemail: 10/19/20__ @ 6:48 PM

I'm here. Your car is outside, but none of the lights are on. Are you here? Jesus…. Why is the front door open?

Voicemail: 10/19/20__ @ 6:49 PM

Syd...I'm in the house. Where are you?

I just called. Your phone is ringing somewhere in here. Sydney! Sydney! Tell me where you are. Make some noise. I'm in the bedroom, can you hear me?

[The voice becomes distant as if he lowered the phone away from his mouth.]

Hey! There you are. Are you okay? You're not hurt?

[There is the sound of a gunshot, a grunt, and then a crack as the phone hits the ground.]

911 Operator: 10/19/20__@ 6:51 PM

911 operator: "911, what's your emergency?"

"Oh my god, I just shot my husband!"

911 operator: "Can you tell if he's breathing?"

"He's not moving. I think I killed him."

911 operator: "Are you hurt, ma'am?"

"He's been leaving me these voicemails all day, saying someone was coming to hurt me. He said to stay away from the house, so I didn't think he'd come here."

911 operator: "But he didn't hurt you?"

"No, I'm fine. I feel dizzy, though. I think I might throw up. There's blood all over the place."

911 operator: "How about you go to another room, okay? Sit down and drink some water. You still have the gun?"

"Yes."

911 operator: "When the officers arrive, tell them you have it, then set it down very slowly. You still with me?"

"Hold on, I think I hear something."

911 operator: "Is it your husband?"

"No. Footsteps in the hallway."

911 operator: "Is there anyone else in the house? Any children?"

"No, it's just me."

911 operator: "Can you leave the——"

"Someone is definitely here. Wait! Stop!"

[There is a scream, the phone falls to the ground, and a moment later there is a thud. A gurgling sound, moaning.]

911 operator: "Ma'am, can you hear me? Are you there? Officers are on the way. Hang in there, sweetheart. Listen to my voice. Hang on."

RED HANDS

1

An old mug shot, a name, a face I haven't seen since junior high. The news anchor speaks while the video shows a shopping mall. Police car lights strobe against the building, the windows. A brief glimpse of a sheet-covered mound in the back of an ambulance before the paramedic closes the doors. People are gathered in the street, huddled together, crying. Some are wearing clothes stained with blood.

A woman with heavy makeup and bed-messy hair says, "I don't think there was a target. He was just shooting at everyone."

She wipes her nose with a tattered tissue. "I couldn't hear anything but the gunshots, one after the other. When he stopped shooting and run off, that's when I heard people screaming."

Another picture flashes on the screen—a woman and two young children, a boy and a girl. The boy looks old enough to walk, but just barely. He smiles at the camera from his mother's arms, a stuffed animal clutched in one hand. The girl is older, and her smile is missing some teeth. She stands there stiffly, arms behind her back, smiling like someone told her to smile, not because she's happy. Her narrowed eyes stare at the camera.

I hope the words don't appear, but they do. Awful words that make my stomach clench. Vomit rises in the back of my throat. I take a drink of whiskey to swallow it back.

"4 Killed, 23 Wounded in Mass Shooting at Westlake Mall."

The reporter says the police are hunting for the killer, and they think he may have crossed state lines. The mug shot flashes on screen again, this time with his name underneath it. Cameron Davies. A name that's been buried in the back of my memory since the year I smoked my first cigarette. Cameron was there when I did. We shared it. I took the first drag, he took the second and passed it to Jessica Eastman, who passed it to Todd Weyers. Deep in the woods behind Jessie's house. The woods where she found the cave.

The cave.

My eyes search Cameron's face, that dead-eyed stare, dark skin under his red-rimmed eyes like he hasn't slept in a long time, maybe not since that day at the cave. I try to find the boy I knew in that face, but it's long gone. The features are all there—same rounded nose, ears that stick out a little too far, dirty blonde hair—but it's like looking at one of those pictures of a missing kid. The ones that show what the kid might look like as an adult. They're similar, but one is from the very real past, while the other is from some non-existent future.

On the TV, a cop examines something on the window of one of the stores. I stop breathing. Splattered on the glass is a bright red handprint, dripping blood down the white paint.

My wife, Deirdre, looks up from her computer and tilts her head when she sees my face. "Bryan?" she says.

"I'm fine."

Deirdre looks at the empty whiskey glass and sighs. Her hand moves to my face. A finger touches my skin and comes away glistening.

2

Jessie found the cave in the woods one day after school but didn't go inside. Not until she rounded up the rest of us.

Todd and I were the only kids in our sixth-grade class whose parents were divorced. I guess it gave us something in common, and we hung around with Jessie because her mom had died a few years earlier. Her dad loved her and tried his best to make up for what she didn't have. He used to throw these big sleepover parties where he'd invite all of us over. He'd make popcorn, and we would watch movies until the sun came up. But Cameron, Cameron had it the worst of all of us. He was small, for one thing, and even though we were all the same age, Cameron looked at least a grade younger. Small and frail, skinny arms, eyes that looked too big in his face.

Cameron's mom and dad were both meth heads, in and out of jail, so he had to live with his crazy aunt in a shitty apartment behind the bar where Todd's dad drank after his shift at the lumber yard. I don't know what Cameron's aunt did for work, but whatever money she had went to buying all kinds of thrift store shit she didn't need. She'd go to garage sales every weekend, load up her car, and make Cameron help carry the junk into the apartment.

I only went inside a few times and had no idea people could live like that. Old magazines and newspapers piled up to the ceiling. Piles of clothes bigger than the leaf piles we'd make around Halloween. Used, grease-stained kitchen appliances with frayed electrical cords. Cardboard boxes that smelled of dust and mildew were stacked on each other to create rooms within the rooms. Cameron had his own bedroom, but it wasn't really his. All he had was a mattress on the floor in the corner. Piles of books, records, snow globes, and trinkets loomed over him when he slept.

A cat lived there, too, even though I never saw it. But I smelled its piss everywhere.

Jessie came to my house first and told me she found something I had to see. She wouldn't say what it was, only that I needed to bring a flashlight. We rode our bikes to Todd's house and begged his mom to let him come outside. She reluctantly agreed, and the three of us rode over to Cameron's.

With all the shit his aunt had packed into her two-bedroom apartment, Cameron didn't even have his own bike, so he rode on my handlebars. Todd, Cameron, and I followed Jessie deep into the woods behind her house. I didn't have to ask what Jessie had been doing in the woods, the wet dirt stains on her knees told me.

Late afternoon sunlight fell through the branches as we rode around the big moss-covered rocks at the entrance of the path. Yellow and orange leaves carpeted the trail, making me think of the four misfits traveling down that yellow brick road to Oz. I said this out loud, and then Jessie wanted to know which one of us was Dorothy. We all laughed, but none of us said who it would be.

I was with Jessie the first time she buried something of her mom's in the woods. It was just a simple bracelet, but something that her mom loved. We walked deep into the trees. Then Jessie fell to her knees and started digging with her bare hands. Tears ran down her face as her fingers tore up the dirt until she'd made a small hole. She lovingly placed the bracelet into the hole before covering it up.

"I'm ready to let that one go," she said, maybe to me. Maybe to her mom.

She never asked me to go with her again, but every once in a while, I'd see dirt under her fingernails and know what she'd been doing.

We knew the trail well, until Jessie made a sharp turn at a tree split and blackened by lightning, and suddenly we were riding into unfamiliar territory. But Jessie knew exactly where she was leading us. I had to pedal hard just to keep up with her.

We rode until the sky turned a darker shade of gray, and then Jessie skidded to a stop and jumped off her bike. She turned around, grinning, arms held out wide.

"Behold," she said, taking a bow, "the Dragon's Throat."

When Jessie moved aside, we saw a dark jagged hole in the rock behind her. A dirt tunnel stretched into the blackness. Strands of green vines hung down around the entrance like tangled, wet hair. Scattered around the entrance were at least a hundred large stones, like they had been blown right out of the dark hole.

"Whoa," Todd said, letting his bike fall. "Did you go inside?"

Jessie shook her head. "I think it goes back pretty far. If you stand near the opening, you can hear echoes."

Cameron folded his arms over his chest, trying not to shiver. "Do you think there are bats?"

Todd took the flashlight off his belt and shined it into the tunnel. He sniffed the air. "It looks like it gets wider."

Cameron couldn't stop the shiver this time.

Jessie got a flashlight from her backpack and joined her beam to Todd's. The curved rock walls bent out of view, down into darkness. There was no wind, but cold air moved from the mouth of the cave as though it was breathing.

"You guys ready?" Jessie asked us.

Cameron's voice shook like he was freezing. "W-We're g-going in?"

Todd turned to him. "We didn't come all this way just to look at it."

Cameron looked at me with pleading eyes, but I wanted to go in just as much as the others. A cave in the woods. A dark entrance that led into the earth. What boy wouldn't want to see that? A boy who lived in a maze with walls made of junk other people didn't want, that's who.

Todd, Cameron, and I lined up behind Jessie. We were all scared, but when I looked back into Cameron's face, he was terrified.

3

Seeing Cameron's face on the news, my heart beats out of time. The heels of my feet go numb. The floor feels so far below me I'm not sure if I'm actually touching it. I make my way through the living room and out to the back patio. A light snow falls from a cement-colored sky. I take a drink of whiskey from my refilled glass. I told Deirdre I'd quit, and I meant it when I said it, but sometimes life throws things at you that just destroy all your plans. Tonight is like that. She couldn't hide her disappointment.

I take out my cell phone and thumb to the contacts. Jessie's number is still in there, but I can't call her.

The year I got my driver's license, Jessie's dad had a breakdown. He got drunk one night and accused her of sneaking out of the house to screw around with boys. She tried to tell him that wasn't true, but her dad wouldn't listen. He went to his bedroom, got the 9mm from the closet, and emptied it into Jessie's body.

The newspaper ran a story the next day. The article said when the cops arrived, Jessie's dad held up his hand, bright red with his daughter's blood, and shouted, "Look at my hand! Look at it!" The sun shone bright on the day of the funeral, and it felt so wrong to be standing in the cemetery on such a beautiful day as our friend was lowered into the ground.

That was also the day I first tried cocaine. Cameron gave it to Todd and me, saying it would take the edge off. It did more than that. It tore through me, lifted me up. I've never forgotten that feeling.

I take a drink and dial Todd's number instead. He picks up right away. "You saw it?" he asks.

"It never left him alone."

Todd sigh distorts in my ear. "Bryan, the cards were stacked against him from the beginning. He made choices."

"Did he?" It comes out as a yell, even though I don't mean it to. "Can you tell me how his life would have gone if we hadn't—"

"I don't believe in that anymore," Todd says evenly.

The falling snow has a sound, like someone moving in soft bedsheets.

"I don't think it matters," I say.

"Cameron completely ripped his head apart with drugs." Todd says, starting to sound annoyed. "There doesn't need to be some other explanation. You could chart his path, Bryan. It was all laid out for him. He just chose to stay on it."

My hand grips the phone tighter. "We need to go back. Check to see if the wall is still there."

"Are you serious?" Todd asks, his voice rising. "Check on the wall? Bry, we're adults, man. You're talking about made-up kid shit."

"The wall, Todd, you remember? You brought salt because you said the devil can't cross salt."

"Bryan, stop," Todd's voice goes cold.

I catch Deirdre watching me through the window. "I brought holy water from Saint Mary's and poured it all over the stones."

"You need to accept that Cameron is mentally ill," Todd says.

"And Jess," my voice chokes up. "Jess brought her mom's Bible, remember? She shoved it between the stones. We knew something was there, and we tried to lock it in, but it didn't work."

Todd doesn't say anything, but I hear him breathing.

My phone is now slick with sweat. "Do you remember who stayed over at Jessie's house the night before—"

"I'm not getting into this with you again."

"The night before Jessie's dad murdered her?" My breath comes out faster. "Cameron was there!" I yell into the phone. "Do you remember?"

Another distorted sigh. "Leave me out of this," Todd says. "And don't call me anymore."

4

It really did feel like walking into a giant throat. Air moved through the dark tunnel, pushing and pulling us as we went deeper. Todd suggested we go single file with the person behind holding onto the waistband of the person in front of him. In case someone fell, he said. But what he really meant was that no one gets lost.

Jessie took the lead, and I told Cameron I'd bring up the back so he could go in front of me. As we made our way down the tunnel, I felt Cameron's body twitching with fear, his sweat-sticky skin quivering against my fingers.

Every cough and footstep echoed. Water dripped from somewhere up ahead, but the noise bounced off the walls and came at us from all around. The ground got slick and wet. Our flashlights picked up the strange grooves on the walls, like the inside of a giant worm. The air, stale and musty, smelled of guano and moist dirt.

Todd, that asshole, he sniffed the air, looked right at Cameron, and said, "Smells like cat piss in here."

Cameron stopped moving for a second, his shoulders slumped.

I said, "Todd, shut the fuck up and keep moving."

Cameron started making small noises when he breathed out. Little squeaks, like a mouse. I did feel bad for him, but we were on an adventure, and being afraid just went with the territory And going anywhere with Todd meant putting up with his shit.

We followed the tunnel until we couldn't see the light of the entrance anymore. The air grew colder, heavier. The ground under my feet got steeper, and I had to walk carefully to avoid slipping on the wet clay. Cameron's legs went out from under him once. His whole body shook as I helped him back up, teeth chattering with cold and fright.

Finally, the tunnel leveled out, and our beams illuminated a round room. High above us, dripping stalactites hung from the ceiling like fangs. Another tunnel in the far wall led down further into the darkness.

Jessie swung her flashlight from the ceiling to the grooved walls. The round circle of light caught something on the stone. A faded painting—that looked like those ancient cave drawings we read about in school—took up one whole section of the wall. The four of us gathered closer to look.

A series of human-looking figures, drawn in rusted red, assembled around a creature that towered above them. Some of the humans bowed, others knelt with their arms lifted, as if worshipping the figure, or begging for mercy. Thin, rounded protrusions covered the creature's body. They stuck out from its limbs and sides. Five rose from the head like a misshapen crown. At first, they looked like flames, but then I leaned in closer.

"Hands," I said.

Jessie stood next to me and reached out to touch the paint.

"Don't," I told her.

Todd and Cameron came in next to us.

"Hands," Todd repeated. "The whole thing is made of hands."

Red hands, one on top of the other, pressed on the wall into the shape of a figure. A single hand, much larger than the others, made up the head. Two dark eyes were drawn in the center. Streaks of red paint ran down the creature's body, fingerprints smeared together.

My flashlight beam kept going higher until it hit the ceiling.

"Holy shit," Jessie said.

She pointed her flashlight up, too, and spread across the rock above our heads was a massive mural made of red hands, only these hands were twisted and broken. The fingers made almost human shapes, hundreds of them scattered around the same figure on the wall. The figure with the crown. Some of these shapes were torn apart, reaching out with bent arms toward the creature.

"How did they get it all the way up there?" Jessie asked.

Something stirred in the corner of the ceiling. I shined my light in that direction and illuminated a pulsing mass of dark, folded wings suspended from the ceiling. Small eyes glowed in the light, bright and curious. A few detached from the rock and flew down, wings flapping.

Cameron grabbed my arm and whispered, "I don't want to be here anymore."

Jessie lowered her light, went over to the other tunnel, and yelled "Bitch!" into it as loud as she could, then stepped back and smiled as her voice echoed down into the earth. Todd followed right behind her and yelled "Fuck!" as loud as he could. We all laughed except Cameron. I motioned to the tunnel, but he just bit his lip and shook his head. I shrugged, leaned my head into the hole, and took a deep breath to yell when something that was not Todd's voice came echoing back.

A deep, ragged sigh. Soft hiss-like whispers in that sound made every hair on my arms stand straight up. Warm air blew into my face, the rancid odor of rotting meat and sulfur.

I took a step back, feeling the ground quiver under my feet. I looked to Jessie and Todd, and they were both staring at the hole with wide eyes. Jessie's mouth fell open like she wanted to say something, as the stirring in the ground grew stronger.

Another sound echoed from the tunnel, a scraping that started and stopped and started again. An image appeared in my mind so clear that I couldn't shake it—a creature sinking its claws into the wet clay and dragging its body up the tunnel. It was the sound my own body made when we played war in the woods and I crawled through the dirt and dead leaves. Only this sound was bigger, heavier.

I heard liquid running into a small puddle and turned to see Cameron standing at the wall with the painting of the creature. His arm was stretched out, one hand flat against the stone. His pale hand inside a red hand on the creature's leg. Cameron's whole body started convulsing. Drool ran from the corner of his mouth. Urine soaked the front of his jeans and pooled on the ground at his feet. I grabbed Cameron's shoulders and tried to steady him. His eyes looked at my face, but I didn't think they saw me.

"Jess!" I called out.

Todd walked backward, keeping his flashlight trained on the tunnel, saying, "What the hell?" over and over.

Jessie moved in the opposite direction, toward the hole, head at an angle, trying to see in further. She squinted into the dark, mouth open, the fingers of one hand opening and closing. I grabbed her arm and yanked on it. "Jess," I said again, "we need to get out of here. Something's wrong with Cameron."

Jessie turned back around and saw Cameron, his eyes rolled back to show only white. The scratching and breathing in the tunnel grew louder, steadier.

"We need to go!" I yelled.

The words barely left my mouth before Todd took off running up the main tunnel. Jessie came over and grabbed Cameron's arm, I took the other, and we half-carried, half-dragged him out of the room. A burst of warm air shot out of the tunnel behind us and hit our backs. The breathing noise followed, frantic and angry.

We scrambled into the tunnel, feet slipping on the slick clay. One long, gravelly breath came from right behind us, the wind of it moving my hair. A wind full of whispers in a language I couldn't understand.

It wasn't in that passageway anymore. It had entered the room.

Jessie and I climbed, shouting for Todd to come back and help us, but we couldn't even see his flashlight. Cameron went limp in our arms, knees dragging on the ground, head hung. I hoped to God he wasn't dead. Jessie couldn't hold onto Cameron and keep her flashlight steady. The beam bounced all over the walls.

The breathing sounded less like an animal now. In fact, it sounded almost human. I glanced back quickly, but the tunnel behind me was pure black. The breathing didn't come closer or move up the tunnel after us. It stayed in that round room.

We kept clambering our way to the cave entrance. My arms and legs burned. Cameron stirred, lifted his head, and looked at me, then Jessie. The bouncing flashlight caught his wide eyes and flared nostrils.

"Can you walk?" I asked him.

His small chest moved fast. He panted like a dog.

"Cameron, can you walk?"

He tried putting his feet on the ground and taking a step, but the motion caught Jessie off guard, and she tripped. Her flashlight fell to the ground. I heard glass crack, and Jessie hissed, "God damn it." Her hands searched blindly until she found the flashlight. She flipped the switch. Nothing. I heard it bang against her palm. Still nothing.

A stillness overtook the tunnel. Pressure built up that sucked air backward from the opening, pulling it against our skin and toward the round room behind us. My ears popped painfully. The breathing wasn't as heavy anymore, it was measured and calm, but still echoing loudly.

I tightened my grip on Cameron's arm and tried to pull him up. All I could see was his outline on the floor. I could hear him breathing faster and faster.

"Come on, Cameron," I yelled. "Get up!"

But he didn't move or couldn't. Jessie and I knelt next to him and started to lift his body when a rush of air came moving up the tunnel. Warm, living. It blew the hair back from my forehead. Cameron screamed once, then he was wrenched from my grip, his fingers dragging marks in the clay. His eyes caught mine, and in them, I saw absolute terror right before something pulled his body backward into the darkness.

I yelled his name as the warm air swirled around us before slowly returning to wherever—whatever—it came from. I reached out to Jessie. Neither of us said it, but we both knew we couldn't go back for him. There was nothing we could do, and that tore my heart up. It felt so wrong. Cameron was gone, but if we went after him, we'd be gone too.

Jessie and I turned around and began running, faster now without Cameron, and made our way toward the bright burning light at the mouth of the cave.

5

I park in the driveway outside Jessie's old house, abandoned since her dad went to prison. He left it in such a state of disrepair that no one would buy it. And after what he did to his daughter, no one even wanted to own the land. Some people want to own a house lived in by a murderer, but not this one.

The moss-covered roof sags down into the leaning porch. The whole house tilts to the right, and the increased weight has blown out half the windows and cracked the siding. The other windows were broken by kids throwing rocks. A rusted wheelbarrow sits upside down in the yard, its metal body punctured with bullet holes. I wonder if that's where Jessie's dad practiced, if he imagined faces when he pulled the trigger.

Inside that house are so many memories. Todd was always a dick to Cameron, but at least he seemed happy among friends. The four of us on the floor in sleeping bags, Jessie's dad sitting on the couch behind us, the TV glowing with images of monsters and robots. Images that kept us terrified and excited late into the night.

I can't help but wonder where Jessie would be now if she were still alive. She probably would have left town and invented something that everyone needed. Something the whole world was missing.

I haven't walked the path since that day, but I still remember where to go. An invisible map, drawn in memory. The woods are thicker now. Undergrowth and brush have covered up most of the ground. I follow narrow deer trails deeper into the trees, and my pulse speeds up when I see the outcropping rising in the distance. The cold, gray stone and snake-like vines. The furry moss has spread over the surface like some alien virus. All the trees along the top are just black skeletons. Leafless branches silhouetted against the sky.

I get the strangest sense that the moments we lived in this small space of the forest, those moments from years ago, they somehow linger. Imprinted in the air, the particles around me. I keep thinking I see the ghosts of our younger selves running down the path, faces pale, eyes wide. Running from something none of us understood.

I know it's probably just my memory aligning with the present, but I still feel like something is in these woods, watching, evaluating me.

I step over a pile of picked-apart animal bones—a deer, maybe—and enter the clearing. My hands start shaking when I see it. Tremors grip my calves and shiver up my thighs. My knees go weak, and I just want to collapse onto the ground.

The cave entrance is a black yawning mouth in the side of the outcropping. The stones we piled up all those years ago, the wall we'd built to keep the evil inside, have been stacked into a pyramid at the center of the clearing. Only this is a structure that should not stand. The pyramid is inverted. The tip is stabbed into the ground, and the flat base points up at the sky, defying gravity.

I walk around the structure, waving my hands to feel for wires, anything that might be keeping this thing upright. At the very top is the largest stone, long and rectangular. I know it's the largest because it took all three of us to move it.

It's floating. The whole god damn pyramid is floating.

I blink once and keep my eyes closed, then press the heels of my hands against my eyelids. I press until white stars explode in my vision. When I open them, the pyramid is still there, and the impossibility of it picks at my brain like a sharp piece of shale, digging into my consciousness.

I reach out one trembling hand. Whatever dwelt inside that cave broke free, then built this to let us know that not even the laws of physics could keep it contained.

My hand shakes more violently the closer it gets to the stones. The fingers distort, they stretch and bend toward the structure. The hand doesn't feel any different, but it looks like it's coming apart.

Then my fingertips make contact with the cold stone and there's a stillness in my head. The pyramid, and the woods, dissolve and vanish. An image comes into focus, clearer than any memory I've ever had.

We're all there, Jessie, Todd, and me. We're young again, collecting all of these scattered stones and piling them in front of the cave entrance. Todd says he thinks that someone else, maybe hundreds of years ago, maybe the Yakama tribe, tried to build this wall once before. But it didn't work.

It takes almost the whole day to stack those rocks, until not even a bird could squeeze inside. When we finish, Todd takes the container of salt out of his backpack. He pours a thick line in front of the wall, then leads us in the Lord's prayer. I sprinkle the holy water all over the stones, and we say the prayer again.

Jessie goes last. She takes out her mom's worn leather Bible and runs her fingers over the name embossed on the cover. She gently places it on top of the wall, and says, "I'm ready to let this one go."

We pray one last time, the three of us standing shoulder to shoulder, believing that we what we've done actually matters.

I yank my hand back…

… and the woods return. As soon as my fingers leave the stone, the pyramid shivers once, and I jump backward just as the whole formation comes crashing to the ground. Several stones crack on top of each other and tumble off into the leaves.

I'm on my back, looking up into the gray sky, into the rolling underbelly of the clouds. Drops of water fall on my face. I gulp in the air and fill my lungs.

"How?" I say out loud. My hand scratches at the leaves on the ground. My fingers feel something, grasp it, and pull it up. It's weatherworn and covered in black mold, but I know what it is before I set it down. The pages are yellow, torn, and eaten through, but some words can still be seen.

Red words. Words that Jesus said.

"When the evil spirit has gone out of a person, it passes through waterless places seeking rest but finds none. Then it says, 'I will return to my house from which I came.' And when it comes, it finds the house empty, swept, and put in order. Then it goes and brings with it seven other spirits more evil than itself, and they enter and dwell there, and the last state of that person is worse than the first."

6

Jessie and I came bursting out of the cave, falling over ourselves to get as far away from the entrance as we could. Todd stood near the trees, one arm across his chest, the other covering his mouth. He came running over when he saw us and helped us up from the ground.

"Where's Cameron?" Todd's voice sounded scared and full of something I later realized was shame. He ran out first, abandoning the three of us to try and escape. "Did you leave him?" Todd asked through his hand, his voice high-pitched and panicked.

Jessie stepped forward and shoved both hands at his chest, knocking him down.

"We didn't leave him," Jessie said. "He was taken. We could've got him out if you hadn't turned pussy and ran."

Todd started weeping silently at first before bawling.

"This is your fault!" Jessie screamed. She clenched her hands into fists and walked around the clearing, head twitching at every small noise from the woods.

"Jessie," I said. "Jessie, we need to get help, call the cops."

She started clawing through the dead leaves, brushing them aside until she found a long tree branch as thick as her arm. She stuck one end in the ground and then stomped her foot against it, snapping it in half. What she held up now looked like a sharpened club.

"What are you doing?" I asked her.

When she looked at me, Jessie's face held more fear and pain than I knew it could. It was a look I'd only ever seen on the face of an adult.

Jessie stared into my eyes, and I knew exactly what she was doing. The guilt burned there, almost as brightly as Todd's—only Jessie intended to do something about it.

She took off toward the mouth of the cave, only stopping to pick up a baseball-sized rock. I ran to get ahead of her and then stood with my arm out. "Hey, think about it for just one second, okay?"

She lowered her head and moved to shoulder past me, but I pushed her back. Anger mixed with all that guilt and fear in her eyes.

"If you go in, you're not coming back out," I say. "You know that. Think of your dad."

Jessie's teeth ground together as she tried to stop her chin from shaking. She wanted to still be angry, but the momentum was gone. At the mention of her dad, water welled up in her eyes. The tree branch dropped from her hand. Her head fell, and I leaned my forehead against hers.

"Goddamn it, Bry," she sobbed. "What is happening?"

I put my hand on the back her head, held her closer and let her cry.

We sat in the clearing, not saying much of anything until the sky turned a darker shade of gray. Todd stood up and brushed leaves from the back of his jeans. He started walking the tree line, hands deep in his pockets.

"Guys," he said. "We really need to call the cops. We're wasting time here."

Jessie sat directly in front of the cave, watching it like it was mouth that might suddenly bite down and swallow us whole. Her whole body jerked when we heard a sound like a bag of cement being dropped on the ground.

Jessie got up and crept over to the dark entrance. A hand went to her mouth, "Jesus," she said. "Jesus. Bry, get over here."

I jumped up and ran over to her and saw what looked like a matted piece of yellow fur on the floor just inside the cave.

"His body just appeared," Jessie whispered. "Like something tossed him here."

Jessie took the flashlight off her belt and shined it into the black hole. The matted fur was connected to a motionless body lying face down in the dirt. While Jessie held the light, I went to the body and gently rolled it over. Cameron's eyes stared, unblinking. I took a step back, trying to think of what we would tell the cops, our parents, when I noticed Cameron's chest rising and falling.

Jessie grabbed his arms, I grabbed his legs, and we carried him out into the dying light of dusk. Cameron looked at the sky, at the foggy light of the moon, and said, "There are thoughts in my head that aren't mine."

7

I walk back to my car in the dark, start the engine, and tear out onto the road, wanting miles between me and that cave.

I pull out my phone and call Todd again. It goes straight to voicemail.

"I know you don't believe anymore," I say, "but please, be careful." The headlights of an oncoming car float in the dark like two yellow eyes.

"The wall…" my voice cracks. "The wall isn't where we left it. It's real, Todd. All of it is real."

My thumb hovers over the red button to end the call, then I say again, "Please, be careful."

I hang up the phone and take a deep breath.

Oh, Cameron, you haven't been alone since the cave. And it's crowded in there now, isn't it? All those thoughts that were never yours. Too many voices are talking all at once.

The house is mostly dark when I pull into the driveway. The curtains are all still open, and a single light glows in the living room window. Maybe Deirdre fell asleep and forgot to close them.

At the front door, I slip my key in the lock, but it turns easily like the deadbolt wasn't locked at all. The door opens to a dark entryway, and an alarm starts going off in the back of my head.

"Deirdre, honey? Are you awake?" I call out.

The car keys clink together loudly as I move them from one hand to the other. My footsteps echo down the hall.

"Deirdre?" My voice comes out through a tightened throat. In the living room, I wince at the subtle but distinctive odor of liquid copper. My stomach lifts inside me, pushes up into my chest.

"Deirdre?" I say again, and the smell gets stronger the closer I get to the living room. The light I'd seen from the driveway is a knocked-over lamp casting a slanted beam against the wall. It makes the room feel so different, a carnival version of where I live.

"Deirdre? Deirdre?" Her name keeps tumbling out. I taste salt on my lips. A chill passes through me as tears run down my chin.

A chair lies on its side, a shattered glass on the floor. The clock on the mantle ticks as loud as a hand knocking at the door. The TV is still on, tuned to the local news, its blue glow pulsing through another color, something darker.

I can't stand. My legs don't work. I collapse to the floor and stare at the large bloody handprint on the TV screen, still wet, still dripping. Todd's face appears behind it, the picture he uses for his business cards.

The news anchor calmly reports, "Local real estate agent, Todd Weyers, was gunned down outside a restaurant earlier this evening. Police are still searching for Cameron Davies, the suspected Westlake Mall shooter, in connection with this killing as well."

I put my forehead on the floor and try not to vomit. I scream my wife's name, knowing she won't answer. I know it as certain as I know Cameron didn't come out of the cave alone.

I get back up, take a step, trip, brace myself with a hand to the wall. The furniture goes blurry. My feet, so far below me, weigh as much as that stone on the pyramid. How much time, how much distance between then and now? I want to go on but don't want to see it.

Drips of blood lead to the bedroom, little red splashes in a crooked line. I follow them to the room, and the tears I've been holding back come pouring out. There is a puddle of blood soaked into the carpet. Red is all over the wall in a pattern. Handprints, one on top of the other, assemble the shape of a tall figure wearing a crown. A crown made of red fingers.

My knees come unbolted. A cold fire courses through my chest and into my arms. I can see a bare foot sticking out from the behind the bed. It's hers. I know it is. I can't see the rest of her, and I don't want to. But I crawl toward her anyway, trying not to look at all the hands on the wall, all that blood. Hands in the same shape we saw on the cave wall.

My wife is on the other side of the bed, face down on the floor. I can barely see through my tears how her head is twisted at a sickening angle. Her open eyes stare accusingly at me. I reach out and touch her leg. The skin is cold. Blood is splattered all over her face and mouth. I feel dizzy and weak. I want to lay down beside her and never wake up.

Something slides along the edge of my vision. A slow, subtle movement. I look over just as the creature made of red hands detaches from the wall and steps forward. A flesh and blood man, completely naked, his body covered in dozens of red prints made with Deirdre's blood.

I know the eyes. I've known them for a long time.

"Cameron...."

What comes out of his mouth is more than one voice. Several voices all mixed like a chorus of whispers saying the same words.

"I know what they know, and I see what they see. I can't carry this anymore. It's time for you to take the burden, to hear all the whispers. It's yours now."

I blink once and he's moved from the wall to right in front of me. So close I can see the fingerprint patterns in the blood that covers his face. His hands grip the side of my head, and he leans in close. His red-stained teeth and bloodshot eyes take up all I see.

We were here at the beginning, and we will be here at the end.

I feel his mouth on my head, teeth digging into my skull. I scream his name one last time before the world goes dark.

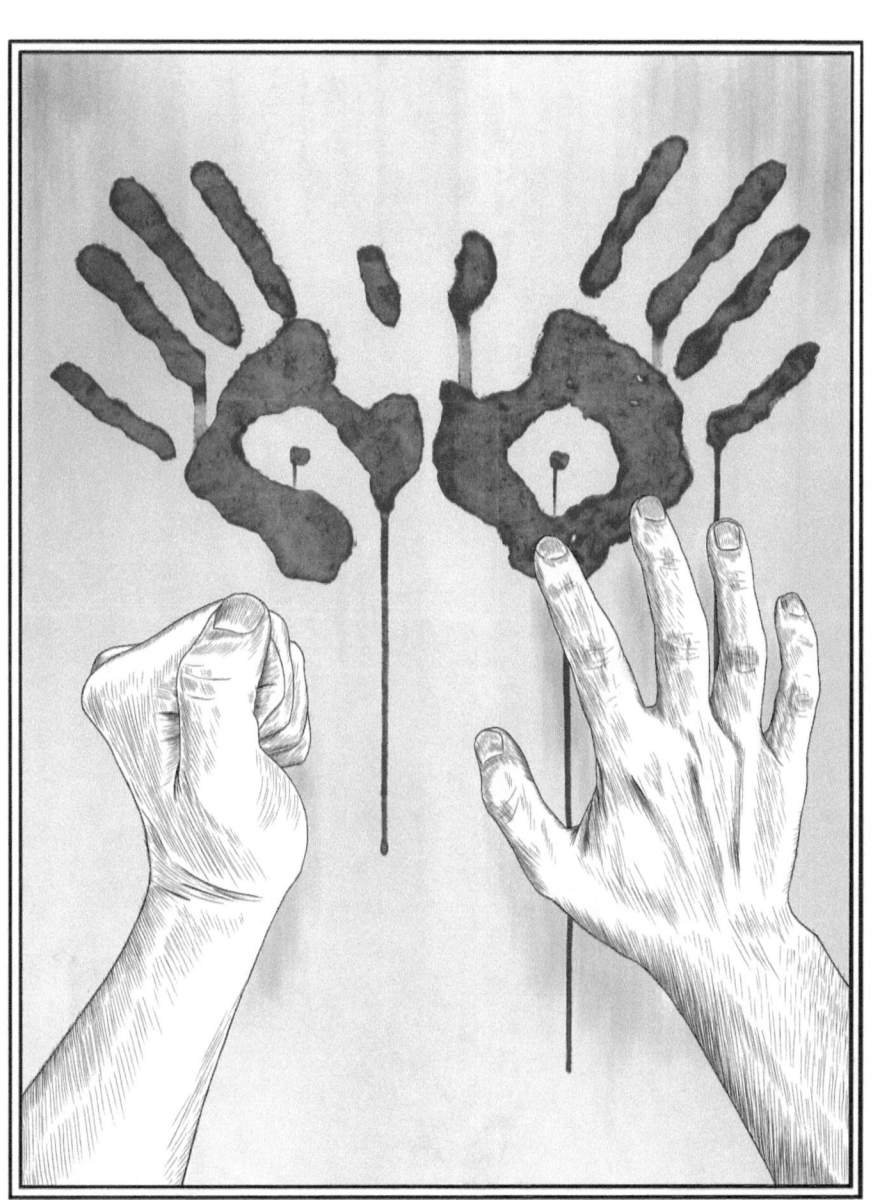

WHITE GLOVE

1

At eleven o'clock in the morning, Danny Parker was well on his way to getting buzzed after finishing his second vodka and soda. The house was empty. His wife and young son left a few hours earlier to go shopping at the mall for Christmas.

Danny sat on the living room couch, laptop open, watching a YouTube video on how to fix a broken dishwasher. Theirs had been on the fritz for a while, but as of this morning, it wouldn't even run.

Danny promised Alisa he'd figure out what was wrong with it. After all, he had the time ever since losing his construction job three months earlier.

On the laptop screen, some guy was stretched out on the kitchen floor, holding his phone underneath a dishwasher and talking about where to hook hoses. Danny sighed. He told Alisa he could fix it even though he knew he couldn't. He hated that about himself, the way he could never admit his flaws.

He clicked off the dishwasher guy, decided to check his email, and found a message—probably spam—from some company he'd never heard of. Included in the message was a video. He hit play.

Bright colors—green, red, white, and gold—and cheerful Christmas music played as a tall man in a black suit strode into view. The man's hair was white like snow, and one gnarled hand was wrapped around a gold-topped cane. He limped through a massive warehouse, past rows of tall shelves filled with brightly colored boxes. Long strands of holly stretched between two giant candy canes that stood as pillars, leading to a fake winter wonderland. Cotton snow covered the floor. Blow-up snowmen stood silent, smiling. A dozen Christmas trees were scattered about. These, at least, appeared real and were covered with lights, ornaments, and tinsel.

"Hello," the man said, "I'm Allistair O'Fallon, owner of the O'Fallon Toy Company."

Workers dressed in elf costumes ran in and out of view, carrying wrapped packages, the bells on their elf shoes jingling. The old man walked through the fake snow, and Danny was struck by how gaunt he looked. The black suit hung on the man's frame like it had been made for a much larger person.

"This has been a hard year for many," O'Fallon said, his voice warm and melodic. "So, I've decided to give something back to the people who need it most."

O'Fallon walked past conveyor belts carrying a variety of toys. Some of the elves boxed them up, wrapped them in holiday-themed paper, and put a bow on top. All of the elves were smiling, their teeth white and shining.

"This year," O'Fallon continued, "I'm going to give every single family in our town a present, a very special gift to open on Christmas Eve night. An early present, you might say."

Danny's tired eyes opened a little wider. He glanced at their Christmas tree near the fireplace they never turned on because gas was too expensive. There were only a couple of small gifts under the lights and ornaments. If this was their town, a free present would be great for Cole. Money was tight even before Danny lost his job, and now the finances were choking them.

O'Fallon stopped in front of a gigantic mountain of gift-wrapped presents, stacked so high it nearly reached the warehouse ceiling.

"To carry out this task," O'Fallon said, "I'll be hiring seasonal drivers to help deliver the presents. This will be done on Christmas Eve, but you'll be home on Christmas morning to spend the holiday with your family. If you're interested—"

Here, O'Fallon's blue eyes looked directly at the camera. Directly at Danny. He sat up straighter.

"—and I hope you are. Call this number—" O'Fallon pointed down as a phone number appeared on the screen "—and apply. This will be a Christmas to remember. I promise you that."

O'Fallon smiled, and his teeth were as white as his hair. It was a nice smile, but the longer Danny stared at the man, the more he found the smile a little creepy. Danny only saw the gold topper to his cane briefly before O'Fallon's hand covered it again, but he thought it might be a gargoyle with a deformed face, and sharp grinning teeth.

The commercial was weird, for sure. But that didn't stop Danny from taking out his phone and dialing the number.

2

By the time Alisa and Cole got home, Danny had polished off his third vodka soda—to celebrate—and was feeling good. That is until Alisa went into the kitchen with a hopeful look and came back out into the living room with an expression that was both disappointed and angry.

Cole told Danny about the toys, decorations, candy, and music he'd seen at the mall. The kid couldn't sit still as he recounted every detail of their trip. Alisa sat on the couch with a sigh and took off her scarf.

"One candy cane," she said. "That's all he had, and he's been bouncing off the walls ever since."

"Where's mine?" Danny asked, grabbing his son and wrestling him into a hug.

Cole laughed. "You don't get one, you're too old!"

Danny stuck his hands into the pockets of Cole's jacket, searching and tickling. The boy giggled and kicked.

"I don't have any," he yelled.

"Ew," Danny said, "your hands are all sticky. Go wash 'em."

Cole got up, stuck out his bright, red tongue, and laughed all the way to the bathroom. Danny laughed, too, still feeling good. He looked over at his wife, and his heart dropped when he saw her staring at him.

"How'd it go with the dishwasher?" she asked.

"Oh," Danny waved a hand, "it's shot. We'll have to get a new one."

Alisa kept looking straight at him. The skin between her eyes folded.

"Did you even try?"

Danny tried to laugh, but it sounded fake. "Of course I did."

"Where are your tools?"

"I put them away already."

Alisa's eyebrows went up. "You put away your tools for the first time in our marriage but still leave a sink full of dishes?"

Danny shrugged and felt the skin of his face getting warmer. "I'm sorry, I just didn't think of it."

"But you knew I would," Alisa said. "If I don't do it, it won't get done."

Danny reached out for her hand, but Alisa pulled it back.

"Come on, honey. That's not true."

"No?" she said. "Let me ask you this: Who do you think will be the one to go pick out a dishwasher, put it on the credit card, arrange the delivery, and then make all the payments on time?"

Danny let his eyes fall to the couch, to the old blue fabric, sun-faded and stained.

"I can't pick up any more shifts, Danny," Alisa said. "So, can you please help out a little more?"

Danny nodded silently. He was about to say something, anything to make her smile, when her eyes filled with tears.

"And drink a little less," she said.

They didn't speak for the rest of the night. They talked to Cole, listened to his stories, and then all of them sat on the couch and watched a Christmas movie on TV that was already half over, but they didn't say a word to each other.

Later, when Danny and Alisa lay in bed, Danny whispered, "I got a job."

Alisa shifted and sat up. "What?"

"It's just for one day but pays really well."

"How much?"

Danny told her, and Alisa's mouth fell open.

"For real?" she said. "No scam?"

"No scam. The only catch is that it's most of the day on Christmas Eve."

Alisa sat all the way up, crossed her legs, and covered her mouth with a hand.

"It's worth it," she said.

"I know," Danny said. "And maybe if I do well, there will be more work in the future."

Alisa turned to him, her eyes full of hurt and hope. "You think so?"

"Maybe. I'll definitely ask, though."

He couldn't see her face in the dark but heard her sniff once.

Danny reached out for his wife, and this time, she took his hand.

3

On Christmas Eve morning, Danny Parker woke up while it was still dark and shuffled to the kitchen. He was about to open the dishwasher and take out a clean coffee mug when he remembered it was still full of dirty dishes.

When the coffee was ready, he poured a cup and went to the living room. He opened the curtains and peered through the window. The lawn was covered in a blanket of unbroken snow, and thick flakes drifted down from a stone-colored sky. He lifted the cup to take a sip when he saw the van parked in his driveway. The words O'FALLON TOY COMPANY emblazoned on the side panel in big, bright letters.

There it was. Just like the voice on the phone said it would be.

Danny wasn't crazy about the idea of some stranger driving over and dropping off a van in the middle of the night, but the voice told him it was how the company coordinated all of this. They didn't want to take any chances that their drivers might be unable to make it to the factory to pick up the vans.

He grabbed his laptop, sat on the couch, and searched for the O'Fallon Toy Company. Nothing came up, which was weird. How could a toy company with the means to give out thousands of free toys not have a web presence?

Next, Danny tried searching for Allistair O'Fallon. He scrolled through the first two pages of results but found nothing related to toys or toy companies. He was about to close the web browser when he saw an image on an article about Irish folklore. An old painting of a tall, thin man with white hair wearing a long, black robe. The gaunt face and mournful expression looked exactly like the man from the commercial. Danny swallowed hard and then clicked on the article.

Allistair O'Fallon, it said, was a monk in the small coastal town of Dungarvan, Ireland, during the winter of 1643. The year had been a hard one for the town. A terrible storm had washed all the fish ashore and flooded the farmlands so the crops were ruined. People were starving and hopeless. O'Fallon gave everything he had to the townspeople to try and ease their suffering.

As Christmas approached, O'Fallon wrote a letter to Saint Nicholas, asking him to visit the town's children and bring them gifts and good cheer.

O'Fallon never received a reply, but rumors began spreading that Saint Nicholas had visited the nearby town of Ardmore on Christmas morning and brought many gifts for the children there. Ardmore was a wealthier town and had been untouched by the storm. Dungarvan's need was so much greater, yet Saint Nicholas had passed them by.

O'Fallon was so enraged that he locked himself away in the friary and would not eat or drink for days. He pored over ancient books and, on the sixth day, using dark magic, summoned the devil and made a bargain. O'Fallon would not die so long as he brought pain and suffering wherever Saint Nicholas brought joy.

Over the years, wealthy towns and villages in Ireland were struck by tragedy each Christmas. Many children died from fever, disappeared into the night fog, or were dragged into the hills by creatures that could not be seen.

Danny finished the article and scrolled back up to the picture. The man in the painting looked so much like the O'Fallon from the commercial that it made Danny feel dizzy. An ancestor, maybe? Or just a coincidence?

That was when Danny noticed the cane the man held and the hideously deformed, golden face on top of it.

Danny spent the rest of the morning trying not to think about the story he had read. He didn't know why it made him feel so uneasy. It was just a folktale, nothing more. The world was full of them. Still, he didn't like the similarities between the painting and the man in the commercial.

After Cole woke up, they had a snowball fight in the front yard. A fight that turned into a battle with some of the other kids on the block while Alisa hid away in their bedroom and wrapped the few presents she'd bought for Cole. None of the big items that were on his list, but still, small things Cole would enjoy.

At 11:30 am, after eating lunch with his family and hand-washing the dishes a second time, Danny hugged Cole and told him he loved him and would see him in the morning.

Danny wore his warm coat and gloves, kissed Alisa, and went to the front door. She followed him and put a hand on his shoulder.

"Hey," she said. "Get home early, and if I'm still asleep, wake me up."

She smiled the same smile that made him fall in love eight years earlier. A smile that didn't have the weight of responsibility and worry pulling down the corners of her eyes.

Alisa leaned in and kissed him.

"I love you," she said.

"I love you too."

She patted his butt and said, "Now go make some money."

<h1 style="text-align:center">4</h1>

The van was unlocked, with the keys resting on the driver's seat on top of a manila envelope. The van smelled brand new like it had just rolled off the lot.

Danny turned around in his seat and whistled. The entire back of the van was packed full of packages, all the same size and all covered in the same wrapping paper. The packages he'd seen in the commercial. Small, square boxes were big enough to fit a basketball and stacked side by side, so tight you couldn't fit in another box no matter how hard you tried.

Danny started to open the envelope, then saw Alisa and Cole watching him through the living room window and waving. He waved back.

He assumed another driver would deliver a present for Cole, but Danny didn't want to take any chances. He grabbed one of the packages, hopped out of the van, and carried the gift to the house. Cole's eyes lit up when he opened the door.

Danny said, "You get to open one present on Christmas Eve, right?"

Cole nodded.

"Here you go. Just wait until I get home, okay?"

Danny hugged his son once more, got in the van, and backed out of the driveway. After turning onto the next street, out of view of his house, Danny pulled to the curb and parked. He opened the envelope and took out several pieces of festive paper printed to look like pages out of Santa's "Naughty or Nice" book. The first page was a letter.

Greetings Driver! I am so excited for you to be part of our delivery team this year. This year will be one to remember for the rest of your life! Before you begin, there are a few rules that absolutely MUST be followed. If you break these rules in any way, you will be terminated without compensation. But I know we won't have to worry about that!

- *You have been given a route for your delivery. You must follow the given route and not deviate from it.*
- *DO NOT OPEN THE PACKAGES!*
- *There are precisely enough packages for the houses on your route. If you keep a package for yourself or your own child, you will be terminated without compensation.*
- *This is a "white glove" delivery service, which means the packages must be hand-delivered to the residents of each house. They MUST not be left outside. If the residents are not home, you must continue your route and return to the unoccupied houses later.*

- *This may take all day and into the night. If that is the case, you will be compensated for hours worked beyond the 8-hour shift. All packages must be delivered by 9 pm.*
- *After all gifts have been delivered, you may return home and leave the van where it was dropped off. Someone will pick it up on Christmas Day.*
- *The van is equipped with cameras. If you break any rules, someone will be dispatched to take your place immediately.*

Well, that about covers it. Again, I am thrilled to have you on the O'FALLON delivery team, and I hope this year is special for all of us.

Damn, Danny thought.

The rules were odd, and specific, and he had already broken one without realizing it. There was no way he could go back and take the present from Cole. Hopefully the company would be understanding. After all, he hadn't even read the rules before he gave Cole the gift.

Paper crinkled behind him, loud in the quiet van. Danny jerked and turned around. Nothing but the packed tight gifts. One of them must have shifted.

The remaining pieces of paper gave him his route, which started on Abernathy Drive. Just a few blocks away in the affluent neighborhood.

There it was again, that sound. The crinkling paper.

Danny hopped out and went around to the back of the van. He opened both doors and pushed on the packages. There was hardly any room for them to move, and they didn't make the sound he'd heard.

Danny got back in the van and turned the radio on to a station playing Christmas music. Might as well get into the spirit of things. After all, he was kind of like Santa Claus tonight.

5

Danny pulled up in front of the first address on his list. He parked along the street, got out, and opened the back of the van. He grabbed one of the packages, careful not to rip the paper, and carried it up the walk.

The box was heavier than he expected, and whatever was inside shifted around, even though he held it steady. He was tempted to shake the box, like he did as a kid, and try to guess what was inside.

Maybe something robotic? The shifting inside had a soft feel to it, but there was also the weight of the thing. So maybe a remote-controlled plush toy or something?

Danny went up the steps and knocked on the front door. A woman, about his age, answered. Her eyes were confused at first, but they softened when she saw the package.

"Hi, Mrs. Ambrose," Danny said. "I'm with the O'Fallon Toy Company, and they've decided to give a special gift to every child in the neighborhood this year."

The woman laughed and smiled. Just past here, Danny could see a man and two children working on a gingerbread house. Some old crooner's voice came from a stereo, singing about snow, sleighs, and jingle bells.

"Oh, my goodness," Mrs. Ambrose said. "What a wonderful surprise! I had no idea. I haven't heard anything about this.

Danny felt a stab of jealousy. Based on the size of the house, and the cars in the driveway, this family didn't need any handouts. He caught a glimpse of their Christmas tree. Presents were piled all around it. Big, small, and everything in between.

Danny handed her the package and tried to match her smile. "There is one rule, though. You have to promise not to open it until nine o'clock tonight.

The woman laughed again and said, "Of course. Thank you. Would you like a cookie for your drive?"

Danny thanked her, said no, and wished her a Merry Christmas. Just a few miles from his house and this family lived in another world.

Back in the van, Danny heard the crinkling noise again, and this time he was certain it came from the back of the van.

Danny leaned back and listened. Something was moving in one of those boxes, maybe even more than one, no doubt about it. There was that papery crinkle, the shifting sound, and something else. A gentle scratching like the sound of a thing wanting you to know it was there.

Danny closed his eyes, and his hands started to shake. He told himself it was because he hadn't eaten in hours. But it wasn't, and he knew it.

He was afraid.

6

Over the next several hours, Danny delivered three-quarters of the packages without incident. All of them went to big, fancy homes. A few families weren't home, so Danny had to make a note on his list and circle back to them later, and so far, he had been able to hand over all of them. Almost as if the O'Fallon Toy Company had known which families would be home tonight.

The sounds from the back of the van continued, so Danny turned the music up and sang along. He kept imagining the small black eyes of cameras mounted somewhere in the van, watching him like the letter said. And there was no way he was going to risk losing out on this payday simply because he couldn't keep his curiosity in check.

Close to 8:30 p.m., Danny pulled up in front of an enormous two-story house with perfectly strung lights and expensive-looking decorations in the front yard.

Danny opened up the back of the van. Only two packages left. He grabbed the closest one, and when he did, something moved inside and the box nearly jerked out of his hands. Conscious movement. Purposeful. He could feel the vibrations of the scratching.

Danny dropped the box on the street and backed away. His heart thumped erratically, and breath poured out of his mouth, silver like smoke. The box skittered along the wet pavement, coming closer, like it was searching for him. All the while, that scratching noise got louder. Then, the box went still.

Each breath of freezing air burned his chest. He wanted to rush over and stomp the living shit out of that package, and whatever was inside.

A thought appeared, and as soon as it did Danny started laughing. He couldn't stop. Why hadn't he thought of it sooner?

What does almost every kid want for Christmas? A dog! Of course, that was the reason for all the rules about not leaving it outside and opening it at 9 p.m. There were probably puppies in the boxes, hamsters, or kittens—something cute, soft, and cuddly.

But what about the noise? There was no whimpering, or mewling, or barking.

No. Danny shook his head. Every belief was a choice, and he chose to believe the O'Fallon Toy Company was gifting children pets. Pets to love and care for. That's what was in the box.

Danny stepped closer to the package and tapped it with his shoe. It didn't move, so Danny picked it back up, holding it away from his chest, and walked quickly to the house. When a man answered the door, Danny mumbled something about a gift and a toy company, handed over the box, and went back to the van. His head hurt and his hands wouldn't stop shaking.

A puppy. I just delivered a really quiet puppy.

Danny got in the van and started laughing again. They were drugged or something. Had to be. Given something to help them sleep, and the medicine was starting to wear off. Some were waking up.

Scratching.

Danny closed his eyes and gripped the steering wheel.

Scratching, faster and harder against the cardboard box hidden beneath wrapping paper.

Danny finally turned and looked behind him. One package left. He looked at the addresses he'd crossed off on his list. He flipped the last page over, looked again. He didn't understand. He delivered to every house on the list. The letter had said there were exactly enough for every address. So, either someone at the company miscounted, or *he* did.

Shit.

Of course it was him. Of course he'd fuck it up. That's what Danny Parker always did. He dreamed and talked big, then he got drunk and incinerated every good thing in his life.

Shit.

Forget it. He'd go home and leave the present in the van. Maybe it was a simple error, and the company would understand.

Danny put the van in drive and started toward home. He made a sharp right turn, and the single box in the back skidded across the floor and crashed into the wall. He heard scratching, like a cat's claws, coming from the package.

He wasn't prone to moments of self-reflection, because they hurt too much, paralyzed him. If he looked too long at himself, Danny would start to feel this burning piece of coal right in the center of his chest. Maybe that's why he drank. The booze doused that coal, but ultimately left him unenlightened, unable to see why Alisa was mad at him again.

What if you're wrong?

The thought came to him, loud and clear.

You don't know what's in those boxes, but you know they're not puppies or kittens. You know it.

A sudden fear gripped him. Fear like he felt when he poured the last remaining drops out of a vodka bottle. The clock on the dash said 8:50 pm.

Cole.

He'd given Cole the first package. How could he have forgotten that? His foot stomped on the gas pedal as the speedometer needle crept higher.

Another turn, but Danny didn't slow down, and it felt like the whole van tilted on two wheels as it tore past a stop sign, past a headless snowman in someone's yard. Christmas lights blurred into green, red, silver, and gold smears as sweat ran into Danny's eyes and stung.

8:53 pm.

Streetlights cast ghostly halos onto the snow, circles of pale light on an otherwise dark street. House after house went by. Houses Danny recognized, because he'd walked up to each one and handed the people who lived there a present.

The box in the back moved on its own. Scratching came from inside. Steady and rhythmic.

Another turn. The tires hit a puddle of slush, and the wheel spun out of Danny's hand. He jerked the wheel left to correct, but the van's back end kept sliding and smashed into a mailbox. The metal box flew into the air and crashed on the sidewalk. Danny didn't even slow down.

8:55 pm.

Danny saw his house up ahead. The only house on the block without any Christmas lights up. Alisa had asked him to do it, but he'd got drunk and forgotten. Just like he forgot he gave Cole the first present.

He slammed on the brakes and came to a harsh stop in the driveway. He had to know what was in the package. He couldn't just run inside and take it from Cole. Danny had given the kid so little. And maybe it was nothing. Maybe his fear was pointless.

Danny unsnapped his seatbelt. Even if he lost the money, he would open that present and see what was inside.

He climbed into the back of the van and stopped breathing when he saw the gift. The wrapping paper was not just torn but shredded, and the cardboard was sliced open, with long, jagged marks.

Danny took a step closer and peered into the box. Empty. He tapped it with his foot. Nothing inside.

8:57 pm.

Clicking just above him. Danny jumped back and looked up. The clicking moved fast, sounded like fingernails tapping on metal. Like something sharp. Danny's hands clenched into fists, and he felt the slickness of sweat on his palms. His breathing was loud in the confined space, and there was a wheeze in his exhales that he didn't like one bit.

Movement from his right, a shift in the shadows. More clicking, and Danny felt a slight rush of air as something moved past him, scrambling along the wall of the van.

He couldn't let Cole open that present.

8:58 pm.

Danny grabbed the handle of the sliding door and was about to open it when he heard a low growl from above his head. He glanced up and saw two yellow eyes looking directly at him. A vague shape in the shadows, clinging to the ceiling with long claws. His first thought was that this thing was a hairless cat with gray, wrinkled skin, but the face was oddly human. Small and deformed, like a piece of fruit well beyond ripe. Pointed ears stuck out on either side of the squished face and twitched with the sound of Danny's breathing.

The same face on O'Fallon's cane.

Danny and the creature stared at each other. The low growl got louder. The mouth opened to show two rows of teeth, like jagged little knives, and before Danny had a chance to throw open the door, the creature leaped onto his face, snarling. Pain, sharp and instant, shocked his system. A flash of cold as claws sliced through his cheeks. Another wound opened on his forehead, and warm blood poured down his face.

Danny fell to the ground and tried to scream, but the creature's arm was in his mouth.

Teeth clamped down on Danny's throat, there was a tearing sound, a small pop, and then a flood of warm liquid pouring down into his lungs. His vision grew dark as thoughts of Cole sparked in his panicked brain.

Cole. Don't open it!

Danny closed his eyes and tried to send his thoughts through the van, the house, and into his son's head.

Cole, get out!

Danny's vision narrowed to a tunnel and all he could see was one yellow eye. His ears worked just fine, filled with the sound of screaming. Not his own, though. Coming from the house, the sound of Cole screaming in pain. Danny tried to speak. Blood gurgled from his open throat.

More screams joined Cole's. A chorus of screams echoed down the street, coming from all those rich houses nearby.

Now, all Danny could see was black, and his consciousness slipped away.

The time on the clock was 9:01 pm.

STRIDOR

1

The first time Dr. Becca Huntley cheated on her husband, it was with another doctor. Not someone she knew, but someone she met at a downtown conference. She stayed at the hotel where the conference was held so she wouldn't have to drive home late at night. Alcohol was involved, of course, but there was something else turning the gears of that bad decision. Gears she did not fully comprehend until much later.

He was a surgeon and a guest speaker who talked about methods to decrease infection in patients with open wounds. The picture used in the program must have been taken years ago because the surgeon's hair was still dark, and his face didn't have the swollen, aged look of someone who had stopped caring for himself. Still, he was a surgeon at one of the biggest hospitals in Portland, and Becca would be lying if she said that didn't make her see him differently.

They met at the reception afterward. She caught him staring at her multiple times as he mingled with other guests. From the moment they shook hands, Becca knew that he wanted her, and she would sleep with him.

She regretted it even while it was happening, but she felt something. She didn't analyze the feeling too much—it was a sort of distant sense of power—and as days passed, the regret faded and left her with a lingering confidence.

If someone had asked Becca why she cheated on her husband, she would have said something about Damien's inattentiveness and his boring, predictable nature. But she wouldn't have said anything about her reasons, which would be no answer at all. The truth was simple: cheating on Damien was exciting. Work, home, and caring for the baby, were not. Each day felt like a repeat of the last, and over time, she began to feel that some other life, some other version of herself, was burning inside her bones.

When Becca was in med school, she thought being a physician would be glamorous, like something from a TV show. Intensity, drama, romance. She quickly found that working in a hospital meant you had to deal with people, lots of people. Patients, nurses, aides, techs, the patient's family, and other doctors. She didn't want that, so she decided on private practice. Pediatrics. She liked kids, they were fun and honest, and of all the patients she cared for during her internship, they were the only ones whose years of poor choices hadn't made them ill or burdened them with conditions no amount of treatment could undo.

Exhausted and hungover, she pulled into her parking space at the clinic and went inside. Her head was heavy, and her eyes burned when she blinked. She couldn't have slept more than two hours in total. Margaret was already at the front desk checking voicemails. A couple of nurses were clocking in and getting rooms set up. Becca's partner in the clinic, Colleen Braeburn, was vacationing in Mexico for the week, so Becca would also have to see her patients.

Once Margaret unlocked the front doors, the patients started arriving, those with appointments and those needing to be seen through Urgent Care. Check-ups, vaccinations, sprained wrists, and endless coughs and runny noses.

Monotony.

She smoothed out her hair with one hand, felt something gritty, and looked down to see a clump of blond hair on the palm. Stress. Had to be. The few times Becca had lost hair like that, it'd been because of stress. She rubbed her hands together and brushed the hair off into the exam room trashcan, where it sat like the husk of a dead thing.

At some point in her life, Becca thought knowing what to expect from a day, a relationship, or a job must be nice. She wasn't sure exactly when that changed, but it did, and the drive to the clinic each morning was filled with dread. Her life started to feel like that movie, the one with the guy who lives the same day over and over. The clinic was the same; she even repeated the same instructions, the same platitudes, and reassurances to parents. She ate the same lunch and charted the same notes. Then she went home to her husband, and he was the same. The only thing that seemed raw, real, and bursting with life was Kelly. Maybe it was her birth that began the shift inside Becca. The pulling away from Damien, her staff, her friends, even her patients. Maybe it was Kelly that sparked something in her, as if the baby exiting her body had left a void, she now had to fill with something else.

A little girl, less than one year old, sat screaming in her mother's arms. Red-faced, eyes clenched tight, hands balled into fists. When the girl tried to catch her breath, Becca heard a distinctive raspy wheeze that sounded more like a sixty-year-old smoker than a baby. The mother had dark circles under her eyes; her hair was frizzy and pulled back into a half-hearted ponytail. She wore sweatpants and a sweatshirt, which bothered Becca, though she wasn't sure why. It wasn't like the doctor's office was a place you dressed up for. Still.

The crying continued as Becca pulled up the girl's chart on the computer. The father stood against the wall, one arm folded across his chest, the other held up to his mouth. Biting his nails. Becca heard the tiny snip of his teeth between his daughter's cries. His hair was unnaturally black, like a raven's feathers, and disheveled. His eyes moved between his daughter and Becca without blinking, as if saying, *Do something. Fix this.*

Becca slipped on a pair of purple gloves and rolled her stool over to where the mother sat. Their last name was Ephrem, which sounded Romanian, maybe? Neither of them had accents.

"How long?" Becca asked, taking the stethoscope from around her neck.

The mother bounced the little girl gently, though it did nothing to stop the crying. "She spiked a fever three days ago, then last night the coughing started."

Becca nodded and rubbed the stethoscope's diaphragm against her pants to warm it up. She knew the girl still had a fever even before touching her; she could feel the heat from her body radiating in the air.

She lifted the girl's shirt and looked into her chubby, tear-stained face. The girl stopped crying for a moment and opened her eyes. Blue. A brilliant blue that looked as unnatural as her father's hair. Babies' eyes were like that, though, like they hadn't been dulled by living.

"Shh," Becca said to the girl, "this won't hurt at all."

Back in med school, she read that the shushing sound used by mothers for thousands of years was not simply a method to soothe a crying child, but a replication of what the infant heard in utero. The gentle movement of amniotic fluid, the sound of an underwater world. The first sound the baby would have heard.

Becca noticed the wheeze again, which indicated an upper airway infection. She gently put the stethoscope on the girl's chest and listened to her left lung. Good airway movement. She moved to the right lung just as the girl caught her breath and let out a scream that distorted through the stethoscope.

Becca pulled the scope away quickly. If the right lung sounded anything like the left, there wasn't any pneumonia, and the girl would be fine. Normally, she'd try again and listen to make sure. But she had been fighting an awful headache all morning, the kind that made her pulse sledgehammer in her temples. She knew hangovers, even though she rarely got them anymore, but this was something different. Something deeper. Her arms and legs felt only loosely connected to her body. Weak, useless things on the verge of collapse.

Was she getting sick, too?

She shook her head a little as she removed the earpieces and pulled down the crying girl's shirt. The mother looked at her expectantly.

No, not illness.

Guilt.

The events of last night left her feeling hollowed out and empty. Driving home from the motel, she knew guilt would come eventually, she was just too drunk to feel it then. She also knew she'd avoid facing it for as long as she could. Admitting guilt would mean taking a good, hard look at herself, her reasons for running around with lit matches, and setting fire to everything good. It would mean Damien wasn't the villain in her story—she was the villain in his. Maybe even Kelly's.

"It's just a little croup," Becca said to the mother. "Give her some Tylenol, some cough medicine, and keep an eye on it for a few days."

The father moved from where he stood against the wall and came closer. His daughter's screams were so high-pitched the sound was physically painful. The inhales between each bout of screaming did sound horrific, but like she was taught in med school, stridor usually sounded much worse than it actually was.

"Is that all it is?" he asked.

His eyes, surrounded by the shadowed skin of a sleepless parent, were heavy-lidded and dark. They stared at her without blinking for a long time.

Becca tried to smile. "Yep. Just a minor infection."

The man's wife looked up at him, her arms rocking their child back and forth as tears streamed down her face. The woman offered a pacifier, but one small hand grabbed it and then threw it on the floor.

"No prescription?" the man said. His cologne drifted into Becca's nostrils, a harsh and pungent odor that made her think of the doctor in the motel. Was it the same cheap brand?

The pressure behind Becca's eyes grew. She wanted to get this girl and her family out of the office as quickly as possible, and then run outside and breathe fresh air.

"No prescription," Becca repeated, wrapping the stethoscope around her neck, then pumping sanitizer onto both hands and rubbing them together.

"If that's all," she said, with the best fake smile she could muster, "you guys are free to go."

The man stared at Becca for so long it became uncomfortable. His eyes peered straight at hers, unblinking, as though he was able to see how badly she wanted them to leave. Becca could have spent more time with the family and further examined the child, but what was the point? Another kid with a cold that would pass with over-the-counter medicine and rest. The room felt cramped and suffocating between the nagging wheeze, crying, and cologne. Flashes of last night kept coming to Becca and making her stomach burn with acid. She had a full schedule and no time, so yes, she wanted to get through the patients as fast as she could.

The man leaned forward and whispered something in his wife's ear, and Becca noticed a silver medallion hanging around the man's neck. A symbol she'd never seen before. At first, she mistook it for the Star of David until she saw the intricacies inside the circle. Six triangles with curved sides, all touching, created the illusion of multiple eyes. Or, perhaps, unfolding flowers. The woman nodded at whatever the man said, and then he bent down to pick up the green pacifier off the floor. He went over to the sink, a breeze of his cologne and body odor following, where he covered the small piece of rubber in soap and rinsed it off before handing it back to the mother.

"Thank you," the mother said quietly as she rose with the child in her arms. The girl sucked noisily on the pacifier now, still rasping in a way that reminded Becca of Damien washing the dishes. The rough scratch of steel wool against a metal pan.

Becca held the door open and let the mother exit the room. The father stopped, standing so close to her that Becca smelled the coffee on his breath.

"Promise me," he said. "Promise me she's okay."

Becca smiled again. "I promise."

The man said nothing as he left the office, but Becca could still hear the wheezing child as the family went down the hall to the lobby.

Once they were out of view, Becca took off her gloves, tossed them into the trashcan, then paused and tilted her head. The clump of her own hair she'd thrown away was no longer there.

Back in her office, Becca collapsed in the chair and made a few chart notes on the computer before checking her schedule. She still had fifteen more minutes before her next patient. She thought about calling Damien to ask if he wanted to pick up anything for dinner, but even the thought of hearing his kind, trusting voice made her heart flutter with guilt.

Again. Guilt.

Instead, she went outside and stared at the gray clouds rolling overhead like smoke from a great fire.

2

The second time, she hadn't meant for it to happen. Nothing ever just happens; there were always decisions that led to the thing happening—but she had not planned it.

She and her friend, Teresa, were going to meet at a downtown bar for drinks and appetizers, but Teresa called and said the babysitter had canceled, and she couldn't make it. Becca was already at the bar when Teresa called, and she saw no reason not to enjoy her night away from Damien and the baby. It had been weeks since she'd had some time to herself. She thought some greasy food with a drink or two, surrounded by laughing voices and loud music, would be just what she needed.

She didn't plan on the guy at the table next to hers looking over and smiling. She definitely didn't plan on smiling back. It didn't even occur to her the smile might have been a little more flirtatious than usual because she was half-drunk.

The guy wasn't handsome. Not as handsome as Damien, anyway. But there was something about him that she liked. Something… careless.

She could tell he liked that she had a wedding ring. For him, it meant that he didn't have to worry about her expecting something from him. It meant that she had more to lose than he did. He said he wasn't married, but she wasn't sure. He was too good a listener to be single. And maybe it was the low light in the bar, but she thought there was a pale band of skin on his finger where a ring used to be worn. He could have been newly divorced, but Becca didn't think so because they went to a motel. If he'd been single, they would have gone to his place, even if it was just a shitty apartment.

Becca thought later that the way it all happened seemed like an inevitability. From the moment he picked up his drink, came over, and sat at her table, the two of them walking outside into the fog-misted night air and stumbling down the street to the nearest hotel, where they clutched at each other's clothes and fell into bed—it all felt pre-planned, as though Becca were playing the role written for her. Later, as she stood in the chipped motel bathtub and let the water run over her body, she wondered when her brain had decided to go forward with the infidelity. She was no expert in psychology, but she seemed to have made the choice subconsciously long before the man ever approached her. Why else would it have happened so fast? Sure, she was a little tipsy, but she'd been far drunker than that before and had never done anything remotely close to cheating on her husband.

Becca unwrapped the small bar of soap and used it to scrub her skin until it was red. She felt nauseous and dizzy. The regret that churned in her stomach had started when she touched the man's skin, and the topography was so different from Damien's that it was startling. His scent, a mixture of sweat, deodorant, and cologne, made her head spin a little. And then there was his breath. Not bad, necessarily, a little sour, and different enough that she couldn't stop thinking she was breathing in another human's breath. She had to push down her disgust to follow through.

After, as they lay in bed, Becca's heart fluttered with fear. Not fear that Damien would find out—he trusted her blindly. Or maybe he wasn't blind; maybe it was because he loved her, and he didn't even think to be nervous about someone he loved so much. No, the fear came from the realization that what Becca wanted from the man and what she got were very different. The stranger was a selfish lover, and all the unspoken desires she had about what something like this would feel like were shattered the moment his lips touched hers. The stubble on his chin scratched her face like sandpaper— Damien was always clean and smooth—and his hands grabbed at her body with aggression. She was not here in this hotel because of who she was as a woman. All of her thoughts, ideas, emotions, and complications meant nothing to this man. She was here because she had taken his hand and allowed herself to be led. She thought she was being clever by withholding her name when he came to her table. But he never offered his name either, and she realized that as she lay beside him, skin still sticky with sweat, and she did not know what to say.

She was not satisfied, although she hadn't really expected to be, but what she felt was more of a loss. Not only did she get nothing, but she also gave up something in the process and got nothing in return.

These are the mistakes that burn a life, a marriage, she thought. *And it wasn't even worth it.*

The worst part, she decided, was that the man started getting dressed before she did. And she was left holding the rough, thin sheets over herself as the man slipped on his underwear (tighty-whiteys, not boxers like Damien wore) and his pants. His paunch was visible in the harsh light from the outside hallway that snuck between the curtains.

He had done this before.

That thought appeared in her mind like a message from one of those old Magic 8 balls.

If this were a TV show, she would feel empowered. But she did not feel empowered at all. She felt dirty and used and stupid. She felt like crying, and so she did, right there in the shower, careful to not get her hair wet. She stood and cried in the shower until the water went lukewarm, then cold.

After, she got dressed and left the room. Becca had paid for the room using her credit card, not the shared debit account, so she didn't worry that Damien would find the charge and question her. He was so trusting, naïve in a lot of ways, and that was something that had started to bother her over the last six months. Years ago, when they were dating, Becca thought his kindness and sincerity were assets rather than detriments, but now, six years later, she had come to see him as vacant and lacking substance. He would trust her just as he always had. She could have robbed a convenience store, done cocaine, wrecked the car, and he would have bailed her out of jail and believed any story she told him about why she'd been arrested.

Why did she want to kick against that so badly?

Becca got in her car and sat there, staring up at the maroon-colored door of the room she'd just left. The details of what happened there were already starting to go fuzzy. Shame had a way of doing that, at least for her. Ever since she was young, she had this strange ability to distance herself from things she'd broken. Maybe she could forget this one too. Call it a lesson.

She started the car and got on the highway. She kept the radio off. She didn't want to hear anyone's voice. It was still early, only 10:30 pm. The baby would be asleep by now.

The further she drove from the motel and the closer to home, Becca Huntley felt anger start to burn inside her. A small flame that flickered right in the center of her chest. She tried to find the source and what fueled it. It wasn't work. Though stressful, the clinic was the one place where she felt in control of things. Damien? Maybe. Things hadn't been right between them for a while, but she wasn't sure he felt the same. The baby? Could be. Becca had been exhausted since Kelly's birth. Long, sleepless nights with an infant attached to her breast drained all her energy. She'd stopped breastfeeding and switched to formula made thick with an oatmeal powder just so she could get some rest. It was something more than any of those things, but she couldn't find what it was.

She parked in the driveway and sat there in silence. A pulsing blue glow between the blinds of the front windows told her the TV was on.

Inside the house, she found Damien on the couch playing one of his stupid war video games. He looked even more ridiculous with that headset on—big earphones and a microphone mouthpiece. He looked up wide-eyed when Becca walked in and dropped her purse on the kitchen table.

"Gotta go," he said into the mouthpiece. "Next weekend?"

He tore off the headset and got up, came over, and wrapped his arms around Becca. She let herself hug him back. God, he smelled good. Familiar. She put her head to his chest, still solid even though he was approaching middle-aged. Handsome, too. Everyone knew it but him. His brownish-blond hair was wavy and a little too long, and he couldn't grow a beard on his boyish face even if he tried. She used to love that about him.

"The kid is fast asleep," he said, one hand massaging her back. "Went down with no fuss. We played with toys for a few hours, watched a hummingbird in the backyard, and listened to some Sinatra. I think she likes his voice."

It felt like coming home...almost.

For a moment, Becca forgot what she had done. She could almost believe that she'd gone out for drinks with a friend instead of finding herself in a motel with a stranger.

Damien pulled back and looked at her. "Did you have a good time?"

That small fire in her chest flared up at the question. She looked over to the kitchen sink, to the pile of dishes soaking there. The door to the laundry room was open, and she saw two baskets full of clean, unfolded clothes.

The rest of the kitchen was so spotless it was obvious Damien had cleaned it. All the toys were picked up and put away in the living room, and she noticed the video monitor on the coffee table so he could watch Kelly while he played video games. Ever since he lost his job, he threw himself into the role of stay-at-home dad with diligence. In fact, he knew more about Kelly's routine and preferences than Becca did. But those two unfinished tasks caused her skin to turn hot. His hand on her back made her feel angry and disgusted.

She pushed away from him. "Jesus, Damien. One night, that's all I ask for, and you can't even do the fucking dishes?"

Damien's face fell. "I'm sorry. I got tired. I was going to do those tomorrow."

Becca stomped over to the laundry room and flicked on the light. She bent over and rummaged through the clothes until she found a pair of wrinkled beige pants. She held them up. "I was going to wear these tomorrow." She held up a finger. "One night, that's all I want. One goddamn night where I don't come home and see all these things that need to be done."

She wanted him to fire back at her. She needed him to. She needed his level of anger to rise and match hers so she could feel justified in tearing into him further.

But he didn't. His kind eyes watched her face carefully. He probably assumed she was a little drunk, maybe thinking she and Teresa had an argument or something.

"Are you okay?" he asked. "It seems like something is really bothering you."

Becca swallowed.

"Look," he said. "I know I can't fix whatever you're upset about, but I can listen if you want to tell me what's going on."

Becca believed him completely, and that made her even angrier. "I just… okay, fine. You don't have a fucking job, Damien. Alright? I work, I run a clinic. You get to be with Kelly all day. Can you just look around and see what needs to be done and do it?"

His eyes clenched momentarily like she'd punched him in the gut. No job. That was his tender spot. The one place she could poke when she wanted to wound him. Remind him that she was the earner, the worker, the doctor. She didn't really feel that way. On her best days, Becca was unbelievably grateful to have a husband who supported her the way he did. He had never once claimed to be insecure about her success. Even when he lost his job as the manager of a high-end plant nursery, he never complained. And even now, she wasn't so sure it was the lack of a job that wounded him rather than what she said meant they were no longer a team; what he did was less important than what she did, and she wanted him to know.

The look on his face was defeat. He had spent all day caring for their daughter and cleaning the house. He sat down at night to do something he enjoyed, and she couldn't let him have that because it was innocent. And she was not. She had nothing else to say, and she was afraid that if she opened her mouth again, something else would come shooting out that she couldn't take back.

She moved past him, quickly. Their shoulders brushed, but he made no move to stop her.

She said, "I'm going to bed," and went upstairs, leaving her husband standing in the laundry room doorway.

Becca checked on Kelly, smelled the top of her head, and tried not to cry.

"Don't be like me," Becca whispered. "Grow up and be something better."

She closed the door softly and went to the master bedroom. She shed her clothes and smelled faint whiffs of the stranger's cologne. It made her gag. She got in the shower again and let the hot water scald her skin until it was red. When she finally crawled into bed, she heard the sound of running water coming from downstairs, followed by the metallic scratch of a sponge cleaning a dirty pan. She closed her eyes, but the tears still burned. She wished Damien was beside her, holding her.

Always pushing everything good away, she thought.

Ever since she was young. At nine years old she gave away her pet parakeet, a bird she loved with all her heart, because she did not want to see it die. The bird went on to live another four years. Years she missed. And she had done the same thing a thousand times since.

She saw the stranger's face when she closed her eyes. Smelled his breath. She woke up every hour on the hour, her stomach clenched with nausea, and she fell back asleep praying that the world would spin backward during the night and it would be yesterday when she woke up, not the cold, harsh light of a new day.

3

Her last appointment of the day canceled, so rather than go straight home, Becca made the ten-minute drive into town, went to a trendy restaurant, and sat at the bar. She ordered a martini and watched people as they came and went. Soft jazz music drifted from the overhead speaker, and if Damien were with her, he'd comment about how devoid of life and creativity the music was.

Soft jazz doesn't even deserve to be called jazz.

Becca sipped her drink and wondered at the lives of the other customers. Some were in groups, many were couples. She asked herself why she'd come here to this place, what was it she hoped to find?

A man, younger than her by several years, came in and sat across from Becca. He wore dark blue jeans and a light jacket. He smiled easily at the bartender, ordered a beer, then looked up and caught Becca's eyes. He smiled again, and she felt a little rush of adrenaline as she wondered if he'd pick up his glass, carry it over, and ask to sit next to her. She wondered what they would talk about if they hit it off.

There wasn't a ring on his finger, and he didn't seem to be waiting for anyone, so Becca did her best to look mysterious and alluring. The man's eyes kept moving between a soccer match on the TV above the bar and Becca. Each time they locked eyes, he'd smile, and she'd smile back, but she had a hard time telling if it was flirtatious. He smiled more or less the same way at the bartender, so maybe it meant nothing. Maybe he was gay and was just being polite.

He kept glancing at the TV and asking the patron next to him about the score. Occasionally, he'd glance over at Becca, catch her watching him, and give that same polite smile. But Becca knew men, and how those smiles hid something animalistic, something feral.

So, she sat and waited for him to make his move. She finished the first martini and ordered another. The alcohol went to her head and made her feel impatient. If he wasn't going to approach her, she'd approach him.

Her fingers wrapped around the stem of the martini glass, and she stood slowly, her head going light. Keeping one hand on the bar, she made her way to the other side where the stranger sat, still nursing that same beer, when something vibrated inside her purse. She set the glass back down, feeling her cheeks blush with embarrassment, and shoved a hand into the purse until she found her cell phone.

She didn't recognize the number and, in her alcohol haze, couldn't remember whether she was supposed to be on-call that night or not. She pressed the green button and held the phone to her ear.

"This is Dr. Becca Huntley."

All around her, voices talked and laughed. A familiar classic rock song played through the ceiling speakers. A crowd cheered from the TV, and a nearby table erupted into applause.

Static.

"Can you hear me?"

She plugged one ear with a finger and strained to listen for a voice. More static.

No, not quite static, labored breathing. The sound of a smoker with emphysema taking a long drag off a cigarette with oxygen tubing snaking into his nostrils. The sound of lungs not getting enough air.

"Do you need help?" she said a little too loudly. Some people at a nearby table turned in her direction with looks of irritation, so Becca tossed a five-dollar bill on the bar and left the restaurant, still holding a finger in one ear.

"I'm a doctor," she said as she stepped out into the cold evening. "Do you need help?"

Silence.

When she looked at her phone, Becca saw the caller had hung up. Through the window, the man still sat at the bar, face turned to the TV. Becca's desperation surprised her. She didn't necessarily want the man, but she wanted him to *want* her. She wanted to know if she could have him if she chose to.

Once she was outside, the spell was broken. She felt foolish and pathetic like a former smoker sniffing the air around an ashtray to remind herself of what she used to have.

I'm married, and I'm a mother, she thought. Then she repeated it like a mantra until she genuinely did want to go home to her family.

It turned dark by the time she made it to where she'd parked three blocks away. As she neared her car, she pressed the unlock button, and the vehicle flashed its lights and chirped in response. She was about to go around to the driver's side when she noticed something on the sidewalk near the passenger door.

What she at first thought was a black, abandoned purse, moved as she came closer. Then she saw the wagging tail and cute face of a small dog. Not quite a puppy, but not much older. She shouldered her purse, knelt, and held out her hand.

"Hello there," she said. "What are you doing here?"

The animal took a few tentative steps toward her, nose twitching. The shape of the head and the ears was familiar, but she couldn't think of the breed. A guard dog, maybe. Its fur was a deep black that looked almost blue in the headlights of passing cars. It came forward, slowly, looking nervous.

"It's okay," Becca said, "I just want to see if you have a collar. I bet someone's looking for you right now."

At the sound of her voice, the animal glanced up, and its eyes were so white that Becca worried there was something wrong with the dog. If it was sick. There were no pupils at all that she could see. The eyes themselves were perfectly round, buried in folds of dark flesh. They weren't cloudy or milky like she'd expect if the animal were blind. Just pure white, and she wondered how it could see at all. Or maybe it couldn't, and it was just following her scent, the sound of her voice.

She continued holding her hand out, making small noises to guide it. She didn't see any collar around its neck, no dangling tags. She'd parked in front of a clothing store with dark windows so the dog's owners would not be inside. It must have run away, then.

When she looked back, the animal's mouth had opened slightly, revealing a set of sharp fangs as white as its eyes. The skin on its brow folded until the eyes changed shape and became threatening and aggressive.

Heat spread over Becca's throat, and she was about to pull her hand back when the creature's jaws opened wider, and it lunged forward. The fangs snapped shut over her hand, and with two small pops, its teeth punctured her skin, driving down into the meat of her palm and nicking bone.

Becca screamed as the creature jerked its head back and forth like it had a small animal in its grasp and wanted to break its prey's neck.

More teeth stabbed into the top of her hand, grinding her bones as they pierced through. She screamed again and swiped with her free hand, slapping the animal across the face. It let out a small yelp, unclamped its jaw, and pulled away.

Becca stood and screamed, "Shit!"

An inch-long tear and four holes leaked blood that ran down her forearm in red rivulets.

The dog lunged forward again, and Becca moved her foot just in time to jam the pointed toe of her shoe right into the animal's stomach. It yelped again and took off, running into the darkness.

An hour later, Becca sat on a bed in the Emergency Department as a doctor finished stitching up the wounds. He wrapped a bandage around it, then gave her the first of four fast-acting rabies shots she'd need since Becca had never been vaccinated.

She'd called Damien and told him what happened. Of course, he offered to come get her and take her to the hospital. She refused and drove herself, mostly one-handed, as she tried to keep blood from dripping on the upholstery.

The doctor was mid-forties, male, with a nice head of slightly graying hair. His breath smelled of peppermint as he gave Becca instructions. Every time he touched her hand, she wished he would hold it and tell her how beautiful she was.

Instead, he declined to prescribe painkillers when Becca asked—even after she told him she was a doctor herself—shook her hand and wished her a good night.

4

Three weeks had passed since Becca met the man at the bar and went with him to a motel. Three weeks since Damien apologized (to her!) for not staying on top of the household chores. That was almost enough to make her confess, but she told herself the guilt (God, how she hated that word) would fade with time.

And it did.

She fell into a comfortable, if boring, rhythm with Damien. They ate dinner together every night at the dining table while Kelly rolled around on a play mat nearby. The dinner was always something Damien made and had ready for her when she came through the door, and she couldn't even enjoy the food without that emotion (she wouldn't name it, wouldn't think it) scratching at the back of her mind.

He'd ask about her day, and she'd tell him the bare minimum. Even that bothered her; small talk seemed such a burden. At some point, she realized she had never asked him about his day. She'd ask about Kelly, but never him.

And that realization, did it just make the guilt worse? She thought it did, so one night she lay in bed staring up at the dark while Damien slept beside her. She tried to think of the affairs (but is that what they were, affairs?) as something in the past. Events that were disconnected from the present moment. If she could find her way back to the place they'd been when things were good, when they were happy, maybe she could forget about them. Maybe she could convince herself she wasn't all the things she believed she was. But still, she felt like an actress on the set of her own life. She wasn't happy or fulfilled, which she couldn't fake.

From that point on, Becca tried to be more engaged in her marriage. She treated her husband kindly and started talking to him at dinner. Things seemed better until she left the office for lunch and ran into an old boyfriend at the restaurant. Married, three kids, the manager of a large downtown bank. She hadn't seen him in over ten years, and Mitchell Brandenburg had aged well. From the tailored suit to the mostly trim figure, it was clear Mitch took care of himself and his appearance.

He had just finished a meeting but stayed and joined Becca for a drink. The conversation was easy and fun. They both brushed over their personal lives and reminisced about old times—the places they'd been, the things they'd done, the people they used to know.

Becca told herself Mitch was just an old friend and did some rearranging of memories and attachments to avoid thinking about how she would feel if it was Damien having lunch with an old flame.

Still, the guilt that had been slowly diminishing over the last three weeks started growing again, like a painful tumor in her chest that took up space and made it harder to breathe.

As she sat across from Mitch Brandenburg, Becca was shocked at how badly she wanted to grab his hand and feel his skin on hers. Sure, it would be wrong, but maybe it could reverse that warm bloom under her ribs. Many women remained with their husbands *only* because they had someone on the side, another person who appealed to the parts of themselves their husbands could not.

Most people from the past that Becca ran into, she found them changed somehow, but not Mitch. He was the same as she remembered, maybe even more himself than he had any right to be. All that charm, that charisma was still present, tempered by age and experience. A little gray shone at his temples in his otherwise dark hair, and Becca wondered what her life would be if she'd never broken up with him.

Why did she? Searching her memory, she couldn't find a good reason. Boredom, if she was honest with herself. Curiosity about what else might be out there. He never cheated on her, never hurt her. She just decided one day that they should separate. Mitch did his best to talk her out of it, but in the end, she wouldn't budge, so he packed all his things and moved out of the apartment they'd shared downtown.

And then they lost touch. Until now.

After lunch, Mitch walked Becca back to her car. He gave her a warm smile and gently touched her arm. She felt a little spark as his fingertips touched her bare skin, and before she could stop herself, she was leaning in, eyes closed, and pressing her lips to his.

Mitch Brandenburg kept his mouth closed and his hands by his side. Becca felt his whole body stiffen. He pulled away and looked at her with sadness.

"I'm sorry if you thought this was something more," he said. "I didn't mean to give the wrong impression."

Becca hoped, prayed, that a dark hole would open beneath her feet and swallow her whole. All her nervousness about making the first move incinerated, and the ashes glowed with shame. No, embarrassment.

She put a hand to her face as Mitch said, "I'm in love with my wife."

"Oh my god," Becca managed. "I'm sorry. I… I don't know what else to say except I'm sorry."

Mitch took one step backward, like Becca might suddenly try to kiss him again. "Look, I know you're not asking for advice but consider counseling, okay? Shauna and I have been going together for a few years, and it really helps keep us centered. Focused."

Becca tried not to laugh behind her hand. The statement was so ridiculous it almost hurt. She and Damien in counseling? Weak people needed therapy, and no amount of talking about problems could make her see Damien as anything less than a weight dragging her down.

"I want what's best for you," Mitch said, looking directly into Becca's eyes. "I want to see you do well."

Becca let her hand fall and suddenly saw Mitch as he really was. His hair had thinned, for one thing. And it wasn't just a little gray, it was a lot. He'd be mostly bald in just a few years, and the weight he'd gained around his middle would gradually spread to his chest and neck. The suit he wore wasn't that nice, and the knot in his tie was so asymmetric it looked like it'd been tied by a child.

She finally did laugh. A harsh and humorless noise that made Mitch blink in surprise.

"All you had to say was 'no,'" Becca said. "You didn't have to be cruel."

She noticed the patch of stubble along his neck that he'd missed while shaving.

"I don't want anything from you," she said, smoothing out her blouse and digging through her purse for the car keys. "I felt bad for you, okay?"

Mitch said quietly, "Okay," and turned to walk away. He looked back once and said, "Take care of yourself," before disappearing into the crowd crossing the busy street.

"Fuck off," Becca muttered.

A tube of lip balm and a pack of gum fell to the sidewalk as she swept her hand back and forth for the keys. She heard the metallic jingling, but her fingers couldn't find them. Finally, she dumped out the entire contents of the purse. Coins, receipts, coupons, a prescription pad, tampons, and a key fob spilled onto the sidewalk. She carefully knelt, grabbed the keys and the prescription pad, shoved them back into the purse, and left the rest where it fell.

She drove back to the clinic in silence, shocked at how angry she felt. How ashamed. Even more than after the night she'd spent with the stranger in the motel. Why? A feeling she hadn't experienced in years, and it ached in her gut like a bad meal.

Rejection.

Becca was only a few seconds away from analyzing what she felt, asking herself where she'd gone wrong when the full parking lot of the clinic came into view. She saw a mother carrying a coughing child, wrapped in a colorful blanket, through the front doors and, instead, pictured Mitchell Brandenburg's doughy face, his droopy eyes, and his asthmatic voice.

She didn't want him. She could do so much better.

Dr. Becca Huntley stayed at the clinic after all the CNAs, nurses, and front desk staff had left for the night. She called Damien and told him she needed to finish up some charting before coming home, and of course, he was understanding and apologetic that she had to stay late. His kindness felt more like an insult, and she hung up the phone frustrated and annoyed.

She logged into a social media account from her work computer and looked up Mitchell Brandenburg. She didn't know why but it was a compulsion that lurked in the back of her psyche.

She found his profile with a few clicks and scrolled through bright, sunny pictures of him, his wife, and his three kids. The wife probably wasn't as thin as she'd been when they first married, but in one photo, she had an arm linked with Mitch's, her head resting against his shoulder as they watched their kids (two boys and one girl) dance on an emerald-green lawn, and her face was radiant. Beautiful and content. She looked... loved.

It's all a lie, she thought. *They're not happy. None of us are happy.*

5

Becca waited until after 9 pm, when Damien would put Kelly down for the night. She pictured the girl's sweet, chubby face, toothless smile, her downy hair and felt something uncomfortably close to guilt.

She deserves parents who love each other.

Becca knew Damien loved her, unreservedly. Whatever she wanted from him, he'd give without hesitation. But she didn't feel the same way about him.

I love him. Of course, I love him.

She gathered her laptop and slipped it into her bag, then took a drink of water and popped two ibuprofen to halt the headache that was coming on. She picked up her cell phone to check the time and saw a picture of her small family. Taken only a few weeks earlier at the birthday party of a friend's child. Damien looked good dressed in a polo shirt and shorts. Becca wore a patterned, sleeveless dress, her long hair cascading over one shoulder. Damien held Kelly, bouncing her up and down to illicit a drooly smile, and then the photo was snapped.

A family portrait.

Damien and Kelly appeared genuinely happy, captured in a moment of joy. Becca, though, looked disconnected from their happiness. She smiled, but it was the rehearsed smile of someone aware a picture was being taken. The two people next to her were lost in each other for a moment outside the camera's eye.

She couldn't look at Damien without thinking of what he should do, what he wasn't doing, and how it affected her. Everything she thought and felt about him was through the lens of a *self*.

Is that love?

The ring of the office phone startled her and set her heart racing. It rang again, a shrill electronic bell that sounded even louder in the silent room.

The caller ID showed a series of asterisks instead of a number. The clinic operated as a primary physician's office as well as urgent care, so it wasn't surprising that some desperate parent would try and call after hours, either needing advice or a prescription.

The phone rang again, and Becca felt the noise in her teeth.

She imagined a harried mother on the other end as her child lay beside her, soaked in fever sweat. She probably looked up the website, saw "urgent care," and decided to call.

Another ring.

Becca picked up the receiver, held it to her, and said, "Hello?"

She knew something was wrong before she even got the word out of her mouth.

Breathing on the other end. But not normal breathing. Like wind through a cracked window, the high-pitched wheeze of someone gasping for breath with a swollen airway.

"Can you hear me? This is Dr. Huntley at the Pediatric Associates Clinic. Do you need help?"

The breathing continued. So loud and so close that it distorted through the speaker. Each breath raspy. Air being let out of a balloon. If Becca could see the patient, she knew the retractions would be pronounced. A deep inhale that didn't bring in as much air as was needed but pulled the flesh inward between the ribs, showing each bony protrusion.

"If you can hear me, you need to get to an ER immediately. They can give you medicine to help with the breathing. You may have an infection, as well. Possibly pneumonia. Please…say something if you can hear me."

The breathing got louder as if the person on the other end moved the receiver closer to their mouth, and the sound made Becca shudder. It reminded her of the panic she felt when Kelly got croup for the first time. When she lay weak and feeble, crying, each breath a harsh and shallow thing. And despite all her training, Becca couldn't shake the feeling that her daughter was in serious trouble. How could a child make a sound like that and be okay? She and Damien ended up taking Kelly to the ER, where she got a dose of the steroid dexamethasone, which decreased the swelling of her larynx and allowed air to get where it was needed.

"Can you hear me?" Becca said again, almost shouting because the breathing was so loud now it hurt her ears.

"If you don't get to the ER right away, things could get bad."

She didn't want to frighten the person on the other end any more than necessary, but the breathing, as best as she could tell, indicated a severely inflamed airway.

The line went dead, and Becca was left holding a quiet receiver.

She gathered her car keys and left the clinic through a side door that locked behind her. It was dark and cold outside. Clouds defined by moonlight drifted across the sky, revealing black space dotted with white stars. Tiny needle punctures in the night.

Damien was either playing video games right then, or he was finishing up whatever chores he didn't have time to get to earlier. Because he was afraid of what his wife would say. How she'd sharpen those tasks into weapons and use them against him.

The clinic parking lot was empty except for her car. An imported vehicle she'd dreamed of owning since she started med school. She never told Damien how she didn't feel any of the joy she expected when she finally signed the paperwork and purchased it. Just one more thing that did nothing to fill the emptiness at the center of herself, a black hole from which nothing escaped.

Keys in hand, she crossed the parking lot. Her car sat bathed in the bright glow of the only streetlight. A row of tall hedges that separated the clinic lot from the business next door rustled with the breeze. Leaves shivering together. Somewhere in the distance, crickets chirped.

The hedges rustled again, but this time there was no breeze. Twigs cracked, and Becca saw motion near the ground as if something was coming from the other side.

She froze and wondered if she'd have time to dig through her purse for the mace. The news was full of reports of women being randomly attacked and robbed, or worse, and she would not go down without a fight.

Mace the bastard and call the cops.

A branch snapped, and a bird resting atop the hedges took flight. Becca watched it rise, a silhouette against the darker sky, and when she turned back to the wall of leaves and branches, she saw a shape hunched low to the ground and two bright white circles trained right on her. Full white, as if the pupils were gone.

The light, she thought. *It has to be the light making its eyes look like that.*

Becca walked faster with one hand shoved deep into the purse. Her fingers felt disconnected from the rest of her. Numb, useless things brushing up against objects but unable to grasp them. Her entire arm was weak, as if she had worked too long, and her blood sugar had crashed.

More rustling, another twig snap. She swung to look at the hedges, but the eyes were gone. It took her brain a few seconds to register the fact that what she'd seen crouching in the brush was not a human face. Her heart thumped wildly and sweat trickled down her back as she fumbled for the keys.

She turned and glanced back as the hedges swayed with the movement of something stalking between them. She caught another glimpse of stark white eyes staring at her.

A head emerged from the branches, black with a long snout, and large, almost bat-like ears that stood straight up. There was something familiar about the beast, and Becca let out a long exhalation when she realized it was a dog. Probably a stray, or maybe lost, hiding until she was gone, and it could look through the dumpster for scraps of food.

The creature came out of the bushes and stood on the asphalt just at the edge of the light. It lowered its head as Becca slowed her walk, its strange white eyes following her movement. She remembered the other dog she'd seen several weeks earlier, and this one looked like it could be the parent of that other animal. Same shape to the head, same strange demeanor, only this one was bigger. Much bigger. She couldn't see the fur pattern well, but even the canine's silhouette looked lean and powerful.

The scars on her hand throbbed a little as she remembered the other dog, the way it had latched onto her flesh. She could still feel the warmth of its breath on her skin, the thick drool that ran down her arm as it shook its head back and forth.

She felt only a little better knowing what had been watching her. "Hello," she said softly. "I'm sorry I don't have any snacks for you." The animal's head tilted at the sound of her voice.

"I'm just going to get in my car and drive home, okay?" she said.

Her shoes clacked on the pavement as she neared the vehicle. She lifted the fob to unlock the door when she heard a sound that made her think the car was already running. A low rumbling, like an idling engine. She paused, hand outstretched, and listened.

It wasn't the car.

She looked over to the dog, and the sound grew louder. A growl, coming from its chest. The mouth parted to reveal long fangs as white as its eyes. It appeared as though the animal was made entirely of darkness and light. Its whole body was as black as a sky without stars, but the eyes and teeth were so bright they seemed lit from within.

Becca ran.

As soon as her legs began moving, the dog came unbolted and shot into the light, tearing across the parking lot with an aggressive snarl. Becca stumbled in her modest heels until first one foot, then the other slipped out of the shoes, and she ran the rest of the way in her stockings.

Her body slammed up against the side of the car as she mashed the fob. The car unlocked with a *beep*. She threw open the door, nearly fell into the driver's seat, slammed the door shut, and hit the lock button just as the creature crashed into the vehicle, causing it to rock, and a demonic face, twisted with rage and covered in black fur rose up into view, bright teeth dripping with strings of saliva.

Becca couldn't help but let out a scream. The animal snarled and snapped, as though it didn't realize there was glass between them, smearing frothy drool on the window.

The light above her car flickered. Something she'd never seen it do, and she had a moment of panic as she imagined the engine sputtering when she tried to start it.

The animal jumped up again, and she heard a metallic screech as its claws scratched along the door. It let out short, harsh barks as it bit at the window. One white eye glared at her, and she felt strange that the dog knew her. That it hated her, and her specifically, for some unknown reason. It wanted to sink its teeth into her flesh and tear away until her screams were choked out by blood loss.

She jammed her finger against the start button, holding her breath and only letting it out when she felt the engine rumble to life. The dog dropped back down out of view as Becca put the car in drive. She looked behind her, hoping the animal would be crushed underneath the tires as she backed out of the space. She punched the gas, and the car lurched forward, slamming into the concrete base of the streetlight. Metal crunched, and she heard the crack of glass as one headlight winked out.

Becca was so pissed at herself that she almost felt like crying. She'd put the car in drive instead of reverse. She pushed the gearshift forward to R and was about to hit the gas again when she heard more snarling and felt the car rocking back and forth. She pushed her face against the glass and looked down to see the dog with its fangs embedded in the front tire. Its head snapped from side to side as the teeth tore away chunks of rubber.

A small pop, then the hiss of air leaking.

She pushed the gas pedal down, more metal crunching as the vehicle backed off the base. She kept the pedal to the floor until the back tires thudded up over the curb and the hedge branches scratched against the trunk like a woman with long nails. Becca put the car in drive and squealed out of the parking lot, the driver's side tire thumping with each revolution.

When she got to the road, she looked back to see the dog standing underneath the streetlight, dark fur glistening, white eyes staring straight at her. She drove as fast as she could, hoping she could make it home before the tire went completely flat. Adrenaline coursed through her veins, making her hands tremble as she gripped the steering wheel. She kept seeing those bone-white teeth tearing at the wheel, and she imagined that it was her leg, her stomach, her face. She felt sick, like she wanted to vomit, as she pulled onto her street. She had no idea how she'd explain what happened to the car to Damien, and that's when she realized her instinct was to lie.

She was attacked by a dog. That was the truth. Why did there need to be another explanation?

She pulled into the driveway, saw the glow of the TV through the curtains, and for once, was glad Damien was still up playing video games. He was awake, and Becca didn't want to be alone.

6

In a dream, Becca heard the robotic bird-like chirp of her cell phone ringing. She tried to stay connected to the images she saw in her sleep—a white sand beach, blue water, a cool breeze, the warmth of the sun—but they faded as the ring came through again.

She jerked awake and sat upright in bed. She searched the nightstand for her phone, but it wasn't there. A band of sunlight streamed into the room between the curtains and stretched along the bed. Damien's voice came from downstairs, talking to someone. Maybe Kelly.

Becca jumped out of bed, snatched her robe from the chair, and was about to run and jump in the shower before she remembered it was Saturday. The clinic was closed.

After using the bathroom, Becca went downstairs. Damien was still talking, firmly telling someone that they needed to get to the hospital. He didn't sound worried, more confused than anything.

She entered the kitchen to see Damien with her cell phone in his hand, and her heart thumped with fear of thinking he went through her texts, maybe her call log. Maybe her credit card app. She tried her best to smile and muttered, "Good morning," as she brushed by him to get to the coffee pot.

Kelly cooed from the living room floor, where she lay on her play mat.

Damien leaned over, kissed her cheek, and said, "Good morning. Hope you slept well."

Becca poured coffee into a cup and added creamer until the liquid turned a pale brown.

"Who were you talking to?" she asked.

Damien handed over her phone. "I got up early and took your phone so you could sleep in."

Again, that feeling. *Guilt.* Of course, Damien wasn't going through her phone. That wasn't him. He knew a ring or buzz would wake her. The phone was always ringing or buzzing. Nights, weekends, didn't matter.

"Who was it?"

"Don't know," Damien said. "There was just someone breathing on the other end. Whoever it was, they sounded sick. Wheezing, I guess, like an asthma attack."

Becca tightened her grip on the coffee mug so she wouldn't drop it.

"Did they say anything?"

He shook his head. "Just breathing. I couldn't tell if it was a prank or not, so I told them to get to the hospital if they were really sick."

Weakness flooded Becca's legs like they'd give out if she didn't sit down right away. She shuffled to the living room and lowered herself next to Kelly. The little girl looked up into her mother's eyes and smiled.

7

Becca took Damien out to the driveway and showed him the damage to her car and the story of how it happened. He listened, in shock, without saying a word until she finished. Then he wrapped his arms around her and whispered, "I'm so glad you're okay. Don't worry about the car. We'll get it fixed."

Damien changed into an old shirt and jeans, jacked up the car, put on the spare, and then drove to a tire store to purchase a new one.

Afterward, they took Kelly to the park and then went on a walk to a farmer's market, where Damien bought fresh vegetables for dinner that evening. Back at home, while Damien cooked, Becca put on some music and danced with Kelly held tight in her arms.

Holding her daughter as they moved to the rhythm, Becca was astonished at the unexpected and overwhelming love that filled her heart. This precious girl belonged to her, came from her. She grew inside Becca's body. Her skin, eyes, hair, fingers, and toes... everything about her was perfect. As perfect as anything could be.

She looked over and caught Damien watching them from the kitchen, a smile on his face. He mouthed the words "I love you," and Becca mouthed them back without hesitation.

After they put Kelly to bed, Damien and Becca sat on the couch with glasses of red wine as jazz played on the stereo. They talked about summer vacation plans and places they could take Kelly. Damien told her that the Westerfield's son would be graduating from college in Massachusetts soon, and they asked if Damien could keep an eye on the house while they were away.

Becca was stretched out on the cushions with her head resting in Damien's lap while he stroked her hair. She couldn't remember the last time she'd felt so relaxed. Maybe it was the wine or the long week, but Becca felt herself starting to drift off when Damien twisted around and moved the curtain.

"What is that?" he said.

Becca sat up. "What's what?"

"In the yard. See it?"

She knelt on the couch, peered through the window to the yard outside, and struggled to swallow as acid burned her throat.

Damien set his wine glass on the sill. "I think it's a dog."

Where the footpath from their front door met the sidewalk sat a large black dog staring straight at them. There was no doubt in Becca's mind it was the same dog from the clinic. Some part of her wished she hadn't insisted Damien sell his 9mm pistol because right now, she wanted to take that weapon, march outside, and blow the fucker's head right off.

"Look at that thing," Damien said, his nose touching the glass. "What the hell is wrong with its eyes?"

The eyes were the same all-white as they'd been when the thing ripped her tire to shreds when it tried to claw its way through the door, but it looked even bigger now. Becca had no idea how that was possible, but even sitting its head would probably be as high as her stomach.

Becca tried to speak, but the words just wouldn't come.

"I think it's a Doberman," Damien said, and Becca was amazed at how unafraid he seemed. And why should he be afraid? They were inside, and the dog was outside.

"I've never seen a pure black Doberman," he said. "Usually, they have some brown markings."

Becca finally found her voice, and it shook when she spoke. "We should call animal control. That's a dangerous breed."

Damien ignored her, climbed off the couch, went to the front door, and slipped on his shoes.

"What are you doing?" Becca asked.

"I'm going to see if it has a tag."

"You can't go out there!"

"If it has an owner, we should call them before we call animal control."

Becca pictured her tire, how the creature's teeth ripped off chunks of thick rubber so big the tire went flat. Damien hadn't seen that. He didn't know what she did. He hadn't seen it snarling or the hate in its eyes. And she couldn't tell him about the nagging feeling she had that it was the *same* dog that wanted to tear her to shreds. That would be crazy.

"Please," she said, trying to catch her breath. "Don't go out there. Please."

Damien turned and looked at her, saw the fear on her face, and put a hand on her shoulder. "Shit, I completely forgot about what happened."

For the second time that evening, Becca fought tears as her husband embraced her.

"I'll call," Damien said. "Okay? I won't go out there and get my hand bit off."

Damien took his phone out of his pocket as they walked back to the couch, and when they looked out the window again, the dog was gone.

8

Becca Huntley tried to sleep, but she kept waking up from nightmares in which she lay tangled in the sheets of a bed that wasn't hers. Moments where the thrill was gone, guilt settled over the dark room like a creeping shadow reaching from wall to wall. A shadow that moved and breathed.

9

There was something wrong inside; she'd known it since she was young. A competition, a prey drive. Other girls, girls at school, probably thought Becca had so much confidence that it twisted into arrogance. In truth, Becca was self-conscious about every single aspect of her life. The absent dad, the mom who worked as a waitress at a shitty diner. The secondhand clothes purchased from thrift shops, holes sewn up by her mom. The crappy apartment in a crappy neighborhood where sirens were more common than the jingle of the ice cream truck.

Yes, she was teased mercilessly by other girls. A constant stream of abuse that was both passive and aggressive, and Becca became convinced whispers were just as violent as a foot sneaking out to trip her when she didn't expect it or fingernail scratches on her face. She preferred the physical fight to the psychological one.

Becca found her weapon when she was fourteen, but looked like she was going on twenty-one. That was when boys really took notice. And they didn't seem to care much about where she came from, who her parents were (or weren't) and whether a stranger had broken in her shoes and then donated to Goodwill.

Fourteen was the year she started wearing makeup. When she realized that how she walked, how she laughed and changed the inflection of her voice, could render a boy speechless and smitten.

That's when she learned how to steal.

It started with shoplifting clothes, shoes, and makeup, and eventually became stealing boyfriends. Everything she wore and how it transformed her behavior felt like armor. Becca would see those girls who thought they were untouchable sitting outside between classes, fighting with a boy whom Becca had charmed.

It was the only time she felt good. The hunt. The kill.

But that wasn't normal, was it?

She truly believed she'd grow out of it someday once she had a good job, a husband who loved her, a home, a child. Now, she had all that and more, and still… still she felt the pull to steal. To sink her teeth into something bloody and tear away at it.

Something was broken inside her. She sat in her office at the clinic, typed Mitch Brandenburg's name into the search bar of the social media website, and gazed at his perfect pictures again. He wasn't really all that handsome. Not her type anyway, and he didn't make her heart flutter like Damien did when he smiled and played with Kelly on the floor. She treated him like shit sometimes, but she did genuinely love him.

What in the hell was she doing?

Becca couldn't answer that question, not even to herself. She felt pulled in a direction she didn't want to go and was powerless to stop. She didn't want Mitch; she wanted to know if she could have him.

Broken. She knew it, so why couldn't she change? And even more than that, why did she believe she couldn't?

She imagined Damien walking through her office door, carrying Kelly in one arm and a bag of takeout in the other. Surprising her for lunch. She imagined him glancing at her computer screen and seeing images of an old boyfriend. There would be nothing she could say to make him believe it was innocent and nothing she could do to erase the hurt that would appear on his face like a bruise.

Sometimes the people we love know us better than we know ourselves, she thought. *Is he really blind to what I am, or does he just pretend not to see it?*

She scrolled through a few more pictures, knowing she should close the internet and get some fresh air. Instead, she clicked the little envelope button to send a direct message and typed: *Mitch, I'm sorry for how I acted the other day. That was inappropriate and out of line. It was just so good to see you and catch up, and I can't help but wonder if there's still something between us. If so, please let me know. I still think about you sometimes. If not, can we just act like this never happened?*

Her finger clicked the send button half a second before her brain screamed to delete the message. By then, it was too late, and the chambers of her heart pumped blood that had suddenly thickened. Her head swam a little, and her neck became blotchy from the rush.

She thought of that old story of the venomous snake who asks a frog to take him across the river. The frog agrees, but only after making the snake promise not to bite him. Halfway across the river, with the snake on his back, the frog feels something puncture his skin. He looks back to see the snake's fangs dripping with blood. As the venom courses through the frog, paralyzing his legs, he says, "Now we're both going to die? Why would you do that?"

The snake replies, "Because I'm a snake."

Becca looked down at the raised hair on her arm and half expected to see scales instead of skin. She's a snake. Always has been. She bites everyone around her, even the ones who could save her. She'd rather drown than change who she is, her nature, and that made tears burn in the corners of her eyes.

Her office phone rang.

10

She somehow knew she wouldn't hear speaking on the other end. A little spark of electricity on the back of her neck told her it would be the breathing voice. A split-second glimpse into a future moment that was about to happen.

"Hello?"

She held the receiver away from her head, and as soon as she heard that air wheezing through an inflamed airway, the electricity sparked over her scalp.

"If you need help, get to a fucking hospital and stop calling me!" she yelled, then slammed the phone down.

It'd ring again. And she knew she'd pick up again. But when that electronic chime rang, it still caught her off guard and made her whole body jump off the chair.

Her fingers wrapped around the receiver and lifted it from the cradle. She thought she'd put it to her mouth and breathe right back at them as loud as she could.

Instead, she heard a voice coming through the speaker. A harsh whisper. "Come home."

Behind it, Becca heard the wheeze. There was a moan in there somewhere, mixed in with the sound of air being squeezed through a tight opening.

Steroids, Becca thought. *Whoever that is, they need a combination of oral and inhaled steroids immediately.*

"Come home," the voice said again. "Your family needs you."

Becca was about to say something sarcastic and cutting when the words finally registered.

"My family? What the hell are you talking about?"

Just breathing now. Louder, right into the speaker.

The room went stifling. Becca inhaled, and it was hot and dry. Her lips stuck together as she tried to think of something else to say. Sweat inched down from her hairline and around her jaw. She wiped her eyes, and her finger came away smeared with mascara.

"They need you." A man's voice disguised in its quietness. Its insistence. And there was something familiar about it, something that made her hands tremble. "Come home."

11

Becca grabbed her purse and ran out through the back door to a low sky pregnant with gray clouds, threatening to rain. She half-jogged across the parking lot, trying not to think about the other night with the dog, and when she made it to her car, she forced herself not to look at the deep, jagged claws marks raked along the driver's side door. But she couldn't help but notice the pinkish holes on her hand, slowly dimming in color from wound to scar.

She got into the car and hit the starter button just as thunder growled through the sky like an angry dog, and rain fell on the windshield with a steady drone.

Her chest hurt as she pulled out of the driveway, almost t-boning an oncoming vehicle that laid into its horn while the driver held up his middle finger, glaring at her until she was out of view.

She pushed a button on the steering wheel and said, "Call Damien," but her voice was froggy with tears and phlegm. She hiccupped a little as she tried to stop crying, and a robotic female voice responded, "I'm sorry, please try again."

"Call Damien!" Becca yelled, and the car speakers came to life with the sound of the phone ringing.

She ran one red light, then another, slowing only to make certain she wouldn't crash, then hit the gas again.

The call went to Damien's voicemail, his calm, cheerful voice saying, "I can't get to the phone, but you can leave a message or send a text."

Becca slammed the heel of her hand against the steering wheel and let out a scream as she pushed the button again. "Call Damien."

She flicked the blinker, switched lanes, and gunned it to pass a slow-moving truck. She switched back to the other lane and pushed the needle past seventy miles per hour.

The phone kept ringing. A chirping that made her fingers grip the wheel even tighter. Were those tears running down her face?

She stole a glance at the rearview mirror, hoping to God a cop wouldn't try and pull her over because they'd end up in a chase.

If she had to guess, she'd say her heartbeat was at least twice the speed of her car. Thump-thumping like the heeled shoes of a doctor walking hospital halls at a brisk pace. Her arms and legs went weak.

Damien's voice, "I can't get to the phone—"

Becca hit the button a third time, "Call Damien!"

Rain rushed into storm drains and collected in puddles that the tires charged through, sending up a spray of water the wipers struggled to clear.

An absurd image popped into her head, and she tried not to focus on it, but the picture developed anyway—an all-black Doberman with pure white eyes, a phone in its paw, saying, *"Come home, Becca... come home."*

Her hands were slick on the vinyl steering wheel, and it almost slid out of her grip as she made a hard right turn onto a residential street. The tires screeched. Her purse flew off the seat onto the floor, spilling its contents.

She turned left down one street, right down another, narrowly avoiding a young boy in a raincoat riding his bike.

Damien's phone kept ringing.

Becca saw their house up ahead. The lights were off, which gave her a strange sensation in the pit of her stomach. She pulled into the driveway and parked, put her head down on the steering wheel, and tried to catch her breath. The muscles in her neck and shoulder cramped and tightened into knots that strained her back. She got out and stood in the rain, let it pour over her face. She imagined opening the door and finding Mitchell Brandenburg and Damien stone-faced and serious side by side on the sofa. Even worse, she imagined the man from the bar or the doctor from the conference. She imagined her mistakes inside her home, her sanctuary, soiling everything good in it.

She would pay every penny she had to make it go away. But it wouldn't fix anything, would it? It wouldn't fix Damien or their small family. It sure as hell wouldn't fix her.

Becca tried to look in through the front windows as she made her way up the walk, but no light glowed around the closed curtains' edges. The house was dark, and the front door was unlocked as she pressed the latch and pushed it open.

12

When Becca was a little girl, she used to play Hide and Seek with her older brother. She'd stand just outside the front door and count to one hundred while David went and hid. The only rules were that you had to hide somewhere in the two-story house, and the garage didn't count.

Once she stepped inside, Becca would be as quiet as she could, and she'd enter each room and stand there. Listening. Each breath a silent, measured thing. It wasn't the listening so much as it was "feeling." She'd feel the presence of another person in the room, another body generating heat, pumping blood, breathing oxygen. It would exist as a faint pressure on her skin, an awareness of sorts that she wasn't alone.

Often, that sense got stronger as she crept to each potential hiding place and eventually found David curled under a bed or behind a dresser to the point that he accused his sister of cheating.

Becca felt that now, as she stepped into her own home. Instantly, her senses were alert to the presence of people other than Damien and Kelly. She knew their sounds, their smells, but there was another scent wafting through the entryway. An odor of sweat and clothing washed with a different detergent. Earthy, herbal smells mixed with food of some kind.

She almost yelled out, "Hello," but stopped herself. She hadn't thought to grab anything that could be used as a weapon, and she didn't want to give away her exact location in case there was someone waiting just on the other side of the living room wall. Waiting with a sledgehammer to bash her head in.

A sound. The small moan of an animal.

Her heart beat like she'd just run a marathon. Pumping in her chest and pounding through her skull. Her shoes clicked on the tile as she approached the living room. The feeling, the sensation of *other people*, grew stronger. She put one hand on the wall, leaned her head into the room, and stopped breathing.

She saw Damien sitting in a chair pulled in from the kitchen table. Silver tape strapped each leg to the chair. More wrapped around his chest and arms, keeping him upright and preventing him from moving more than just his hands. A bundle lay across his lap.

Kelly, Becca thought. *Thank God.*

Another strip of silver tape covered Damien's mouth. Strings of blood ran down from a gash above his eye and over the tape. He looked up when he saw Becca's head come around the corner, and his eyes widened in fear.

A few of the other kitchen chairs were toppled over. A ceramic bowl lay shattered on the kitchen floor, lettuce and salad dressing strewn about.

A home invasion? A robbery?

She was about to run to him and tear the tape off his mouth when she noticed the two people standing behind Damien, hidden in shadow. Becca froze. Her right hand clenched into a fist.

Two dark silhouettes, one tall and one short.

They stepped forward into the light in unison, and it took Becca's brain a second to find their faces in her memory: a man and a woman, shoulder to shoulder.

The woman cradled something in her arms, and she rocked gently back and forth, a familiar motion to soothe a child to sleep. She looked straight at Becca, her eyes cold and watery.

The woman's husband came forward, stopping at Damien's side. Gray light streaming in through the glass of the front door glinted along the blade of a large knife gripped in his hand. The man's black hair hung in greasy strands around blue eyes so pale they almost looked like stone. His mouth twitched, and he grimaced as if he was holding back tears. He looked different than the last time Becca saw him. He was even more tired and worn down as if he hadn't slept in days, perhaps weeks.

Their last name came to her in a haze of fear. *Ephrem.*

Becca held up her hands, afraid to move too suddenly in case that knife would flash through Damien's throat and leave him gasping for breath through a bloody hole in his neck.

"Listen," Becca said softly, trying to make her voice not shake. "If your little girl is still sick, we should call an ambulance and get her to a hospital."

The man continued staring at her. His eyes narrowed.

"How did you find where I lived?" Becca asked.

The man remained silent, and Becca moved one foot along the carpet, testing to see if he'd let her.

She kept her hands raised, "I just want to check on my daughter."

Tears streamed from Damien's eyes. Glistening lines ran down his cheeks.

Becca moved her other foot, bringing her within slashing distance of the man with the knife.

"I just want to check on her, okay?"

The man said nothing.

Becca's eyes moved from Damien down to the bundle on his lap, and she couldn't hide or control the choked gasp that came out of her.

A dark, leathery face looked up at her. The eyes were closed, but the toothless mouth hung agape, giving her a glimpse of the black tongue inside. One hand lay curled against its chest, the fingers discolored and wrinkled like an old woman's.

Becca fell to her knees and reached out. Fine threads of hair broke apart and turned to dust as she stroked the infant's head. She let out a sob. Tears and snot dripped from her chin. Damien's chest shook as he moaned through the tape.

Becca could not understand. She'd seen their daughter just this morning, and she was fine. Why hadn't Damien called her if something was wrong?

Her vision narrowed and grew dim as she looked up at the man with the knife. He continued staring at her, watching every muscle spasm that wracked her face.

Then she heard that small sound again—the peaceful sigh of a sleeping baby—and Becca's eyes snapped up to the woman behind Damien, a bundle cradled in her arms. Its head turned just enough for Becca to see the profile—the lips, the nose—and she could barely speak the child's name.

"Kelly."

13

"We trusted you." The man's voice was calm as his other hand dug into the pocket of his pants and came out holding a cell phone.

Becca opened her mouth to speak, but the man interrupted.

"That same night, after we left your office, her breathing got worse. We gave her medicine, like you said, but it did nothing. She wouldn't stop crying, and that made her breathing even worse."

He held up the phone and pushed a button. The same raspy wheeze Becca heard whenever she answered an unknown number came out of the speakers.

Stridor. A constricted airway. Breath squeezing through a narrow passageway. Ribs pressing against the skin, bending the flesh around each curved bone.

The man's wife clenched her eyes shut and turned her head away.

"She did not make it through the night," the man said, as he pressed the button again.

"I'm so... so—"

The man screamed, "I could smell the alcohol on your breath!" His spittle reached her face. "I could feel your judgment as you listened to our little girl's lungs, and it was you who deserved judgment." The man pointed to his own ear with the tip of the knife blade. "You hardly listened at all. You put the stethoscope to her chest and said she'd be fine. Why? Because you didn't want us there."

The man came around Damien's chair and knelt in front of Becca. His eyes pulsed. "I saw it, but it didn't come to me until much later." He put one hand on his chest, the left side. "You only listened to one lung. If you'd moved the stethoscope to the other side and listened… really listened, you would have heard my daughter drowning. You would have heard fluid inside her lung."

Becca broke into tears; she couldn't fight it anymore, and the man watched as her face contorted in pain. His own face was expressionless.

He stood and reached into his other pocket. "It's been following you ever since," he said. "With every mistake, it gets bigger and bigger. Stalking you, waiting." His fist opened, revealing strands of blond hair tied at one end with dark thread. He dropped it to the ground, and Becca remembered the clump of her hair that went missing from the trashcan.

"Please," Becca began, but the man lifted the knife and made a hiss that stopped her.

Asleep, Kelly squirmed in the woman's arms.

"You took our daughter," the man said, "and now we will take yours."

Becca's stomach twisted as she tried to catch her breath. "No, no! Please, I'll—"

A low growl came from behind her, the sound of a chainsaw idling inside the throat of a beast. Vibrations ran through the floor and up the palms of her hands as something heavy moved down the hallway.

She turned and saw the darkness shift and move as two stark, white eyes hovered in the air. Fangs the size of knives glistened in the low light. More vibrations came as the thing rushed down the hall. Its shape became clearer: the animal that bit her, that attacked the car, that sat sentry outside her home, only the creature had grown so massive that the tips of its pointed ears grazed the ceiling, its raven-black fur blended into the darkness, making it appear as though it were made of the dark. Pure dark with eyes and teeth.

Becca turned to plead with the man and saw him leaning over the dead child resting on Damien's lap, his lips pressed to the wrinkled skin of the girl's forehead. Tears dripped on her face.

The woman wrapped the blanket around Kelly's head, and Becca let out a howl, thinking *She's going to smother her, to kill her the same way her own child died, struggling for air* She jumped to her feet and rushed toward the woman, screaming the whole way.

The heavy footsteps from the hall grew faster, and the rumbling growl got louder. Becca managed to grab the woman's shoulder and tried to pry Kelly away, but she sensed something behind her and felt moist, warm air on the back of her neck. She turned and had to lean back to see the beast in total. It towered above her. Thick ropes of drool fell from its curled lips. The creature lowered its head until the white eyes stared into Becca's, and in a moment that seemed to exist between heartbeats, she saw every mistake like they were high-definition photographs, and the shame that flooded through her nearly drowned all her fear.

Until the creature's mouth opened and moved toward her, sucking in rays of dim light from the room, and she saw stars swirling in the back of its throat.

Looking at Damien, her mind sparked with everything she wanted to say to him, then to Kelly, sleeping peacefully in the woman's arms.

Be better than me, Becca thought. *Be better.*

The dripping teeth came closer, and Becca closed her eyes.

A couple exited the house and made their way down the concrete path to the sidewalk. The man kept his arm around his wife's shoulder as an excruciating shriek came from inside the house. The man knew a neighbor would hear the screaming and call the police. He quickened their pace.

The woman's muscles tensed, her face twitched at the sounds of pain, the corner of one eye trembled. The man pulled her close and kissed her forehead.

A name screamed at maximum volume with a raw throat became a gurgle and then silence. A few tears slipped from the woman's eyes as she gently rocked the child she held. The little girl, wrapped in a soft blanket, opened her large blue eyes and looked up at the woman. There was no judgment or fear. Even the gasping voice from the house, saying, "Help," did not seem to faze her. Her small legs kicked.

"Shhh," the woman said. "Shhh, Katya."

She glanced over at her husband to see if he approved. He smiled and squeezed her shoulder.

The baby stopped moving and focused on the woman's face, looking right into her eyes. The cold turned her tiny nose red.

"You like that name? Katya? It is your name now."

FULL FATHOM FIVE

1

Before he went by the name Julian Le Sang, in fifth grade, the boy I knew as Julian Schechter couldn't stop picking his nose. Before he was famous, before he stopped making public appearances, before his name was all over the news in big, bold headlines that made you believe he was some kind of psycho, before all that, he was just a shy kid with a bad habit.

The last time I talked with him was about six months ago. I'd been laid up in bed fighting the flu for several days, and when the phone rang, it was Julian. I wasn't surprised.

We talk several times a year. It's not something we ever planned, but he always calls exactly when I need to unload. He called after my first miscarriage. He called after my company downsized and I was left without a job. He called after my second miscarriage, after my son Alex was born, and again after my husband left me.

In fifth grade, he sat right behind me in Mr. Murphy's class, and I could hear the moist, sucking sound of Julian's finger digging around in his nostril, and then that distinctive wet pop when he pulled it out. This would be after recess when we were all outside playing four-square or basketball in the non-stop Portland drizzle. Everyone had runny noses when we came back inside the warm classroom.

I always thought of nose-picking as something done with a purpose. You know, when you get those thick, dried-up boogers that take up space like a small stone? You want to get it out, get rid of it, and move on. But it was something different for Julian.

Okay, let's start with this: Julian didn't have many friends. Or any friends at all, really. He was that kid everyone forgets they had a class with until years later in high school, hanging out in Greg Lester's parents' garage, and someone mentions him. Everyone makes that "ooohhh" sound as his face slowly materializes in their memories like an image on a Polaroid. But no one really remembers until Greg says, "Remember how he'd pick his nose until it'd bleed?"

That one detail is the only reason Julian stood out to most people at all. I wonder if maybe the nose-picking was partly a reaction to the fact that he blended so seamlessly into the background of our lives.

Until he didn't.

Greg was right. Julian would pick his nose so frequently, and so furiously that blood was almost always running out of his nostrils. Bright red trickles curving around his lips. It got to the point where Mr. Murphy had to buy extra boxes of tissue just for Julian. Even wrote his name on a box in black marker. I think Murph met with Julian's mom a couple of times about the nose-picking because I saw her come to the school, and Julian never got in trouble, never purposefully drew attention to himself. But after one of these meetings, Murph brought a new trashcan into class and placed it right next to Julian's desk.

A trashcan just to hold all the bloody tissues.

To make matters even worse, Julian had chronic allergies. Which meant he sneezed. A lot. And when he did, blood would spray out of his mouth and nose, covering his desk in tiny red droplets. One time, after school, I got home and changed out of my white t-shirt. Mom came to me with the shirt later and asked if I was okay. I said, yeah, why? She showed me the back of the shirt, and it looked like someone had taken a paintbrush dipped in red and flicked it at the fabric. Julian's blood splattered all over it.

Why am I writing this down now? I'll get to that eventually, but I should mention that Julian and I never stopped being friends. I got as close to him as he let anyone get. Our friendship started because I felt bad for him until I learned that Julian didn't feel bad for himself. He had every reason to, but self-pity just wasn't built into him. Anger was, and I think we all saw glimpses of that in his art over the years. You don't create the kind of work he does if you're not killing something inside yourself—a feeling, a memory.

So, back to fifth grade and the nose-picking boy.

The first time I ever talked to him was at recess. It was one of those rare December days when it was cold enough to freeze puddles to ice, but the sun was shining, and kids were running around the playground playing tag, shooting down the slides, smacking the tether ball around the tall pole. Seems that everyone was in some sort of group, except for one kid walking the perimeter of the soccer field by himself. Skinny kid, bad complexion, black hair hanging in his eyes. Head down, slow steps, one finger jammed up his nose.

I'm not sure why I went over to him other than the fact that Mom told me almost every day before school to be "a friend to the friendless." I imagined what it would feel like to be the person no one else wants to be around, so I ran across the blacktop to the soccer field and caught up to Julian Schechter. He came to a stop as I got close, but he didn't see me. He was holding out his right hand, palm up, and staring at it.

"Hey. Julian, right?" I called out.

He didn't look up, just lifted his left hand and looked at it, then turned his attention back to the right. He tilted it slowly in the sunlight. His eyes narrowed.

He startled a little when I came right up to him.

"I'm Marcy," I said, out of breath. "I sit right in front of-"

"I know who you are." He shoved his hand close to my face. "What does that look like to you."

I took a step back because his hand was covered in blood splatter. At first, I thought he'd cut himself on something and was about to suggest we go to the school nurse when I noticed the thin trickle of blood running from his nose.

To be honest, I thought it was a test to see if I was there simply out of pity, which I was, but he seemed to be saying, "This is me. Can you handle who I am?"

My stomach felt a little funny (I've never liked the sight of blood), but I leaned in anyway and squinted at Julian's hand. Looking for what, I didn't know.

"A tree, maybe?" I said.

Julian turned his hand around and looked at it again. "That's not a tree. Not even close. Is that what you see?"

"I don't know," I told him. "What do you see?"

That's when his interest in the blood vanished, and his cheeks turned bright with embarrassment. "Nothing, I just… I just thought it looked freaky."

"Freaky, how?"

He went to wipe his hand on his shirt, stopped, and wiped it on his pants instead. He looked at me, and I suddenly felt that he was older than me, much older. Not his size (if anything, I was a couple inches taller), but his face, his expression. It was such an adult look of irritation.

"What do you want, Marcy? Did your friends send you over on a dare to find out how weird I am?"

I felt bad he might think that about me, but why wouldn't he? No one talked to him for any reason, ever.

"No. I was just… curious, I guess."

"Curious?" He laughed, but it was a fake laugh, forced.

"It's okay," I said. "I can go."

I started walking away. Julian let me take a few steps, before he said, "You really want to know what it looks like to me?"

I turned around, and I didn't know what I expected to see, but it wasn't the anxious boy looking at me. He held up his hand with the smeared blood on the palm.

"I see glass," he said, his eyes widening like he was surprised to hear himself. "I see Mr. Murphy's face all cut. His eyes are open, but I don't think he's alive. His nose is—" Julian put two fingers to his own nose and pushed it to the side, like it's broken.

Inside, I'm thinking I need to tell my parents about this the moment I get home. Maybe even fake being sick and call from the nurse's office.

Instead, I said, "Yeah, he's a tough teacher. Can be pretty harsh sometimes."

Julian shook his head. "It's not what I want. It's what I see."

He held out the hand to me. The blood had turned darker as it dried. "When I look at this, it's like someone drew a picture in blood, and that's what it shows me."

In fifth grade, I had no idea what violence looked like, but I did know desperate and scared because that's what I saw on my father's face before he committed suicide when I was in third grade. And that's what I saw in Julian's face.

Okay, he saw something. But he really didn't want to see it. In fact, it terrified him.

His eyes filled with tears. "I don't know what this means."

"Maybe it doesn't mean anything."

Julian shook his head again, this time so hard that the tears slid sideways into his hair.

"I saw Grandma Martha's lungs right before she died. I saw Brody's tumors."

"Brody?"

"Our dog."

"Is he—?"

Julian nodded and closed his eyes. More tears leaked out.

He let his hands fall to his sides. The fingers curled into fists, and I wondered for a second if he was going to hit me. His eyes closed tight, and his teeth clenched together.

"Please, please don't tell anyone. I shouldn't have told you. I just needed...I needed to say it out loud. Hear what it sounded like."

I took his right hand, the bloody one, and held it as he cried.

The next day, Mr. Murphy wasn't at school. The principal came to our classroom and told us he had died. A car accident, a head-on collision when another car swerved into his lane. There was nothing he could have done to stop it from happening. As the principal spoke, I reached one arm behind me and grabbed Julian's left hand. His right hand was busy, digging in his nostril. I know because I heard the soft sound of blood dripping onto his desk.

2

Belief is a strange thing, isn't it? Most of the time, I don't think you have a choice in the matter. I could be wrong, but I don't think people can be convinced of anything they didn't convince themselves about first. Think about people holding signs outside a big corporate store. Does anyone drive by, see those signs, and change their mind? Maybe the sign is more for the person holding it than anyone else.

The point is, I believed Julian, and I didn't decide to believe him, it was just there inside me. I believed him even before we were told about Murph's death. It was the look on his face when he held out his bloody hand to me. His eyes, his pained expression. The fear and desperation. Whatever he saw, he didn't want to see it. And he needed someone else to know what he carried.

Then Murph's car accident happened, and I had this brief glimpse into what it might feel like to know things you weren't supposed to know.

We became close friends after that. I hesitate to say "best" friends because I never knew exactly how Julian felt. And that's something you need to know about him. Being close to Julian is not the same as being close to other people. He never invited me over to his house, though he came to mine a couple times. Mom said he was "sweet, but awkward." Which was true. I don't know what his family life was life because he never talked about it, but I don't think it was all that good. His clothes were rarely clean, and sometimes, he wore the same pants and shirt to school two days in a row. Wrinkled, like he'd slept in them. His hair was often greasy and uncombed, but sometimes it wasn't. I assumed his parents were divorced, but looking back, I'm not sure why I thought that. Maybe because I only ever saw his mom, and he never talked about his dad.

I realize I'm making Julian sound like the weirdo without any friends, but I guess that was true for me, too. Before I met Julian, I spent most lunch breaks by myself. Ever since my dad killed himself, other people seemed gray and lifeless, two-dimensional. I'd look at the kids in my class and see people who had no idea what real pain felt like. They'd never lost anything they couldn't get back.

Julian was the first person I met who seemed to understand that kind of hurt. He glowed with it, to be honest. It made his words, his mannerisms, his behavior unpredictable. He didn't care about offending anyone with what he said, which should come as no surprise if you've seen his art. He didn't change as he got older. All those pieces were present even as a kid. They just grew and assembled into something bigger and bloodier when he became an adult.

Somewhere in junior high, he stopped being so obvious about the nose picking. It didn't go away exactly, but he started getting interested in girls, and with that came some self-awareness. I came to understand, though, that picking his nose wasn't just a gross habit, it was the result of all the creative electricity that flowed through him. It needed somewhere to go, some movement in his body. Once he stopped picking (at least in front of people), his legs started bouncing up and down constantly, and he'd pick at the skin around his fingernails. Just picking and picking until there was torn, bloody skin. The papers he turned in were almost always stained with bloody smears and fingerprints. That habit never went away. The cuticles would scar and scab, and then he'd pick those. His nails were warped and misshapen from the constant abuse. But I never saw a finger up his nose again after seventh grade.

So, the big question is "Did it happen again?" Did he see death in his blood?

I think he did before we got into high school, but he never told me the specifics. There were a few days, though, when he was distant and irritable. That wasn't uncommon, but he had the same sort of desperate look he had that day on the soccer field. Like he knew something he shouldn't know. After days like that, I'd be on high alert, waiting for the axe to fall on someone around us. It never did, as far as I know, and that's when I started to suspect his vision might extend beyond our town and the people around us.

The first one he told me about was halfway through our freshman year. This girl in our Biology class, Jackie Mokely, was only fifteen but looked, dressed, and wore makeup like she was much older. She was always dating one upperclassman or another, some jock with a car who could take her off campus for lunch. I don't know how many boyfriends she burned through before she landed on Brett Andrews, but he was the last. A senior from a rich family with a shiny new car, he walked around campus with his arm wrapped so tight around Jackie you'd think he was going to break her. I won't bore you with the details, but he treated her like shit. He was an absolute dick, and everyone knew it. Arrogant and shallow, a terrible combination.

I always felt bad for Jackie. Sure, she was beautiful, but I couldn't help but wonder what had happened in her life to make her think someone like Brett was what she deserved.

It was a Monday when Julian met me at my locker before first period. He looked sick, feverish. The skin on his face was blotchy and red, his dark hair wet with sweat.

He pushed in close so no one could see the 3x5 card he handed me. His B.O. mixed with the smell of his unwashed clothes and made me feel embarrassed for him.

I took the card and whispered, "Deodorant, Jules. Get some."

"I will, I will."

"Serious. Get some today. You reek."

His face went a little redder, but I'd learned that no bullshit was the only way to get through to Julian. His brain blocked out anything that sounded dishonest, which is why he never heard the nasty stuff people said behind his back, or even to his face sometimes. But if you said what you meant, Julian listened.

I held up the card covered in dried blood. Drips and smears. "What am I looking at?"

He put his mouth so close to my ear I felt the rough skin of his lips. His fingers gripped my arm. "Jackie Mokely."

"No shit?"

"Drugs, I think. I see her lying on the floor, eyes open, foam coming out of her mouth."

I looked back at the card. "You see all that?"

Julian wiped his nose, and his hand came away wet with blood. His fingernails were all chewed to hell.

"I don't understand how you can see a person in this mess," I said.

"What does it matter?" Those gnarled fingers made their way into Julian's mouth, and his teeth searched for bits of skin to gnaw.

"I bet it's Brett," he said. "I bet that douchebag gives her something."

I held the card up to the light, like an invisible message might be there. Something that would start to glow. Julian put his hand on my arm and lowered it.

Not right then, but later, I learned what he saw—or...how he saw it—not the mechanics of it, but the details. It was blood at first, the same thing I saw, but the longer he stared at it, whatever "it" was, the blood formed patterns and shapes. The strands of red connected, twisted, until an image emerged. So clear, it looked like it was drawn in ink—red ink.

But I didn't know that then. Neither did Julian. Or, I should say he knew but didn't know how to say it. All he knew was he saw something.

"You have to tell her," I said.

Jules nodded, and his teeth snipped through a piece of fingernail. It sailed through the air in slow motion, a crescent moon-shaped thing tumbling over and over before hitting the floor and becoming lost.

"Hey Jackie, just wanted you to know I saw your death in my blood."

I raised my eyebrows.

He turned to my locker, put his forehead against the cool metal, and banged it once.

"Shit."

"You can't ignore this."

"I know."

"What if nothing changes?" he said.

"What if something does? You have a... what's the word? Responsibility."

The word I was searching for was "moral obligation," but I'm not sure that word entered my vocabulary until much later.

When Julian turned back to me, his eyes were filled with tears.

"I never wanted this," he said. "I never asked for it."

I used his own words against him. "It doesn't matter."

He banged his forehead against the locker one more time, took the bloody card from my hand, and walked down the hall into a crowd of people laughing, shoving, running. Like that piece of fingernail, Julian seemed to move in slow motion while everything around him flowed in normal time. He didn't have his backpack on, but he was carrying some-thing. Something heavy.

Jules spent the rest of the day trying to find the courage to say something to Jackie. As fate would have it, he passed her alone at her locker right before last period. He stopped and looked at her, at her face covered in thick makeup. Her sparkly eyes and long eyelashes. He didn't know her, and she didn't know him.

"Jackie," Julian said. "Please be careful. Whatever that means to you, just please be careful."

According to Julian, she didn't laugh or smile. She actually looked sad, and she said, "Thank you."

We figured if something happened, it would be over the weekend… parties and all, you know? Julian spent most of the time at my house. We agreed not to talk about Jackie.

I was trying to learn how to paint, so Jules picked up a brush and started messing around with it. I had a little potted plant sitting on the table, and no matter how hard I tried, I couldn't seem to make my hand move in a way that would create a plant on the paper.

Eventually, I gave up, stood, stretched, and went over to Julian's side of the table. I held my breath. He wasn't painting, not really. He was making these dark red watercolor strokes that were bold at the top and faded near the bottom. He somehow made one color look like seven different shades. It wasn't the technique or even the art that was so impressive, it was the small empty spaces between the strokes. Each one seemed to contain a world, a figure, a face, a tear, a hand, an object. I took a few steps back to see if it was an optical illusion, but it was all still there.

We never really talked about it because we didn't need to. Whatever Julian did, something inside him came pouring out. Whatever it was, it filled him up, and it was bigger and wider than what most of us have. It saw the world, maybe even time itself, in all the brushstrokes and blood drips.

On Monday morning, we came to school all tense. Just waiting for the principal to call an assembly and tell us that Jackie had died. But the announcement never came, and we passed Jackie in the hall on the way to class. Looking just as bright and beautiful as ever.

The following weekend went exactly the same way. We stressed and worried, but then school started back up and Jackie was fine.

Julian wondered out loud if maybe the images weren't always right, and I wondered the same thing, until six weeks later, Jackie didn't come to school on Monday. Whispers and rumors spread through the halls, and by the time we found out the truth, no one could believe it.

Jackie's dad had abandoned his family when Jackie was only three. Her mom remarried a decent man, and they all went on with their lives. Apparently, Mr. Mokely had been in and out of jail ever since, and he blamed his ex-wife for all his troubles. One warm spring night, only a week after his last stint in the clink, R.J. Mokely decided to drive to his ex's house. Once inside, he pulled out a gun and tied Jackie, her mom, and her stepdad to chairs around the kitchen table and forced them to drink the Drano he found under the sink. R.J. stood by and watched them all suffer and die right before he put a gun in his mouth and blasted his brains all over the ceiling.

Julian's face went pale when he heard the story. Like every drop of blood inside him had drained out. He looked like someone who had been locked outside in the snow for hours. Dozens of kids rushed past us, talking, crying, embracing each other.

Jules leaned over and whispered in my ear. "I told her to be careful. But there was nothing she could've done to stop this."

I was about to say something, anything, to take some of the guilt off him, but I knew he was right. He had seen what only one other person had seen, and that was the person who killed her. Beautiful Jackie, convulsing so violently the ropes that tied her to the chair cut into her wrists and ankles. The chair fell over. She hit her head on the floor, and the tender skin above her eye split open. She choked, gagged, and must have felt holes burning throughout the soft tissue of her esophagus. And those wide-open eyes, they would have seen her father standing over her, watching.

Thankfully, Jackie's younger half-brother survived because he was at a friend's house just down the street. I've always wondered what happened to him. Maybe I'll look him up after I finish writing this down. It's cliché, but I hope he found some peace, someone to love him and help repair all the hurt he must have felt.

Jackie Mokely's death was the last "blood ticket" (his term, not mine) that Julian showed me for three years.

3

I was lying in bed when he called this last time. Bottles of Tylenol, Advil, and cough syrup on the bedside table. A growing pile of crumpled tissues next to me. The TV played some home remodeling show I wasn't really paying attention to. Thankfully, Alex was sleeping and hadn't shown any signs of being sick.

I should mention here that Alex loved Julian, even though they'd only met once. Julian flew out and stayed with us for the week, and those two spent the entire time drawing, playing video games, having conversations about who-knows-what? Talking to adults has always been challenging for Julian, but he was the most *himself* I've ever seen when spending time with Alex. Who would have known that a seven-year-old boy could bring out that side of him? Right before he left, I let Julian paint the words *Everything Matters* on the wall above Alex's bed. Inside each letter was an image of something Alex loved. A soccer ball, bugs, a video game controller, paintbrushes, books, and a silhouette of me. Alex loved to lay in bed and stare at that mural. Whenever Julian called after that, his first question was always, "How's the little man?" And after we caught up, I'd hand the phone over to Alex and they'd talk for an hour.

That night, when the phone rang, I didn't want to pick it up. I didn't want to talk to anyone. My throat hurt too bad, and I felt like a claw was digging sharp talons into my skull. But then I saw Julian's name on the screen.

It had been six months since we'd talked and he sounded older, tired. Maybe I sounded the same to him. I told him I was sick and took the day off work to recover. He said he was sending me a text, a picture of a "blood ticket" and he'd explain it after I had the chance to look at it. My phone buzzed against my ear with the text, and I looked at what he'd sent me. Then he started talking.

I'll get to that soon, first, back to where we were.

So, a lot of people don't realize that Julian didn't always do the kind of art he's known for now. At least, that's not how he became known. I don't really know much about painting, so my descriptions may be off, but you'll get the idea.

How he made his name was by painting what he called "outlines," or "empty space" pieces.

We were in his mom's garage the first time he showed me one. Dozens of canvases were leaned against the walls, face-forward, so I couldn't see them. Cans and tubes of paint lay scattered all over the floor. Brushes stuck out of jars half-filled with water. And this canvas leaned against an old dresser he used to store his supplies.

This painting was of a woman standing in front of an open window, curtains blowing in a breeze. An old fold-up table with a coffee cup and a dying plant sat against the wall. A wall with peeling wallpaper. It looked like an old apartment in some city or town that wasn't ours. The woman, such as she was, stood in front of the window, one arm held up by her face, cigarette between her fingers.

But she wasn't there. Not really. You could see pieces of her outline—her hair, the curve of her hip, the shape of her hand—but through her body, you saw what was behind her. Curtains, a wall, a windowsill, glass. Pieces of her appeared and disappeared along the shape of her. All of it rendered in brushstrokes that made the scene look more real than real. To be honest, I thought I was looking at a photograph.

I felt a breeze blow over my skin, and the hairs on my neck went electrified. I shivered, felt cold. I turned around and the garage door was still closed. I swear the breeze came from the open window in the painting, and I felt a cold sort of sadness, maybe even a little fear, as I looked at the woman who wasn't there.

"It's called 'Invitation'," he told me.

I approached the painting. I wanted to touch it, to remind myself that it was nothing more than paint on a canvas.

"She looks like a ghost."

Jules shrugged. "Maybe she is."

"Is she?"

"She's whatever you need her to be."

I snorted. "That's the most pretentious, asshole artist answer you could possibly give."

Julian's face went a little red. He took a pack of cigarettes out of his jeans, lit one, and spit out a piece of tobacco.

"You always want answers," he said.

"Well, you made this. It has to mean something to you."

He came closer and stood beside me, and the way he stood reminded me of that specter in the painting. Hip cocked to one side, arm held up, one elbow resting in his hand.

"If I told you to picture Mount Hood right now, do you think you could?" He asked.

I could. As soon as he said, "Mount Hood," I saw the snow-covered peak in my head, clearly. I nodded.

"Okay. So, what does that mean?"

"What do you mean, 'What does it mean?'"

"You're picturing something, it must be important to you."

"I'm picturing it because you told me to."

He inhaled then blew out smoke. "I gave you the image. So, if you were to paint that image, what would it mean?"

I stole the cigarette from his fingers and took a drag. I pointed at the canvas. "Who gave you this, Jules?"

He put both hands on his hips, stared at the thing he had created, and said, "I don't know. It was just there," touching two fingers to his temple like a loaded gun, "and I painted it."

He took the cigarette back. "And that's that answer, Marcy. That's what it means. Now you've seen it, and it belongs to you."

A few years later, "Invitation" really did belong to me. A gift from Julian before he moved to New York. In fact, I'm looking at it now. It's hung on the wall in every apartment and house I've lived in. My ex-husband hated it. Can't say I blame him, but I came to love it. I could sell it now and get a fortune, but I never will.

You know those faces carved into marble? The ones that seem to follow you with their eyes as you walk by. This painting has that kind of quality to it, but it's hard to explain. Someone is there in frame, but they aren't at the same time.

I still think about what Julian said in the garage, and knowing him, he wasn't just talking about the painting. The boy I met on the soccer field saw things. They appeared in his head and he had no idea who put them there. As he got older, he tried to figure out how to pull them out of his head and put them on canvas. "Invitation" was the first time he succeeded. I bet somewhere in the world is an apartment that looks just like the one in the painting, and the people who live there occasionally feel a chill even though the windows are closed. And maybe sometimes the person who lives there gets a little jump scare when they think they see the outline of a woman standing by the window. But then they realize it was just the curtain fluttering, throwing a shadow on the wall. Their heart rate is still high, but they laugh out loud just to hear a voice and go on with their day. But at some point, it'll happen again, and maybe they'll tell a friend the story of how the apartment is haunted. They may even try to take a picture, but it'll be all blurry. The closest and most accurate representation of what they saw and felt is hanging on my wall.

The only way it could ever be captured.

Speaking of ghosts, it was only after Julian's mom died that he decided to move. Once she was gone, he had no family left. He didn't even know where his dad was and had no brothers or sisters. There was nothing to keep him in Oregon, and when he asked me what I thought about him leaving, I told him to go. I believed in him then, like I believe in him now. I knew he had a unique talent that comes along rarely, and I don't just mean the "blood ticket" stuff. He is a genuinely gifted artist, as almost everyone knows by now.

I never did ask if he saw his mother's death before it happened. Splattered in a red mess on the garage floor after a bloody nose or smeared on a napkin at a fast-food restaurant. I never asked if he saw her heart attack on one of the 3x5 cards he kept in a rolodex on his bedroom desk.

But if I had to guess, I think he knew.

He wasn't himself about a week before she died. Moody, withdrawn, irritable. I thought he was just in one of those sleepless creative bursts he got into sometimes. But after he called and told me she was gone, I knew he'd probably been carrying the weight around that whole time.

We talked pretty frequently after he took a Greyhound across the country and got a small apartment in New York City. It wasn't long before he got an agent, changed his name to Julian le Sang, and had work hanging in swanky galleries. He'd email me articles, reviews, and photos from events. He was featured in magazines and journals. It was so strange to see portraits of him, slick, professional photos taken while he stood next to one of his paintings. That's about the time he started dressing in all gray. Gray pants, shirts, jackets, hats, and shoes. Still as skinny as ever, Julian started to look like his own shadow cast on a sidewalk. A stony, expressionless face with eyes that looked distrustful of whoever was snapping his picture.

The paintings were all variations on what he'd done in "Invitation."

This was all part of what art critics have referred to as Julian's "outline" period. And maybe it was...maybe Julian was already an outline of what he'd become. Because within a few months of breaking into the bigtime, Julian began a new phase and started creating art that would make him infamous.

4

To whoever is reading this now: I don't know where he is, okay? Not exactly. He called, we talked. The end. Over the years, various art magazines and newspaper journalists have asked to interview me about "the Julian I knew." As if he was two different people. Look, the Julian I knew is the Julian the world saw. Only they didn't know what to make of him. He didn't change, but the world's perception of him did. Nothing I can do about that.

He called the day before his new exhibition was scheduled, not to warn me necessarily, but to let me know what to expect. He didn't want me to be surprised.

"You've already seen it," he told me. "Just not on this scale."

I asked what he meant by "scale."

He said, "The bigger the canvas, the more you see."

Thinking about what Julian could see, *had* seen, I asked if he'd ever tried to look for his own death.

He sounded genuinely surprised. "No way, I wouldn't want to know. That's all I'd see. I'd think about it every hour of every day. It'd probably paralyze me. No, I'd rather leave that a mystery."

He paused, then said, "Would you want to know?"

I said, I think I would. It's a stupid analogy, but there's a reason that soap opera used it. Sand through an hourglass. If I could see all those grains slipping from top to bottom, slowly filling up, I think I'd use my time differently. Which is a strange thing to admit because it means I know I'm not using my time wisely right now. There are so many things I want to do, to see. People I want to spend time with. Even apologies I need to make. Wrongs to make right and all that. If I knew that seven years, or however long, was all I had left…God, I'd quit work and start living.

Julian laughed and said he was trying to do exactly that right now, without knowing when he was going to die. But, no, he'd never tried to see his own "blood ticket." Most likely, he never would.

Then he told me what he had done. What he'd made. Still, I wasn't quite prepared for how it would feel to see his new art.

The morning after the exhibition opening, the news was ablaze with reports from the event at the gallery, complete with dozens of pictures taken there. Many of the major newspapers showed pictures of all the ambulances parked outside the gallery, with headlines that said things like *63 Faint at Julian le Sang Exhibition, 3 Dead*, and *le Sang's Latest Artwork Causes Mass Hysteria*. Some of the tabloids went more for shock with *Bloodbath in Soho*.

There were pictures of well-dressed bodies strapped down on stretchers being wheeled out of the gallery and loaded onto waiting ambulances. One woman fell to the ground and had her ribs crushed, which punctured her lungs, and another man slipped or was pushed and fractured his skull on the corner of a table. The man who died of a stroke was a wealthy art collector much beloved by the community, and his death made Julian something of a villain for the snootier among them.

Some of the other pictures were taken inside the gallery after it had been cleared by the police. It looked like an earthquake had hit. The floors were covered in broken glass, spilled wine, and hors d'oeuvres. A few of the high tables had been knocked over. A statue valued at over $20,000 lay shattered. A woman's lone shoe, bright pink, was abandoned in the center of the room, looking almost obscene.

And then there were the pictures of the art itself. Large canvases between eight and twelve feet in height and width—ten of them in all, stationed throughout the gallery.

Let me pause for a second. I thought I heard Alex moaning in his sleep. And you've already seen the art, and like anything grotesque, it becomes less so the longer you're exposed to it. But that initial shock of seeing something your brain isn't ready for, the creak of your neural machinery as it tries to collect data, process it, file it under something non-threatening…that is something special. Something many of us spend our lives chasing. I suppose it's why some people love extremely violent horror movies—they want to be shown gory death in a way they've never seen before.

So, imagine you'd never seen the art Julian le Sang became famous for. Imagine you were one of the upper crust in evening wear, clutching a long-stemmed glass of expensive wine, talking with your boring friends about your boring life. You want to support young artists because you want to pretend that you understand what it is they're doing, even though most of it looks like it was painted by a chimpanzee. But you want to be at the ground level of whatever's going to happen, whatever that means. So, you're there, and you're waiting for this artist (whose work is much better than so many of the other artists' exhibitions you've seen in the past), and he's got that mystique that makes work collectible, which makes it valuable. And he has this sort of tragic rock star look. Like he might die young. He only dresses in gray (it means something!), wears sunglasses indoors, and says cryptic things to reporters. But remarkably, none of it feels like an act. This guy is the real deal, quirks and all.

Yeah, yeah, of course, he's late. Like any headlining band knows, you have to make an entrance. Ten works are hung on the walls, all covered with gray (gray!) sheets. All of them are connected by a thin wire stretching from piece to piece, so once this Julian le Sang (what kind of name is that, is it French?) can pull one cord and simultaneously bring all the sheets down.

Mingle, mingle. Talk, talk. Drink, drink. Laugh, laugh. It's all so grand and magnificent and shallow. Doesn't everyone look amazing? Aren't all our children amazing? Our homes, jobs, cars, golf scores, sports teams, stock portfolios… all of it, just fucking amazing.

But none of us are amazed, are we?

In our gleaming, sanitized world, there is nothing pulsing with life.

A hush moves through us, like a physical thing with wings soaring through our midst. Conversations come to a stop mid-sentence. How many people are here? Two hundred, three hundred, maybe? All of us go quiet, and we go still. A door opens at the gallery's far end and a man comes out. We know who he is. Gray suit and waistcoat. Gray shirt, tie, and shoes. No sunglasses tonight, though, and his eyes are a pale blue. Bright, too bright. They look like small sky-colored stones in his pale face. Pale like he hasn't seen daylight for weeks.

And what's this? A girl next to him? Beautiful, long black hair cascading down her shoulder like a 1950s movie star. Her dress is gray to match Julian's, and she has one delicate arm linked through his. So now we think he's not gay, at least (hurray!), and this makes us all feel a little better somehow, but also a little disappointed because if he was gay, we would tell everyone we were supporting a gay artist. Alas, it was not to be. But still, here he comes, and we hear his shoes click-clack on the floor, or maybe those are the woman's. She looks foreign. Russian, maybe. Her face has a severe expression that makes us think she's not comfortable in this crowd. We like her for that because she recognizes what we are.

The gallery owner waits until Julian and the woman reach the center of the room, where a small pedestal rests. Upon it rests a large gray tassel attached to the wire.

The gallery owner holds his hands together as if in prayer and says, "Ladies and gentlemen. The Rogue Gallery is proud to welcome Julian le Sang."

You know he wants to say more, but the short speech makes us think Julian told him to keep it brief. Julian himself says nothing. The woman disentangles her arm from his, and Julian steps forward to the pedestal. Those eyes (good God, they're intense) search all of us. Our bodies, our faces, our posture, our clothes and jewelry… all of it. Are we being judged? It feels like it, but why? Perhaps because nothing in his presentation makes us believe he's grateful we are here. It's as if he was expecting royalty to show up, and only peasants arrived. Maybe we're imagining it, but the feeling is there in the atmosphere when he reaches for the tassel and gives it a pull.

The sheets seem to fall in slow motion, dramatically, slowly revealing the art beneath them. Inch by precious inch. What we are expecting, we don't know, but it's not what we see. Nothing but shades of red as the sheets slide away. Collectively, we take a sharp breath in and hold it. Most of us, anyway. We turn from one canvas to the next and see more red. Then to the next, and the next, and the next. All ten of them, various sizes, are covered in shades of red. Dark, light, thick, and thin. This series of paintings was created with an entirely red palette.

Julian stands there with his hands folded at his waist. He says nothing. He waits. For what we don't know, we feel he's giving us an opportunity to figure out what this is—what all of it is.

Someone—let's just say it's a woman, although it could have just as easily been a man—steps away from the crowd and moves closer to the largest painting. It's abstract, that much is clear. There is no image we're supposed to see and understand. Not like his previous work. This is, as we say in the art world, "challenging." It forces the viewer to do work, to bring something to the proceedings. You are not allowed to simply be a by-stander. You must engage with the art in order to truly see it.

So, this woman, she still carries her glass of wine in one hand. She tilts her head and observes all the puddles and lines on the canvas. Thousands, maybe millions of tiny crimson drips dot the white space. The center of the work is a mass of ropy lines crisscrossing each other, stretching across the canvas and back again, getting lost in an intricate network of other lines—all red. Some so dark they're nearly black, while others are so light they look almost orange. The very center is a congealed mass of red, thicker at one end. Small clear-ish bubbles catch the light, and they look three-dimensional. Real bubbles frozen in time. They shimmer. In fact, the whole piece does. It shines under the light, and every detail seems to lift off the surface of the canvas and hover. That network of lines is like a spiderweb, something you fall into.

The woman looks down at the reddish-purple wine in her glass, then back at the art. She sways a little, maybe the high heels, maybe the alcohol. She turns to the crowd, and her face has gone pale. She lifts a hand to her forehead as if feeling for a fever. The glass slips from her fingers and shatters on the floor, shooting tiny shards into the crowd. A man yells out. He slaps one hand to his cheek, and blood leaks from between his fingers, runs down over his knuckles. At the sight of blood, the crowd takes a step backward.

We stare.

The woman lies forgotten on the ground.

The blood covering this man's fingers is familiar, somehow.

Our eyes move from the man to the art hanging on the walls. We know what it is. That isn't paint—we always knew it wasn't. Deep in our subconscious, we knew. We'd never seen paint like that.

Blood.

All ten canvases absolutely covered in blood.

Breath rushes out of us, all of us together.

Then chaos.

5

When the first articles came out, they were all about the mad rush for the doors after the art had been unveiled. The trampling, the "stampede," as it was called. The pushing, shoving, hitting, scratching. The stepping over and on top of bodies. The woman who fainted and cracked her skull. The man who had a stroke and was left dying as everyone else ran outside. The other two killed in the melee. But not much was known about the art itself until later, when some of those in attendance were interviewed.

Blood.

Was it really blood, or just paint made to look like blood?

"Like a crime scene," one woman said.

"A massacre," one man said.

Reporters contacted Julian's agent and asked for a statement about the art. Was it blood or not?

"It is blood," the statement read. "My own blood. Every drop of color on the canvas is from my veins."

When reporters asked for some remarks on the violence at the exhibition, Julian refused. Not even a statement to offer his condolences to the families of those who died and the others who were injured. Nothing.

That was the last thing Julian ever said publicly. Not long after the gallery fiasco, he called and told me he had no idea what to say.

"It's art," he said. "I have no control over how people react. I made it—it's out there. What people do with it now is up to them. They can accept or get angry about it, but I won't be caught trying to explain or apologize for it."

It was almost a year before I heard from him again. During our conversation, I asked what made him shift to painting in blood after all these years creating genuinely beautiful art.

He explained that he had never stopped seeing death in his blood. Specific death. Actual people. Sometimes, it would be in the blood from his chewed-up fingernails. Other times, it would be from accidentally cutting himself with a knife while stretching canvas. Whenever the crimson liquid came leaking out of him, he saw it creating shapes—faces, moments in time, instruments of death.

"The other work stopped speaking to me," he said. "It went silent. I could paint the images, but they felt lifeless. I got some of those lancets that diabetics use to prick their fingers. You know the ones? They put the drops of blood on a small strip that goes into a machine and measures their blood sugar. I bought some and started pricking a finger once a day. I let the blood drip onto 3 x 5 cards, and within seconds, I started to see something. Every single time. I'd squeeze and squeeze, drop after drop, until the image was complete. Then I'd leave it out, and once it was dry, I put it in this old filing cabinet I got that had been used as a library card catalog. I have hundreds of those cards now. Thousands. I write a brief note about what I see. Okay, like this one from today…I wrote, 'middle-aged woman, bed, pill bottles' and today's date."

It wasn't long before Julian wondered how far this (Gift? Power? He didn't know what to call it) extended, and the only way to find out was to test its limits. He created an account with an online medical supply company. He watched some videos and learned how to insert a needle into his vein so that he could hook himself up to a bag and fill it, like they do at blood drives. He bought an extra refrigerator so he could store the blood.

His theory was, "The bigger the canvas, the more you see."

I asked if he had ever researched his ability, read articles or forums, or watched videos about it. He told me he had never looked into it. He didn't want his perception of what he could do to be influenced by what other people said, especially when it could all be made up.

The first large canvas he ever attempted was ten feet wide by two feet high. A long rectangle that he placed on the ground and hovered over, holding a chilled bag of his own blood. He later got an IV pole to hook the bag on, but that first time, it was suspended from two curled fingers. His other hand held tubing that he had fitted with a valve he could turn to make the blood flow. He dripped and splashed the cold, thick liquid onto the canvas and watched as it ran in rivulets down the textured surface, forming tributaries and puddles. Some of the blood splashed and sent droplets into far corners. Some lines congealed quickly, and then other lines crisscrossed those.

Eventually, Julian knew the artwork was finished. How he knew, he couldn't say. A feeling, maybe. A tingling at the back of his neck that told him any more blood would ruin the image. Then he stepped back and looked at what he'd made.

It was blurry at first, but the longer he stared, the clearer it became. And when it did, he fell to his knees and cried.

Faces (two hundred and seventeen exactly) lined up in rows, screaming in pure terror. Their expressions were frozen in the moment of death. Some of their eyes were shut tight. Some faces were peaceful, others weeping. Men, women, children, babies. There was water in there somewhere, rushing in. Debris—metal, glass, plastic, fabric, small pieces of luggage.

Julian wasn't entirely sure what he'd seen, but it was all over the news the next day. A 747 airliner flying out of Delhi experienced a mechanical failure and crashed into the ocean. All three hundred and eight people on board died. Julian said he only counted two hundred and seventeen because all he saw was third class. He wondered if a bigger canvas would have shown him the whole plane, a theory he was never able to test.

A few weeks later, he painted a terrorist bombing in Dubai, but he only saw a few of the conference rooms, and he later found out more people died than what he saw in the art.

The nonspecific nature of the images bothered him more than anything. What he saw were the people, not the flight number or the name of the building. How could he stop something from happening if he had no idea when and where it would occur? The plane crash happened the next day, but like with Jackie Mokely, the bombing took weeks to happen.

I asked Julian if maybe he was seeing events that would eventually transpire somewhere in the world because… those things, tragic as they are, happen.

"Twelve weeks," he told me. "Never more than twelve weeks. Every painting happens within that time frame. And I read multiple articles about the plane until I was able to verify…two hundred and seventeen people in third class. What I saw was accurate, and I think other people can see it too. Sort of. Their brains know they see something, but they just don't know what it is. But they know it's bad, and that unknowable leads to a kind of panic."

He believed that it was the hazy, half-understood vision that caused the stampede at the gallery. Was it the blood that drove them to hysterics, or did they see something? All of those eyes, in one place, staring at one thing. Did each of them see a piece of the puzzle, a piece that psychically assembled with all the others until the crowd saw a death image? A "blood ticket"?

Julian spent almost a year painting with his blood before that showing, and he learned that a bigger canvas yielded mass casualty events, while a smaller canvas typically revealed a single death, sometimes two. But the smaller canvas could also show more detail: location, landscape, furniture, and sometimes…the weapon.

"What I don't have an answer for," he told me, while I put the phone on speaker and coughed into my pillow, "and I don't know if I ever will, is the question of whether I am causing these things to happen, or just seeing them before they do."

He lost nights of sleep, wondering if that plane crashed because he painted it. He took a twelve-week break from art—as an experiment—and kept a close eye on the news. Of course, he saw tragedy on every website and in every newspaper, but none of them gave him that electricity on the back of his neck. None of them made his heart skip beats, and somehow, he knew it was because his blood wasn't connected to them. Whatever that meant.

I had no idea what to say. I didn't doubt Julian at all. I'd been there from the beginning. I knew what happened to Mr. Murphy and Jackie. I'd seen enough strange things of my own to know the world, the universe, did not play by our rules. Never had. So, when I said, "That is so weird," it wasn't out of disbelief, it was simply because I didn't know what else to say.

There was silence on the phone for almost a minute. I heard a breeze blowing over the speaker on Julian's end.

I said, "You got quiet."

Finally, he said, "Tell me again."

"Tell you what?"

"Tell me that you'd want to know."

I hesitated. "Know what? How I die?"

"Yeah."

My heart moved up a few more inches, and my breath became shallow. "Yes. I want to know."

He let out a long sigh. His voice shook when he spoke. "I've been painting small 'blood tickets' again at night when I can't sleep. The other night, I thought about you. I've wanted to call for months but couldn't. I wanted to make sure you were okay, you know?"

This is it, I thought. Whatever he sees next will deter-mine the course my life takes until the end. He saw me. He saw me dead. I am about to know what so few people ever get the chance to know. My whole body was vibrating, just humming with what he knew, what he would tell me.

"I didn't see you, Marcy."

I held my breath.

"I saw Alex."

All strength went out of me. I fell over onto my pillow, tears pouring out of my eyes. I tried to breathe but couldn't. My legs kicked against the blanket. A moan came out of me like I was a wounded animal. Sound disappeared from the room. The clock stopped moving.

"I painted him three times to be sure, Marcy. I'm so sorry."

I buried my head in the pillow and screamed for as long and as loud as I could. Minutes went by as I sobbed, and all I could hear was Julian's distant voice saying, "I'm sorry," over and over again.

"Where is he?" I asked. "When it happens."

"He's in a hospital. He doesn't look in pain. He looks peaceful."

The tears came again, a flood of them. More tears than I thought my body could hold came pouring out of me.

Julian was many things, but attuned to the emotions of others, he was not. So, you'll understand that it means something when I say he comforted me that night. I don't know how much time went by as I mourned this thing, this death, that hadn't happened yet. And Julian stayed on the phone with me through it all—every scream, every sob. Even when I blamed him, he remained silent and listened. Then he comforted me some more.

I didn't think about this until later, but at one point, he said, "Maybe it's for the best, Marcy. Who knows what the future will look like?"

After we said our goodbyes and hung up, I went to Alex's room and crawled into bed with him. I held his small body next to mine, but I did not sleep. Not even when the sun rose, and light blazed through the crack in his curtains.

6

Three weeks later, Alex started complaining of pain in his ribs. Then his spine. Later in his ankles. I took him to the doctor, and x-rays showed nothing. Another doctor, more tests.

We got a call to come to his office, and he delivered the news there.

Myeloma. Cancer of the plasma cells. Advanced.

My reaction probably wasn't typical for a mother in this situation. I knew it was coming, I just didn't know what *it* would be. I'm not lying when I say there was some relief in finally knowing. I didn't have to wonder anymore. The bullet that would kill my child had a name.

That night, I sat with Alex at the dinner table and explained to him what the disease was and how it would eventually end his life. Judge all you want, he'd know soon enough anyway, and I didn't want him to be scared.

I quit my job the next day and bought an RV. We would fill every minute of every day that Alex had left. Yes, we'd do treatments because you can't ever let go of hope, but it wouldn't define us. I wouldn't let it. We'd drive and drive and drive. We'd stop wherever he wanted, do whatever he wanted. Rollercoasters, fairs, zoos, parks, museums, forests, lakes, rivers, the world's biggest ball of yarn. Anything and everything.

We'd drive through autumn rain and winter snow. We'd sing songs and dream dreams. Some days, I'll forget about the end. Some days, I won't.

One night in a hotel, I thought about the fact that we all knew we were going to die. It's the only certainty in life. But we so rarely consider it in any meaningful way. It's something far off. But the reality is that none of us know when we go. We live like it's distant when it could be tomorrow. This knowledge should change us, somehow. Reconfigure our small, selfish minds into something bigger and wider.

We don't have a destination, Alex and me. We're in New Mexico right now. Alex is asleep beside me as I write this. I have both hands wrapped tight around whatever time we have left, and I will not let go for anything. I haven't heard from Julian since, but I didn't expect to. He said he wouldn't be able to call for a long time. I hope he's okay, wherever he is.

The air in New Mexico is really dry, and I've had a bloody nose since we arrived. There's a tissue on the bed next to me, stained with my blood. I pick it up, unfold it like a strange flower, and stare at the patterns, the splatter of bright red, and I look for something… some vision to tell me that the end isn't coming.

I don't see anything.

The end is coming. It's always coming.

Alex, I'll do my best to keep it in the rearview mirror, forever chasing us down.

As the sun rises, we'll put on some rock 'n' roll and drive.

And we'll keep on driving until the end.

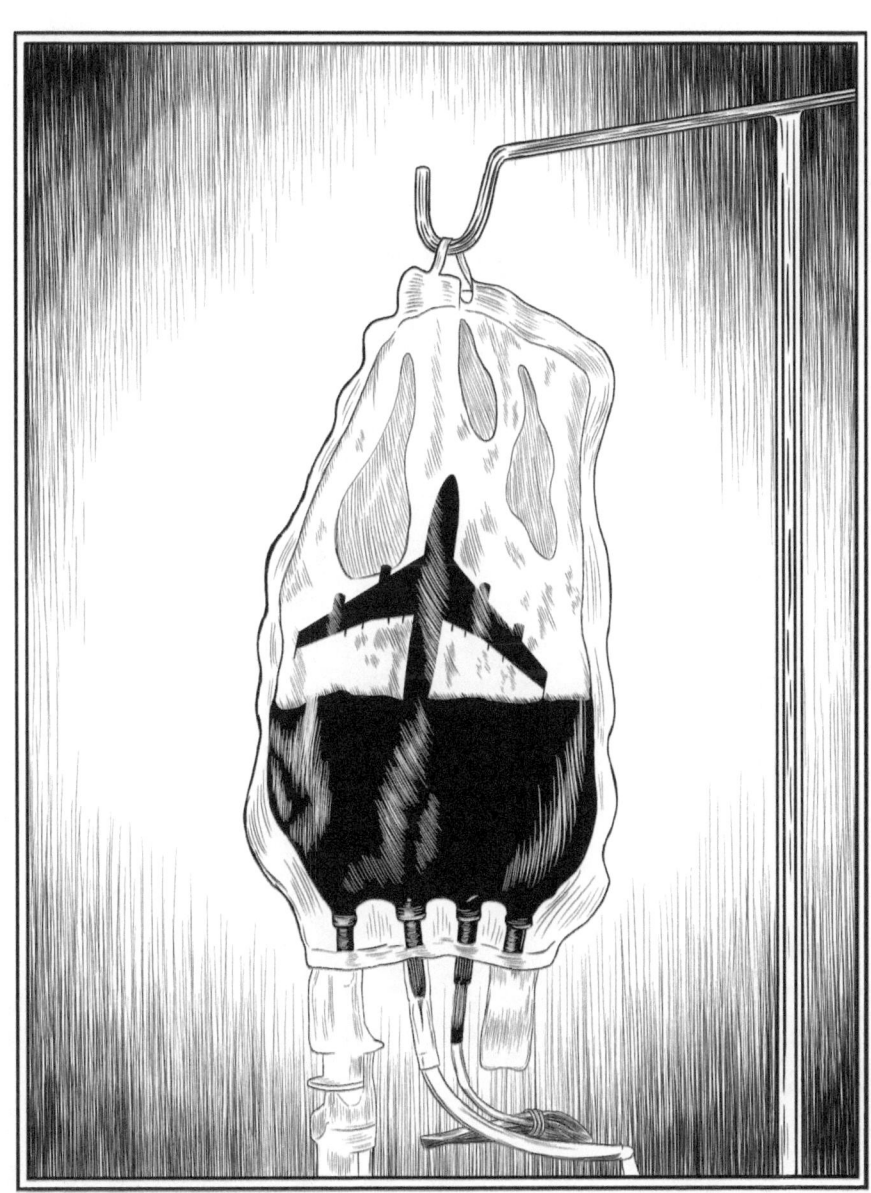

AFTERWORD

I once met a man who believed he was possessed by a demon. It
started when he was fourteen, and he and his family had just moved
into a new home. This man, let's call him Scott, went exploring
with his brother and sister, and they discovered a large crawl space
underneath the house. Big enough to stand upright, but not really a
basement. Scott made his way around support beams, thinking how
clean the dirt was, how there was no debris or rat droppings that he
could see. His younger siblings chased each other down the length of
the house, their laughter coming back to Scott in dead echoes.

He moved slowly. His stomach suddenly started to hurt. His head
ached. He was about to turn around and leave the crawl space when
his shoe scuffed through some whitish dust on the ground. He took a
couple of steps and saw more of the chalky dust curving in thick lines.
Then other lines—straight, intersecting. He turned in a circle, and the
particles drifted into his nostrils. They smelled like something burned,
like ash.

He backed away until he was outside all the disturbed white dust, and he could finally see what he had walked through.

A pentagram, broken now by Scott's footsteps, drawn on the dirt in that strange white substance.

Scott hunched over, vomited, and passed out.

Later that night, as Scott lay in bed with a fever, he started having visions. Clear, vivid pictures that filled his head with images of a terrible and violent event. He saw bodies on fire, falling from the sky. Black smoke billowing. Rubble, twisted metal, shattered glass. He heard a voice whispering to him, so close he couldn't tell if the speaker was right next to his ear or inside his head. The visions went on all night, and Scott barely slept.

And he barely slept for the next twenty years. Sometimes, the visions would subside for a few weeks, but when they came back, they'd be more horrifying and grotesque than ever. Over time, he started to see a figure within these nightmares. A shadowy presence that stood just beyond where he could see. Watching him. Scott came to believe this shadow was the voice that spoke in his head, telling him that everything was meaningless, that existence was nothing but pain and misery followed by death, then eternal darkness.

And this isn't even the interesting part of the story.

By the time I met Scott, he was in his thirties. A hollowed-out shell of a man with dark circles under his eyes and a nervous energy that made his body twitch whenever he spoke. When I met Scott, he told me someone was trying to kill him. Not just anyone but a secret government agency.

According to Scott, he had gone to the FBI and told them he had proof that demonic forces were real. The FBI then contacted a dark agency that dispatched a team to investigate. Several men broke into his apartment in the middle of the night, covered his bed in plastic, tied him down, drugged him, and then one of the men (wearing a white collar) stepped forward and began to perform an exorcism.

Scott felt something being pulled from him, violently. Something deep inside his chest, its claws scratching for a way to stay connected. He screamed and thrashed as the priest stood over him, reciting Latin and dousing him with holy water. A thick, black, tar-like substance came pouring out of Scott's mouth, so much so that it formed a puddle on the plastic and soaked his clothes.

The other men stood around the bed, watching, until this substance came out. They took some canisters out of their duffel bags and collected as much of the black liquid as they could. Then Scott was untied and given a shot of something that sent him spinning into darkness.

All of this happened only a couple of weeks before I met Scott. He was terrified the men were going to come back because he believed some part of the demon remained inside him. Growing stronger with every passing day. After the exorcism, the whispering stopped for a few days. But he heard it again, faintly, as if it were calling to him from across a chasm. He knew it was only a matter of time before that voice was clear and strong again.

He put five extra locks on his apartment door. He propped a couch up against it before going to sleep at night. He stopped going to work. He thought the injection gave him multiple heart attacks.

Why am I telling you about Scott? I could tell you about Martin, instead. A former Army Ranger told me his friends in the CIA took him by helicopter to a remote clearing in a southern Washington forest, where he sat on a grassy hill at three in the morning and watched as a family of Sasquatch grazed for food. One of them waved at him.

But I won't tell you about Martin, and here's why: I didn't believe Martin's story. Or, I should say, I didn't believe he believed it. Scott was different.

I've heard a lot of crazy stories in my life. I'm sure you have too. But, I have never heard one so wild and told with such conviction as Scott's. I should mention here that Scott was crying the entire time he told me about what had happened to him. There was no act, no drama in his presentation. He kept saying, "I don't even know why I'm telling you this. You won't believe me. No one ever believes me."

He showed me a printout of his blood work. No drugs. Scott said he never did drugs, didn't drink alcohol. So, what do I make of it? Mental health issues? Abuse, maybe? A broken mind?

I don't know. And I don't need to know.

Scott's story was fascinating and revealing, maybe even more than he intended. As I type this now, I sincerely believe that Scott believed every word he told me. That was the most unnerving thing. To hear a story so outside the realm of reality, but to be so convinced by the conviction of the teller that I was able to suspend any doubts. What I saw was a man telling me about a darkness inside him that nothing would get rid of. It ate into his thoughts, infected his dreams, destroyed relationships, and left him broken.

Someone once told me that fiction is the lie that tells the truth truer.

Maybe every story reveals something about the teller, whether we want it to or not. Maybe the most important thing is that *we* believe it, even if it's impossible and frightening. *Especially* if it's impossible and frightening. In order to tell stories of the creepy and fantastic, the dark and the macabre, an audience needs to know it isn't a joke.

I suspect this is true of living, as well. If I believe every moment matters—every second of every single day—do I somehow create a world in which the outcome is less important than the moments that connect and stretch out over time?

I sincerely hope you've enjoyed the stories in this book. None of them are true, but I believe in them all.

STORY NOTES

CORPORATION

What does it profit a man to gain the world and lose his soul?

TRIGGER

I've always loved stories where the voice carries half of the narrative. I was thinking a lot of Joe Lansdale when I wrote this one, of the way he inhabits a character's voice—and their particular syntax, their view of the world, becomes the engine that drives everything.

Going into it, I knew that these two brothers were tasked with burying the family dog, but they eventually came to believe that what they were burying wasn't the dog. From there, I uncovered the horrors right along with Travis and Jonah. This piece is the longest in the book because it felt like the opening of a much bigger story. I wanted to see what happens to these brothers, and maybe someday I will.

THE GOLDEN RULE

Of all the things we've lost in the Internet Age, the Golden Rule is the one I mourn the most. An experiment in voice. The broken English became almost a form of poetry.

THE DEVIL ON THE STAND

The oldest story in this collection. It's a simple concept—the person who sees something (a danger) no one else can—and it's been done before in a variety of ways. I read a fascinating article about how courtroom sketch artists were a dying breed, and it *is* a sort of antiquated means of capturing specific moments in time. It seems that these artists are used even in trials that are televised or where photography is allowed. Yet, these artists still toil away, sketching defendants, prosecutors, witnesses, and judges. I also noticed that, much like police sketches, courtroom sketches have a similar style and feel. No matter the case, no matter the people involved, to my eye, they all seem to be drawn by the same artist.

Maybe, at its core, this is a story about how what we see is often marred by our perception. We accept what's easy to accept, but sometimes truth is much less attractive and far more complicated. The simple narrative is always easier to swallow.

BOO!

Speaking of perception... what a kid sees and understands about the world of adults is always interesting to me. Children tend to see the best in a situation that is obviously wrong simply because most are not yet trained to recognize all the lies and manipulations of their elders.

Again, a simple concept—a kid confuses his mother's affair for ghosts in the house and seeks to find evidence.

There's something heartbreaking about a child's innocence in the face of adult indiscretion. They can't always understand the reasoning, or logic (or lack thereof) of why an adult would sacrifice so much for so little. And what a tragedy it is when the child is no longer a child and learns those lessons in full.

A SHARP BLACK LINE

Just outside Portland, Oregon, there is a place where the Willamette River divides the city of West Linn in two. Throughout this stretch of river are several small islands that you can get to only by swimming or kayaking.

During the fall, when it rains for days on end, the river rises and thick fog rolls over the water and makes it look like the Willamette is a river of smoke.

One day, during a storm, I went to a boat dock and watched as the fog drifted. It swirled and moved like something alive, and within all the silver I saw a glimpse of some trees, a shoreline. Then it was gone again, vanished into the fog.

I kept watching but the island never reappeared, and I started to wonder if I'd actually seen anything at all.

That's how this story started. The image of an island that materialized in the fog during a storm. What lived on that island?

By now, you already know. But I didn't when I first started writing the story, and that's the part I love most about writing—having a question, and the only way to find the answer it to tell the story, discover it.

CHARWOOD

It's almost cliché to say, "Kids are resilient." And maybe that's just a simplistic way of saying, they can endure a lot of pain and heartache, and continue to look for the beautiful in the world. A wonderful trait we seem to lose the older we get. Still, all of carry scars from childhood. Some of us more than others, and what a rare thing to look at those old wounds and know we can face whatever pain is waiting for us in the future. Some allow that pain to define them and shape every action, every relationship. Others, some I know and love, become indestructible forces for good despite childhoods that should have broken them.

I like to think that Kayla, wherever she is now, still carries some hurt, but she's okay. She fought back against the smoke that would have choked out her ability to become someone more than just the sum of all the bad things that happened to her.

CRATE 42

Sometimes, it's a fun challenge to set a word limit for a story and try and see how much of a narrative arc you can fit into, say, one thousand words. Some stories seem to know exactly what they want to be, and that was the case with "Crate 42." I knew it wasn't meant to be very long, so I set a limit of one thousand words and went over on the first draft. Then I went back and trimmed until I got down to 990 words. And that is the version you've read.

The idea itself came because a publisher had an open call for an anthology, and they wanted stories about a single person stranded on a deserted island. Alone. And it had to be horror.

Immediately, the idea came of a man transporting something bad on a plane that crashes into the ocean and leaves him stranded with the one thing in the world he did not want to be anywhere near.

We never see what's in Crate 42, but I wonder if maybe it's the chest we see in the basement of the pawn shop in "The Golden Rule."

I'm grateful to Max Booth III for giving this story a home in *Dark Moon Digest*.

HOW WE LEARN

This story is an example of starting with a simple concept and having no idea where it's going. Some stories, I see certain moments, beats, and have a vague understanding of how we move from point A to B. But this one, I had no clue. I just saw two kids running away, hand in hand, from a burning house and I knew two things right away: First, they set the house on fire, and it wasn't the first time they'd done it, and second, they weren't normal kids. From there, I followed them on their journey.

An interesting fact: I wrote this story two years before the COVID-19 pandemic, when wearing masks would become common place. At the time, the thought of seeing a young kid in a surgical mask would look out of place. Maybe there's a metaphor in there somewhere. Maybe not.

There is something powerful about growing up and learning that what you think, do, and say can have consequences in the real world. We've all been given these incredible tools of language and communication. How unfortunate that we often wield these tools as weapons, and how painful to learn that the words we say can start fires.

An idea I find fascinating is the transitional period between child and adult. There's no clear line we cross from one to the other. It tends to be a series of lessons that we learn along the way, and at some point, we are no longer blissfully ignorant children but adults with all the weight and responsibility of being one. Often, those lessons are painful, tragic even. Sometimes, they're beautiful. But they are almost never forgotten. And they, in turn, are the very foundation of who we become as people.

We learn by failing, sure. But we also learn by getting it right, sometimes.

WARLOCK

The Oregon coast is a strange and wonderful place and the towns that populate it are full of character, weather-beaten, and storm-blasted. Many of these towns seem frozen in time. The wooden siding on the buildings is gray and warped. The craggy beaches, full of rocks and boulders, move from sand to forest with hardly any transition.

Often overcast and rainy, the Oregon coastline has always felt ominous to me in a way that's hard to explain. In other words, the perfect setting for a story.

By now, you know what that story is about, and I was really interested in the idea of a child making a deal he doesn't fully understand and the parent being unable to explain how truly horrifying that deal could be.

I think one of the most difficult things for a parent is to allow their children to grow up and make mistakes. We want to save them from the pain of bad decisions, but that pain is a lesson far greater than any speech we could give. The wounds, which eventually turn into scars, are invaluable as they become adults. Some we save them from, but there will always be others we never see coming.

LION'S DEN

Some people are afraid of snakes or spiders. Some people read and watch horror to have a specific fear realized on the page or screen. An unstoppable killer wielding a knife, an old house full of ghosts. Demons, vampires, werewolves, creatures of the dark. I love stories with these elements, but they fascinate me. They don't frighten me. What I am most afraid of is Time. To me, it is more terrifying than any other monster. An unstoppable force that destroys everything eventually, and all we know about it are the rules we've created to try and make sense of something none of us understand. It is invisible and indifferent. It latches on to us and follows us from cradle to grave, robbing our youth, our loved ones, and our memories until we can't run anymore and end up caught in its slipstream.

Like most of these stories, "Lion's Den" started with a simple idea: what if there was a secret government agency that used remote viewers to gather intelligence? Psychic spies? (You may also notice that this unnamed agency shows up in several of these stories.)

The other part of the idea was this: how would a remote viewer know if what he was seeing was the past, the present, or the future?

Sure, if you saw the world being destroyed by a nuclear holocaust, you could infer it was the future. But what about other events that happen on a daily basis, like car accidents? How would you know? What if you sometimes saw the present, and other times it was the past or future?

I think maybe the present is really all that matters because it is the aspect of Time in which we are active participants. One of the greatest tragedies I've witnessed in life is a person who carries the Past, like a burden, into the Present rather than leaving it where it belongs. Loss, grief, pain, betrayal—they can become a sort of identity that prevents us from being fully aware of the fleeting beauty of the Present moment. I am not convinced that these burdens brought forward from the Past do not shape the Future in some way.

DEEP DOWN

A Frankenstein's monster built out of phantom limbs, not the physical pieces themselves, but the astral form that an amputee often feels. Created by some shadowy government organization for violent purposes.

Telling the story through voice messages was not meant to be a gimmick. When the idea first occurred to me, I imagined a man's voice calling his wife, but she wouldn't pick up. He needs her to hear him, so he begins talking to her the only way he can. I couldn't see any other way to tell the story. A story I meant to be a fun, weird tale began to say something meaningful to me anyway. Bitterness is a poison that infects our lives in ways we don't fully understand until one day, we realize it's burned through the parts of ourselves that are most important to us.

RED HANDS

Another story of children being shaped into adults by events they cannot control. Probably inspired by school shooters, if I'm honest. Wondering, processing, how some people (adults included) become broken. If you take one hundred kids and abuse them, beat them down, and neglect them, a certain percentage will become violent, right? How many kids carry deep wounds into adulthood, wounds that become infected and, in turn, infect who they are as people? Some studies have investigated the correlation between childhood abuse and adult dysfunction. There is a clear connection. Break a child, and often, you will create a broken adult. What an uphill battle. What a war to fight, to become someone stronger and better than what the statistics say you will be.

I often wonder if some of the most horrific acts of violence that flash across the news are the result of violence that took place behind closed doors. Hidden violence. Hidden wounds.

I imagine Cameron is something like that. A man who never came to terms with his past, who let all those hurts define him until he couldn't see any other version of himself. And what does a person like that do? They externalize their hurt. The pain is so abstract by that point, so nonspecific, that it becomes the world that has hurt them. So, the world will suffer. Of course, I could be completely wrong, but something rings true in this.

This story was adapted into a wonderful audio drama by the fine folks at The NoSleep Podcast, and I was, once again, absolutely honored to be part of it.

WHITE GLOVE

Oddly enough, this story started with the theme instead of the concept. I was thinking about how much of our society is driven by the idea that we should constantly desire what we don't have. No matter what it is, there is someone out there who has it better. I was wondering how I could put that theme into a story when this one came to me. A Christmas story about greed, the chasm between those who are wealthy and those who are not. Hopefully, it's a fun and creepy holiday story that'll make you look at the gifts under your tree a little differently.

I originally sent this out to subscribers of my newsletter around Christmas time.

STRIDOR

Like so many of the stories in this collection, "Stridor" starts with a what-if scenario. In this case, the scenario is: "what if guilt were a physical thing that stalks us?

When I was six years old, I was riding my bike down a dirt alleyway that ran behind some houses in my neighborhood. As I passed one particular house, I heard a low growling that grew into frantic barking. A black dog broke through the wooden fence and chased me down the alley, teeth bared. I pedaled as fast as I could, but the dog still managed to lunge and sink its fangs into my calf. I kicked the animal away and rode all the way home with a shoe full of blood.

Even though this memory wasn't forefront in my mind while writing "Stridor," I'm sure it was there subconsciously.

To six-year-old me, the dog was huge. But I'm not sure that's true.

FULL FATHOM FIVE

Anything I want to say about this is in the story.

ACKNOWLEDGEMENTS

I would like to give my sincere thanks to Joe Sullivan and John Brhel at Cemetery Gates Media for publishing the first edition of this collection, and to Steve Berman for giving this new edition such a great home.

I'm grateful to David Mack for creating the original cover art, and to Ben Baldwin, who took a ridiculously long letter I wrote him full of ideas and images and turned it into the chilling and beautiful art on the front of this book.

To Ryan Mills, whose art I'd seen online and absolutely loved. He has this incredibly unique black-and-white style that is simultaneously detailed, realistic, and dreamlike. I asked Ryan if he would be interested in doing some illustrations to accompany each of story. He agreed, and what started as a chance encounter has grown into a wonderful friendship. We've emailed, texted, and talked endlessly about books, stories, and artwork. We've passed ideas back and forth, ideas that sometimes turn into drawings or stories. I love each of the illustrations for different reasons. Some are precise, others are abstract. Each is distinctly Ryan. It is truly an honor to have such wonderful art alongside these stories, created by such a wonderful person.

My thanks to Phil Haagensen, another chance encounter that has become an invaluable friendship. Phil is the kind of early reader that every writer dreams of having. Honest, insightful, and observant. Phil read all these stories and offered thoughts and suggestions that improved them all.

Ross Jeffery, I will never stop thanking you for your support and encouragement.

Michael Marshall Smith, Philip Fracassi, Scott J. Moses, Scott Cole, Janelle Janson, Brennan LaFaro, Eric LaRocca, Sadie Hartmann, J. Grell, Kev Harrison, Brad Proctor.

I am grateful to Chuck Palahniuk and The Lie Factory (Dan Frazier, Jeremy Barlow, Scott, Tricia Callahan, Bennett Mohler, Nic Turner, Justin Klutka, Sunshine Barbito, and Michele Boldt) for reading early versions of these stories and helping me learn what worked, and what could be better. All of these benefit from your feedback.

To Cursed Morsels, Dead Headspace, Paper Cuts, Talking Scared, Scaredy Cats, and all of the other podcasts that have given allowed me to talk about books. Thank you.

I am grateful to all the readers, reviewers, and bloggers who have been so supportive. My deepest thanks to all of you.

And my thanks to The NoSleep Podcast, *Dark Moon Digest*, *Aphotic Realm Magazine*, *Haunted MTL*, and *Flame Tree Press* for publishing some of these stories in their original forms.

To Mom and Dad Wright, everything important I learned from you two.

To Mom and Dad Jones, for your love and support.

To Liam and Quinn, you both have brought so much depth, joy, and light to my life. I am grateful to be your dad.

Rae Lyn, thank you for marrying me. Ours is my favorite story. I love you.

ABOUT THE AUTHOR

Tyler Jones is the author of *Criterium*, *The Dark Side of the Room*, *Almost Ruth*, *Turn Up the Sun*, *Heavy Oceans*, *Longsight M40*, *Midas*, and *Night of the Long Knives*. His work has appeared in numerous anthologies and on *Cemetery Dance*, *LitReactor*, and *The NoSleep Podcast*.

He lives in Portland, Oregon.

ABOUT THE ILLUSTRATOR

Ryan Mills' published work includes interior illustrations for the extended editions of *Criterium*, *The Dark Side of the Room*, and the novel *Almost Ruth*, as well as front and back cover art/design for Enter Softly by Tyler Jones. He also contributed illustrations to the StokerCon 2022 Souvenir Book, from Burial Day Books. In his free time, he has a passion for reading Stephen King and a wide variety of horror novels, and for interior design. He lives with his husband and their retired greyhound, Noodle.